Nokee | The Last of
The Great Lakes
Mound Builders

# Praise for
## Nokee: The Last of The Great Lakes Mound Builders

"*Nokee: The Last of the Great Lakes Mound Builders* is a deeply compelling historical novel that … skillfully weaves themes of cultural survival, ancestral knowledge, and the complexities of intertribal life during early colonial disruption. The story combines a passion for storytelling, historical detail, and emotional depth. … It highlights the enduring strength of Native communities … and carries the potential to serve as a meaningful bridge to deeper, more meaningful conversations centered around Indigenous history, representation, and survival."

—**Kelsey Wabanimkee, Anishinaabe, Great Lakes Area**

"*Nokee: The Last of the Great Lakes Mound Builders* is a masterful historical fiction that will capture the reader with its powerful story of survival enmeshed within a fascinating historical framework. Mr. Rheaume›s finely crafted story of a tribal chief fighting to protect his people resonates at the deepest human levels of existence. … Through finely crafted details of the lives of those directly impacted … it's nothing less than a novel that will change how the reader views a crucial period of American history."

—**William Murphy, author of ten books and numerous journal and magazine articles on history, travel, and environmental issues—inducted into the Michigan Environmental Hall of Fame in 2018**

"*Nokee: The Last of the Great Lakes Mound Builders*, a powerful debut novel set in the 17th century, captivated me immediately. It is historical fiction at its best—well researched and yet entirely readable, a rare combination! The author shows a dazzling fluency in Native terminology and culture, along with a passion for the flora and fauna of the Great Lakes region. Rheaume has created vivid characters that jump off the page, their universal humanism would be believable in any century and in any setting."

—**Joshua Veith, author of the Sudden Quiet trilogy**

# Nokee

## The Last OF THE Great Lakes Mound Builders

Stephen J. Rheaume

M·P·P
www.MissionPointPress.com

Copyright © 2026 by Stephen J. Rheaume
*All world rights reserved.*

This is a work of fiction. Names, places, and incidents are the products of the author's imagination or are used fictitiously. Any resemblance to actual events or locales or persons, living or dead, is entirely coincidental.

No part of this book may be reproduced, stored in a retrieval system, or transmitted in any form or by any means electronic, mechanical, photocopying, recording or otherwise, without the prior consent of the publisher.

Readers are encouraged to go to MissionPointPress.com to contact the author or to find information on how to buy this book in bulk at a discounted rate.

## Mission Point Press

Published by Mission Point Press
2554 Chandler Rd.
Traverse City, MI 49696
(231) 421-9513
MissionPointPress.com

Cover Design: Jeanne Calabrese Design
Interior Design: Jeanne Calabrese Design
Map on cover: *Partie Occidentale de la Nouvelle France ou du Canada (1755)* by Jacques-Nicolas Bellin (reissued by Homann Heirs, Nuremberg). Public Domain. Wikimedia
Commons, Geographicus Rare Antique Maps.

Hardcover ISBN: 978-1-965278-97-0
Softcover ISBN: 978-1-965278-98-7
Library of Congress Control Number: 2025921435
Printed in the United States of America

*Nokee: The Last of the Great Lakes Mound Builders is dedicated to all who feel the stirrings of a story, a developing tale waiting to be told, a great quest that must be shared, keep writing…*
*Don't just wish for it, make it happen!*

# Contents

Nokee  **1**
The Fight for Survival  **10**
Shadow Walker  **21**
The Great Circle  **31**
Father Agard – Paris  **46**
Young Jesuits  **51**
Quebec City  **56**
Two Routes to the Soo  **65**
Day of the Dead  **78**
Lacrosse  **94**
Cat People  **107**
Detroit and the Mounds  **117**
Morningstar  **133**
Long Way Around  **147**
Pine Lake  **161**
Facing the Enemy Within  **174**
Peace Delegation  **187**

The Great Council  **198**
On to the Soo  **218**
The Long Winter  **228**
Green Bay  **240**
Recovering from the Loss  **256**
Reunited  **267**
The Chosen One  **277**
Tionontati the Storyteller  **287**
Kickapoo and the Dakota Sioux  **298**
Preparing for War  **309**
Father Allouez  **320**
Mississippi River  **327**
Father Marquette  **340**

Epilogue  **352**
References  **355**

*This book is a novel. Although historical individuals and events are incorporated into the lives and travels of my fictitious characters, all encounters and dialogues with historical individuals are a product of my imagination. It is not the author's intention to depict or change historical records. This book is fiction.*

# Nokee

It was early September in 1654, and the last descendants of the once-mighty Michigan Mound Builders were concentrated in a single village in the southwestern corner of the Lower Peninsula. On the shore of Paw-Paw Lake, a short distance from Lake Michigan, Little Bear lives with his father, Mahtowa—Bear—a Sauk peace chief, and his mother, Manomin—Good Berry— the daughter of a deceased Mascouten chief. Their marriage united the two tribes together in a common defense against their blood enemies, the Ottawa and Chippewa.

Due to European diseases and the never-ending wars, the Sauk and Mascouten populations had dwindled. The Sauk warriors, renowned for their bravery, did most of the fighting for the village. The Sauk shaved their heads, leaving only a strip in the center, which they styled to stand straight up by combing in red dye mixed with bear grease. They were a terrifying sight to behold in combat.

The Mascouten had long black hair, and though they were farmers, they were also well-trained with their bows and arrows. The Mascouten cleared openings in the prairie by burning and created large, raised garden beds, often in geometric shapes. They grew a mixture of crops but were best known for their large fields of maize—corn.

Little Bear, the oldest of Mahtowa and Manomin's two sons, was in his fourteenth cycle of the thirteen moons—what Europeans would understand as fourteen years old. He was looking forward to his coming-of-age ceremony in the fall where he would finally receive his adult spirit name. Little Bear had grown to dislike his childhood name. Now almost six feet tall, being called "Little" felt wrong.

Each fall, the children anxiously awaited the first ripening wild paw-paw fruit from the grove along the river bottom. Paw-paws taste like a cross between a banana and a mango. When ripe, they turn yellow with brown spots and have a strong but pleasant aroma. The fruit was a valuable food source in the village, and children were only permitted to pick the ripe paw-paws they could reach from the ground. With his generous nature, tall body, and long arms, Little Bear became quite popular with the younger children when the fruit was ripening.

One day, in the fall of Little Bear's fourteenth year, he was hunting rabbits with his bow and arrows when he heard screams at the paw-paw patch. As he neared the grove, he saw a group of children hanging from the upper branches of the paw-paw trees. Disgusted with this violation of village rules, he hastily approached the patch to give the children a piece of his mind. As he stepped into the opening, he froze.

Under the tree was a massive black bear. As the children climbed higher, shaking the branches, the beast greedily gorged on the falling paw-paws. Seeing Little Bear, the bruin rose on his hind legs and made a deep popping sound with his jaws, a clear gesture of his displeasure and a warning that he would defend his food source at all costs. Little Bear drew his bow without thinking and sent an arrow deep into the beast, striking its heart. The bruin flipped in the air, made a horrible guttural growl, hit the ground spinning, and crashed into the brush.

As the children in the trees cheered, Little Bear stood trembling, listening to the final death moans of the terrifying creature—a sound he would never forget. Little Bear's fame spread quickly throughout the village, and the story was told and retold. In each version, the bear became bigger and closer. At Little Bear's coming-of-age ceremony, the tribal council unanimously agreed. His spirit name would be Nokee—Bear Paw—a combination of the fierce bear and the paw-paw tree. It was a name Nokee proudly accepted.

• • •

Life changed dramatically for Nokee over the next year. He no longer had to help the women with routine tasks around the village. Instead, he trained with the warriors, went on hunting trips, and began learning how to flint knap—the art of making arrowheads. But what Nokee enjoyed the most was the time he spent in the sweat lodge with Tionontati, the village's ceremonial chief, spiritual leader, and storyteller. Tionontati was a fourth-degree Midewiwin and a member of the Grand Medicine Society, gifted with supernatural powers and the ability to heal the critically ill.

Nokee especially enjoyed Tionontati's stories of ancient times. He told of a time when his ancestors were part of a great nation. They ruled the land with thousands of the finest warriors, built grand cities, and amassed great riches. Tionontati spoke of how he and the other Midewiwin would gather every fifth summer for a pilgrimage around the Great Circle. They would travel up the Grand River to its headwaters, stop at all the ancient cities along the way, and pay homage to their ancestral spirits of the past. Then, they would portage into the St. Joseph River and return home. Tionontati would often bow his head and lament that the pilgrimage was no longer possible, as the Ottawa and Chippewa now controlled those lands—a fact that Nokee came to deeply resent.

In the fall of Nokee's sixteenth year, he sat comfortably in the sweat lodge with Tionontati, listening to one of his stories. Suddenly, they heard excited shouting. As Nokee stepped out of the sweat lodge, he saw the village warriors returning from their five-day mission to repel the encroaching Ottawa to the north.

Days before, they had received word that a small group of Ottawa, traveling with French fur trappers, had crossed the Grand River into the Land of the Mascouten. Chief Mahtowa had left with his best warriors to drive the invaders back across the river. They believed that the intruders wanted to trap beaver. Nokee was still mad that his father had not let him go along with the war party, having insisted that Nokee's training was not yet complete.

As the warriors drew closer, Nokee could see his father's arm and side were bleeding. Nokee grabbed Manomin and Tionontati, and the three raced to Mahtowa's aid.

"Mahtowa, are you alright?" cried Manomin.

Mahtowa lowered his head and said, "I will live. I cannot say the same for some of the others."

"Where are they?" asked Manomin with a horrified look. "You left with fifty warriors. I see less than twenty returning."

"Father," Nokee said. "I should've been with you! You know I'm ready to fight. I have proven myself in many mock battles during our training."

"No, Nokee," responded Mahtowa. "There was nothing you could have done. We lost ten men in the first attack."

"How?" Manomin asked, tears in her eyes.

"The French! Five French trappers were with them, and they've given the Ottawa muskets. Our scouts were wrong. They weren't there to trap the beaver. They had two hundred warriors headed for our village with one purpose: to drive us from our land. They were already at Lake Macatawa when we intercepted them. They would've been here in less than a day if we had not stopped them.

"Those muskets were longer and could shoot farther than I remember. Our men couldn't get close enough to attack. The Ottawa warriors were wearing full-body war paint and were intent on killing as many of us as possible. We had a tough time retrieving our dead and wounded before we fell back.

"I left half of our remaining force out there to watch for any signs of their war party advancing. The rest of us stopped only long enough to cremate and bury the ashes of our lost brothers at the mound site near the mouth of the Kalamazoo River. I fear this is only the beginning."

Mahtowa had seen muskets before. Twenty summers ago, when the Chippewa and a couple of French trappers had attacked his village on the Upper Grand River, the French were carrying Dutch arquebuses. But those weapons were heavier, less accurate, and took longer to reload, which gave the Sauk warriors a chance to rush and overtake their foe.

"If they launch a full-scale attack on our village," said Mahtowa, "our people will have nowhere to hide, and our numbers are too few to repel such firepower in the open. Notify everyone that we must quickly break camp. We'll move south and live with our Miami trading partners at Three Rivers."

Without hesitation, all the villagers began the arduous task of breaking camp. The villagers were accustomed to moving in the winter while they pursued larger animals for food and hides. However, they lived comfortably in well-built shelters near their crops in the summer. All of that was about to end.

Mahtowa demanded they gather as much as they could quickly carry. The chief knew the invaders would destroy everything that was left behind. The plan was for the entire village to move out at first light; however, troubling news came during the night as the scouts returned.

One scouting group reported that the Ottawa invaders knew they had lost the element of surprise. They had halted their advance at the mouth of the Kalamazoo River, waiting for more forces to storm the village. Another group reported seeing a large group of Chippewa traveling southwest down the Kalamazoo Trail. The Ottawa warriors had sent word to the Chippewa to join them in the attack. The scouts believed the Chippewa would reach the Ottawa warriors' location by mid-morning. A third group of scouts reported that the Potawatomi, located south of the Mascouten village, had allied with the Ottawa tribe. The Potawatomi had agreed to establish a line along the Lower St. Joseph River to block the Sauk and Mascouten retreat. Soon, the fleeing villagers would have no chance of escape.

Chief Mahtowa quickly called a council meeting of the clan leaders. Tionontati was the first to address the council. "The night our warriors left camp, I had a dream that I've been trying to understand. A dark cloud approached our village with sweeping winds, tremendous thunder, and a flashing sky. Dark Forces arose from the ground and descended upon our village. In a flash of light, our village was gone. I now believe it was a premonition from Gitchee Manito of a foreboding future."

Mahtowa stepped forward to speak. "It's now apparent that this is not just an invasion to take our land. It's a full-scale plan to exterminate our two tribes. However, the Ottawa chief may have just bought us time. If the Ottawa force holds back, waiting for the Chippewa to arrive, that should provide us with enough time to slip out toward the east. My Miami friend, Chief Myamick, at Three Rivers on the Upper St. Joseph River, will offer us refuge and protection. But we must move tonight."

Mahtowa considered his options. What would he do if they were suddenly under attack in the dark? What would be the best move if the attack came later that day? He estimated he had eighty Sauk warriors and fifty Mascouten archers. He asked everyone to leave their fires burning in their lodges. If the Ottawa scouts were watching the village and could see or smell that smoke, they might assume everyone was still there. *A decent head start could mean the difference between success and failure*, thought Mahtowa.

As Mahtowa walked out of the council meeting, he saw Nokee sitting on a log, still brooding about being left out of the fight. "Son," yelled Mahtowa. "I want you to oversee the evacuation of the women and children. Make sure they stay together and keep moving. I don't want anyone to fall behind and get lost in the dark."

"Put Mother in charge of that," shot back Nokee. "I'm a warrior, and I plan to fight if it comes to that."

"My son," said Mahtowa, shaking his head. "You wear the tattoos of a peace chief on both arms. Someday, you will lead this tribe. Always remember that the sign of a good chief is not how hard he fights but how hard he fights to protect his people. Without our women and children, we can win all our battles but still lose the war." Nokee gave an audible huff as he headed toward the emptying lodges to do what his father had asked.

• • •

Well before daybreak, three hundred Sauk and Mascouten villagers were on the move. The night was cool and windy, and Chief Mahtowa planned to use the weather to their advantage. It's hard to move so many people without making substantial noise. However, the wind would mute their sound if Ottawa scouts were nearby. The villagers barely spoke as they crept forward, expecting an enemy attack at any moment.

They traveled east through the open prairie along the Paw-Paw River until they reached Pine Creek. As dawn broke in the eastern sky, they turned south and entered an old-growth white pine forest. Walking beneath the monarch pines was easy in the brush-free understory, where the ground was carpeted by a thick mat of soft pine needles. They reached the St. Joseph Trail at sunrise. The trail ran east and west across the entire Lower Peninsula. It had been created generations ago by the Mascouten, Sauk, and Kickapoo as a major trading route between the tribes.

Mahtowa repeatedly urged his people to keep moving. "We must hurry until we reach the intersecting trail from Grand Rapids. There, we can turn south, and in a half day, we will arrive at the main camp of the Miami tribe on the St. Joseph River."

Mahtowa estimated it would usually take the villagers three days to make a trip like this. However, they would need to do it in half that. His biggest concern was the time spent on the St. Joseph Trail. He was sure the Ottawa warriors would pursue them from the west. If the Chippewa came down the connecting northern trail, they would be cut off. Being caught between two armies would ensure their doom. Their only chance was to reach the intersecting trail before the Chippewa warriors arrived. He knew that once his villagers turned south, they would be in the lake country—the land of the Miami. The Miami warriors were a powerful force. Mahtowa was sure the Ottawa and Chippewa would not follow them there for fear of starting an unnecessary war.

• • •

At the abandoned Mascouten village, the Ottawa scouts watched silently from a distance as the first light of day began to spread. The scouts had been deceived by the rising smoke from the lodge fires and were now returning to report to their chief. They were so pleased with their report that they saw no need to hurry.

The Ottawa war party had moved further south overnight to the Black River. They were now less than a half day from the Mascouten village. Still, it was mid-morning before the Ottawa scouts reached their chief to deliver their findings. They reported that the villagers had no idea what was coming.

"My chief," said Odawa, the leader of the scouting party. "We can wait for the Chippewa to arrive."

Chief Atowas grabbed Odawa by the shoulders. "Were any of your scouts seen?"

"No," replied Odawa. "We saw no one."

Chief Atowas looked concerned and continued to query Odawa. "Where did they station their guards?"

"We saw no one, just the smoke rising from their lodges. Everyone was asleep."

"You idiot!" screamed Chief Atowas. "You should be ashamed of yourself. You've fallen for the oldest trick in warfare. If you know your enemy outnumbers you, you abandon your village. You can rebuild. You can't replace your people. They could be half a day ahead of us now."

Chief Atowas gave the order to move out, thinking there might still be time to trap the villagers between his warriors and the Potawatomi.

Atowas thoughtfully rubbed his chin. "Chief Mahtowa is crafty. If he has detected our plan, Mahtowa will move his villagers to the east. He'll seek safety with the Miami."

"You!" Chief Atowas growled, pointing at Odawa. "You will leave immediately to intercept the Chippewa, who should have arrived this morning at the mouth of the Kalamazoo River. Tell Chief Twakanha that the Sauk and Mascouten are escaping on the St. Joseph Trail, and we are pursuing them. He must move his force east, traveling cross-country at great speed. When they reach the Three Rivers Trail, turn south toward the St. Joseph Trail intersection. If his warriors hurry, they can trap Mahtowa's people between our two forces and finish them forever. We'll try to catch them on the Trail. That will force them to slow down and fight, thus buying his Chippewa force more time to arrive."

"What if the Chippewa warriors reach the intersection and Mahtowa does not go that way?" Odawa asked, concerned. "Or suppose Mahtowa and his people have already passed through that area before the Chippewa arrive?"

"Then Chief Twakanha will kill you," Chief Atowas said dryly. "And it will save me from doing so myself."

It was midday when Odawa reached the Chippewa force, which was waiting at the mouth of the Kalamazoo River. The Chippewa had traveled through the night to join the Ottawa warriors, hoping to launch a morning attack on the village. Chief Twakanha was furious when he heard what Odawa had to say. His forces could easily have been positioned to block the retreating villagers—if only the Ottawa chief had counseled him before launching his attack. Instead, the Ottawa had crossed the Grand River alone to fight the Sauk warriors and tipped them off to the plan. Chief Twakanha estimated that the journey would take an entire day. The best he could do would be to send twenty of his best runners armed with muskets. Even then, they would not arrive until after dark.

Chief Twakanha grabbed Odawa by his bear tooth necklace and pulled him close. "You'll run with the advanced team. You had better not slow them down. The rest of my war party will follow as fast as possible. Is that clear?"

Twakanha knew the plan was unlikely to succeed. However, his hatred of the Sauk ran deep. Being unable to witness the extermination of the Sauk was not acceptable to Twakanha.

# The Fight for Survival

The fleeing villagers had made substantial progress on the St. Joseph Trail. The mood was upbeat, and everyone was confident they had tricked the Ottawa force. They would soon be safe in Miami country, hopefully before dark. But Mahtowa was not so optimistic. He knew the Ottawa warriors would not be fooled for long, and they would most certainly pursue them. All he could do was urge his people to keep moving.

It was late in the day when they finally reached the massive Kalamazoo moraine that separated the Paw-Paw River basin from the Kalamazoo River basin. On top of the moraine, they could see the intersecting trail in the distance. Everyone shouted with joy—everyone except Mahtowa. He studied the land ahead for any sign of opposing forces. Seeing none, he tried to relax—but that sense of ease evaporated when Nokee approached him, visibly frustrated.

"Father, the women and children are begging to stop long enough to rest and fix something to eat."

"No," replied Mahtowa. "We must reach the intersecting trail and turn south. Then, once in Miami territory, there will be time for rest. We must keep moving!"

But when Mahtowa turned around, the women were starting fires to cook their evening meals. Mahtowa, realizing he was losing control of his exhausted people, relented and agreed to a short break. There was still a shred of daylight left, and from their elevated position, Mahtowa could see a long stretch of their back trail. He asked Tionontati to go to the eastern edge of the ridge and watch for any sign of the Chippewa to the north.

The wind was beginning to pick up at the top of the moraine, so the women set up their three-legged mobile shelters, wrapping them with elk hides to block the wind and protect their cooking fires. They reheated their smoked meat and brought out their clay pots, each filled with cornmeal wraps to roll the meat.

Manomin gently tapped Mahtowa on the shoulder and pointed west as the group sat down to enjoy a little well-deserved rest and food. "Mahtowa," she whispered, "why do those trees look like they're moving?"

Mahtowa dropped what he was eating and jumped up. Straining his eyes against the setting sun, he yelled, "Those aren't trees—the Ottawa warriors are coming!" At that, all the women and children started running toward the other side of the ridge.

"No," pleaded Mahtowa. "Stop running! Tionontati, you must stop them. They mustn't run."

Tionontati raised his staff and yelled, "Stop, or I'll strike you down myself."

Mahtowa ran into the center of the crowd: "Listen to me. Look at that open prairie up ahead. If they catch us out in the open—and they will—we will have no chance. They'll shoot down our warriors and kill or capture our women and children. We must fight them here on top of this hill. We must fight them on our terms."

"How?" asked the clan leaders. "You just told us they'll defeat us in the open with their many muskets."

"Listen," said Mahtowa with a sense of assurance. "I have a plan, but it will take everyone's help. At Lake Macatawa, they saw only fifty warriors. They killed ten of us before we could get near them. If we make them think we have only forty fighters left, they might become overconfident and make a fatal mistake."

"Nokee," shouted Mahtowa. "Quickly place five spears in the ground across the ridge top, evenly spaced fifty paces apart."

When the spears were in place, Mahtowa instructed three Mascouten archers to try hitting the second spear. Two arrows smacked the spear, and the third grazed it. Then Mahtowa asked three Sauk warriors to throw their spears, and all three spears landed next to the second marker.

"Now we know our effective killing range," said Mahtowa.

"If we can get them trapped within fifty paces of us, we can fight them. I'll stand with forty of our fastest Sauk warriors at the top of the west side of the ridge and wait for the Ottawa to come running up. Before they top the ridge, we'll fall back, staying out of range of their muskets."

The clan leaders looked puzzled. Mahtowa, seeing their expressions, said, "Don't worry, we'll fight, but at the right moment. At the second spear, we will place two groups of twenty archers—one fifty paces north of the trail and the other fifty paces south. They'll remain motionless, hidden in the tall switchgrass. Manomin will oversee the archers.

"At the third spear, we'll hide two groups of twenty Sauk warriors, one on either side of the trail. Tionontati will oversee the spear throwers. They must remain hidden until Tionontati gives the word to charge. The women and children must stay visible at the far eastern end of the ridge. When the Ottawa force tops the ridge, they should start retreating. That should trick the Ottawa into thinking our women and children are fleeing in panic.

"My forty warriors and I will retreat across the ridge to the eastern side and form a tight horizontal line with our long elmwood shields and spears. If the Ottawa force responds as they did at Lake Macatawa, they'll stop at the third spear. There, one hundred paces away, they will wait for our charge."

Mahtowa nodded at Tionontati. "We'll charge when you hear us quit pounding our shields with our spears. At Lake Macatawa, I saw that the Ottawa aren't as well-disciplined with their muskets as the French. They'll fire first. With a little luck, our long wood shields should absorb their first volley at that distance.

"Manomin," Mahtowa said with a confident smile, "when you hear their muskets roar, your archers must rise on both sides and fire a swarm of arrows into the Ottawa. Tionontati, your hidden Sauk warriors on both sides of the trail should rise and charge at that moment. Run straight at the Ottawa, throwing your spears, and attack them armed with your short shields and war clubs. If our timing is right, my warriors and I should reach their front line before the Ottawa reload. We'll decimate their numbers, and our archers will shoot down any that try to flee back to the west."

• • •

The Ottawa force was still far off when the Mascouten archers and Sauk warriors took their positions, ready for battle. Mahtowa called Nokee over and told him he had a critical role for him and the nine youngest Mascouten warriors, all still in training.

"Nokee, ready your comrades and gather ten little clay pots with lids. The ones that the women keep their cornmeal wraps. Also, get ten of their gourds filled with sunflower cooking oil and meet me at the western front of the moraine. But you must hurry. There's little time to waste."

"Father," argued Nokee. "We are ready to fight!"

Mahtowa put his hand on Nokee's shoulder. "Son, the task I'm about to assign you and your young warriors may be the most dangerous part of my plan. If you fail, it could cost us the battle."

After Mahtowa quickly laid out the plan to Nokee, the band of young men grabbed their supplies and took their positions. Mahtowa asked the women to leave their three-legged shelter poles in place but to take their elk hide covers with them as they moved to the opposite side of the ridge. The women were to fill the base of their structures with dry-grass bedding. He wanted it to look like they planned to spend the night on the ridge. It was important that the Ottawa felt the villagers were running for their lives, leaving whatever they couldn't easily carry.

A stiff west wind was blowing in Mahtowa's face as he and his forty warriors stood waiting at the top of the ridge. The sight of the Sauk warriors standing there inflamed the Ottawa chief's anger. He ordered his force to quicken their pace.

Nearly two hundred Ottawa were approaching, their eyes filled with rage. In the past, two hundred Ottawa would have been no match for Mahtowa's current one-hundred-and-twenty-member force. The Sauk were fearless fighters. With muscular bodies and long arms wielding shields and stone hammers, they would destroy their enemies in hand-to-hand combat, often defeating three foes for every one of their own. However, things were different now. Muskets had changed the balance of power—but Mahtowa was determined to take it back.

When the Ottawa were one hundred paces away and coming up the ridge fast, Mahtowa and his men fell back. His warriors needed to be past the third marker when the Ottawa force topped the hill. Mahtowa told his braves to run fast enough to stay out of the range of the muskets, but not so fast that the Ottawa felt they couldn't catch them. When time came to fight, Mahtowa wanted their enemies out of breath.

As Mahtowa reached the fifth marker, his force spun around and formed a line. They began beating their spears against their long shields, chanting their war song. As Mahtowa had predicted, Chief Atowas and the Frenchmen halted the assault near the third marker and began shouting orders. Speaking in Ottawa, the Frenchmen ordered the fifteen warriors armed with muskets not to fire until the Sauk charged closer. They instructed the Ottawa archers to wait until the Sauk were within fifty paces before releasing their first volley of arrows.

Mahtowa focused on the western side of the ridge. When he saw the first puffs of smoke coming from the three-legged shelters left behind, he told his men to prepare to charge. Earlier, Mahtowa had instructed Nokee and his young warriors to fill their small clay pots with hot coals from their evening cooking fires. They were to hide at the side of the trail, and when the Ottawa force ran past, clearing the top of the ridge, they were to run as fast as they could to the ridge top and crawl through the grass to each of the three-legged structures. Then, they would empty their jars of sunflower oil on the dried-grass bedding and dump their pots containing burning coals.

"It's important that you then crawl off to the side and wait for the fighting to start," Mahtowa insisted. "When you hear the muskets fire, swing around and join the Mascouten archers."

When the first wave of smoke drifted into the Ottawa force, Mahtowa watched the Ottawa and Frenchmen spin around to see what was happening. When they did, Mahtowa gave the order for his force to charge. As Mahtowa had predicted, the trigger-happy Ottawa turned back and fired at the charging Sauk. The lead balls from the muskets buried deep into the Sauk's wood shields but didn't penetrate.

He heard a Frenchman scream, "Reload quickly! Reload!"

At that moment, Manomin's archers rose from the grass and fired their bows. Their arrows penetrated the exposed backs of their Ottawa enemies with deadly results. The Ottawa archers returned a volley of arrows; however, they were shooting blindly into the grass, as the Mascouten archers had already ducked and taken cover behind their shields. The Ottawa arrows fell harmlessly around them.

As thick plumes of smoke drifted into the Ottawa force, chaos broke out as visibility dropped to near zero. When Mahtowa and his warriors were fifty paces away, he ordered them to throw their spears into the panicking Ottawa force. The five French trappers shot wildly into the smoke, resulting in only minor wounds to two of the Sauk.

At that moment, Tionontati gave the order to charge in from the north and south. Running at full speed, Tionontati's men threw their spears into the tightly packed Ottawa, killing dozens. As Tionontati's force smashed into the Ottawa force's side flanks, Mahtowa's men crashed into their front line from the east.

Within a matter of minutes, half of the Ottawa force lay dead or dying, and the rest were retreating. As they ran back to the west, past Manomin's archers, the Mascoutens picked off another twenty or so with their bows. Mahtowa's forces sounded a roaring cheer, knowing they had delivered a devastating blow to their pursuers. Mahtowa considered pursuing the Ottawa force but then thought better of it. His warriors had decimated the Ottawa, suffering only a handful of losses.

Mahtowa was about to give the order to fall back and head for the intersecting trail when he noticed something. Through the smoke, he saw Nokee and the other young warriors burst out of the grass where they had been hiding. Ignoring his orders, they rushed to attack the last of the retreating Ottawa.

"No, Nokee! No!" Mahtowa shouted.

But it was too late. The four surviving Frenchmen reloaded their muskets and spun around. Three muskets fired, and three of the youth fell. The fourth Frenchman readjusted his aim and fired at the charging Sauk peace chief. Nokee heard the musket erupt, then saw his father stumble into the tall grass. Before he could comprehend what had happened, the retreating Ottawa had knocked him and the six young Mascouten onto the ground. They quickly bound the youths' hands, tied tethers around their necks, and led them away.

"Father, I failed you!" Nokee muttered, tears forming in his eyes. "I let my pride get in the way and blatantly disregarded your orders. I put us all in unnecessary danger. Please forgive my selfish stupidity."

• • •

Tionontati and Manomin ran into the tall grass to search for their fallen chief. By the time they found him, he was dead. Manomin, wailing in sorrow, fell to her knees. The victorious celebration ended abruptly as the warriors now stood silently at the side of their chief.

"What should we do?" asked a distraught voice in the crowd.

"Who will lead us?" cried a clan leader.

"The rules of the village council still stand," demanded Tionontati. "Mahtowa was our peace chief. By council law, his oldest son Nokee is now our chief."

Manomin, suddenly realizing that her son wasn't there, screamed. "Where's Nokee?"

No one had seen Nokee since Mahtowa had asked him to collect the pots and oil from the women.

Tionontati feared the worst. "Find Nokee!" he shouted.

Everyone began searching the dead for any sign of the young warriors among the fallen. Before long, Tionontati and Manomin heard a distressed scream from the western side of the ridge.

"They're over here!" shouted one of the women. "I've found them, and one is still alive."

Manomin closed her eyes, praying quietly. "Please, let my son be alive."

As they approached, the woman was standing over the bodies of two young warriors. A third, Measita, lay dying with a musket ball in his stomach. The young warrior's mother pleaded with Tionontati to heal her son. "Do your magic," she cried.

But Tionontati knew there was no magic cure for this type of wound, not from a musket. Aid and comfort were the best he could offer. Tionontati knelt and asked Measita what had happened.

Measita's voice strained as he spoke through the pain, brave till the end. "We just wanted to be part of the fight, so we rushed the stragglers. We didn't see the Frenchmen with muskets in the group. When we did, it was too late. They shot us down and captured the rest of our group."

Tionontati held Measita in his arms as the young man began coughing up blood. "Did they take them alive?"

"Yes," Measita gasped. "I heard them say, 'keep them alive. We'll trade them to the Chippewa.'" Measita's body began to shake. He took his last breath and passed into the spirit world.

Muskuta, the village war chief, addressed Tionontati. "I'll take our Sauk braves and go after them. Our two forces are now favorably matched in numbers, and we'll crush them to avenge our fallen leader."

Tionontati paused thoughtfully, then asked uneasily, "How many muskets did the Ottawa leave behind?"

"We've taken five from dead Ottawa fighters. A very fine one was found on a dead Frenchman."

"That means they still have fourteen muskets. How many warriors did we lose?"

"Counting Mahtowa and these three, we have ten dead."

Tionontati hesitated, then asked, "Did anyone see where the Ottawa went?"

One of the Mascouten archers from the north side of the battle spoke up, "When they hit the bottom of the ridge, they turned north."

"North! The logical reason for that would be if Chief Atowas knew the Chippewa would soon arrive and join the fight. Mahtowa was right," sighed Tionontati. "Muskuta, you knew Mahtowa as well as any of his fighters. What do you think he would say we should do?"

"He would say that our first duty is to get our villagers safely into Miami country. Then plan our revenge."

"I thought the same. If the Ottawa join with the Chippewa this evening, the Chippewa will certainly have more muskets. The Chippewa chief, Twakanha, might try to shame Chief Atowas, who has suffered two embarrassments in one day. He'll want him to pursue us into the Miami territory. However, Chief Atowas will refuse. He now knows our strength and fears the strength of the Miami Nation. The Miami scouts may already know of the forces that have amassed at their northern border. They may already be preparing to defend their land."

Tionontati turned to the villagers gathered around him and raised his voice so all could hear. "Council law says that if our peace chief is dead, his oldest son takes his place. If there are no sons, the ceremonial chief is in charge until our council chooses another peace chief. However, Measita told us before he died that Nokee was still alive. Therefore, as your ceremonial chief, I'm temporarily in charge until Nokee returns.

"I appoint Muskuta to lead our people south into Miami country. Take our ten beloved dead, including our Great Chief Mahtowa. Before the evening moon rises, you'll reach Gourdneck Lake, the site of one of our ancestral burial mounds. Camp there for the night, and tomorrow, cremate their bodies on top of the mound. Honor them with the appropriate grave goods and cover their bones and ashes with Mother Earth. Then proceed as quickly as possible to Three Rivers and seek the protection of Chief Myamick."

"When you arrive at Three Rivers, tell Myamick what has happened and present the five muskets to each of the clan leaders. Present the Frenchman's musket as a personal gift to him. That should win his favor. Manomin and I will stay behind and follow the Ottawa to see if there is a chance to free Nokee and the six young warriors."

"But Tionontati, what can two of you possibly do?" asked Muskuta.

Tionontati just smiled and said, "Why, Muskuta. I'm a fourth-degree Midewiwin and a shadow walker. I can do amazing things. Now go before the Chippewa show up."

Manomin gathered Mahtowa's medicine bag, copper crescent-moon necklace, and white peace pipe. "All these things now belong to Nokee, our new peace chief," she said.

The villagers collected the dead and quietly moved down the ridge toward the intersecting trail. Manomin and Tionontati headed north, following the fleeing Ottawa. In the dark, the villagers quietly walked south into Miami territory. They stationed scouts along their back trail to watch for any pursuers, but saw no one. When they reached Gourdneck Lake, the exhausted travelers camped for the night.

In the morning, they found the tall burial mound at the western outlet of the lake, just where Tionontati said it would be. They spent the morning gathering and assembling the large piles of wood needed for the funeral pyres. Then, they solemnly laid their dead on the elevated wood platforms and placed grave goods next to each one. Special attention was given to the body of Mahtowa so that those who met him in the spirit world would know he was a great chief and mighty warrior. His shield and spear were laid across his body, and they placed his war club next to his side. While the fires burned, they sang the ancient burial songs and began their ceremonial dance. As the sun set, they covered the fallen's ashes with earth and continued the mourning ceremony late into the night before finally resting.

• • •

As daylight began to break, the exhausted villagers awoke to frantic shouting. "Prepare for war! The enemy is upon us."

Muskuta leaped from his bed and prepared to fight. Quickly scanning the horizon, he saw that hundreds of warriors had encircled their camp during the night. But instead of grabbing his spear, he smiled and picked up his peace pipe. Standing there in front of his warriors was Myamick, the Miami chief. The Miami had spotted the smoke from the funeral pyres the day before and had come prepared to drive out the intruders.

Muskuta yelled to his people: "Stand down. These people are our friends."

Muskuta quickly assembled his clan leaders and approached Chief Myamick with the six muskets. Chief Myamick was pleased with the weaponry, especially the musket that had belonged to the French trapper. They sat in a large circle, smoking tobacco, while Muskuta recounted the events of the past few days. News of Mahtowa's death deeply saddened Myamick. The boldness of the Ottawa and Chippewa forces so close to his northern border also troubled him.

After listening attentively, Chief Myamick spoke, his voice soft. "Muskuta, I assure you that your people are welcome to stay with us in Three Rivers. You may stay until you gain your strength and heal your wounds. But you can't stay forever. Miami Country is no longer safe. The Miami people are fighting battles on all fronts.

"The Iroquois are driving vast numbers of people west. The Neutrals allow various Huron factions to cross the Detroit River and flood our territory. The once-mighty Fox Nation to the north has grown tired of constant war with the Chippewa. They crossed into the Upper Peninsula and moved west. Their absence has left the north open to a steady flow of Chippewa and Ottawa. They cross over, in ever-increasing numbers, at the Straits of Mackinac. To our south, roving bands of Iroquois frequently try to pass through our territory, and so far, we've been strong enough to fend them off.

"Muskuta, your people and ours have been friends and trading partners for generations. However, with the decreased strength of your people, the Potawatomi have moved north, up the Lake Michigan shoreline, and now control our western border. If Ottawa, Chippewa, and Potawatomi have joined an alliance to come after you, we can't defend against them all.

"I will tell you this. Last summer, a group of Kickapoo from Saginaw Bay passed through our land on their way to the other side of Lake Michigan. They told me they had been forced out of their homeland by the Chippewa, who now control that area. They said that a large group of Kickapoo, Sauk, and Mascouten now live on the other side of Lake Michigan. That may be the safest place for you and your people to settle."

# Shadow Walker

Far to the north, Tionontati and Manomin continued shadowing the Ottawa force. After the battle, Chief Atowas led his battered warriors up the Grand Rapids Trail. It wasn't long until the Ottawa force joined the Chippewa advance war party. The meeting was contentious from the start.

When the Chippewa heard what had happened, they mocked the Ottawa as weak and stupid. "How could two hundred warriors be defeated by a village of old men herding women and children? You probably had your muskets pointed the wrong way and shot yourselves. With our twenty warriors, we could've held them until Chief Twakanha arrived. He will not take your failure lightly."

Chief Atowas feared that fighting between the two forces might break out at any moment. Atowas called for his guards to bring the prisoners forth, then addressed Jibewas, the leader of the Chippewa advance force. "We've brought seven Mascouten prisoners for Twakanha, and one of them is the son of Mahtowa. Chief Mahtowa is dead. We can present your chief with the new Mascouten-Sauk peace chief. Do you want to be the one who takes this gift away from him?"

"He lies!" Nokee screamed. "My father is alive, and he'll come after us. You will regret this day."

One of Jibewas's men shoved Nokee to the ground and, in a flash, had a knife on Nokee's throat. Jibewas raised his hand and told his warrior to wait. "Prove what you say is true," he said, turning to Chief Atowas, "or I will have this worthless scum killed."

Chief Atowas pulled Nokee up by the hair and shoved him

forward. "See, he bears the marks of a peace chief." On each of his arms were the unmistakable tattoos of a black bear with a long white peace pipe. Such tattoos were well-recognized marks given to future peace chiefs at their coming-of-age ceremony.

"I believe this scum may be of value to Chief Twakanha," said Jibewas. "I'll spare his life. Get those prisoners out of my sight and see they don't escape. I assume your men are capable of handling that?"

As soon as the captives were gone, Jibewas turned to Chief Atowas. "Now, how can you prove that Mahtowa is dead?"

Chief Atowas called for the French trapper who had shot Mahtowa to step forward. The Frenchman confirmed that he had killed Mahtowa with his musket—he saw him fall dead. All the Ottawa nodded in agreement and let out a cheer of support.

"Give me that musket," Jibewas demanded. "Chief Twakanha will use it to kill the new Mascouten-Sauk peace chief and capture his spirit power."

At first, the trapper refused. However, Chief Atowas made it clear this was not a negotiation—it was a demand. The trapper went silent and quickly handed over the musket. Atowas, pleased with the quick response, gave the trapper a replacement musket from one of his warriors. Jibewas ran his hands up and down his coveted prize.

The two tribes spent the night on opposite sides of the trail. Tionontati and Manomin saw no chance to rescue the young prisoners. Both sides had posted double guards due to distrust of each other and Nokee's threat.

Early the next day, Chief Twakanha and his sizeable fighting force arrived. Surprisingly, Twakanha had brought a delegation of Potawatomi chiefs with him. Chief Twakanha was outraged when he heard the news of the failed Ottawa attack. He had been so confident of a victory that he had arranged a multi-tribal meeting to decide how to divide the newly acquired territory amongst the tribes. Instead, he had to deal with a botched attack and the thought that his blood enemy had escaped at full strength. The failure made his warriors question his wisdom, and the Potawatomi chiefs wondered why they were there.

Chief Twakanha knew he had to act quickly to reestablish his authority. He demanded his war party leader to give him a full report. Jibewas appeared tense as he approached Chief Twakanha. "My Chief, your warriors traveled at great speed throughout the day without stopping until we intercepted the retreating Ottawa. We considered killing this rag-tag force when we heard what had happened. We would've done it, too, just for you. But then they told us Mahtowa was dead and that they had captured Mahtowa's son, the new peace chief. We made them turn over the musket that killed Mahtowa. I now present it to you—it holds great power."

Chief Twakanha stood quietly as all eyes and ears turned toward him. He knew he needed to devise a way for all parties to save face. He asked Chief Atowas to explain, for all to hear, how this could have happened.

Chief Atowas called for Odawa, his lead scout who had traveled with the Chippewa warriors, to step forward. Chief Atowas turned to the group, raising his voice. "Great chiefs have great scouts. The information they provide can often make the difference between success and failure. Timely delivery of that information is everything. Odawa, what time did the Sauk and Mascouten leave their village yesterday?"

"Before morning light, my Chief," replied Odawa.

"Odawa, what time did you report to me?"

"Around mid-morning, my Chief."

"Odawa, what time did you report to Chief Twakanha?"

"Around midday, my Chief."

"Odawa, what would've happened if the Chippewa force had arrived at the intersection before sunset?"

"They would've trapped the villagers between our two fighting forces. Together, we would've easily destroyed our enemy."

"Odawa, if you were chief and your lead scout delivered bad information, and that bad information resulted in a humiliating defeat of your force, allowing the enemy to escape virtually unharmed ... what would you do?"

"I would make sure it never happened again." Odawa took his knife out of his belt and handed it to his chief. Chief Atowas took the knife and thrust it into Odawa's chest, striking his heart.

As Odawa fell dead to the ground, Chief Atowas shouted to the shocked crowd, "Let this be a lesson to all scouts. You'll pay with your life if you deliver your chief inaccurate or untimely information."

Chief Twakanha, satisfied with what had just happened, asked Chief Atowas to join him in a private counsel. As soon as they were settled, Twakanha spoke first. "I've brought many warriors. My fighting force outnumbers your battered warriors two to one. My men want me to seek revenge for your failure and kill all of you here and now."

Chief Atowas stared hard into the rival chief's eyes. "We'll fight to the death, and you'll shed more blood than you think."

"I hoped you would say that, and I respect your courage. I've thought of a way for all to come out of this with our honor intact."

Chief Atowas narrowed his eyes. "What do you have in mind?"

• • •

At the end of their meeting, the two chiefs emerged. Chief Atowas, grinning softly, was the first to address the group. "Chief Twakanha has invited all of us to join him at his tribal fishing village at Grand Rapids. There, we'll hold a multi-tribal council meeting to divide up the land taken forever from the Fox, Kickapoo, Sauk, and Mascouten. The Great Chief Twakanha has made a fair offer that benefits us all. He has proposed that all rivers north of the Grand River, which flow west, will now be the undisputed territory of the Ottawa." A great cheer broke out among the Ottawa warriors.

"He also has proposed that all westerly flowing rivers south of the Grand River will now be the undisputed territory of the Potawatomi." The shocked Potawatomi delegation was ecstatic with the announcement.

Chief Twakanha stepped forward. "The entire Upper Peninsula and all rivers, north of Lake St. Clair in the Lower Peninsula, including the entire Saginaw River basin, will now be the undisputed territory of the Ojibwa and Chippewa." The Chippewa warriors stood there in silence.

"United, the new Alliance of the Three Fires will join forces with the Neutrals at Detroit and drive the Miami tribe out of the Lower Peninsula. All Miami lands will become the land of the Chippewa Nation." At that announcement, a great cheer broke out among the Chippewa warriors.

The mood of the three tribes changed from contentious to upbeat as the group prepared to move north to Chief Twakanha's fishing camp at Grand Rapids. Twenty summers ago, the Chippewa had driven the last of the Sauk from the area and took over their territory. Chief Twakanha's main camp was in the Saginaw River basin. During their final push to remove the Sauk, they discovered a small fishing village at the rapids. The Sauk used the site to harvest the abundant Coaster Brook Trout. Generations of Sauk had made rock fences in the rapids to guide the spawning trout into rock-lined pools where they could easily spear them. The Chippewa regarded this precious jewel of their conquest with great reverence.

Coaster Brook Trout were large, colorful, tasty trout that came up the Grand River in the fall from Lake Michigan to spawn in the rapids' gravel beds. The Chippewa women like to eat them fresh or smoke them and wrap them in corn husks. Once smoked, they could be stored in underground storage pits for months.

In addition, the Chippewa had figured out that if they dumped their wooden buckets of fish entrails into the woods, they could set up bait piles to attract bears. Once the bears grew accustomed to feasting on the bounty of flesh, hunters would lie in ambush and slay them with their bows and arrows. The area had become quite a resource for the Chippewa tribe to fill their fall food cache before returning to their winter camp on the Saginaw River.

Chief Twakanha sent runners ahead to inform the villagers that his force was returning along with one hundred and twenty Ottawa and Potawatomi. The villagers at the rapids began preparing for a Great Council meeting, ensuring there was enough food and drink for all. Twakanha also sent orders for seven posts to be set in the ground in front of the council house for the sacrifice of their seven prisoners.

When the three groups arrived, they were all served generous portions of baked trout, fresh-cooked bear meat, corn cake, squash, and boiled beans. The seven prisoners were given dry smoked meat and water and tied to the interior posts of one of the lodges. After everyone had finished eating, the chiefs and clan leaders entered the large council house and began their discussions. Almost immediately, the talks grew contentious when the

Ottawa chief demanded compensation for turning over the prisoners. The Chippewa insisted that the Ottawa were a retreating army rescued by the Chippewa. Therefore, they should forfeit all rights to the prisoners. The Potawatomi refused to get involved in the discussion, and the argument continued late into the evening.

While the arguments raged on, Nokee and his fellow hand-bound warriors sat quietly, trying to appear brave but fearing what would come next. They could hear angry voices rising, but the words were indistinct. Yet they were certain of one thing: their futures looked bleak. One of the young men broke the silence. "What do you think they'll do with us?"

"I heard the Chippewa chief tell his messenger to place seven posts in the ground," Nokee said. "That can only mean that they are planning to kill us."

After a long pause, Nokee lowered his head and said, "I'm so sorry I got all of you into this. None of this would've happened if I had followed my father's orders."

"Don't blame yourself," said one of the warriors. "We all trained together and were itching for a fight. We all agreed to attack the Ottawa."

"True," replied Nokee. "But our chief trusted me with your well-being. My vision was clouded. I failed to live up to my father's orders."

After thinking for a time, Nokee said: "And yet what you said is true. We've all trained to be warriors and were looking for a fight. So, let's give the Ottawa and Chippewa one last fight they will remember."

"How?" the group whispered in unison.

"I managed to hide a small knife in my leggings that they didn't discover. If I can get my leg up to someone's hands, they can use it to cut their bonds and free the rest of us. Then, when the tormentors come to get us, we rush them. They will most certainly kill us, but it will be on our terms." All nodded in agreement to the plan.

• • •

Chief Twakanha had enough of the squabbling in the council house. He ordered a group of Chippewa women to prepare three Wampum Belts.

"Each Wampum Belt must be three feet long," demanded Twakanha. "I want one foot blue, one red, and one white. A Wampum Belt will be presented to each tribe to signify the unbreakable Alliance of the Three Fires."

Then Chief Twakanha turned to address the council. "The blue on the belt will represent the Chippewa, the red the Ottawa, and the white the Potawatomi. We will tie the seven prisoners to the seven posts, and each tribe will deal with their two prisoners in any way they wish. Finally, the seventh prisoner—the son of Mahtowa—I will kill, capturing the spirit power of the Sauk and Mascouten forever."

The Potawatomi and Ottawa agreed to the new alliance. When the Wampum Belts were ready, Chief Twakanha ordered the seven prisoners to be brought out and tied to the posts. At that moment, one of Twakanha's warriors ran into the council house, wild with anxiety.

"The prisoners are gone!"

What began as a congratulatory celebration quickly descended into a flurry of accusations.

• • •

Minutes earlier, as the guards outside the prisoner's lodge strained to overhear the heated conversations coming out of the council house, no one noticed that a Shadow Walker had entered the camp. Slowly, a knife blade cut through the cattail-wall mats of the prisoner's lodge. The young Mascoutens, already freed from their bonds, rose and readied themselves to fight to the death. But instead of facing their tormentors, Tionontati pushed his head through the wall mat and signaled for silence. He motioned for the young men to slip out of the back. With silent footsteps, they followed him to the river. Their hearts raced as they reached the bottom of the rapids, where Manomin waited with five of the Chippewa's light-and-fast birchbark canoes. She had punctured all the other canoes with her knife to prevent the Chippewa from quickly following them.

As the group prepared to shove off, Tionontati put his hand on Nokee's shoulder. "Nokee, you'll not be going with us."

Nokee shot a questioning look at Tionontati and his mother. Tionontati locked eyes with Nokee and spoke softly. "Last night, I had a dream. Gitchee Manito, the Great Spirit of the Midewiwin Order, came to me. He told me you must undertake a great journey before being accepted as chief of our tribe. Your path lies up the Grand River. You are to make the Great Circle, visit the sacred places, listen to the guiding voices of the spirits, and find your way back to the Miami Three River camp on the St. Joseph River. You'll receive help from unexpected people and places along the way. Trust your heart. When you finally return to your people, you'll be recognized, and there will be much joy."

Tionontati handed Nokee a two-foot-square piece of deer hide. "Take this. It will help you find your way. The spirit told me that our path was downriver. Your path is up. He promised me that if you do this, we'll all meet again."

Manomin handed Nokee her fine-woven shoulder bag with geometric shapes and a black bear stitched on its front cover. Nokee dropped the piece of deer hide into the bag and peered inside. Stashed within were a leather water bag; a small tool kit for making arrowheads and arrows; a block of flint; a strike-a-light fire starter; three small stackable wooden bowls; a flat cooking stone; his father's knife, medicine bag, copper-crescent necklace; and a white peace pipe. There was also a handful of elk jerky and six small cornbread cakes. But the most precious item was at the bottom: his mother's ultra-lite, ultra-warm, rain-repellent bobcat blanket. Nokee was flooded with memories of the soft warmth the blanket had provided, of how Manomin would wrap him in it during his childhood.

Nokee was torn between pride and sorrow. "I can't take your blanket. It was a gift to you from Father."

With tears in her eyes, Manomin wrapped her arms around him, sharing her warm spirit with him for what could be the last time. "Take it; it will keep you warm during your travels. I now trust my care to Tionontati. You must do the same."

Manomin handed Nokee his bow and quiver of arrows, which they had retrieved from the tall grass at the battle site. "Nokee, my son, my chief, may the spirit of Manito travel with you."

Nokee stood frozen in shock. His mother had just confirmed what Nokee had refused to accept; his father was dead. The final moment they'd shared was receiving orders from his father—orders he had disobeyed. Nokee didn't deserve to be chief. He wasn't ready. Someone older and wiser should take his father's place. Time seemed to freeze as a torrent of unanswered questions swirled through his mind. By the time he came to, the four canoes had slid quietly into the fast-moving current and were about to disappear into the darkness.

Nokee, his head still in a fog, crossed the river in the fifth canoe and looked toward the woods. Once on the other side, he stabbed holes in the canoe and set it adrift. Then he began to run. He ran until his breath came in ragged gasps and all sense of time and direction was lost.

Finally, on the verge of collapsing, Nokee came to a clearing in the woods and fell to the ground. As his conversation with Tionontati raced through his mind, his despair gave way to anger.

"Why did they have to leave me?" Nokee mumbled. "Why couldn't Tionontati have stayed with me? I've always thought this Great Circle was nothing more than one of Tionontati's stories. ... How can this be the path I'm supposed to follow?"

As he felt the forest close in around him, shrouding his path forward, his mother's words pierced through the darkness. *Son, I now trust my care to Tionontati. You must do the same.*

Nokee looked up to the night sky, suddenly feeling small and ashamed beneath the glinting stars. *Tionontati and my mother have risked their lives trying to save the other young warriors and me. None of this would've happened if I had followed my father's instructions. Tionontati is a fourth-degree Midewiwin, a seer of things to come. He has never steered the tribe wrong. If this quest is mine and mine alone, I must accept it.*

Tionontati had told him the story many times, how the Midewiwin would gather every five years and travel the Great Circle. Tionontati once said they did it in a single moon cycle.

*I can do it in less time.* As part of his warrior training, he had spent two weeks alone in the woods with nothing but a knife. He and the other young men survived by finding food and shelter, proving that they could live off the land. Nokee tapped his shoulder bag, courage rising once more within him. *This will be easy.*

Then, another great wave of guilt swept over him as he realized the danger the others were in because of him. They had deliberately left no doubt about which direction they were heading and their mode of transportation. When Chief Twakanha and Chief Atowas figured out what happened, they would send every available warrior after them. They will be relentless in their pursuit, and if they catch them, the escapees will suffer a most horrible death.

Nokee, exhausted, couldn't think of it anymore. He reached into his mother's shoulder bag, wanting to wrap himself in the warmth of her blanket. As he pulled it out, two of the corn cakes fell out. Nokee's stomach growled. He had forgotten how hungry he was. He gobbled down the cakes and ate two pieces of elk jerky before drifting into a deep sleep.

# The Great Circle

Nokee woke with a jolt as daylight broke on the eastern horizon. He found himself drenched in a cold sweat from a terrifying nightmare. He'd seen himself standing on the shoreline of Lake Michigan when he spotted four canoes paddling away. His mother waved to him, so he jumped in and started swimming toward her. However, the canoes continued moving west. Finally, he grew tired and sank below the waves. The water became darker and darker until he was gone.

Every dream carries meaning—Tionontati had taught that to Nokee long ago. If he were here now, perhaps he could explain it—but he wasn't. This was Nokee's quest, and he would have to pursue it alone. Whatever the dream meant, he would have to uncover it for himself.

Now more than ever, Nokee was convinced that Three Rivers was the direction Tionontati's group would take. *Tionontati knows the Grand River system better than anyone*, thought Nokee. *They'll travel at night and hide their canoes in the woods during the day. Soon, they'll abandon their canoes and travel south through the Land of the Mascouten. Once safe in Miami Country, they will head straight to Chief Myamick's camp. I need to do the same. It will take them as much time as it takes me to make the Great Circle. We should all arrive at Three Rivers at about the same time.*

Nokee, confident his plan would succeed, reached into his shoulder bag and ate two corn cakes and a few pieces of elk jerky. He wasn't concerned about food. He knew he could acquire all he would need with his bow and arrows. Rabbits, hares, grouse, nuts, and seeds were readily available at this time of the year. His confidence was growing by the minute.

As he stood and took in his surroundings, he was stunned. The clearing he had slept at last night held a dozen or more mounds. From where he stood, he could count six large structures and numerous smaller ones. Old-growth pines circled the opening, but the mound site was without trees. Nokee remembered Tionontati telling him how the Midewiwin would visit and care for the ancient burial sites on their pilgrimages.

Nokee took his time walking around the area. It turned out there were sixteen mounds in all. He did an estimate in his head: If a peace chief lives an average of thirty years, and each chief starts a new burial mound, there must be close to five hundred years of history here. However, four of the burial mounds were different. Each was the same height and had a ramp that led up to a sealed chamber. It looked like the design was for individuals of immense importance.

Nokee considered what this could mean. Burial mounds were supposed to hold the cremated remains of anyone who died the previous year. Everyone in the village would participate in the annual burial ceremony and help in the recapping process to prepare for next year's burials. But not these chamber mounds. Why were these people so important? Where were the rest of the people buried? He would have to ask Tionontati about this later.

But what fascinated Nokee most was a large boulder in the center of the burial mound complex. The obelisk was slightly tipped to the side by the exposed roots of an ancient beech tree that had grown next to it. The tree looked to be hundreds of years old. That meant the stone must have been placed there long before the tree.

On the sheared-off face of the large stone were animal shapes representing the various clans that had lived there. Nokee identified a deer, bear, cougar, wolf, swan, bald eagle, perch, bass, and sturgeon—nine different clans. An average clan can have over fifty people in it. That would mean there must have been close to five hundred people living in this village. *Tionontati told me over a dozen villages like this were on the Grand River system and likely a similar number on other major rivers in the Lower Peninsula.*

*If all villages were of equivalent size, that would mean that their total population must have numbered in the tens of thousands.*

That afternoon, Nokee foraged as he hunted for wild turkey. He gathered chicken-of-the-woods mushrooms, wild grapes, and rose hips for tea. Before long, he found and shot his prey, then returned to the clearing with the mounds to start his fire. He had been careful to collect dried oak and hickory for the fire—any other wood would produce too much smoke. As the sun dipped below the treetops, he roasted enough fresh meat for his meal, smoking the rest for later use. Nokee kept a close eye on the smoke, making sure it didn't drift downwind along his back trail. His pursuers would most likely be coming from that direction.

Adding the last two corn cakes to the meal made for a fine evening feast. After enjoying his nourishment, he leaned back against a tree and assessed what supplies he had at his disposal.

Nokee reached into his mother's shoulder bag and pulled out his father's medicine bag. He knew that a proper medicine bag must contain at least one item from each of the four kingdoms: Plant, Animal, Mineral, and Human. He spread out his mother's blanket on the ground and dumped out the contents of his father's pouch. Medicine bag items can never touch the ground, or their power will drain back into Mother Earth.

From the Plant Kingdom there was a small leather bag of tobacco and a cord made from twisted butterfly-weed fiber. The cord was thin and light but extraordinarily strong. From the Animal Kingdom there was a bone from a bear penis, symbolizing strength and fertility, and the orange incisors of a beaver, used for perforating or etching items. From the Mineral Kingdom there was a long turkey-tail-style spear point made of chipped flint. It had been handed down from chief to chief for countless generations, symbolizing spiritual connection to the ancestors. There was also a small copper implement—a celt—for working wood.

From the Human Kingdom came three personal items close to Nokee's heart. The first was a small, artfully crafted silver bear, suspended from a leather strap. It had been his father's spirit animal. Now, it would serve as Nokee's guardian spirit as well. The second item was his father's copper crescent-moon necklace, six inches across and warm with memories of his father. Nokee lifted it gently and placed it around his neck. Finally, to his delight, he found the arrowhead that Nokee had given to his father after Nokee had killed the bear at the paw-paw patch. Satisfied, Nokee reloaded everything into the pouch.

The last thing Nokee removed from his mother's bag was the piece of deer hide Tionontati had given him back at the river. Unfolding it with care, he found a map of the Great Circle etched in black wood ash. He was struck by the amazing detail—each twist and turn of the Grand and St. Joseph River systems was precisely marked, and each tributary river he would be crossing had a name. What caught his eye was the small circles showing the location of every mound center along the route. He studied the map and determined he must be at the mound center located southeast of the Grand River rapids.

• • •

By now, darkness was setting in, and it would soon be time to move on. Determined to leave no trace of ever having been there, he dug a small hole to bury the ashes. At the bottom of the pit, he felt something sharp prick his finger, drawing blood. He picked it up and held it in the fading daylight; it was a thin, well-crafted, corner-notched projectile point with serrated edges. It was the length of an index finger, wider at the base and tapered to a sharp point. It looked like an aspen leaf. On the back was a jagged N, most likely carved with a bear claw. *Too large for an arrowhead*, thought Nokee. It must belong to the people who once lived here.

He cleaned the point and placed it in his newly acquired medicine bag. As soon as he did, a sudden burst of wind rattled the beech leaves and branches above, sending down a shower of beechnuts.. Nokee took this as a good sign and gathered a couple of handfuls of high-energy nuts for later use. *Now I have my connection to the ancestors*, thought Nokee. He covered the pit with earth and leaves, leaving no trace of his presence.

It was dark when Nokee stepped back onto the Grand River Trail. He headed east, moving slowly, watching and listening for any signs of danger ahead. He traveled a long way without encountering anything unusual. When he reached the Thornapple River, he paused for a moment. This part of the river was shallow enough to wade across. As he stepped into the cool water, Tionontati's words echoed in the back of his mind: "This you must do. You are to travel up the Grand River, make the Great Circle, visit the sacred places, listen to the guiding voices of the spirits, and find your way back."

Nokee pulled out the map that Tionontati had given him. The nearest mound site was located at the mouth of the Thornapple River. He backed out of the water and turned north, choosing to follow the Thornapple River downstream.

It was an unusually warm early September night. The sky was clear, and the half-moon lit Nokee's path as he moved silently through the night. As he neared the place where the Thornapple empties into the Grand River, he stepped into a clearing. Sure enough, he found mounds encircled by a ring of boulders.

There were three mounds at this site. All resembled the unfamiliar chamber mounds Nokee saw last night. They were the same size and style of construction, each with dirt ramps and sealed chambers.

Nokee spent time carefully examining the area, and the more time he spent in the presence of the mounds, the more questions he had. *Did these people share the river sites with my ancestors? Or did they come long after them?* Nokee made a mental note to look for similar mound types at other sites. He was already excited to ask Tionontati about them.

He took out his map and copper needle. Carefully, he etched a line through the three circles to indicate chamber-style mounds. He did the same for the site he had visited last night.

Still exhausted from two days of captivity, Nokee leaned back against one of the mounds and fell asleep. He dreamt of great chiefs lying inside this mound. They were in log coffins surrounded by the finest-crafted grave goods. There were assorted items and tools of silver and copper: long white flint spear points, knives, and well-designed decorated clay pots at their sides. Turtle and conch shell bowls, bone pins, hammerstones, and antler billets were neatly stacked nearby. A pile of aspen-shaped projectile points lay next to the entrance.

Nokee snapped awake—he had slept longer than planned. With only an hour of darkness remaining, he hurried upstream along the Thornapple River, hoping to cross before daybreak. As he neared the river crossing, he heard voices traveling east on the Grand River Trail. He was certain they were Chippewa, returning to Saginaw Bay from their Grand Rapids fishing camp. Although their languages differed slightly, they were similar enough for Nokee to catch parts of the conversation.

The group, composed of women and children, moved quickly, their voices full of lighthearted talk. Once their voices faded into the distance, Nokee began to backtrack toward the Thornapple mound site. He would cross the Grand River there—the trail was no longer safe. As he neared the river's edge, he froze. A moment before they came into view around the river bend, he heard the rhythmic splash of canoes paddling upstream. Nokee dove into the nearby brush, his body pressed against the damp soil.

As they came into view, he recognized them as Chippewa warriors returning home from their fishing camp. Their large cargo canoes sat low in the water, weighted with heavy camp supplies, including substantial amounts of preserved bear meat and smoked fish.

Nokee lay hidden and listened for any talk about how they had captured the escapees or suspected that he had separated from them and traveled upstream. He heard nothing that indicated either. After all the canoes had passed, he found a floating log and covered it with a tag-alder branch to camouflage him and his equipment as he swam across the river. He wanted it to look like a beaver had gathered branches for their winter food pile in case another canoe happened to appear unexpectedly. None did, and he breathed a sigh of relief as he safely reached the other side.

• • •

Nokee spent the next ten days traveling along the north side of the Grand River, heading east. He would visit mound sites on the Flat, Maple, and Looking Glass Rivers. At each location, Nokee recorded the number and type of mounds he encountered.

When Nokee reached the big bend in the Grand River where the river curved south, he saw signs of fresh fire pits. Nokee immediately expected the worst. If his enemies had figured out that he was heading upriver, he was in grave danger. His suspicions were justified the following afternoon when, from his daytime hiding place, he heard voices and saw an Ottawa hunting party moving slowly along the south bank of the river.

"I must be more careful," whispered Nokee.

Nokee was unaware of the deal Chief Twakanha had made, making all westerly flowing rivers north of the Grand River the undisputed territory of the Ottawa tribe. These Ottawa had moved into the Big Bend area on the Grand River to assess the sincerity of the Chippewa offer.

He had planned to visit the mound site near the mouth of the Red Cedar River but determined it would be too risky. Tionontati's map showed another mound site at a large lake northeast of the Big Bend. He decided to visit that site while skirting around the Ottawa's inhabited area. From there, he could turn south and rejoin the upper reach of the Grand River.

When Nokee arrived at Pine Lake, he found a lake teeming with ducks, geese, swans, and cranes. The north and west sides were lined with towering white pines, while the south and east sides encompassed a large marsh. Nokee worked his way around to the south ridge of the lake. There, he found an American chestnut tree surrounded by fallen chestnuts. He gathered a couple of handfuls of the tasty nuts to roast later.

Nokee headed to a small island where he could safely spend the day hiding. The opportunities to gather food in the wetland seemed endless. He put an arrow through a fat sandhill crane, found freshwater mussels in the shallows, and pulled cattail roots. Then he picked staghorn sumac clusters, wintergreen berries, wild plums, wild cranberries, and spicebush branches.

Nokee stripped out the breasts and legs of the crane. He sliced the breast meat to cook on flat rocks in the coals. He cooked the crane legs on a hickory stick supported over the flames by two forked posts. After cleaning up the cattail roots, he placed them in the coals. When cooked, he stripped off the outer burnt skin and ate the starchy potato-like center. Nokee mashed the sumac clusters and wintergreen berries in one bowl and added water. In another bowl of water, he placed the cranberries. He brought the mixers to a boil by adding small fire-heated stones. With spicebush branches, he fished out the cooled rocks and replaced them with hot ones when needed. The spicebush branches added flavor to the mix.

While cooking his dinner, he split open the mussels and placed the half-shells in the coals. They were a delightful pre-dinner treat. After sandhill crane breast, cranberries, cattail root, and sumac and wintergreen tea, Nokee relaxed with roasted chestnuts and wild plums for dessert. *It was a fine feast*, he thought to himself. *I could live like this forever. Who needs to be chief?*

As darkness set in, Nokee left his hiding place to continue searching for the Pine Lake mound site shown on the map. Nokee hadn't gone far when he tripped over a half-buried boulder in the dark. As he stood up, he saw a boulder-lined trail running east. Though many of the boulders had fallen over or were sunk deep into the leaf litter, it was clear to Nokee that someone had placed them there long ago. *This must be the boulder-lined trail Tionontati told me about in his story of Pine Lake*, Nokee thought.

Nokee followed the winding trail east through the woods until the path opened into a large prairie. As the full moon slipped out from behind the clouds, Nokee saw seven mounds of assorted sizes. Six were in the traditional cone-shaped style. However, the one on the western end of the group was a chamber-style mound. It had a ramp leading to a chamber framed with thick, square-cut rocks. A huge boulder, shaped like the face of a great chief, blocked the entrance.

This site was the largest mound center that Nokee had visited yet. It was almost five hundred paces long. Nokee remembered Tionontati telling him of a sacred place in the center of the Great Circle. It was a place where the Midewiwin would meet every five years on the day of the Summer Strawberry Moon. Tionontati said it had been the heart and soul of the once-great Sauk Nation.

Nokee wondered: Could this possibly be that place? He wished he had listened to Tionontati's stories more closely, and that Tionontati was there to explain all this. One thing he knew for sure was that he felt a strange connection to this place. Nokee planned to study this site until he could decipher its meaning. He would not allow himself to return to Tionontati without insight into the burial mounds.

What made this site unique from the others he had visited was a tall, flat-topped hill located south of the seven burial mounds. Nokee estimated the hill to be about thirty paces wide, forty paces long, and about as tall as an oak tree. It must have taken years to build. The mound didn't appear to be intended for burials, but for ceremonial purposes. Atop the ceremonial mound were two stone altars surrounded by a ring of stone benches. One altar faced east, and the other faced northeast toward the burial mounds. Studying their alignment, Nokee wondered what the purpose of these structures was—and just as importantly, who had constructed them. Did the Midewiwins build these altars, or were they maintaining ancient artifacts of the past?

It wasn't until the following morning that the purpose of the structure became clear. As the sun rose in the east, a ray of light pierced a hole in a boulder and lit up a chiseled mark in the eastern facing altar. The altar was aligned perfectly for singling the days of equal light and darkness—the beginning of spring and fall.

Nokee spent the rest of the day continuing his investigation of the site. Three groundwater-fed streams crisscrossed the area, one marking the north border and the other marking its south. But the stream in the center of the complex was the most interesting. That one originated from a rock-lined spring next to the mounds.

While looking into the bubbling pool of water, Nokee noticed numerous crafted items lying at the bottom of the spring. He could envision the sacred ceremonies that had taken place here. The villagers would have lined up to offer items blessed by the priests. They would have asked for special favors from the Great Spirit or wished to make amends for some evil past deed. Nokee spotted a large chunk of red jasper carved into the shape of a bear. He reached for it but quickly withdrew his hand from the spring. Taking an item from a sacred place could provoke the Dark Forces to place a terrible curse on you—one that might follow you for the rest of your life. Nokee felt he was cursed enough as is—he had no need for any more negative energy.

For two more days, Nokee expanded his search of the area. Two trails intersected at the mound site. The Pine Lake trail that he had followed to the site continued east. The north/south trail connected the Red Cedar River to the south with Vermilion Creek to the north, a tributary of the Looking Glass River. Nokee looked at Tionontati's map. If his ancestors ruled the land from Saginaw Bay to the shores of Lake Michigan, this would have been the center of that realm.

At the end of the fourth day, Nokee sensed it was time to move on. Though he left the site with more questions than answers, he felt confident that Tionontati could help him find a satisfying explanation. Besides, he thought it would be best to get to Three Rivers—his mother would soon be worried about his whereabouts.

• • •

Nokee headed south toward the Red Cedar River. He turned east on the Grand River Trail and headed upstream a short distance until he reached the mouth of Deer Creek. Tionontati's map showed a small burial site at the junction of Deer Creek and the Red Cedar River; however, Nokee would never find it in the dark. So instead, he continued south, following Deer Creek to its headwater, then turned due west until he reached the rapids on the Upper Grand River. Nokee located the mound site indicated on the map and spent the rest of the night there. There were no chamber mounds at that site.

He had traveled a long way that night and was exhausted. However, sleep did not come easily. A feeling that his journey was taking too long had taken root within him. In his dreams he heard whispers from his mother, calling for him to hurry home. "The villagers need their chief," she cried. "They're growing restless without you."

Nokee estimated he still had another five or six days before reaching the Miami village at Three Rivers. The nights were getting colder, and even his bobcat blanket was not enough to keep him warm. He dared not light an evening warming fire until he reached safer territory. It would take at least one exceptionally long night of travel before leaving the land his enemies controlled. He would heed the message from his dreams and forgo any further mound studies. It was time to return to his tribe—time to become chief. The next night, he deliberately quickened his pace. Though his muscles ached, he reached the land of the Miami Nation before dawn. For the first time in a month, he built a fire and slept warm and worry-free.

From that point on, Nokee felt confident he could travel during the day. He estimated he had only about half a day's travel southwest on the Sauk Trail before he would intercept the St. Joseph River. From there, he would be reunited with his tribe in two days.

*Oh, what stories I'll tell them*, he thought. Nokee smiled when he realized that Tionontati won't be the only one to tell stories of the Great Circle in the sweat lodge. It was the first time he'd smiled since his capture.

Pleased with himself, Nokee retrieved his father's peace pipe from his mother's bag and assembled the three sections. He figured if he was going to be the leader of the tribal council, he had better learn to smoke. He loaded the long pipe with tobacco from his medicine bag and lit the peace pipe. After taking a big draw, he nearly coughed his head off.

"This isn't the pleasant experience I was expecting," Nokee said to himself. "I'll need considerable practice to not look like a fool." He added wood to his warming fire, put away his pipe, and fell asleep.

In the morning, he awoke to the distinctive sound of muskets cocking. Opening his eyes, he saw six Miami warriors pointing their weapons directly at him.

"I'm glad to see you guys," Nokee said without stirring from his grass-mat bed.

"Don't move, you worthless spy," Oumami, the leader of the group, shouted. "Your luck has run out."

"I'm no spy. I'm Nokee, peace chief of the Mascouten and Sauk tribe," responded Nokee with a newfound sense of dignity. "Surely, Tionontati and my mother told you I would be coming this way?"

The men looked at each other with questioning stares.

"Prove it," said Oumami.

Nokee had his bobcat blanket wrapped around his shoulders like a cape. Slowly, he let it slide open. On both shoulders were the tattoos of a peace chief, and around his neck hung his father's copper crescent-moon gorget.

"I recognize that," said Oumami, pointing to the gorget. "The last time I saw it was when your father and Tionontati visited our village. How did you escape? Muskuta told us that the Ottawa captured you after your father died on the St. Joseph Trail."

Nokee sat up with a puzzled look. "Surely, Tionontati told you how he and my mother freed us at the Chippewa village."

"Like I said," responded Oumami. "I haven't seen Tionontati since he and your father visited our village almost a year ago."

"That can't be right! Are you telling me the others haven't arrived? After Tionontati rescued us, he and my mother escaped down the Grand River with six young warriors in Chippewa canoes. Tionontati insisted that I head upstream and make the Great Circle—a vision quest to communicate with our ancestors. Tionontati knows the Grand River and the land of the Mascouten better than anyone. There's no way the Chippewa could have captured that group. We must quickly return to your village and tell the others to search for them."

"Nokee, I'm afraid I have more bad news for you. Your people are no longer there."

Nokee jumped up and grabbed Oumami by the arm. "What do you mean they're no longer there?"

"They've all moved west before the Iroquois could prevent them from leaving. The Iroquois advance from the east in ever-increasing numbers. They attack villages and take prisoners. The villagers either join the Iroquois raiding parties or are put to death. In addition, the Chippewa, Ottawa, and Potawatomi have joined forces in the Confederation of the Three Fires. They've demanded that our chief turn over your people, or they will attack. The Miami tribe can't afford to be at war on all borders. Chief Myamick told your people they must go now while he could still protect them. Soon, their path west will be closed. They could not wait any longer."

"If what you say is true, I'll hunt for Tionontati and the others myself. They're out there somewhere. I can feel it!"

"I would not recommend that course of action. The Iroquois are everywhere, as are their spies. The Iroquois send out their prisoners to locate villages and assess a village's strength. Then they swarm that village like a horde of locusts."

"Did my people say where they are going?"

"I did hear Chief Myamick tell Muskuta that a group of Kickapoo had passed through our village last summer. The Kickapoo told Myamick that others of your kind live in the land of Illinois. Muskuta said he would take his people there."

"His people!" snapped Nokee. "Muskuta isn't chief, I am. Who put him in charge?"

"Muskuta said it was Tionontati's request," replied Oumami. "Tionontati told him it should remain like that until their rightful chief returns."

Nokee took a step back. It was too much information to process all at once. Had he misinterpreted his dreams? His mother and Tionontati drifting west in their boats might have been a sign that they had been captured and killed. It might have been their spirits he saw leaving this world. His mother pleading with him to hurry back must've been a warning that the villagers would soon leave without him. She must have known that his opportunity to be chief was rapidly disappearing.

If all this was true, then Tionontati's dream of reuniting must have been meant for the spirit world. *If Tionontati had let me travel with them, I could have helped save them*, Nokee thought. *If I had not spent so much time traveling the Great Circle and studying the ancestors, I would be with my tribe. Maybe Tionontati was wrong about all of this.*

There was so much to consider. Nokee spoke little as he traveled back to Three Rivers with the Miami men. He could only think of Tionontati's last words: "You must first undertake a great journey before being restored as chief of our tribe. You are to travel up the Grand River, make the Great Circle, visit the sacred places, listen to the guiding voices of the spirits, and find your way back to Three Rivers on the St. Joseph River. You will receive help from unexpected people and places along the way. Trust your heart. When you finally return to your people, no matter how long it takes, you'll be recognized, and there will be much joy."

His doubts about Tionontati's words were a storm roiling in his mind. As he entered the Miami village at Three Rivers, Chief Myamick embraced him. "Nokee, it brings immense joy to my heart to see that you're alive. Your father was a great warrior and a dear friend of mine. The blood of a warrior runs strong in your veins. You will make a great chief."

"I am not so sure," Nokee said. "They thought so highly of me that they left me, my mother, Tionontati, and six young warriors for dead. Muskuta has claimed he is chief and took my people away. In my mind, Muskuta is a back-stabbing snake."

"Nokee, you must understand. Your people had no choice. The Iroquois are at our doorstep, and travel becomes more dangerous with every passing day. Soon, the weather will worsen, making your people's journey impossible. I sent one hundred warriors with them as protection until they reached our border with the Illinois tribes. Chief Echohawk of the Peoria-Illinois is a friend of mine, and he'll guarantee your people safe passage.

"Before Muskuta left, he asked me to watch for any sign that you or your group might still be alive. He requested that if any of you show up, tell them to stay here at Three Rivers, and he will send word on where the tribe has settled. Muskuta is an honorable man. He'll be thrilled you are alive."

"We'll see about that when I catch up with him."

"Nokee, I understand your anger. But if what you say is true, and you believe your mother and friends are still out there, stay with me and wait for them. Chief Muskuta will send word as soon as safe passage is possible."

For now, Nokee decided to stay and wait. The days became weeks, the weeks became months, and the months became years. The Iroquois attacks increased, and no one from Nokee's village ever came. Over time, the Alliance of the Three Fires united with the Miami tribe to keep the Iroquois at bay. Nokee jumped at every chance to fight the Iroquois with members of the new alliance. As much as Nokee hated the Chippewa, Ottawa, and Potawatomi, he blamed the Iroquois for his continued separation from his tribe.

• • •

For the next ten years, Nokee fought fearlessly. He became a skilled warrior, capable of leading large defensive parties. He had learned much from his father, having watched him deploy sophisticated tactics against the Ottawa on the St. Joseph Trail. Nokee knew the Iroquois had guns, and lots of them. Full-frontal attacks would spell death for him and the other warriors. So, he trained his forces to become excellent at ambushing. Soon, the Iroquois learned to stay far south of Miami territory as they pushed west, attacking the Illinois tribes.

Chief Myamick grew very fond of Nokee and treated him like the son he never had. Myamick was known as the sonless chief, for he had sired only daughters. Secretly, he hoped that Nokee would one day marry one of them. Eventually, Nokee forgot about his past and became a member of the Miami tribe.

# Father Agard – Paris

In 1654, the same year that Nokee shot the great bear under the paw-paw tree, events thousands of miles away were set in motion that would impact Nokee's life in unimaginable ways. At the Roman Catholic Abbey of St.-Germain-des-Pres, in the Latin Quarter of Paris on the left bank of the Seine River, Father Aton Agard sat in a small classroom, preparing to address his eighth-grade class.

He had been instructing the fourteen-year-old male students at the abbey for as long as anyone could remember. Teaching students at this critical age offered the church its best chance to steer these young men into a life of devotion. Father Agard loved his work, and his students appreciated his teachings, as evidenced by the number of them who became Black Robe Jesuits. He taught them history, geography, reading, writing, and math skills that he believed would bring glory to France and perpetuate the Catholic faith for generations to come.

Looking around his class that morning, Father Agard was pleased by the potential of these young men. In the front row was Henri Hébert, whose father owned a series of apothecary shops around Paris. In the second row sat Pierre Pajot, whose father worked directly for the young French King, Louis XIV. The Pajot family was known for putting on the annual Paris Carnival. However, the Pajot business recently acquired great fame for its spectacular fireworks displays at the coronation. The Boy King now requested the Pajots' pyrotechnic skills at every special social event.

Toward the back of the room sat a student whose father had made a fortune in the fur industry as a member of the Company of One Hundred Associates in New France. Next to him was a youth whose father owned the largest vineyard in Paris. The parents of these young men were an impressive mix of merchants, financiers, and the wealthy.

Father Agard began, as he always did, by clearing his throat. "Class, this week, in our first history lessons, we will discuss the discovery of the Americas. In particular, the history of New France. My past students have told me that this period in history was what they found most interesting. The truth is this subject fascinates me as well. We'll learn about the French explorers who blazed new trails across the wilderness. They saw incredible things and created great riches for themself and our country. At the same time, we'll hear stories of the Recollect friars and Jesuit priests that followed them, bringing the word of God to the Indigenous people of New France.

"As eighth graders, I don't expect you to remember everything I tell you. However, I expect you to remember important names and write a sentence or two on their major accomplishments. So, take out your notepads and copy these names."

As the students hurriedly copied the list, Father Agard turned to Henri Hébert and said: "And, of course, we'll include Louis Hébert, the first apothecary and farmer of New France." At that point, Henri Hébert blushed. Pierre Pajot turned to Henri with a disgusted look and stuck out his tongue.

Pierre Pajot raised his hand.

"Yes, Pierre."

"My father says ..." Pierre paused. "That there can never be peace with the Natives because they have no souls. He says we should catch them, put them in cages, and sell tickets at the carnival for people to see them."

Father Agard scowled at Pierre and barked: "Mr. Pajot! Do you believe God created all things?"

Pierre grudgingly responded: "Yes, Father. We learned that in first grade."

Agard stared at Pierre and asked: "Then do you believe that God would put souls in certain people and not others?"

"Well, no, I guess not," Pierre responded sheepishly.

"Well, neither do I! We, the people of faith, believe that all humans have souls and all souls are worth saving. That is why our brave Jesuits and friars spent so much time learning their native languages. They lived with the Indigenous people in their villages, working tirelessly, trying to understand their beliefs. Our Jesuits use *syncretism*, which means they blended aspects of native belief with teachings of the Christian faith. For example, if the Natives believe in different gods, we teach them that our God is the God of all. He welcomes all of them into his kingdom. Does that make sense, Pierre?"

"Yes, sir," replied Pierre respectfully. This time, it was Henri Hébert who gave Pierre a dirty look.

After school, Henri and Pierre quietly headed home, milling over what they had just learned. Henri was the first to speak. "That was great hearing about those first explorers. I can't wait until tomorrow to hear about Louis Hébert."

"Oh, I bet you can't," snapped back Pierre.

"What's bugging you?" Henri asked, surprised.

"You know darn well!" moaned Pierre. "I'm as much related to Louis Hébert as you are, and you just sat there soaking up all the glory. We're cousins, for God's sake."

"Second cousins, actually," grinned Henri.

"That's beside the point. Jacqueline Pajot, Louis Hébert's mother, had a brother. That brother was my great-grandfather. Nicolas Hébert, Louis Hébert's father, had a brother. That brother was your great-grandfather. Call it what you want—we're cousins."

"Yeah, yeah. You have reminded me of that one hundred times since we met in first grade. I'm the one that should be mad at you!"

"Why's that?"

"Because you embarrassed me when you made that stupid statement about Natives not having souls. You knew that would tick off Father Agard."

"Yeah," Pierre said, laughing. "I like getting under his skin!"

• • •

Although the two boys loved to argue, they were the best of friends. They went everywhere together, and people were always surprised to see them apart. Yet, in many ways, the boys were exact opposites. Henri had well-kept dark hair, was tall, thin, and a better student. He was quiet and observant. Henri always had his nose in a book and loved telling Pierre about the latest adventure story he was reading.

Pierre was shorter. His red curly hair and freckled boyish face seemed out of place with his muscular-looking body. Pierre spent most weekends loading and unloading the heavy mortars used in his father's pyrotechnic business. He was more outgoing than Henri, loved clowning around in class, and was less inclined to turn in assignments on time. He believed in living adventures, not reading about them.

Over the next seven years, the two boys grew into fine young men. Henri Hébert continued to be an outstanding student. He excelled in math and literature, but medicine and science were always his greatest passions.

Pierre Pajot was a brilliant student, aided by his impressive photographic memory. He aced every test he took but often received less than top grades because he refused to finish homework assignments on time. He would tell his teachers, "Homework is boring and a waste of my time. History, humanities, and world geography are more my forte." In addition to his native French, Pierre was fluent in English, German, Spanish, Dutch, and Latin. He told anyone who would listen, "Someday, I'll travel the world."

Henri kept himself busy with his studies through secondary school and helped his father in his apothecary business. In his free time, Henri drew pen and ink pictures and continued to be a prolific reader. He especially enjoyed reading about the French coureurs des bois and their encounters with the Indigenous peoples.

Pierre spent his free time with gypsies. They taught him numerous card tricks, cups and ball games, and puppetry skills. He loved showing off his newly acquired talents at the annual spring carnival. For a while, Pierre worked as an assistant chef at a restaurant in Paris, then decided to help his father's business. His job was to mix the various ingredients and assemble the pyrotechnic rockets needed to produce the spectacular fireworks shows for the young king. Henri was constantly trying to get Pierre to concentrate on his studies. Pierre, in turn, was pushing Henri to have more fun. The boys continued to grow up as opposites but were inseparable in everything they did.

In 1660, Henri was submitted as a candidate Jesuit at the Novitiate Society of Jesus in Nancy, France. Unwilling to let Henri travel the world without him, Pierre asked his father to pull some strings with a member of the king's court to have his name submitted as a candidate. Henri and Pierre's parents both had hopes that their oldest sons would continue in their family businesses. However, a son becoming a Jesuit brings tremendous pride and status to the family. When the boys entered the novitiate, the parents of both boys walked around the streets of Paris beaming with pride.

# Young Jesuits

Born to a prominent family in Laon, France, on June 10, 1637, Jacques Marquette read every edition of *The Jesuit Relations* he could access. He was fascinated with the missionary work the Jesuits were doing in the New World and set his mind to become part of it. From his youth, he had attended daily mass and school at the Cathedral of Notre Dame in Laon. At seventeen, his father, Nicolas Marquette, seigneur of Tombelles and councillor of Laon, asked the presiding bishop to recommend young Marquette as a Jesuit candidate for entry into the Jesuit Novitiate Society of Jesus.

Jacques understood that becoming an ordained Jesuit was a long and arduous process, usually taking ten to seventeen years of study and ministry. Still, he had every intention of becoming a full-fledged Jesuit priest.

Upon acceptance, Marquette began his two-year formation at the Novitiate as a Jesuit novice. At the end of the two years, he attended his Vow Mass and took his First Vows, committing himself to a life of poverty, chastity, and obedience. He received a small metal cross—the Vow Cross—which he would wear around his neck for the rest of his life, a symbol of his unwavering commitment to his faith.

Unfortunately, events in New France continued to delay Marquette's dream of traveling to the New World. The Iroquois attacks were becoming so frequent that the governor-general of Quebec decided to ban all travel into Huron country. The successful colonization of New France was at a turning point. Around Paris, the talk was that France had taken all it could when the getting was good. Some believed France should pull out and leave that mess for the Natives to figure out. Others thought France should stay and fight.

In 1662, King Louis the 14th, now twenty-two years old, declared absolute rule. For seven years, his council had told him to distance himself from New France. The French court was encouraging the king to spend more money on the welfare of the local French people. The king was aware of the local sentiment but was unwilling to give up on New France.

Suddenly, everything changed when word drifted back from Quebec City that Joseph Hébert, great-grandson of Louis Hébert, had been captured and killed on the Ile d'Orleans by a band of Oneida Iroquois. Louis Hébert, the first apothecary and farmer of New France, was a legend in the eyes of the French people, and the news outraged the locals around Paris. A rising tide demanded adequate troops be sent to control the marauding Iroquois and restore the fur industry. Stories of great riches in furs in the Upper Great Lakes area sparked a new public interest in returning to New France.

At last, this was the opportunity the young king had been waiting for to assert his dominance in the New World. He ordered his defense minister to send a sizable French fighting force to take control of the situation.

That fall, French troops started showing up in Quebec City in ever-increasing numbers. Their mission was to defeat the Iroquois or reduce their strength. At first, they didn't rely on their native Indigenous allies to guide them, and finding the Iroquois proved immensely difficult. Eventually, they started using their allied Indigenous scouts to locate Iroquois encampments. However, the Iroquois would abandon their villages and disappear into the woods before the slow-moving French military could arrive. All the troops could do was burn the Iroquois villages and destroy their food supplies.

Removing the Native American villages and food supplies became the French soldiers' most effective tool. It forced four Iroquois tribes from the League of Five Nations to discuss peace with the French. But not the Mohawk Iroquois, the most fearless of the five tribes. They never forgot nor forgave Champlain's attack against them in 1609, when he killed three of their chiefs near the shores of Lake Champlain.

In 1663, with the military campaign well underway, the king sent Nicolas Perrot, a French explorer, fur trader, and diplomat, to New France. Nicolas Perrot's instructions were to take the lead in re-establishing contact with the displaced Native Americans in the west. In a policy reversal, the king permitted Perrot to trade guns for furs with the tribes he found there. The French didn't want to make the same mistake they had made earlier by standing by and watching only the Iroquois obtain guns through trade with the English and Dutch. Quickly, Nicolas Perrot became known as the gun-trafficking fur trader.

• • •

In 1665, Nicolas Perrot returned to the Upper Great Lakes area to guide Jesuit Father Allouez to Chequamegon Bay at the western end of Lake Superior. There, Father Allouez started the La Pointe du St.-Esprit mission for displaced Ottawa and Huron Indians. That same year, Henri and Pierre completed their fifth year of study in France and became deacons.

When the Bishop of Laon reviewed the list of new Jesuit deacons, he came across the names of Hébert and Pajot. Both of their last names were from distinguished families in Paris. After doing a little research, he discovered that both Jesuits were related to the famous first apothecary and farmer of New France.

The bishop knew of the king's desire to put a positive public spin on his efforts to eradicate the Iroquois and spread Christianity, and these two Jesuits would serve that purpose perfectly. He immediately wrote a letter to Cardinal de Retz in Paris telling him of his findings.

Shortly after that, Marquette received a letter from the Jesuit General in Rome, telling him he had been re-assigned to missionary work in New France. The Jesuit general had agreed to Marquette's transfer if he was willing to team up with two young deacons also slated to head for New France. All three would complete their theological studies in one year before shipping out.

Marquette, not known for being a team player but desperately wanting the missionary assignment, reluctantly agreed to the terms. Upon arrival at Pont-a-Mousson, he met, for the first time, Jesuit Deacons Henri Hébert and Pierre Pajot. Their first meeting didn't go well.

As Marquette marched into the room wearing his full clerical garb—a black robe—his face was red, and he was short of breath. He immediately launched into an angry tirade. "Who in God's name arranged for the two of you to attend theologian school in such short order? And who thought you deacons—so minimally trained—could survive, for even a day, in the wilds of New France? I've prepared my whole life for this moment. I will not be going there to be anyone's nursemaid!"

The hackles on Pierre's neck immediately went up, but Henri, the most composed head in the group, stepped between the two of them. "Jacques, calm yourself! We can explain the whole process, but I need a minute with Pierre. Please excuse us for just a moment."

As soon as they left the room, Pierre blurted out, "There's nothing likable about that man. I don't think we should trust Marquette with any information."

"Pierre, you are too quick to judge people. He's here to assess our strengths and weaknesses. After all, we'll be traveling and spending considerable time together—Lord knows how long. And Marquette is right. We know little about where we are heading and what to expect when we get there. We are going to need his help."

"That man is ill-natured and disagreeable," Pierre said, folding his arms.

"I know. I've talked to some other Jesuits here, and they all say Marquette is obsessed with starting missions in New France. He doesn't want anything, including us, to get in his way. Besides, I hear he's a sextus."

"A what?" Pierre asked.

"A sextus," Henri explained. "That's a person who spends six years in their regency. That's enough to make anyone a bit edgy."

"That's one more reason to stay clear of him," Pierre said.

As they re-entered the room, Marquette stood up, impatiently waiting for an explanation. Henri spoke first. "We are here because of a request made by the bishop. He told us he had reviewed our records and noted our desire to be foreign missionaries in New France. Cardinal de Retz in Paris asked the bishop to assemble as many Jesuits as possible and have them ready to travel to New France within a year. The bishop informed us that it would be difficult and dangerous work, but, if we were successful, he would see to our ordination as priests at the end of four years of missionary service. We both readily agreed to the assignment."

"The bishop personally told you this?" asked Marquette cautiously.

"Yes, he personally delivered us our new orders." Pierre nodded in agreement.

At hearing this, Marquette's demeanor did a complete turnaround, and his mood and disposition mellowed. Pierre wasn't so forgiving, but Henri convinced Pierre to listen to what Marquette had to say. After a few tense moments, the three men sat down and began comparing stories about school life at the Novitiate Society of Jesus in Nancy, France. They shared their reasons for wanting to go to New France and talked about their experiences growing up. It wasn't until Henri Hébert mentioned the ongoing trouble with the Iroquois and the recent death of his cousin Joseph Hébert that Marquette put the big picture together.

"What Henri forgot to mention," Pierre said, "is that Louis Hébert's mother, Jacqueline Pajot, had a brother. That brother was my great-grandfather."

Marquette appreciated what these new additions meant for him. He had just received the best public relations gifts he could have hoped for.

Over the next year, the three theologians spent many days together in prayer and studies, preparing for the adventure of their lives.

# Quebec City

In January 1666, Jacques Marquette received word that Rome had approved his ordination to the priesthood. The ceremony was scheduled for March 7 at St. Etienne's Cathedral in Toul, France—just months before he and a group of Jesuits would depart to New France. At last, this was the news that Jacques had been waiting for to set his plan in motion.

Cardinal de Retz attended Marquette's ordination, and at the end of the ceremony, he handed Marquette a sealed letter. Marquette was to deliver the letter to the bishop in Quebec City upon his arrival.

Henri and Pierre asked Marquette what this letter was about, and he responded, "Men, I think I just bought us a ticket to the western edge of the New World!"

On May 1, Father Marquette, Henri, and Pierre arrived at the French seaport of La Rochelle with over a dozen Black Robe Jesuits from across France. The sea crossing was rough, and many of the Jesuits, unaccustomed to life at sea, were seasick most of the voyage. When they reached Quebec City, they learned that Bishop François de Laval had already left Quebec to travel west with Father Allouez to the Upper Great Lakes. The bishop wanted to see firsthand the sites Father Allouez had identified as needing missions.

Father Marquette was shocked by the news but was put at ease when he heard that the bishop had arranged a welcoming party for the newly arriving Jesuits. The governor-general, his intendant, and numerous other public officials would be in attendance. Marquette saw this gathering as an opportunity to forward his objectives.

The governor-general, recognizing the value of the Louis Hébert connection, had invited five well-known Quebec City residents, all related to Henri and Pierre. Among them was Louis Hébert's granddaughter, Elisabeth Couillard Guyon, accompanied by her oldest living son and grandson, both named Joseph. Also present was Pierre's uncle, Thomas Pajot, along with his twenty-four-year-old son, Thomas Pajot Jr.

The party started quietly, with fancy hors d'oeuvres, pleasant introductions, and soft violin music playing in the background. The tranquility lasted until Henri and Pierre met Thomas Pajot Jr., one of the coureurs des bois who had recently returned from Sault Ste. Marie with lots of stories to tell.

Henri and Pierre latched onto Thomas, barraging him with dozens of questions. His stories of the thrills and misadventures on the river captured everyone's attention, as all ears turned to hear what he had to say. Soon, all the new Jesuits were sitting on the floor in front of Thomas, while other guests gathered behind them. Pierre noticed young Joseph Guyon, only eleven, was trying to get closer so he could hear. Pierre, who always had a soft spot for the children, waved young Joseph over and gave him a seat next to him.

Sensing the excitement in the room, Thomas Pajot Jr. looked directly at the newly arriving Jesuits. "You're lucky you showed up when you did. The past two years were extremely bad around here. No one could leave Quebec City for fear of the Iroquois attacks. The trouble began the previous winter when a French regiment of four hundred men, led by Lieutenant General Alexandre de Prouville, traveled south to attack a large Mohawk village. With all due respect, those soldiers weren't seasoned bushmen. That first assault on the Mohawk Iroquois didn't go well! The French met a much larger Iroquois force than they had expected. The Iroquois sent their war chief, Chief Canaqueese, with a delegation to offer peace. However, it was only under the conditions that the French allowed the Iroquois into the fur trade. They wanted to be the middlemen doing the fur collections.

"The French commander refused," Thomas said with a

dramatic flair. "A heated discussion ensued. Alexandre de Prouville, seeing that he was outnumbered and outgunned, withdrew his forces. But before he left, he took Chief Canaqueese and the entire Iroquois delegation prisoner. This ill-planned decision resulted in the Mohawks declaring full-scale war against the French."

"However, the following spring," said Thomas Pajot Jr., lowering his voice to build suspense, "Lieutenant General Alexandre de Prouville, with his twelve hundred soldiers in twenty-four companies, began the relentless pursuit of the Mohawk Iroquois. Using Algonquin scouts, the French forces intercepted and crushed the Mohawk raiding parties. The French forces conducted marches across New York, burning Iroquois villages and destroying their food sources. In the fall, the Mohawk finally realized that the English would not come to their aid, so they surrendered to the French. We still hold Chief Canaqueese here in Quebec City. The Lieutenant General is negotiating with the Iroquois for Canaqueese's release if the peace holds."

Thomas Pajot Jr. paused before continuing. "What this means to all you Black Robes is that if you train up here in Quebec City before going out into the bush, you now have a pretty good chance the Iroquois won't chop off your heads!" Thomas then let out a roaring laugh.

• • •

While Thomas was toying with the crowd, Marquette saw the opportunity he was waiting for and slid over to where Governor-General Daniel de Rémy and his intendant stood. Father Marquette handed Cardinal de Retz's letter to the governor-general.

After reading the letter, Daniel de Rémy stared at Marquette. "The only instructions Bishop Laval left me with was that the new Jesuits are to stay in the Quebec area for the next two years while they learn the different Indigenous languages. How you go about planning your stay is your own business. You produce a plan, and Bishop Laval can modify it when he returns."

This news was music to Father Marquette's ears. The next day, Marquette gathered his two deacons and asked for an immediate meeting with the senior Jesuits, three of which had been recently called back from their missionary work with the Seneca and Oneida due to the increased hostilities in New York. Marquette proposed that in addition to Huron and Algonquin, he and his two deacons needed to learn a third language.

"I'll add Montagnais," Marquette said confidently. "Pierre should study Iroquois because he is already fluent in Dutch. He could learn Iroquois from the imprisoned Iroquois Chief Canaqueese, who is half Dutch."

Pierre smiled and turned to Henri. "Henri has always had a soft spot for the underdogs. He should take a stab at learning Siouan from the displaced Tutelo from Virginia." Everyone laughed, but Henri thought the idea was intriguing. The senior Jesuits saw no harm in Marquette's plan. Since they would spend the rest of the year in Quebec, they offered their services as Huron and Algonquin language instructors. Jacques Marquette, Henri, and Pierre spent the rest of the evening grinning, unable to hide their excitement.

The three Jesuits went to work learning the Indigenous languages. They spent that fall hanging around and assisting the displaced Huron and Algonquin people seeking refuge around Quebec City. Pierre met with the imprisoned Chief Canaqueese and quickly bonded with the chief. Pierre, a natural linguist, was surprisingly quick at learning the Iroquois language. Within three months, he was quite capable of carrying on a conversation.

By October 1666, it was safe for Father Marquette to travel up the St. Lawrence River to Trois-Rivieres to meet the famous missionary Father Gabriel Druillettes. Father Druillettes had spent the past twenty years bringing the word of God to the Montagnais and Algonquins. He traveled with the Montagnais and Algonquin people throughout eastern Quebec and Labrador. He endured unbelievable hardships along the way, especially during the winter months.

Father Marquette cherished the time he spent learning the different languages with Father Druillettes, especially the evening stories Father Druillettes would tell. Tails of running down moose on snowshoes with the Montagnais, eating the leather from his shoes to prevent starvation, or sleeping with the dogs to stay warm kept Marquette on the edge of his seat. Father Druillettes's stories of the strange lands and the people he had seen fascinated Father Marquette.

But Marquette was not content with merely learning the languages and listening to stories. He wanted to put what he learned into practice. So, every Sunday, Marquette would cross the St. Lawrence River by boat or on the ice and participate in offering Holy Mass at a small church in Cap-de-la-Madeleine. There, Father Vachon would minister to the fur-trading colony, as well as a small group of Algonquins and Montagnais. Father Marquette would spend the afternoon with Father Vachon and his Indigenous parishioners. He would listen, learn, and practice his newly acquired language skills. Marquette spent one year with Father Druillettes before he felt he had mastered the various languages.

• • •

While Marquette was away, Henri concentrated his time with the senior Jesuits. He would sit around the woodstove with his superiors on the long, frigid winter nights, discussing the habits of the Indigenous people.

"I want to learn the Algonquin and Huron languages," stated Henri. "However, I also need to understand the meaning and feelings behind the words. I want to know about their religious beliefs and how they are similar or different from what we Jesuits offer."

Henri got Pierre involved in the discussion groups. It was at one of those evening meetings that Henri and Pierre first met the Jolliet brothers. The Jolliet brothers were born in Quebec City and spent their summers playing games with the Indigenous children on the Ile d'Orleans. It was there that both boys learned to speak various Indigenous languages. Their stepfather never had time for the two boys, so, on their 10th birthdays, he enrolled them in the Jesuit school for youth in Quebec City and insisted that the boys become priests.

At the Jesuit school, the boys learned English and Spanish. Science, philosophy, religion, and music were also part of the curriculum. Louis Jolliet became well-known as a talented organist.

In 1662, Louis Jolliet took his first vows, and in 1664, Adrien Jolliet did the same. By 1666, Louis Jolliet had become a deacon.

Henri and Pierre were fascinated by the Jolliet brothers from the first time they met. In addition to having lived through the tumultuous times of the fur industry and the results of the brutal wars with the Indigenous people, both were fantastic storytellers. Growing up in Quebec City, the brothers had heard all the frontier stories and met many legendary coureurs des bois who had traveled the lands to the west.

Henri watched the fire in the Jolliet brothers' eyes when they talked about how they couldn't wait to be a part of the action. Many nights, Henri, Pierre, and the two Jolliet brothers would stay up late into the evening talking about their hopes and dreams. They enjoyed their long nights together, even though they knew they had to get up early each day to attend 6:00 a.m. Holy Mass.

During one of those nighttime discussions, Henri casually asked Pierre, "Were you joking when you suggested I learn to speak Siouan? If there are indeed displaced Tutelo in the Quebec area, I would love to learn their language."

"Yeah, I kind of was," replied Pierre. "But I did hear from Father Jacques Fremin that a group of Siouan-speaking women and children are living with the Oneida."

Louis Jolliet nodded. "It's true. Last summer, I visited a small village for displaced Tutelo people with Father Jacques Fremin. The Tutelo spoke a form of Siouan. I would gladly guide Henri there if he can get permission from the senior Jesuits."

When Henri approached the Jesuits with the idea of meeting the Tutelo people, Father Jacques Fremin told him he was planning a four-month visit there next spring. He said he would be happy to take Henri along. Henri was ecstatic. It would be his first adventure into an official Indigenous encampment.

• • •

In May 1667, Father Jacques Fremin, Henri Hébert, and Louis Jolliet left for the Tutelo Sioux village in New York. Henri was surprised at the terrible condition of the people. The Tutelo Indians were originally from Virginia and were fierce warriors and excellent artisans. The flint-knapped arrowheads made by the Tutelo were valuable trade items. However, the Dutch and English traders had addicted the Tutelo to whiskey and rum, after which they were driven from their homeland by the expanding European settlers to parts unknown in the west. If it hadn't been for the kindness of the Oneida Iroquois, they most certainly would've perished during the winter.

By relying on the apothecary skills he had developed working with his father, Henri Hébert slowly nursed the women and children back to health. Over time, the Tutelo villagers became trusting of Henri and his healing methods. In turn, Henri communicated better with the people and soon was on his way to learning their Siouan language.

When Henri, Louis, and Father Fremin returned to Quebec in September of 1667, Marquette was back from Trois-Rivieres. He was now fluent in Montagnais and five different Huron and Algonquin dialects. Pierre and Henri updated Marquette on their mastery of the Iroquois and Siouan languages. Father Marquette was pleased.

Marquette explained to his two young Jesuit assistants that while staying with Father Druillettes, they had planned two travel routes to the Upper Great Lakes. Marquette suggested that if they split up, they could maximize their opportunity to visit many different tribes. That two-pronged effort would help them determine where new missions were most needed.

Henri seemed a bit uneasy about the new plan. "I thought Bishop Laval made the assignments for where the Jesuits go."

"That's true," Marquette said. "However, Father Druillettes told me he had received a letter from the bishop that said he wouldn't return to Quebec until late next summer. He asked Father Druillettes to oversee the St. Lawrence River missions in his absence. I asked Father Druillettes to allow us to accompany the fur-trading convoy heading to the Soo next spring. He was hesitant at first, but I convinced him we would be in a perfect position at the Soo to quickly start any new missions that Father Allouez and Bishop Laval had planned."

"Father Druillettes did have one precondition," Marquette said.

"What precondition?" Henri asked, suspicious.

"He wants us to spend the next six months teaching at the Jesuit school for youth here in Quebec City. Bishop Laval wants his new Jesuits to see firsthand the damage that the trade of alcohol for furs has done to the Native population. To see how it has destroyed Indigenous families. The bishop is pushing hard for a decree that will ban the trade of alcohol to the Indigenous people."

Henri couldn't agree more with what the bishop was promoting. He related what he had seen at the Tutelo village, and Henri was the first to embrace the new assignment. The next day, Louis Jolliet, Jacques Marquette, Henri Hébert, and Pierre Pajot showed up at the Jesuit school for youth to offer the group's service. It turned out that Father Druillettes was spot on; the situation was worse than they thought. They found the school overcrowded with child refugees. They heard Montagnais, Huron, Algonquin, Iroquois, and Siouan languages drifting through the halls.

Marquette called his three deacons together. "Our help is desperately needed here, but that doesn't mean we can't learn from this ourselves."

"What do you have in mind?" asked Pierre.

"I can't think of a better place to practice our language training," Marquette said. "At the same time we are teaching them, they can teach us. But we'd be wasting an opportunity if we only seek to learn a language. We must talk to them and befriend them. We can learn about their customs, history, religious beliefs, travel patterns, friends, and enemies. We all need to agree to keep meticulous notes, to document everything. If we hope to get continuing support for our missions, we must publish this information in *The Jesuit Relations*. We must show the world that we can bring Christianity and the comforts of civilization to the Indigenous people without destroying their culture."

Pierre bonded with the children almost immediately using the universal language of magic. He would pull items out of a children's ears, make things disappear, and turn handkerchiefs into flowers. Pierre was a master at the ball and cups game and even better at guessing what card you had in your hand. On special occasions he would put on fireworks shows using homemade rockets he knew how to assemble.

But the thing the children enjoyed the most was Pierre's

puppet shows. Pierre even got Henri into the act. They would throw their black robes over a couple of chairs, and with a box of cutout stick figures and hand puppets, they put on splendid shows. Sometimes, it would be about a brave warrior saving a village from a hungry bear. Other times, it might be about tribal wars ending in peace. Depending on the group they had in front of them, they practiced speaking different Indigenous languages. Other times, in mixed Indigenous groups, they would say nothing and let the action figures speak for themselves. It turned out that laughter was the best gift the four Jesuits could give these traumatized children.

At the end of the six months, the Jesuits all agreed that they had enjoyed their time at the youth school and hated to see it end. However, by March, Father Marquette was getting anxious. He knew he had to act quickly, or his missionary plan would soon fall apart.

# Two Routes to the Soo

In the spring of 1668, the signed peace treaty with the Five Nations was in place, and the Jesuits were now free to move about New France without fear of attack by the Iroquois. The Iroquois had agreed to stop all hostilities against the French, their fur-trading convoys, and the Christian tribes. However, the French had not anticipated that the Iroquois interpreted this to mean they were free to attack the non-Christian tribes to the west. The Iroquois had every intention of conquering those non-Christian tribes and making them part of the Iroquois Nation. Undeterred by this information, Father Marquette gathered his three deacons to discuss his next move.

Marquette carefully arranged three stools in a half circle and directed Henri, Pierre, and Louis Jolliet to have a seat. He wanted their full attention. "I've talked to one of the French regiment captains," stated Marquette excitedly. "He told me the French Carignan-Salieres Regiment will return to France this summer because of the signed peace treaty. Thank God they are leaving four companies in Quebec City, approximately two hundred men, just in case any trouble breaks out.

"I've been told that Governor-General de Rémy had decided one platoon will travel with the fur traders heading west this spring. When the convoy reaches the Ottawa River, half of the soldiers will travel up the Ottawa River and head for the mission at Sault Ste. Marie. The other half will travel the southern route to Detroit. Reports are that a group of coureurs des bois have successfully set up trading posts at both locations. Each holds large shipments of furs, waiting for safe passage back to Montreal.

"This is the opportunity we have been waiting for," Marquette said, clenching his fist. "We must be ready to leave with that convoy at a moment's notice. When they reach the Ottawa River, they will split up. Louis Jolliet and I will travel with the soldiers heading north to the Soo. Henri and Pierre will follow the other soldiers, taking the southern route to the western end of Lake Ontario. There, the convoy will continue west on the foot trail to Detroit. At that point, I want Henri and Pierre to separate from the convoy, travel up the Niagara River, and visit the Seneca Iroquois. Henri should have an in with them after his stay with the Tutelo tribe in Oneida country.

"Then, I want the two of you to travel down the southern shoreline of Lake Erie on your way to Detroit. The captain informed me that the Seneca Nation had virtually destroyed the Erie tribe to their west. He told me that a remnant of that tribe is still on the southwest corner of Lake Erie in the Bass Islands. Reports from the coureurs des bois say the Erie tribe is in desperate straits and could use your assistance. Once you reach Detroit, you can travel north along the eastern shoreline of Lake Huron and join us at the Soo Mission.

"I must remind you," Marquette said, "it's of utmost importance that we document the customs and the conditions of the tribes we meet. Take copious notes on their appearances and religious practices. Carefully note which tribes are willing to accept the Christian faith. We'll use this information to plan where to establish new missions. Once you show up in the Soo, we'll combine our research. Then we can pass on this latest information to the *Journal of The Jesuit Relations* in Paris.

"Louis Jolliet and I will stay in Sault Ste. Marie," continued Marquette. "We'll assist Father Claude Dablon, who is trying to establish an Ottawa mission there. If Bishop Laval decides to return early, we hope to intercept him and receive any new assignments he has prepared for the four of us. We'll continue to discuss this plan at great length over the next month as we prepare for departure. Henri and Pierre, you must be very meticulous about your equipment list. You'll have a long stretch of travel on your own. Are there any questions?"

"Yeah, only about a thousand," shouted Pierre. "I'm good at directions. But come on! How will we find our way?"

"I've already thought about that," Father Marquette said. "I'll hire a couple of coureurs des bois to be your guides. With the Iroquois peace treaty in place, many coureurs des bois are no longer afraid to travel in Iroquois-controlled areas. They can harvest wild game with their muskets and build cooking fires without fear of attack. You should be safe and eat well.

"Besides, there'll be four of you traveling together. Four is a sacred number among Indigenous people. Take, for example, the four cardinal directions: north, south, east, and west. Or the four forces of nature: earth, wind, water, and fire. And the four kingdoms: plants, animal, mineral, and human. Because of that belief, the four of you will be perceived as a peace delegation and allowed safe passage."

Until now, Louis Jolliet had been sitting quietly. But as Marquette finished excitedly outlining their venture, he rose and addressed the group. "I've been waiting for the right time to tell you this, but I cannot wait any longer—this is as good a time as any. I'm dropping out of the religious order, as is my brother Adrien." You could have heard a pin drop in the room as the three other Jesuits sat with their mouths open.

"What?" Henri said. "You have dedicated years of your life to study. You are within reach of priesthood—and don't forget all the good you've already done, bringing joy to the children at the youth school. You can't leave us now!"

"Thank you for that, Henri. But this is not a decision I've made lightly. After our father's death, Adrien and I wanted nothing more than to be just like him—to grow up involved in the fur trade, to become a coureur de bois, to trade with the Indigenous people and see distant lands. That was all we talked about as children.

"When Adrien told me he was leaving with the soldiers this spring, I knew what I had to do. I had to follow my heart and do the same. We have already sent our resignation letters to Father Druillettes. He'll deliver it to Bishop Laval upon his return."

For a long moment, Pierre was shocked into silence. "I never saw this coming."

Henri was more sympathetic in his response. "God knows the job we're about to undertake will be the most demanding thing we've ever done. If your heart is not fully into this, I believe it would be impossible to accomplish what we hope to achieve. I saw the fire in your eyes when you and your brother told the stories about the coureurs des bois, and I feel your passion has not left you. It is simply that God has chosen a different calling for you. I believe that whatever you decide to do, you will achieve remarkable things. If there's anything I can do to assist you, I will. My hopes and prayers go with you."

"Let us not rush ahead of ourselves," Louis Jolliet said. "We are still going with you. My brother and I will have two fur-trading canoes traveling with the spring convoy. You three Jesuits will be bringing the word of God, while we will bring the trade items that'll make the lives of the Indigenous people more comfortable."

Father Marquette stood up and walked out of the room without a word.

Louis's eyes followed him to the door. "I hope I did not hurt him."

"Don't worry about it," Henri said. "We'll talk to him. You must understand that he has been planning this day since we met him in theology school three years ago. His whole purpose in life is to create missions and spread our Catholic faith. He can't imagine anything being more important. Giving up that opportunity is not something that Father Marquette can easily accept. And besides, he can be a little pushy at times."

"A *little* pushy!" cried Pierre. "The man has a one-track mind. Every move Marquette has made to date has been to get us to this point. Thank God his intentions are good. God help us if they aren't." Louis and Henri almost fell off their chairs laughing.

"Yes," Pierre said, "we'll talk to him. I'll tell him it's good to have trained Jesuits running a fur-trading business. Would he rather have a bunch of drunken, corrupt coureurs des bois trading whiskey and rum for furs and sexual favors? That'll get him thinking. Don't worry, Louis, Father Marquette will come around. Besides, all three of us will need help from you and your brother in deciding what critical items we need to pack."

• • •

A couple of days later, Louis Jolliet presented a list of trade items he and his brother had assembled. The list contained long guns, pistols, black powder, lead, traps, bells, beads, axes, kettles, salted pork, salt, pepper, mixed spices, sugar, flour, salted butter, pipes, tobacco, and yards of cloth. In addition, there was an extensive list of personal items that were critical to surviving in the wilderness.

They would be traveling by canoe, which made transporting these things possible. However, Henri and Pierre would branch off from the Detroit-bound convoy at the western end of Lake Ontario. There, they would be forced to undertake a tough portage over the Niagara escarpment and would need to be selective about what they could bring. Louis Jolliet suggested they send half of their gifts and trade items with the soldiers going to Detroit. Henri and Pierre could pick them up in Detroit for the second half of their journey to the Soo.

Jolliet paused for a moment and said, "Some of the best items to impress the chiefs are copper cauldrons and French ceramic confit pots. While they are difficult to transport, they have immense value to the tribal leaders."

The following week, Father Marquette informed Henri and Pierre of a change that put their minds at ease. "I've talked to the Jolliet brothers," Marquette said. "Jean Talon, the intendant of New France, has announced which fur traders will go with each group. Louis Jolliet and Jacques Largillier will take their crew up the northern route. Adrien Jolliet, Thomas Pajot Jr., Jean Plattier, and Jean Tiberge will take their group down the southern route.

"I see this as an excellent opportunity. As you know, our young king dissolved the Company of One Hundred Associates in 1663 and created the French West India Company. Adrien Jolliet and Thomas Pajot Jr. are new to the company and want to make a good impression. So, I asked Adrien and Thomas if they would be interested in being hired as your coureurs des bois. I told them that your travel plans would take them to new lands recently opened to the French fur-trading industry. If they go with you, they'll have the first chance at brokering a trade deal with the Seneca, Erie, and possibly the Shawnee tribes."

"What did they say?" Henri asked excitedly.

"The two of them discussed it with Louis Jolliet, and he agreed. Louis Jolliet saw it as a chance to subsidize their young company. The fur collected during that trip would be pure profit if their salaries were prepaid. It would prove that their company can be profitable." Henri and Pierre were ecstatic about the news.

Having already secured funds through Father Druillettes, Father Marquette and the Jesuits began assembling their needed items. Top on their list were their rosaries and their Roman Catholic Bibles. Marquette packed a portable altar and wine so he could say Holy Mass daily. Each Jesuit brought a compass, strike-a-light, flint, tinder box, two wool blankets, pipe, and tobacco. Additionally, each would carry two small copper kettles, a knife, a small axe, and pieces of rope.

For clothing, they would be wearing their black robes but thought it prudent to add two sets of pants and shirts, an oil-skin long coat, leggings, boots, and a wool hat. Leather-bound notebooks and a supply of ink and pens would allow for copious note-taking. Henri announced he was bringing two medical books. One was *The Treatment of Common Ailments*. The other was a fifty-year-old copy of *The Medicinal Plants of Canada*, published by Louis Hébert and Henri's great-grandfather. Pierre was more secretive about the wooden box he added to his pack.

Next was a discussion on food items. The coureurs des bois guiding them would be responsible for hunting wild game. They would also provide a half barrel of salted pork, dried peas, cornmeal, flour, baking powder, seasoning, salt, sugar, coffee, and lard to prepare the evening meals. Breakfast would consist of cornbread, coffee, and whatever meat was left from the evening before. Each Jesuit was on their own regarding lunch. Most wilderness travelers relied on jerky and pemmican for lunch, which they ate while on the move. Pemmican, a mixture of fat and protein, could be stored for long periods without spoiling.

Father Marquette had purchased a hindquarter of a moose, a deer, and a large tub of rendered bear lard from the local hunters. They stripped the moose meat into pieces, seasoned it, and hung it over the fire for twelve hours to make jerky. The deer meat went into pemmican. Pemmican was made by slicing the deer meat into strips and drying it over the fire. Then, the dried venison was pulverized into powder using Henri's mortar and pestle. Next, they added dried huckleberries and crushed black walnuts for flavor. While Henri was making the powder mix, Pierre was slowly heating bear lard. When the lard had melted, they carefully poured the hot liquid into the pan containing the powdered mix until all the powder had absorbed the fat. When the pemmican cooled, the team cut it into squares, then wrapped and packed it.

For gifts, the Jesuits purchased ten white-Kaolin-clay pipes, ten packets of glass beads, ten jackknives, ten French felling axes, ten silver beavers on chains, ten small mirrors, and a pile of colorful ribbons. They also included three bags of small metal crucifixes, which the Jesuits could distribute to the tribes to wear around their necks.

Father Marquette acquired ten medium-size French copper cauldrons with hanging handles and ten French confit pots. The porcelain confit pots had glazed yellow tops and earthenware bottoms. They filled the confit pots with rendered bear lard and placed each pot in a copper cauldron. Then, they filled each copper cauldron with cornmeal to protect the porcelain pot and provide an additional food source. The Jesuits divided the lot in half and planned to send half with Father Marquette and half with Henri and Pierre. Henri and Pierre planned to split their lot in half and send half of it to Detroit with the soldiers.

Two days before the platoon was ready to leave, the governor-general gave an order that caught the Jesuits off guard. He insisted that all Frenchmen leaving Quebec City without a military escort must be armed. Henri and Pierre protested, claiming they had no intentions of shooting anyone and were unfamiliar with weapons of war, but the governor-general wouldn't budge from his position. He had received word that the Iroquois were attacking the non-Christian tribes to the west. He knew if word reached Paris that Jesuits were in danger, support for the fur-trading industry would again collapse.

Henri and Pierre feared their plans were falling apart. After thinking for a moment, Pierre said, "The decree said that we must be armed, but it didn't say armed with what. I've got an idea. Henri, you keep packing and leave this up to me."

The next day, Pierre returned to the rectory with two guns:

one an old musketoon, and the other a more modern flintlock musket. Neither looked to be in decent shape or of any interest to the soldiers. When Henri saw them, he threw his hands into the air and started to walk away.

"Wait!" Pierre shouted. "They're not what you think."

"They sure look like guns to me," Henri replied.

"Good. I was hoping you would say that. I bought these from the blacksmith in town and had him do a few modifications." Henri looked skeptical but cautiously intrigued.

"Do you see the stock on this musket? I had him take off the heavy metal butt plate, which shortened and lightened the stock. Look at the trigger and hammer. I had him weld them in place. This gun is inoperable. Here, hold it like a walking stick."

Henri took the gun and held it out like a staff. "Good," said Pierre. "I had him leave it a little longer because you are taller than me."

"Why would I carry a useless gun?"

"Ah ha. Here is the best part. I had the blacksmith weld an iron crucifix on the bayonet." Pierre showed Henri the bayonet with the cross and placed it on the musket. "Here's your peace rifle and walking stick. If you remove the bayonet, the governor-general will never know the difference, and you'll meet his order."

"What about the other gun?"

"It's a Spanish musketoon," said Pierre. "Don't you remember old Father Agard telling us how Champlain would carry around an arquebus when he attacked the Iroquois? This gun functions like an arquebus, only shorter. It also has a much larger barrel bore."

"It looks more like a shotgun than a musket to me."

"Right again. I had the blacksmith modify this one as well. The trigger and matchlock are also immobilized. Like the other one, this gun doesn't work. I had him add two 3-foot-folding hollow rods to the front. I can now stand it up like a tripod."

"I don't understand how that could possibly be useful," Henri said.

Pierre pulled out the wooden box he had kept secret for several days. When he opened it, Henri saw it contained a jar of rice husks coated in black powder, various kinds of black powder-coated fuses, glue tape, and a stack of ball-shaped cups. There were also six small, labeled tins. The tins read: sodium chloride - yellow stars, copper - blue stars, strontium - red stars, aluminum - white stars, calcium - orange stars, and barium - green stars.

"Why are you bringing all that stuff?

"To make these," said Pierre, as he pulled a handful of walnut-size paper balls with short fuses out of his pocket.

"You're bringing *fireworks*?" Henri asked, clearly shocked.

"Yes, this gun will function as my mortar. With a little black powder down the barrel and a touch of a lit wick to the flash pan, I should be able to send these small balls hundreds of feet into the air. I also had the blacksmith make us a bag of copper shot rather than lead; we can flatten and shape a handful into copper arrowheads to show the Indigenous people. And Henri, don't forget to fill your powder horn with black powder. With my fireworks show, we now have a beneficial use for it."

Henri just shook his head, smiled, and said: "Pierre, I'm never going to take the showman out of you, am I?" They both sat there and had a good laugh.

• • •

On May 20, 1668, Father Marquette and his two deacons met at the Quebec City riverfront. Pierre and Henri had briefed Marquette and the Jolliet brothers about their modified guns and were told not to make a fuss at the docks. The *engagés*—hired French citizens who carry cargo and help paddle canoes—had been there all morning, loading supplies, trade items, and large canoes. The team planned to sail to Montreal, portage the canoes and gear over the rapids, and then split into two equal groups. Governor-General Daniel de Rémy was there to wish his men success on their mission and pray for their safe return.

As the group of Jesuits boarded the ship, the governor-general narrowed his eyes at Henri and Pierre. Fortunately, it was a rainy morning, and the Jesuits wore their oil-skin long coats. Henri and Pierre had tucked their guns beneath their coats, with only the barrels showing.

After the governor-general addressed the crowd, he walked directly toward Father Marquette. Marquette stepped intentionally in front of his two deacons and greeted the governor-general with a smile and a handshake. "Good morning, Governor. What a wonderful speech. May God bless all those who travel today."

"My thoughts exactly," Daniel de Rémy replied. "I would like your two deacons to do me a favor. They'll enter the land of the Seneca when they reach the Niagara River. There, the Seneca will surely intercept them and take them directly to Chief Mingwe's camp. He's a fine fellow—we met him while signing the peace treaty with the Five Nations last year. Rumor has it that the Mohawk Chief Thayenda is staying with Chief Mingwe. Unfortunately, Chief Thayenda wasn't comfortable attending the ceremony and fled west. I ask that your two deacons present Chief Thayenda with a gift. It's the same gift I gave the chiefs from four of the five nations. Tell him it symbolizes our lasting peace and willingness to trade."

With that, the governor-general handed Father Marquette an English-style tomahawk peace pipe. The head of the axe, forged from metal and with silver inlays, featured a raised pipe bowl on top and a four-inch-wide cutting edge on the bottom—symbolizing both war and peace. The axe head was attached to an 18-inch engraved ash-wood handle, its inter-heartwood core hollowed out with a hot iron poker. A silver mouthpiece adorned the opposite end. It was, without question, a splendid pipe. Marquette accepted the tomahawk pipe and passed it to Henri.

Henri, who had not said a word, blurted out, "Sir, we'll deliver it to Chief Thayenda. You have my word." Pierre elbowed Henri to shut up as the governor-general nodded before walking away.

The ship's journey to Montreal was uneventful. Upon arrival at the foot of the Lachine Rapids, the crew began unloading their cargo. The convoy spent the rest of the day making the portage. They had brought four thirty-six-foot-long, twenty-man voyageur canoes for the French soldiers and engagés. Each canoe weighed three hundred pounds empty, and it took eight men to carry one canoe.

These canoes could transport ten 100-pound tightly bound packages of food, equipment, trade items, guns, and three barrels—one barrel of rum, one of salted pork, and one of rock salt.

All these items had to be portaged by leather straps worn across the engagés' foreheads to support the packages on their backs. Henri, Pierre, Adrien, and Thomas would be responsible for their gear and smaller eight-man canoe with a collapsible mast and sail.

The two groups split up when they reached the Ottawa River, one heading north to the Soo and the other south to Detroit. The plan was for each canoe to stop for a smoke break every hour. By doing so, they could maintain a six-mile-an-hour pace. Voyageurs measured distance travel by how many pipes it took to get from one place to another.

• • •

In two days, Henri and Pierre's group entered Lake Ontario. The sheer size of the lake overwhelmed Pierre. "Henri, look at this immense body of water. It's a freshwater ocean. If you put the entire French Navy in here, the fleet would look like a dot on a map."

"True," Henri said. "And if you added up the moose, bears, wolves, and beaver we've seen, they would outnumber the sailors it would take to crew those ships!" Both men laughed.

"Henri," Pierre said, his tone suddenly more serious. "Ever since Marquette headed up the Ottawa River, I've pondered what he said when we first met him at theologian school. Remember how he questioned if two minimally trained deacons could survive, for even a day, in the wilds of New France? Until now, Marquette directed our every move. For our sakes, I hope he was wrong. We don't know where we are heading or what to expect when we arrive."

"I know," Henri said, his gaze sweeping across the endless expanse of water. "I can't help but feel the same. I don't know how we'll do it or whether we'll survive this trip. But what keeps me going is the feeling that we owe our Indigenous allies immense gratitude. Ever since we've seen those poor children, I can't help but feel that for all the good they've done for us—trapping, processing, and delivering furs—they have received nothing but ill tidings in return. They've suffered diseases that killed them by the thousands and watched as their ability to defend themselves against the Iroquois has greatly diminished. Ultimately, they lost everything, and many had to leave their homeland. The least I can do is volunteer to help them in any way I can."

"Well, bless your soul, Mr. Hébert," said Pierre, with a grin. "The blood of Louis Hébert runs strong in your veins, and you have the fortitude of Champlain. Your dedication has restored my faith. Someday, New France will recognize your efforts and place a statue of you on the streets of Quebec City. When they do, I expect to have mine placed next to yours. It will be grander and fashioned of solid gold!" The sound of laughter and the swishing of paddles echoed across the water.

Following the north shoreline of the lake, they stopped whenever they encountered an Indigenous fishing village. Henri and Pierre would hand out small metal crosses to the chiefs they encountered. The chiefs could use these to show raiding Iroquois bands that they were Christian people under the protection of the French Army. With each cross, they added a copper musket ball. They would inform the Indigenous people that the French were back and ready to trade. They told the villagers to spread the word that their convoy would return to the area to trade in two or three moons.

Each morning, Henri and Pierre would start their day with the Liturgy of the Hours prayers and bless the convoy for safe travel and success on their mission. Their days were long. They would start at 5:00 a.m. and paddle for three hours before stopping for a breakfast of peas, salted pork, and corn biscuits. Lunch was eaten on the move, usually consisting of pemmican or jerky. Dinner did not occur until long after dark. Sleep was sparse, spent under the stars beneath a blanket or an overturned canoe if it was raining. When they encountered Indigenous fishing villages along the way, the coureurs des bois would trade for meat or fish for the evening meal. If not, they would eat what the French called rubbaboo stew, which they made by combining flour, water, maple syrup, and chunks of pemmican.

Each night, Pierre would get out his journal and map where they had traveled, noting interesting land features they had seen that day. Henri would sketch the Indigenous population's dress and record their customs. After the evening meal, Lieutenant

DeMarre would order a round of rum for the officers, coureurs des bois, and the engagés. The lieutenant would offer the Jesuits a shot of rum. Henri would refuse, feeling it was shameless to drink in front of the Indigenous people. Pierre happily accepted both shots of rum for himself.

One evening, Henri scolded Pierre for drinking in the presence of their Native guides. "I can't believe you do that right in front of them. You know that many tribes have forbidden the use of alcohol."

"Yeah, I have heard that," Pierre said, slurring his words. "I've also heard that one of those tribes is the Iroquois. The way I figure it, if I'm going to be captured and killed for drinking, I might as well be drunk when it happens!" Henri turned away in disgust.

# Day of the Dead

In five days, Henri and Pierre's group reached the other side of Lake Ontario. At the western shore, they met the Wyandot, a tribe best known for the fine tobacco and corn they grew. They spoke a dialect that was a blend of Huron and Iroquois. The French called them the Neutrals because they would trade with anyone, including the Iroquois. This practice of open trade kept them at peace with their neighbors for many years. However, in the 1650s, the Neutrals suffered constant attacks by raiding Iroquois war parties and were forced to surrender to the Seneca Iroquois tribe. Now, they were part of the Seneca Nation.

Henri took out his journal and drew a picture of a Neutral warrior, then wrote:

> They wore little other than a loincloth, leggings, and moccasins. The men were proud of their tattoos covering most of their bodies. Their heads were shaven, except for a tuft in the back that grew long on the warriors. They had great affection for dogs, which ran freely, barking at the French strangers.

Lieutenant DeMarre was quite surprised at the enormous number of Neutrals gathered there. Makeshift shelters filled the shoreline, and others circled the village. He called over one of his Huron scouts. "What's going on?"

"They're here for the Feast of the Dead," replied the scout. "Many people have fled their villages due to war and diseases. They come here to rebury the bones of their dead. They now hold this ceremony every other year on the first full moon in June.

"This ceremony is very sacred, involving eight days of mourning and preparation and two days of celebration and gift-giving," continued the interpreter. "We've arrived on the fifth day. Visitors are welcome. We've come at a most opportune time."

Henri leaned over to Pierre. "Did you hear that? They are celebrating the Feast of the Dead. Father Marquette told us to document their religious practices. I must get an invitation. What the scout said is true. We've come at a most opportune time."

Pierre looked at Henri, shocked and confused. "Feast of the Dead! Do they eat their dead? Or do the dead eat the living?"

"No, you fool! Don't you read your history? Recollect Gabriel Sagard and Father Jean de Brebeuf wrote about these ceremonies and gatherings in *The Jesuit Relations* in the 1620s and '30s. They reported that when villages move, the inhabitants bring their dead with them. They dig up their relatives, clean their bones, and rebury them at their new home. It is quite an elaborate ceremony."

"And you want to watch that?" replied Pierre, horrified. "Count me out! I'll find another way to be of assistance."

"If you are so squeamish, I'll attend the ceremony alone. I must speak to the chief of this village."

Lieutenant DeMarre sent his two Huron scouts to the village to ask for a counsel with their peace chief. Shortly afterward, they returned with Chief Kondiaronk at their side. "Welcome, my French friends," Kondiaronk said. "You have come at the most sacred time of mourning and celebration for my people. You'll see how we celebrate the lives of our dead and honor their connection to the spirit world. The riches of our nation will be on display. Come, celebrate with us. There will be drink and food aplenty."

Lieutenant DeMarre signaled for the engagés to bring forth the gifts. On the rocky shore, he unrolled two wool blankets. One had six French flintlock muskets, six powder horns filled with black powder, and six bags of musket balls. On the other were three iron axes, four jackknives,, one pound of glass beads, and three necklaces supporting three-inch-long solid silver beavers.

Lieutenant DeMarre, speaking through his interpreter, said, "These gifts are for you and your people during this most special time. It's only a small sample of the wealth our great leader wishes to provide you with as we restart our fur-trading operation. We only ask that you allow us safe passage on your land trail to Detroit. Please keep watch of our canoes. We'll return this way in two moons and be ready to trade more of what you see here."

Chief Kondiaronk looked at the interpreter and spoke in an angry voice. Lieutenant DeMarre turned to the interpreter, confusion evident on his face. "Doesn't he like the gifts? Those guns are an extremely generous peace offer directly from the governor-general himself."

"No," said the interpreter. "That's not it. You insulted him by not accepting his invitation to honor their dead."

Henri quickly jumped in. "Lieutenant, have your interpreter tell Chief Kondiaronk my team will stay. I'll graciously accept his invitation to the ceremony."

Pierre looked at Henri and shook his head before turning back to the lieutenant. "Lieutenant DeMarre, I speak fluent Iroquois. With your permission, I'll tell Chief Kondiaronk that Henri and I will attend so your convoy can move out in the morning with safe passage." The lieutenant agreed.

"Great Chief Kondiaronk," began Pierre. "We, your French friends and allies, are most fortunate to have come to your shores at such a momentous time. The Black Robes," pointing toward Henri and himself, "will stay with you and your people while you honor your dead. We are the spiritual leaders of this convoy, and our God will surely bless the souls of your departed. When the mourning period is over, our team will celebrate with you. We have magnificent items to bestow upon you. You'll be the envy of your people. The convoy must leave in the morning to bring supplies to your western brothers in Detroit. Those exiles are now in desperate need after the Iroquois forced them to abandon their villages. But fear not—the convoy will return here in less than two moons. Your people will have time to gather their furs, and the French will have many useful items to trade."

Chief Kondiaronk smiled. "Black Robes, you are welcome in my camp. Your people have done good things to help my people in the past. Bring your team of voyageurs to our council house, and we'll smoke, eat, and remember the old times."

Pierre informed the lieutenant that the chief had agreed to the safe passage of his convoy. The lieutenant immediately started making plans for the convoy's departure in the morning.

The soldiers and engagés would stay on the beach, readying their gear. The lieutenant, the Jesuits, and the coureurs des bois would join Chief Kondiaronk for dinner.

• • •

When they arrived at the council house, the women had already started to cook venison strips on flat stones in hot coals. The men sat on cattail mats on the floor and passed around a long-handled peace pipe. Pierre deliberately sat near the half-open door to watch the women preparing the food.

While the meat was cooking, the women dug a hole in the ground and placed an elk hide over it, forming a kettle. They filled the hide kettle with water and began adding ingredients. First, they added dried beans and corn soaked in a wooden bucket. Then, sliced arrowhead tubers and dandelion roots. They poured in six cups of birch tree sap and added wild onions and leeks. While they stirred the mixture, they kept adding and replacing hot stones from the fire to bring the concoction to a boil.

As the meat cooked, Pierre watched the women place small, rolled balls of dried coltsfoot leaves on stones by the fire. After the coltsfoot caught fire, they would dump the coltsfoot ashes into the stew. Pierre would later discover that this method of using coltsfoot leaves created a form of salt. When the roots and tubers were tender, the women added the cut-up chunks of venison.

As the stew simmered, the coureurs des bois discussed the trade value of furs with Chief Kondiaronk. The fur industry back in Europe wanted either luxury furs or felt. Fox, bobcat, marten, mink, and otter were lucrative luxury furs for French men and women. Beaver pelts became felt. They sheared the long guard hairs and compressed the underfur into felt. As beaver felt hats became increasingly popular, the beaver became the king of furs. Beaver pelts became the standard for all North American financial transactions. The value of one beaver pelt became the standard unit of currency for all other types of fur.

The coureurs des bois gave Pierre a list to read to Chief Kondiaronk. It contained items available for trade and their cost in furs. The price list was created by Intendant Jean Talon and approved by Governor-General Daniel de Rémy before departure from

Quebec. It read: one-made beaver equals one beaver pelt, two foxes, two bobcats, two otters, three marten, or seven minks.

| Trade Item | Cost for each Item |
| --- | --- |
| Flintlock musket | 14-made beaver |
| Pistol | 7-made beaver |
| Blanket | 7-made beaver |
| Cloth 1-yard | 3.5-made beaver |
| Copper kettle | 1.5-made beaver |
| Jackknife | 0.25-made beaver |
| Powderhorn | 1-made beaver |
| Black powder 1-lb | 1-made beaver |
| Shot 1-lb | 1-made beaver |
| Hatchet | 1-made beaver |
| Net line 1-spool | 1-made beaver |
| Files (set of 3) | 1-made beaver |
| Scrapers (set of 3) | 0.5-made beaver |
| Rum 1-gallon | 4-made beaver |
| Tobacco 1-lb | 2-made beaver |
| Clay pipe | 1-made beaver |
| Twine 1-spool | 1-made beaver |
| Strike-a-light steel | 0.25-made beaver |
| Flint (PK) | 0.83-made beaver |
| Hawk bells (pair) | 0.83-made beaver |
| Fishhooks (PK) | .071-made beaver |
| Glass beads 1-lb | 2-made beaver |
| Mirror | 1-made beaver |
| Beaver trap | 3-made beaver |

When Pierre finished reading the list, Chief Kondiaronk argued the cost per item was too high. But everyone there knew that trade item prices came directly from Quebec City. They were the same across New France, and no amount of negotiating would change the outcome. Besides, the chief knew he had just received gifts worth over 150-made beaver. After a short negotiation, the chief agreed to the terms of the French, and together, they ate their fill of fine stew and corn cakes.

In the morning, the convoy set out on the overland trail to Detroit with thirty-one of its original thirty-five members. The lieutenant, his sergeant, Jean Plattier, Jean Tiberge, and three Huron guides led the way. Following them were ten well-equipped foot soldiers and fourteen engagés carrying a total of 1,400 pounds of trade items and gear on their backs.

Adrien Jolliet, Thomas Pajot Jr., Henri Hébert, and Pierre Pajot stood silent as they watched the convoy disappear over the first hill. The plan was for the Detroit convoy to travel around fifteen miles per day with short stops at Indigenous villages they encountered along the way. At that pace, they estimated it would take about two weeks to walk the two hundred miles to the trading post at Detroit.

The two Jesuits and their coureurs des bois would take the smaller canoe and travel the four-hundred-mile route along the southern shore of Lake Erie. The four of them should arrive in Detroit in about three weeks. The convoy planned to stay in Detroit for two weeks, allowing adequate time for the two groups to reunite before the convoy headed back to Quebec City.

"Now, are you still glad you promised the governor-general that you would deliver the peace pipe to the Mohawk chief?" Pierre said with a chuckle as he nudged Henri.

Henri didn't reply. Instead, he pointed toward a commotion at the far end of the village. At first, the four Frenchmen thought Chief Kondiaronk had changed his mind and was assembling a war party to go after the convoy.

But Pierre quickly corrected them. "Those sounds aren't the cries of war. They are more like sounds of pain and suffering."

"It's starting," Henri said.

"What's starting?" Pierre asked, puzzled.

"The Day of the Dead," Henri whispered. "We must go and join them."

• • •

Chief Kondiaronk had announced that all the expected villagers had arrived, and it was time to display the dead for all to see. Songs of mourning broke out across the area as village representatives started loading two-man travois with the bones of their deceased relatives. Henri and Pierre slowly approached the group of mourners. Adrien Jolliet and Thomas Pajot stayed with the canoe.

Before abandoning their villages, the displaced Neutrals exhumed the bodies of their dead from their original graves. The village women carefully cleaned the bones of any remaining flesh and skin. The bones were then rewrapped in beaver-skin bundles and transported to their new home for a communal burial. This ceremony not only brought the spirits of the dead together but also reunited the living in a communal celebration between villages.

Soon, everyone was ready, and the burial procession began to assemble. Each village had selected two warriors to drag the travois holding the bones of their dead. The crowd moved slowly up the shoreline to a secluded bay overlooking Lake Ontario. A large, freshly dug pit ringed with tall posts containing crossbars stood waiting. The mourners immediately began hanging the beaver skin bone bags on the wood posts and stringing gifts for the dead on the crossbars.

Some bags had skulls, arms, and leg bones attached to them. Others contained only the bones of the deceased. Regardless, the focus seemed to be on the amount and quality of the gifts presented to the dead. The crowd moved post to post, evaluating the offerings and commenting on the wealth and importance an individual must have had during their lifetime. The various village shamans were beating drums, shaking rattles, and chanting songs of the dead. The mourners screamed, wailed, and told stories of the dead until sundown. Then, everyone quietly returned to their campsites.

The following morning, all the villagers were back at the burial site. Everyone wanted to see the additional offerings made during the night. Often, the relatives of the deceased waited until darkness to place their most impressive gifts. Fine-crafted pottery and baskets, shell necklaces, feathered headdresses, and decorated weapons of war impressed the crowd.

The burial ceremony began after a lengthy period of viewing the dead, accompanied by music, songs, and screams of sorrow. The village shaman carefully removed the bone bags from the cross bars and ceremonially lowered them into the pit. They added gifts, food items, and essential tools needed in the spirit world. The posts and crossbars were dismantled and stored. Then, all in attendance filled the burial pit with dirt. At that point, the mourning period was officially over. The crowd returned to Chief Kondiaronk's village for the gift exchange and the Great Feast.

The gift exchange was the part that the villagers looked forward to the most. The village overflowed with joy as they lavished their children with presents. Wood-carved toys, cornhusk dolls, and strings of beads made from freshwater mussel shells delighted the children. Gifts for adults, on the other hand, were carefully planned to impress. Meticulously crafted arrowheads, clay pottery, and smoking pipes were proudly exchanged.

Henri nudged Pierre. "Now would be a suitable time to give Chief Kondiaronk the gifts we have brought him." Pierre agreed and went to fetch them from the canoe. When Pierre returned, Henri and Pierre approached Chief Kondiaronk. In a loud voice, Pierre said: "Oh, Great Chief, we want to thank you for your kindness to the French convoy. The ties between our two nations remain strong. We Black Robes have also brought gifts for you. They are small compared to your great wealth, but we hope you'll accept them as a token of our appreciation."

A crowd gathered to see what the two Black Robes had to present. When Pierre pulled the copper cauldron out of his pack, you could hear whispers of approval in the crowd. Its shiny, bright copper gleamed in the sun. Pierre tapped it with a stick so all could witness the sound of metal. The Chief looked thrilled with the gift.

"But wait, Great Chief," said Pierre. "We have one more item to present to you as well." Henri reached into the cauldron filled with cornmeal and pulled out the confit pot. You could hear a gasp come from the crowd. The Indigenous people treasured ceramics. None had seen any finer than this.

Pierre pointed out that the pot contained the freshest of bear lard. "This lard is excellent for preparing many fine French dishes." Pierre noticed the puzzled look in the clan chief's eyes—it was clear they had never tasted French food. He made a mental note to change that.

Chief Kondiaronk accepted the gifts with a wide smile. He held them up high so that all could see. A great cheer arose from the crowd. Chief Kondiaronk turned to the two Jesuits and said, "Now, I must offer you something in exchange."

Pierre quickly responded. "Great Chief, allowing us to join your people in your most sacred ceremony is gift enough. However, if you could spare the necessary ingredients, there's something I would like to prepare for you."

"The riches of the Neutral Nation are available to you. What do you seek?"

"I saw you have river mussels and mushrooms," said Pierre. "If I can have them, a few wild onions, garlic, chives, and maybe a nest full of fresh duck eggs, I could prepare you something wonderful. Oh, and I suppose you don't have any fresh buttermilk. Do you?"

"As I said, the riches of the Neutral Nation are great. You may be surprised. Come, gather your two friends. The four of you will eat with me tonight at the Great Celebration."

• • •

For the past two days, while the crowd attended the burial, many of Chief Kondiaronk's villagers had been preparing for the Great Celebration. The men set long nets stretched along the shoreline of Lake Ontario to catch the spawning smallmouth bass. They deliberately slit open some female bass and hung them in the net. The scent of the female spawn attracted more males than females. This practice was a way to maintain a renewable resource without overharvesting.

The men had soaked yesterday's catch in a salt brine overnight, then smoked them in a log smokehouse using oak, sassafras, and hickory chips. The men baked the morning's freshly caught bass fillets on four-foot-long split-cedar planks placed over a long trench fire. The fillets were basted using a mixture of maple syrup and dried crushed wintergreen and spicebush berries.

While the men were busy with the fish, the women cooked fresh bear and deer meat on greased flat rocks in the fire. The women were proud of the tender fawn meat they were preparing. The Neutrals had a custom that was strange to Henri and Pierre. A hunter must kill the first young animal they see in the spring, or that animal will warn others of its kind to stay away. A hunter's success for the year depends on this. Luckily, one of the hunters had killed two doe and their fawns that morning.

In addition to the meat, the women prepared enormous quantities of flatbread. They picked a basket of fresh watercress and added wild leeks, chives, onions, sunflower seeds, and dried cranberries to the salad. They then tossed it with maple syrup vinegar dressing. The women served the feast on cedar-wood plates with hot ginseng-root tea. It was the grandest meal any Frenchmen had ever eaten in the wilderness.

After dinner, the men sat around the fire smoking their pipes, while the women stored away the leftover food. Then, it was time for songs and dance. The men started the circle dance with chants and drums. Then, the women and children joined in with rattles and reed pipes. The four Frenchmen were thrilled with the display.

When the dancers tired and sat down for a rest, Pierre reached into his pack and brought out his game of ball and cups. Pierre slid the three cups around and let the observers guess where the ball was. What began as a game of entertainment quickly turned into a betting sport. Soon, a crowd of men was betting whether the ball was under cup one, two, or three. Pierre's carnival skills allowed him to keep the winners and losers on an even keel. Henri cringed, aware that Pierre was controlling the outcome. However, in the end, all seemed happy.

Pierre, thrilled with the attention, asked Henri to help him set up the puppet show. Henri shook his head. "I'm not sure that is a wise move. This day is a solemn occasion. Do you really think we should be trying to make them laugh?"

"Of course we should," Pierre said. "Nothing is better for the soul than a good laugh. We must win them over as friends to save their souls. Nothing builds friendship like laughter."

While Henri cut two four-foot forked sticks and a crossbar, Pierre wowed the crowd with carnival magic tricks. They pushed the forked sticks solidly into the ground, and the two Jesuits threw their black robes over the crossbar. After setting up elm-wood buckets for seats, they'd put together a decent stage for their show.

They reenacted their old favorites, loved by the schoolchildren in Quebec City, using Pierre's stick puppets. The Frenchman chased by the black bear made everyone giggle. The warrior killing and carrying the bear over his shoulders made everyone cheer. But the skit that they got an unexpected reaction from the crowd was the Iroquois attack on a Huron village. The wounds from that war were still too fresh.

Pierre whispered to Henri, "Quick, do the peace scene." An Iroquois and a Huron warrior entered the puppet scene. In the middle stood a Jesuit with a peace pipe and gifts for both sides. "There would now be lasting peace," they yelled, both praying this resolution would lift the tension. Much to their relief, the crowd let out a roaring cheer.

After the show, Pierre addressed the gathered village chiefs and clan leaders. "You've met our soldiers and fur traders. Now you've had a chance to meet the Black Robe Jesuits. We are here to bring you the word of our great Christian God, the God of all gods. He loves all people. He will surely welcome all the departed souls you reburied into his great kingdom. The French soldiers told you they made a treaty with the Iroquois League of Five Nations. That's true. But the soldiers didn't tell you that the Iroquois have only agreed to spare Christian tribes allied with the French. Our job as Jesuits is to bring you into the great circle of Christian tribes. To become part of the Christian tribes, our God asks for only two things:

"One, recognize him as the God of all gods. He created the spirits that watch over your wind, rain, sky, water, sun, moon, fire, and thunder. His power is greater than the stars in the heavens.

"Two, treat all people like you want them to treat you. Avoid war and killing. Seek peace. The men must take care of their children and wives. Be faithful only to her. Be true to your word, and don't take or desire things that don't belong to you.

"If you do these simple things, you will join his Christian tribe.

You'll have the protection of the French soldiers. Before we leave in our canoe tomorrow, we'll perform baptisms at the shoreline of the Big Lake. Every chief or clan leader baptized will receive one of these necklaces bearing a silver cross. Wearing these crosses signifies you are Christians, and the League of Five Nations raiding parties will leave you alone."

Then, in a loud voice, Pierre said: "Our great God has taught His many Christian tribes a prayer that he wishes all of us to say each day. It goes like this ..."

Pierre, using hand gestures, recited the Lord's Prayer in Iroquoian. "Our Father, who art in heaven, hallowed be your name. Your Kingdom will come; your will shall be done, on earth as it is in heaven. Give us this day, our daily bread, and forgive us for our trespasses, as we forgive those who trespassed against us. Lead us not into temptation, and deliver us from evil. Amen."

Then, to make his point, Pierre asked Thomas to step forward and say the Lord's Prayer in Algonquian. Then Adrien said it in Montagnais. Henri in Siouan. Pierre finished by saying the prayer one more time in French.

"As you can hear, the reach of our God is vast," Pierre said. Pierre had one more carnival trick up his sleeve. He set up his musketoon mortar and warned the chiefs and clan leaders, "This next demonstration will be loud and scary," Pierre said. "But fear not! No one will be in danger." Unfortunately for the Jesuits, gossip quickly circulated amongst the villagers that the Black Robes were great sorcerers and were about to perform powerful black magic.

When everything was ready, Pierre stood there with his wild red hair, goggles, and a white spark-resistant apron pulled over his black robe. He looked more like a Parisian clown than a Jesuit. Yet somehow, that costume transformed Pierre into a carnival salesman ready to launch into his routine.

With a smoldering wick held in his hand, Pierre said, "Our God is the almighty creator of all things. He commands the lightning and thunder."

Pierre touched the burning wick to the musketoon's flash pan filled with black powder. The mortar boomed, and the thunder ball soared hundreds of feet skyward. When the ball exploded, it created a thunderous roar and a bright white flash. The crowd dropped to the ground in fear.

Thunder balls contain black powder-coated rice husks and small metal balls. All ball-style fireworks use a mortar and a charge of black powder to launch them. When the black powder ignites, it lifts the ball and lights a delayed fuse in the projectile. When the delayed fuse reaches the inner core, it sets off a secondary charge that ignites the metal stars. The color of the burning stars depends on the metal type used in their construction.

Seeing the crowd's reaction, Pierre loaded his mortar with a ball labeled barium chloride and said: "Fear not; Our God is also benevolent. He fills the land with green plants and trees that feed all living things." Pierre touched the wick to the flash pan, and a shower of green filled the sky.

Next, Pierre loaded a ball labeled copper chloride. "Our God created the blues of the oceans and the sky. So that the birds can soar, and the fish can swim." As Pierre finished speaking, the crowd watched a beautiful veil of blue as it came drifting down.

Finally, Pierre loaded a ball labeled strontium carbonate. "However," yelled Pierre, "he is a fair and just God. He captures the departed souls who ignore his teachings. Those that murder, rape, take, and destroy are placed in the hottest of fires. Their spirits burn in hell forever." Pierre lit the mortar, and the ball burst into an umbrella of burning red fire.

At the end of the display, somewhat shaken, Henri looked at Pierre and said: "Wow, do you think you properly represented our Catholic faith?"

"Of course I did," replied Pierre. "Do you not remember what old Father Agard told us? He said, 'Our Jesuits use syncretism, which means they blend aspects of native belief with Christian teachings.' I was using syncretism to make my point. That gives me quite a bit of leeway in our teaching. Don't you agree?" Henri didn't respond. It would take some time for him to think about this.

• • •

While the four Frenchmen were packing their things, Chief Kondiaronk held a council meeting with his visiting chiefs and clan leaders. When it was over, he approached the two Jesuits. "We, members of the Neutral tribes, have decided to join your Christian tribe and receive the protection of your God and the French army. The Seneca say we are now part of their nation. But we know we are Neutrals. We seek only to be at peace with the Iroquois, the French, and your God. We'll come to your baptism in the morning and wear the metal cross. We'll pray that your God can protect us."

Pierre looked at Henri and whispered, "Syncretism." Henri looked up at the sky and made the sign of the cross.

Chief Kondiaronk turned to Pierre. "Have you forgotten what you asked for earlier in the day?" The chief clapped his hands, and two women appeared. One carried a basket of fresh duck eggs, wild onions, garlic, chives, and leeks. The other held a gourd filled with liquid.

"What's in the gourd?" asked Pierre.

"You asked for milk, and the riches of the Neutral Nation have delivered," replied Chief Kondiaronk.

Pierre waved the jar under his nose. It had a rich smell, more like heavy cream, but pleasant. It smelled like goat's milk. "Incredible!" said Pierre. "How in the world did you get milk?"

Chief Kondiaronk smiled. "You know that tender fawn meat you had this evening for dinner? The warrior that killed those fawns this morning also killed their mothers. He extracted their milk sacs for you." Henri turned pale and suddenly felt sick. Pierre could see that Chief Kondiaronk was proud of what he had just provided—any hesitation in accepting these gifts would be a great insult. Pierre smiled and graciously accepted them.

"Great Chief, these are fine ingredients. With these, I can prepare a mussel and mushroom bisque, just like in France. However, it would require one more thing on your part. I feel ashamed to ask this, as you have already done so much for us." Pierre stood there with his fingers crossed, hoping the chief would decline his offer.

"What more do you need?" Chief Kondiaronk asked.

"I would need to use your new copper cauldron and some of that bear lard."

Chief Kondiaronk ordered two women to go to his lodge and

retrieve the requested items. He then looked at Pierre and said, "If we Neutrals are to be partners with the French in trade, peace, and religion, I might as well understand how you French eat."

"I'll be back shortly," Pierre said. "I need more things from our canoe before I get started."

When he returned, he washed and scrubbed the two dozen freshwater mussels to remove any sand, then placed them into the cauldron. He added chopped onions, garlic, and a pinch of mixed spices. Pierre added four cups of water and steamed the mussels until they opened. He then strained the broth through a double cloth and set the mussels aside to cool.

When the mussels were ready, Pierre removed them from their shells and diced them. Then, the diced mussels and broth went back into the cauldron. Pierre added four tablespoons of salted butter, a teaspoon of chopped onions, a teaspoon of chopped leeks, and a half pound of chopped morel mushrooms. He moved the cauldron to the fire's edge and added two beaten duck egg yolks, four cups of doe milk, and ¼ teaspoon of black pepper. When the milk was hot, Pierre added two tablespoons of chopped chives and served the bisque with hot biscuits smothered in salted butter. Pierre and Henri grinned as they watched the chief and clan leaders taste the soup. What started with skepticism and apprehension quickly turned into smiles.

When the council finished discussing what they had just tasted, Chief Kondiaronk approached the two Jesuits and said, "Again, you have presented me with a delightful gift. I feel I must return the favor, but I sense your apprehension about my offers. Therefore, I'll offer you something I think you'll not refuse. Tomorrow, when you leave for the Seneca village, I will send with you our finest warriors. Chief Mingwe wants the Seneca, Mohawk, and Neutrals to have a tewaaraton tournament. Our team can guide you up the Niagara River, help you make the portage around the falls, and introduce you to the Seneca chief. He will have heard of the power of the Black Robes, gods of thunder. He'll want to meet with you before your journey into Lake Erie. Also, the Mohawk chief, Thayenda, has moved his people there. Be careful around him—he doesn't like the French!"

Henri swallowed hard and stepped forward. "We will graciously accept your offer!"

# Lacrosse

The following morning, the Jesuits and their two coureurs des bois had a hearty breakfast of leftover smoked fish, fried salted pork, biscuits, and two duck eggs per man. As they finished packing their canoe, a group of chiefs and clan leaders showed up to receive their baptism. The ceremony proceeded without issue, and each received a metal cross, which pleased them very much. Then, sixteen men showed up carrying a long canoe. Fourteen were handsome young warriors dressed in brightly colored feather costumes and heavy body paint. They were the finest looking warriors any of the four Frenchmen had ever seen. Two of the men were older. One was the apparent coach, and the other was a traditional healer whose job was to yell chants of support to his team while cursing the other team's players.

The first people to play lacrosse—or *tewaaraton*—were the Algonquin tribes. It involved hundreds of men playing on huge game fields. The purpose was to strengthen young men for war while building bonds and creating solidarity amongst clans and villages. After thousands of Native Americans died from European diseases and Iroquois raids, lacrosse had all but disappeared. However, the Iroquois League of Five Nations adopted the game and had turned it into something resembling a major sporting event. It was now a way for tribes to display their finest athletes. When the Seneca absorbed the Neutrals into their tribe, they expected the Neutrals to send a team to special celebrations. The arrival of the Black Robes, gods of thunder, would require such an event.

After saying goodbye, the Frenchmen and the tewaaraton team launched their canoes. They traveled quickly east along the southern shoreline of Lake Ontario, and the Frenchmen struggled to keep up with the athletic young men. By midday, they were at the mouth of the Onguiaahra—the Niagara River. They started paddling upstream, but the strong current slowed them down. Soon, the river narrowed, and the banks grew steeper. Eventually, the river's current became so ferocious they had to beach their canoes and travel on foot. In the distance, they could hear the roar of the falls. The Neutrals' tewaaraton team dragged their large canoe into the woods and flipped it over, leaving it there for their return journey.

The four Frenchmen shouldered their heavy packs and prepared to make the overland hike to the falls. Henri used his rifle with the bayonet crucifix as a walking stick, and Pierre carried his musketoon over his shoulder. Adrien and Thomas each carried two flintlocks—one ready for use, the other wrapped in a cloth sleeve.

As they headed up the portage trail, they were surprised to see six tewaaraton players pick up the Frenchmen's eight-man canoe and follow them up the steep Niagara escarpment. Even while carrying the canoe, the warriors moved with such speed that Pierre and Henri found it hard to keep up. However, Henri reminded Pierre of the words Father Druillettes had told Marquette, "Do your share of the work and don't slow down the Natives when they are on the move." The two Jesuits pushed on.

While the group walked across the escarpment trail, Pierre could not help but take frequent glimpses of the river flowing through the gorge below. He made mental notes of the number of twists and turns of the rapids. He planned to document all this in his journal that evening. Just as the sun began to set, they arrived at the western side of the falls. The site took their breath away. Pierre sat down to make an entry in his journal, accompanied by sketches of the waterfalls.

> Two great walls of water, separated by a rocky point, plunge hundreds of feet into a swirling mist. A veil of water rises high into the air, pierced by an incredible rainbow. The volume of water rushing over these two cliffs is beyond measure. The roar is so loud one

cannot hear himself speak, much less continue a conversation with his companions. Only the finger of God could create something so beautiful.

The Seneca encampment lay upstream of the falls, at the mouth of a large river—the Welland River. As they approached, they saw an enormous wooden palisade enclosing a vast village. The Seneca were the largest tribe of the Iroquois League of Five Nations—they numbered in the tens of thousands.

The Frenchmen could see dozens of longhouses lined up in neat rows through the open palisade walls. It was the grandest Native American village that the Frenchmen had seen. A welcoming party was already waiting outside the village—scouts had likely sent word as soon as the Neutrals entered Seneca territory at the mouth of the Niagara River.

Chief Mingwe, muscular and of average height, stood just beyond the walls, flanked by a large crowd that had gathered to greet the visitors. His face was painted, and his shaved head bore a tattoo with a tuft of hair on top. Numerous feathers were tied in a circular whirl in his hair, standing up like a peacock's display. He had a Dutch knife in his belt and held an arquebus in his right hand. Beside him stood a giant of a man, his tattooed face stern and his shaved head topped with a rooster-tail comb running down the center. He carried an imposing wooden club with a metal spike jutting from its end.

Pierre nudged Henri. "That must be the Mohawk chief you are meant to meet. Good luck presenting the governor-general's gift." Henri tensed, wiping the sweat from his brow.

Beside the two chiefs stood three tewaaraton teams, adorned in their full regalia and waiting to compete against the Neutrals. Each team member flexed their muscles, showing off their athleticism as their healer introduced them. As each player stepped forward, they added an item of value to a growing prize pile. The undefeated champion team would get to select items from half of that pile. The loser of the championship game would get to take half of the remaining half. What was left went to the winner of the rematch between the two losers from the first day.

Henri took note of the items in the pile. There were guns, bows, arrows, stone clubs, clay pottery, food items, and even trade items obtained from the English and Dutch. Henri drew pictures of each team as they were displayed for the crowd.

It was now time for the Neutral team and their French travelers to be introduced. The crowd booed and jeered as the Neutral players stepped forward. Then, Chief Mingwe approached the two coureurs des bois. Speaking in Iroquois, he said, "I hear from our Neutral brothers that the French are ready to trade again. Does that offer extend to the Iroquois people as well?"

"What you've heard is true," Adrien replied in fluent Iroquoian. "All that the French have to offer to the Algonquin, Huron, and Neutrals, are now available to your people. The trade price will be the same across all nations. Thomas and I will gladly explain those trade prices when you are ready to take counsel."

"Will those trade items include guns?" Chief Mingwe asked.

Responding in a strong, clear voice, Adrien said, "Yes, if the Iroquois keep peace with their neighbors and don't attack the Christian tribes that wear the silver metal cross. Our Lieutenant-General Marquis de Tracy sends you a gift with his offer to trade freely."

Adrien and Thomas pulled the cloth sleeves off their second flintlocks. "This peace rifle is for Chief Mingwe," Adrien said, "and the other is for Chief Thayenda." The watching crowd let out a gasp. The flintlocks were the same model used by the French military; however, they had been custom-made with silver inlays in the forearm and stock. The powder horns were etched with animal figures and filled with black powder. A bag of patches and musket balls accompanied each rifle.

After studying the firearms, Chief Mingwe placed a hand on Adrien's shoulder. "Tell your great chief we'll trade with him. He offers fine gifts. Now tell me, fur trader, how do you speak our language as if you were one of us?"

"I grew up on the Isle of Orleans near Quebec," Jolliet said. "I have many Iroquois brothers."

There was a long pause, the crowd waiting to see if Chief Thayenda would speak. Seeing his opportunity, Henri shouted in French, "I, too, have a gift for Chief Thayenda from our great governor-general." Henri reached into his pack and pulled out the tomahawk peace pipe he had promised to deliver. Pierre quickly interpreted in Iroquois, and Chief Thayenda accepted the pipe. He held it high for all to see. It was an exact copy of the one Chief Mingwe had received at the treaty signing.

"The Mohawk Nation will trade with the French as well," Chief Thayenda said. The crowd erupted in excitement.

"Black Robes," Chief Mingwe said, "tonight, you and your fur-trading friends will eat with Chief Thayenda and I, and we shall talk trade."

That evening, the four Frenchmen sat around the council house fire with the chiefs and clan leaders. During dinner, Adrien and Thomas discussed the trade value of beaver pelts and promised that the French convoy would return with items to trade next spring.

After dinner, Chief Mingwe laid out the program for the next three days. "Tomorrow will be a day of rest and preparation for our Neutral friends. But fear not, great excitement will fill the village as we show off our next generation of tewaaraton players. At midday, our twelve to fifteen-year-old males will divide into two teams and play until the mid-afternoon. Following the youth tournament, our sixteen to twenty-year-old males will compete and show their potential to become members of our adult teams. Hundreds of players will be on the field at the same time. The tournaments provide great war training for our young warriors, and it binds our clans together. There will be celebrations and gift-giving throughout the day."

Seeing an opportunity to make a good impression, Henri pulled the second copper cauldron out of his pack and presented it to Chief Mingwe. The copper gleamed brightly in the firelight. Chief Mingwe looked thrilled with the gift, and the crowd nodded approvingly. Henri reached into the cauldron filled with cornmeal and removed the confit pot containing bear lard. A gasp rippled through the lodge, followed by a flurry of excited whispers.

Chief Mingwe looked at Pierre and said, "The Neutrals have informed us that you used a similar pot to cook their chief French food. Will you be doing the same for me?"

Pierre paused for a moment. "I would gladly cook for you if I can have a piece of that leftover turkey we ate tonight. However, I'll need a little help gathering other necessary items."

Chief Mingwe called for his two best hunters. "These warriors will escort you tomorrow morning to hunt a large, fresh tom turkey. Wear your black robe and blacken your face with charcoal. Be ready well before dawn. Tell the women the other items you seek, and they will gather them for you."

• • •

An hour before sunrise, Pierre—still drowsy from travel—was up and ready to go. But when he stepped outside, he nearly had a heart attack: two warriors, their bodies camouflaged with lines of charcoal and brown paint, emerged out of the darkness, bows and arrows in hand. One warrior was carrying a bird-shaped frame made from willow branches and covered with the skin of a hen turkey. The other had a turkey wing taken from an earlier kill. Both warriors wore turkey calls on cords hanging around their necks.

Pierre had seen Indigenous peoples with wing-bone calls before but had never seen them used. He was aware that they crafted them from the wing bones of a tom turkey. After boiling the meat off the wing bones, they scrape them clean. Then they cleaned out the soft marrow from each bone, then cut the ends square. The three pieces were tightly bonded together with pine resin. Bear lard preserved the calls and gave them a smooth, translucent sheen. Wing-bone calls work by sucking in air with short, kissing smacks that produce soft yelps startlingly similar to those of a hen turkey.

After greeting one another, the three men set off into darkness, leaving the village behind as they climbed a long ridge. They didn't pause until they reached an open overlook. As the first hint of morning light appeared on the horizon, a tom turkey gobbled from a tree further up the ridge. The two hunters took off on a dead run toward the gobbler, with Pierre close behind.

When they were about one hundred paces from the bird, the hunters guided Pierre to a large tree with a greening bush nearby and motioned for him to sit. They instructed him to remain perfectly still. After moving forward and placing their decoy on the ground, they advanced another twenty paces and knelt behind large white pines, thirty paces apart.

Pierre watched as the warrior on the right raised his wingbone call and began producing soft hen yelps. The gobbler, still in the tree, responded with a series of thundering gobbles. The tom seemed highly interested in this new receptive hen in his area. However, the hunter on the right called sparingly. He did not want the hen he was imitating to sound over-interested. The tom turkey needed to come to them.

Tired of waiting for the hen, the gobbler flew down to see what was taking her so long. When the hunters heard the big bird hit the ground, the man on the right flapped the turkey wing against his body—the "hen" was leaving the roost. At the same time, he let out a series of excited fly-down yelps and cackles. To complete the well-rehearsed charade, the hunter on the left added a series of calls that mimicked a hen walking away.

The tom was properly fooled. As it approached, the braves let go of their calls and readied their bows. When the tom saw the hen decoy, he immediately went into a full strut—gobbling, puffing out his chest, and fanning his tail feathers. As the tom passed between the trees, the two hunters released their arrows. The tom flipped in the air, crashed to the ground, and then scrambled to get up. Before Pierre could so much as blink, one of the warriors was standing on the head of the dying bird. Pierre estimated the bird weighed around twenty pounds.

Pierre set out to create a meal worthy of a chief, and after several hours, he had prepared a meal that drew admiring looks from everyone within smelling range. As Chief Mingwe sat down to watch the start of the youth games, Pierre served him hot turkey soup, warm soda bread smothered in salted butter, and maple-flavored squash. The chief and all that tasted Pierre's creation marveled at his culinary skills.

For the rest of the afternoon, the villagers and the Frenchmen watched an impressive display of strength and endurance the likes of which they'd never seen. Hundreds of youths battled back and forth, every goal scored followed by loud cheers from the crowd. Armed with mesh-headed sticks and a round stone ball covered in deer hide, the teams moved in waves across the field. For the most part, the referees ignored the constant body checking, tripping, holding, and sticking. Many players left the playing field with cuts, broken bones, and head injuries, but fortunately no deaths occurred that day. After the games, joyous celebration ensued, with all players honored through chants, feasting, and dancing.

Pierre and Henri joined the festivities by putting on their puppet show for the children. They began with the Frenchman running from the black bear and the brave warrior saving him by slaying the beast. The children all laughed. They dropped the war skit and added in the story of how man first acquired fire.

Henri later entered the story in his journal:

> Long ago, the world was dark and cold, and men had no fire for heat or cooking. However, the top of the nearby mountain bellowed out smoke and glowed at night with melting fire. Men wanted the fire, but approaching it was always too hot. The animals saw man's desire and made a pact with men. If the animals could bring fire to the men, the men must agree to respect animals and treat them with kindness.
> 
> So, the animals decided that the snowy owl would fly to the mountain and bring back a burning stick. When the owl reached the mountaintop, the heat was unbearable. Several times, he flew down to retrieve a burning stick. But each time he tried to approach, he singed the edges of his feathers. He had to give up the attempt. From that day forward, the snowy owl would wear black-tipped feathers on its snowy white body.
> 
> Next, they sent the gray rattlesnake. Slithering low to the ground, the snake avoided the heat. However, the snake's body burst into flames upon grabbing a lump of burning wood. The snake dropped the glowing ember and rolled down the hill to extinguish the fire. From that day forward, he wore burnt black stripes across his gray body.
> 
> All the animals had given up hope. Then the little brown spider said he would go. Everyone laughed. What could a little spider do? The spider ignored them and went anyway. As he approached the top of the mountain, he didn't rush in like the owl and the rattlesnake. Instead, he waited patiently at the edge until a tiny ember popped off a burning log and rolled toward him. The spider quickly spun a silk web around the ember, carrying it down the hill on his back. He gave the fire-starting ember to man, but alas, the ember had burned the spider's body so badly that he would forever remain black.

The Jesuits ended their show with stick puppets bringing a peace pipe and gifts for the villagers. Pierre followed up the miniature theatre performance with magic tricks for the children and his ball and cups game. Once again, a crowd of men had gathered round to bet on Pierre's game.

After a while, Chief Mingwe approached and interrupted Pierre's game. "Black Robes, gods of thunder, word has reached me that you are great sorcerers that do powerful black magic. Will you call down the sky fire for us?"

As Pierre happily began loading his musketoon, Henri tried to hide his displeasure. He remained unconvinced that Pierre's "black magic" was truly a boon for their Lord—or whether it might one day come back to haunt them. After Pierre lit his last mortar and the ball burst into an umbrella of red fire, he smiled, certain he had made his point. Henri wasn't so sure.

• • •

At sunrise on the second day, the real games began. With fewer players on the field, the matches were easier to follow—but the intensity among the adults was ten times more brutal. Once the games began, nothing interrupted them. Players with bloody and bruised arms and legs just kept playing. The only time the referees would stop the game was when more than half the offensive team flooded the defense's goal. Even that was seldom penalized.

Throughout the day, Henri drew pictures of the games in his journal. Pierre caught himself rooting for the Neutral team, resulting in troubling stares from the crowd. The Neutrals easily beat Seneca's second team that morning. The Seneca's first team defeated the Mohawk team in a close afternoon match. The Mohawk team called foul, saying the referees were biased. Grumbling could be heard coming from the Mohawk camp throughout the night.

On the morning of the third day, the Mohawk team thoroughly trounced Seneca's second team. That restored the Mohawk's honor and put an end to their quibbling. In the afternoon, the two winning teams from the day before played. It was the most brutal game of all. The defenses of the Neutral and Seneca teams were well matched, resulting in a low-scoring game. The pitched battle seesawed back and forth, but in the final minute, the game remained tied.

Chief Mingwe's son, Mingo, was the star player for the Seneca team, playing brilliantly on both offense and defense. In the final seconds of the game, the Seneca team launched their final offensive drive. Mingo made a ferocious, twisting leap and sent the ball sailing past the Neutrals' goalkeeper for the winning goal. As he fell, he collided with two Neutral players and crashed to the ground, hitting his head and neck. The Seneca crowd roared in celebration and flooded the field to congratulate their team. However, an uncomfortable silence spread throughout the crowd. Mingo could not get up.

Chief Mingwe and members of his medicine society rushed to Mingo's side. He was out cold. At first, they tried to wake him, but stopped when his body suddenly started convulsing. The chief ordered the team members to carry his son to the Medicine Society's lodge. Henri followed them, watching closely. He was concerned about the care the injured player would receive.

Henri saw the medicine men put on their "false faces," wooden masks that are meant to scare off the dark spirits that have taken over a sick person's body. Carved out of living trees to capture the healing power of nature, they were painted red or black and adorned with long, black fibrous strips of inner bark to resemble hair.

The tribal healers mixed potions and sprinkled ashes on Mingo's body. They shook turtle rattles and wampum prayer beads as the lodge filled with tobacco smoke and chanting. Henri, no longer able to see what was happening, returned to his campsite. He told Pierre about his concerns and his desire to help.

"You have a kind heart, Henri," Pierre said, "but we're here to watch, listen, learn, and document their customs. Father Marquette told us to teach them about the saving power of our God. But we are to do it in a way that doesn't alter their way of life. It's best that we stay out of this." Henri left Pierre without a word. He needed time to think about his next course of action.

In the morning, talk around the camp centered on the condition of the chief's son. His health had worsened. The traditional healers had failed to draw the dark spirits from Mingo's body, and they were losing him. As Pierre sat there casually eating his breakfast, Henri broke the silence. "Pierre, I've given thought to what you said last night. I must agree with most of your conclusions ... but you left out two things. We must also provide aid and comfort to the Indigenous people. You have a gift for explaining the power of our great Christian God. You tell the people that our God is fair and just, but God is also benevolent. Your methods are unorthodox, but they resonate with the people. I wish I had your communication skills. However, I come from an extensive line of apothecaries. I have the gift of medicine. If I do nothing, I betray myself and the gift that God has given me."

Pierre was taken aback but recovered quickly, flashing a smile. "Henri, you have always tried to bring out my better side. I'll talk to Thomas and Adrien and ask for a two-day delay in our departure. You and I will ask Chief Mingwe if he'll accept our help."

"Our help?" Henri said, with a questioning look.

"Yes, Henri. You'll need me as your interpreter. Your Iroquoian is terrible!" Henri and Pierre both laughed.

After speaking with Thomas and Adrien, the two Jesuits went directly to Chief Mingwe. They found not just a chief, but a father who was overwhelmed by the thought of losing his son. After Pierre told him that Henri had the power of healing and wanted to help, he gave them a solemn look, his eyes tired from grief. "Black Robes, my son is my heart and soul. If your black-robe magic can save him, I will allow it. What do you require?"

Using Pierre as his interpreter, Henri said, "First, I need to evaluate your son. If there's hope, I may need help from the women of your village."

"Everything I have at my disposal will be available to you," Chief Mingwe said as they hurried toward the Medicine Society's lodge.

Upon arriving at the lodge, they were met with a heavy haze of smoke. Henri passed six shamans chanting their healing prayers as he made his way to Mingo. His breathing was labored, and he drifted in and out of consciousness. His neck was swollen.

"This man needs more air," cried Henri. "I'll have to reduce that swelling, or he will suffocate. Open the doors on both ends and clear out this smoke. Give me room to work." Chief Mingwe gave the order to clear the room. There was initial protestation from the spiritual leaders, but they eventually complied with the chief's order. Henri sent Pierre back to their camp to fetch Henri's pack.

When Pierre returned, Henri was holding a bucket of warm water. He gently washed the ashes off Mingo's neck and shoulders with clean cloths, carefully cleaning the wounds he had received during the game. Henri also found a large bruise at the base of Mingo's neck. Henri fished a small wooden medical box out of his pack. It contained a small mortar and pestle, and six small containers of salves and lotions. One of the bottles, labeled "wound lotion," had been created by renowned French surgeon Ambroise Pare. It contained a mixture of egg yolk, rose oil, and turpentine. Henri cleaned and treated Mingo's wounds, then wrapped them in clean dressings.

Henri dumped out the dirty water and asked the women to prepare a vapor bucket with clean boiling water, juniper berries, and spearmint leaves as quickly as possible.

While Henri was waiting, he opened a jar labeled Tubocurarine Chloride. It was used in Europe as a muscle relaxant for skeletal tissues. The Spaniards had brought it back from South America, where Indigenous peoples extracted it from the skin of poisonous frogs to create poisons for arrows. However, it was known to reduce swelling when used in small concentrations. Henri gently applied the compound to Mingo's neck.

Henri asked the woman assisting him for two more things. The first was to keep replacing the cooling rocks in the vapor bucket with hot ones. The second was to take a front leg from a recently killed deer and tie a cord to it.

"Throw it in the marsh and bring it back to me in four hours," Henri said.

Henri established a strict regimen of applying the muscle relaxant every four hours until the swelling went down. After the second treatment, the woman returned with a deer leg. Henri gently rolled Mingo to his side. He extracted a dozen leeches from the leg and placed them on Mingo's bruised neck. The leeches sucked out the excess blood, reduced the swelling in the tissue, and promoted healing by allowing freshly oxygenated blood to reach the damaged area.

Henri and Pierre spent the night with Mingo, praying the rosary, applying the salve, and changing his dressings. In the morning, the swelling had gone down, and Mingo was awake, responding well to the treatment. Chief Mingwe was overjoyed. He spent the entire morning talking with his son. He told Mingo how the Black Robes had pulled him back from death's grasp.

The spiritual leaders were not as thrilled. They saw this as a direct threat to their standing in the tribe. Dissent over the foreigners' meddling crept through the village, smoldering at first—then erupting into a raging fire.

When Chief Mingwe heard of the growing unrest, he was outraged. He ordered ten of his most trusted men to ready a lake canoe that would provide safe passage for the Frenchmen down the south shoreline of Lake Erie. As Thomas, Adrien, and Pierre loaded the canoe with their belongings, Henri boiled an extraction of hemp root and wintergreen leaves to ease Mingo's pain. Henri instructed the women to give Mingo two ounces every four hours for two days.

As the Frenchmen were about to embark, Chief Mingwe approached the shore. "My French friends, you've come here in peace, bearing fine gifts and promises of open trade. You've saved my son's life—I will be forever grateful. We will trade with the French and honor the treaty protecting those wearing the silver cross around their neck. I'm sending my most elite warriors with you. They will safely guide you to the Cuyahoga River, the edge of our territory. From there, you'll enter the land of the Erie Nation, the Cat people.

"They have a fortified village located in the Bass Islands. Approach them from the Big Lake with your sail raised and white flags of peace. Don't tell Chief Marameg that you have come from the Seneca village—that will not go over well. We crushed them in a great battle ten years ago, and they still consider us their blood enemy."

# Cat People

In four days, the two canoes reached the mouth of the Cuyahoga River, and the Seneca warriors turned around and returned home. At the end of the fifth day, the four Frenchmen could see the Bass Islands in the distance. As Chief Mingwe suggested, they circled out and approached the islands from the west. During the journey, Adrien Jolliet devised a plan. They would tell Chief Marameg that the French had set up a trading post at the straits of Detroit and that the soldiers sent them here to offer open trade. Henri hated the idea of lying. However, Pierre tried to convince Henri that they were providing honest and helpful information. In the end, Henri's objection was overruled by the rest of the group.

As the Frenchmen's canoe approached the shore, Chief Marameg stood waiting with three hundred warriors armed with bows and arrows. Adrien stepped out of the canoe into the shallow water, raising his voice for all to hear. "Great Chief Marameg, we come in peace. We bring gifts and offer you trade with the French. The French soldiers established a trading post at the straits of Detroit. They have valuable items to exchange for fur. May we come ashore and tell you more about it?"

Pierre leaned over and whispered to Henri, "I'm glad he mentioned the soldiers. They look like they could come to Detroit and take whatever they want."

Chief Marameg studied the French coureurs des bois and their two Black Robe friends. "You may come ashore in peace. However, leave your muskets in your canoe. We know all too well how your muskets bring death. We learned that from the murderous Seneca to the east."

What happened next surprised everyone in the canoe. Adrien held out his flintlock and offered it to the chief. "Take it; it's yours as a sign of our peaceful intentions."

Chief Marameg took a long look at Adrien. "Any man that would give away his weapon to avoid a fight is either a fool, or a seeker of peace. I see you have a pistol in your belt. That means you aren't a fool. For now, I will accept you as a peacemaker. We will feast tonight and talk trade. Leave your weapons in your canoe. I assure you—no one will disturb your things."

When they entered Chief Marameg's lodge, they found him sitting on a cougar skin blanket lined with bobcat fur. Dinner consisted of fire-grilled steaks covered with wild onions, leeks, and mushrooms sautéed in bear lard. There were several sides, including wild rice, poke greens, and cornmeal ash cakes. A dried cranberry cornmeal pudding was their dessert.

After dinner, Adrien and Thomas talked about the trade items that the French had waiting in Detroit. They discussed the value of beaver pelts and other furs. Chief Marameg told them that his people had amassed a large pile of trade furs, which he would show them in the morning. The two coureurs des bois reiterated the invitation to escort the chief's traders to Detroit.

Pierre was more focused on the dinner he had just eaten. He was fascinated with the sweet-tasting meat. He asked if it was elk. "No," replied Chief Marameg. "It's *tatanka*. The French trappers call it *boeuf*—buffalo."

"Tatanka!" Pierre exclaimed. "Are there any more around here? I would love to see one."

"No, not anymore," the chief said. "We travel south and trade with the Shawnee to get this meat. Two days ago, we encountered a Shawnee hunting party following a small herd north as the beasts grazed on the greening spring grasses. Those Shawnee are now only one day south of us."

Henri decided it was the right time to present their copper cauldron. As he pulled the last of their three kettles out of his pack, the chief smiled with delight. But the room went silent when Henri reached into it and extracted the confit pot. The glazed yellow top and lug handles glowed in the firelight.

The chief was thrilled with his gifts. Chief Marameg turned to

Pierre and said: "My black-robed friend, tomorrow, there will be a full moon. I'm sending five of my archers south to sit over the gut piles and butchered bones of the tatanka that the Shawnee killed. The great cougar cats will feed on the remains when it is dark. You may accompany them if you wish. If you do, you might get to see your tatanka." Pierre jumped at the opportunity, and Adrien agreed to accompany him.

• • •

The following morning, Henri awoke at first light. Arising from his ground mat, he noticed a group of men gathered at the shore of the lake. As he approached the beach, he watched the men remove spawning catfish from fenced enclosures offshore. Occasionally, they would throw a giant, well-rounded catfish back into the water. Henri asked why, and they replied that they were releasing the females to reproduce.

Henri examined the cage traps and noticed they were made of closely spaced sticks embedded in the sand. In the center was a small, enclosed circle surrounded by a larger fenced square with small openings on both ends. The center circle held a spawning female. When the shoreline waters warmed, her scent would attract the males into the larger enclosure. The men would approach the traps from both sides with gates, trapping the males inside. They would then net out the male fish while releasing the occasional female that entered with them. This process would be repeated every morning for two weeks until the spawning season ended.

While Adrien and Pierre were preparing to leave with the hunting party, Henri came running back. "Pierre, you must see the catfish they are catching in the Big Lake. They're huge."

"That'll have to wait," Pierre said, smiling. "The hunting party is ready to leave. But maybe when we return, we can show them what a French-style catfish celebration is like."

Henri spent the rest of the day moving about the Erie villagers. In his journal, along with drawings of Erie warriors, he wrote:

> The men shave their heads except for a long ponytail that protrudes from the center-back of their heads. Their hairpieces often contain an eagle feather or two. They have tattoos on their foreheads and

decorate their clothing, bows, and quivers with tails from bobcats, raccoons, and mink.

Thomas Pajot spent the day with Chief Marameg. Marameg led Thomas to a longhouse filled with a breathtaking array of tanned fur. There were cougars, wolves, foxes, bobcats, mink, and over one hundred made beaver skins. It would be a fortune in furs if Adrien and Thomas could deliver this fur cache to Montreal. A find like this would win the two men permanent positions in the French West India Company.

Meanwhile, the Erie hunting party had spent most of the day heading south before finally reaching the tatanka bone piles in the late afternoon. As darkness fell, five archers took up positions at the various carcasses and waited. Adrien and Pierre stayed at the hunting camp and tended the fire. By midnight, under the light of a full moon, three great cougar cats had been shot and carried back to camp. There was a grand celebration as they skinned the large cats and ate cougar meat cooked over the coals.

As dawn approached, everyone was exhausted and quickly fell asleep with full bellies. Adrien awoke in a daze to the feel of whiskers on his face and the smell of hot breath. He instinctively sat up, startling the calf that had been sniffing him. He heard stomping and a deep snort to his right. There, less than ten yards away, was a stray tatanka cow. He was between the cow and her calf, and she was about to charge. Instinctively, Adrien drew his pistol from his belt sash and shot the cow behind her ear. She dropped like a rock.

Chaos broke out in the camp as everyone jumped up to see what had happened. Two warriors quickly killed the confused and scared calf. Then shouts of joy rang throughout the group. One man slit open the rib cage of the great beast and removed its still-beating heart—Adrien learned that a bison's heart will keep beating for five minutes after death. The man handed it to Adrien to take the first bite. Fighting back the impulse to vomit, Adrien bit the buffalo's heart and wiped the blood off his face.

Pierre was astonished by the size of the cow and whipped out his journal to sketch a drawing of it. Adrien and Pierre stood back, amazed at the speed at which the Erie men skinned and butchered the two animals. Within the hour, the calf was being slowly roasted over the fire.

Everyone was so busy that no one noticed twenty horses carrying Shawnee riders watching them from the ridge. The Shawnee had heard the pistol shot and came to investigate who had entered their hunting grounds. They rode slowly down the hill and circled the camp.

The Shawnee leader, Tecumtha, got off his horse and scanned the campsite, eyeing the corpses of the tatanka and the cougars. "Who killed the tatanka?"

Adrien stepped forward. "I did! I awoke between the cow and her calf. I had to kill her with my pistol or risk injury."

Adrien held up his pistol for all to see. Tecumtha was familiar with long guns. They had captured a half dozen muskets from Iroquois raiding parties traveling through their territory. But he had never seen a hand pistol before. "You killed the tatanka with that? Show me how."

Adrien reloaded the weapon and aimed at a pile of bones, blowing them into pieces. The horses startled at the shot, and the Shawnee men laughed at the little gun. In another surprise move, Adrien turned and handed the pistol to Tecumtha. "Here, it's yours now. It's payment for killing your tatanka cow."

Adrien slowly drew his French Biscayne axe from his belt sash. He carefully handed it to the chief. "This is for killing her calf."

A Biscayne axe is forged from iron ore obtained from the Spanish mines at Biscay Bay and was a formidable weapon. It supported a one-pound, razor-sharp four-inch blade attached to a two-foot black-stained hickory shaft. The axe is perfectly balanced for throwing and is more useful in hand-to-hand combat than a gun.

Tecumtha looked surprised and addressed the leader of the Erie hunting party. "My brothers from the Cat Nation on the Big Lake to the north, you have generous friends. I see you have killed three great cats. Old Chief Marameg will be pleased. I commend the archers for killing the beasts that prey on our newborn calves. That stray calf wouldn't have made it a day with all the wolves prowling during daylight and the cougars at night. May we join you for some of that young meat on the fire?"

Adrien and Pierre let out a deep sigh. Everyone was laughing as the two groups sat down to eat. It was like old friends getting together. After they consumed the calf, Chief Tecumtha turned to Adrien and asked, "Is this your first kill of a tatanka?"

Adrien smiled and nodded. "Yes, in fact, this is the first one I've ever seen."

Chief Tecumtha looked at him sternly. "In our tribe, the killing of a man's first tatanka is an important thing. It's a time for great celebration. Therefore, I also have a gift for you." Tecumtha went to his horse and brought back a full-length tatanka blanket. "This will keep you warm at night, even in the coldest weather." Adrien, speechless, graciously accepted the gift.

• • •

They were met with a cheering crowd when the cougar hunting party returned to the Erie village. Not only did they return with three cougar cat skins, but they also brought back hundreds of pounds of fresh tatanka meat for all to share. The women went right to work, smoking and preserving the meat. Chief Marameg declared a day of celebration.

Pierre approached Chief Marameg. "I would like to prepare a celebratory French-style dinner for you and the five successful hunters. I'll make the hunting party deep-fried catfish and hush puppies, so long as I can use your new copper cauldron and a little aid with a few ingredients." Henri, Adrien, and Thomas all smiled and clapped their hands.

Pierre joyfully went down to their canoe to gather a few needed supplies. He collected four wood bowls, a small trade kettle, and some essential ingredients. He had planned this meal from the moment he saw the dead tatanka cow and calf. At the kill site, Pierre wanted nothing to do with the biting of the bloody beating heart; however, he had enthusiastically asked the butchering team for the cow's milk sac. He had salvaged over a quart of creamy milk and stored it in his leather water bag.

He hung the cauldron and the smaller kettle over the fire. Half the bear lard went in the copper cauldron and the rest went into the trade kettle. While the bear lard was melting, Pierre mixed measured amounts of cornmeal, flour, salt, potash, and sugar in one bowl. Then, he added one finely chopped onion, chives, two duck eggs, and one cup of tatanka cow milk in a second bowl. He told Henri to wait until the fish had finished cooking before combining the two bowls.

Pierre added cornmeal, flour, salt, mixed spices, one duck egg, and cow milk to a third bowl. The fourth bowl held only cornmeal. Pierre cut the catfish into strips and dipped them into the third bowl. He then rolled the fish strips in the cornmeal bowl and placed them in the copper cauldron. Pierre asked Henri to mix bowls one and two and bring them to him. With a wooden spoon, Pierre dropped walnut-sized balls of the batter into the boiling lard in the smaller trade kettle.

The women brought Pierre two cattail woven baskets, and Pierre placed the deep-fried fish in one and the hush puppies in the other. Pierre handed the baskets to Chief Marameg and asked him to share them with his returning warriors. The dinner crowd marveled at the taste as they ate their fill.

After dinner, Pierre announced to the crowd that the Black Robes would now provide tonight's entertainment. They began with the puppet show, which made the children giggle and warmed the hearts of their smiling parents. Then Pierre did magic tricks. Finally, he brought out his ball and cups game. As always, the men enjoyed that game the most.

Then Pierre set up in preparation for his fireworks show. It always amazed Henri how Pierre could tailor his performance from one group to the next. Pierre began by saying: "You have met our fur traders. Now, you can meet us, the Black Robe Jesuits. We are here to bring you the word of our great Christian God, the God of all gods ..."

After the show, Henri seemed troubled. Sensing something was wrong, Pierre approached him. "Henri, what's bothering you? Things are going our way."

Henri looked at Pierre and said: "You mean going your way."

Pierre furrowed his brows. "Not another one of those speeches on how I do all the talking, and you feel left in the shadows, is it?"

"No, no. It is how we hand out baptisms and medals like prizes at the carnival. Do you remember the stories of our early Jesuits? They worked extremely hard at educating the Indigenous people about our Catholic faith. They sought conversions first, then performed the baptism. We baptize and hand out protection medals with no way of guaranteeing the Iroquois will recognize them as Christians without our missionaries being present."

Pierre shook his head. "You used three words that you need to reconsider: Catholics, missionaries, and Christians. Please note I never used the word Catholic. To become a Catholic, you must receive the three sacraments of Christian initiation: Baptism, Confirmation, and Eucharist. That is achieved only through a process of preparation. That preparation comes from the teaching and guidance of our missionaries."

"Remember the words of Father Marquette. He urged us to take copious notes on their appearance and religious practices. To carefully note which tribes are willing to accept the Christian faith. We'll give this information to the bishop so he can plan where we'll establish new missions. These people have agreed to accept that our God is the God of all gods. Right now, they're willing to take baptism and wear the Christian cross. That's all we can do with our little time with them."

Henri bowed his head, made the sign of the cross, and said, "Pierre, I accept your explanation. I must understand that God works in mysterious ways."

• • •

The following morning, the four Frenchmen woke up and saw six long canoes ready and fully loaded with bundles of fur. Ten men stood waiting next to each canoe. Henri, Pierre, Adrien, and Thomas quickly finished packing and headed down to meet them. Chief Marameg and his clan leaders stood proudly next to his trading envoy. Henri and Pierre baptized Chief Marameg, his war chief, and the four Rock, Cord, Deer, and Bear clan leaders. The six crew leaders, one from each canoe, were also baptized. All received their metal cross and wore them proudly. A large crowd had gathered to see the canoes off, and a rousing cheer filled the air as the six trading canoes and the four Frenchmen headed for Detroit.

The seven canoes reached the Detroit outposts on Belle Isle in two days. A guard sounded the alarm that a fleet of Indigenous people was approaching from downriver. The troops mustered into a defensive position, fearing an attack on the post. Then the lookout tower reported that the lead canoe carried two coureurs des bois and two Black Robes, and a great cheer went through the troops. The southbound voyageurs had arrived. Lieutenant DeMarre put on his bright-colored military jacket and cap, adjusted his wide-brimmed feather-plumed hat, and prepared for the official welcoming of the new arrivals.

Before the lieutenant was ready to greet them, a group of soldiers, engagés, and fur traders were already helping the canoes land onshore. Lieutenant DeMarre came strolling down the path with his arms spread wide, speaking loudly in French, so all could hear. "Welcome, welcome, to the largest trading post on this side of Montreal. The riches of France are stored here and are available to our friends in the south. Come, smoke the pipe of peace, and tomorrow we will exchange."

Pierre was aware of the show the lieutenant was trying to put on, so he turned to Chief Marameg. Translating in Iroquois, Pierre said, "Chief Marameg, our military leader and his fur traders welcome you and your warriors to the Detroit Trading Post. They have dozens of valuable items to show you and promise a fair trade for your fine collection of furs. Come ashore in peace. Set up your camp here on the south side of the island. Tonight, we shall smoke tobacco and share food. Tomorrow, we will trade."

The French had picked a perfect location to establish a trading post. The Chippewa, Miami, Ottawa, and Potawatomi shared the area and passed through frequently. In addition, many Neutrals fleeing the Iroquois crossed the Detroit River from Canada and settled on the Michigan side. All this had created a bonanza for the fur traders that set up the post two years ago. However, they could not safely ship furs or receive new trade goods from Montreal until the treaty with the Five Nations was signed. Now that the French soldiers were there, they had tons of trade items and half a dozen tribes ready to trade. Even better, they had a military escort to ensure the furs reached the market.

The following morning, a frenzy of trading began. The Erie men acquired long guns, pistols, black powder, lead, traps, bells, beads, axes, kettles, ribbons, mirrors, and tobacco. The French received a fortune in furs. Lieutenant DeMarre was thrilled with the report he received from Adrien and Thomas. They had arranged for a fur trading rendezvous with the Seneca next spring, delivered the wealth of the Erie Nation to his doorstep, and made peaceful contact with the Mohawk and Shawnee Nations. The lieutenant proudly declared, "Tonight, we feast and celebrate. Things are looking up, boys!" All the men let out a cheer.

# Detroit and the Mounds

As soon as the Erie finished loading their canoes and headed south, preparation for the evening festivities began. Pierre volunteered to assist the platoon's cook by helping in the kitchen. The rest of the men set up tables outside and collected wood for a huge bonfire. When everything was ready, all were issued two shots of rum, and the platoon fiddler began to play, accompanied by two men with harmonicas. The engagés stomped their feet and danced, knowing their bonus pay would triple if they could deliver these furs to Montreal.

The lieutenant asked Henri to say the Catholic grace when dinner was ready. Henri made the sign of the cross, bowed his head, and began. "Bless us, O Lord, and these, thy gifts, which we are about to receive. From thy bounty, through Christ, our Lord. Amen."

The lieutenant added the prayer of the French soldiers. "May the souls of our faithfully fallen, at the mercy of God, rest in peace, now and forever. Amen."

The men raised their glasses in a resounding toast. "All hail the glorious dead!"

Dinner began with steamed freshwater mussels drizzled with lemon juice. Next came squab—young pigeon—roasted with juniper berries smothered in wild onions, leeks, and chanterelle mushrooms. The sides included squash cooked in molasses and maple syrup, supported by a large bowl of salted pork and bean soup. They finished with French wine and bread pudding containing dried cranberries, plums, and huckleberries.

After dinner, Pierre launched into his usual routine, minus the puppet show and sermon. The magic tricks made everyone laugh. The ball and cups game captured the men's interest. However, the lieutenant had forbidden gambling to prevent fights between the men. Pierre could see that side bets were taking place. So, he again steered the results, and most players broke even.

As the evening sky darkened, Pierre set up his musketoon mortar. Henri cringed, thinking the lieutenant would catch on to the fraud they had played on the governor-general back in Quebec. But if the lieutenant suspected anything, he never let on. Pierre then proceeded to put on the first fireworks ever seen over the skies of Detroit. The men cheered as Pierre rapidly fired fireballs of red, white, and blue into the air.

Pierre, now feeling the effects of too much rum and the thrill of the crowd, threw caution to the wind and set up his grand finale. He moved his mortar near the fire and told everyone to step back. The excitement was palpable as Pierre loaded a double charge of black powder in the musketoon. Pierre placed three thunder balls in the barrel and attached a long fuse to the flash pan. He lit the fuse and jumped back. When the powder ignited, the musketoon exploded, sending the coals from the fire ten feet into the air. Two of the three balls had made it out of the barrel. The coals from the fire glowed red as the first ball flashed white and the second burst blue. The crowd went wild. However, Pierre's musketoon had seen its last show.

• • •

After the show, Henri asked Lieutenant DeMarre: "Where did all this gourmet food come from? How is this meal even possible?"

The lieutenant laughed. "Since we got here with the trade goods, word has gotten out amongst the Native communities. We've been visited almost daily by various tribes and bands. We only allow one group on the island at a time—we don't want to start conflicts between the tribes or cause inter-tribal disputes. We're here to foster peace, not start wars. The Potawatomi villagers bring us fruit and vegetables, the Chippewa supply waterfowl, Neutrals provide fresh fish, and the Miami hunters bring the bear and elk meat. Life has never been so good on the frontier."

Henri turned again to the lieutenant and asked: "Where did you get the squab? It was delicious!"

Lieutenant DeMarre rubbed his hands together. "Now that's an interesting story. Two days ago, a group of Miami villagers brought a supply of meat. Trading was going well, and we acquired some tasty elk. Then, a couple of canoes crossed the river uninvited. It was that Tutelo tribe, the turtle people. They're a rough bunch that roams the thumb area just north of here. I've heard that they've gotten hooked on rum and smoke that *kinnikinnick,* a mix of hemp weed and tobacco."

Henri interrupted the lieutenant. "Did you say Tutelo? Is that the same Tutelo tribe that used to live out east? We spent time at a mission in New York with the Tutelo women and children. Apparently, the Tutelo men had abandoned them there."

The lieutenant shrugged his shoulders. "It's possible. The men who run the post say that the group is new to this area. They speak a language that our interpreters have a tough time understanding. I can't verify anything about their women being abandoned, but they have Chippewa women traveling with them. The women do most of the talking during trading."

Henri was visibly troubled. "They're Eastern Sioux. I speak Siouan. I need to talk with them."

Lieutenant DeMarre shook his head. "I recommend you stay away from both groups, especially that tall Miami leader. He's trouble. He cares about nobody but himself."

Henri looked confused. "What do the Miami people have to do with the—"

The lieutenant cut Henri off. "That's what I'm trying to tell you! The Tutelo had just returned from a place they call Mudwayaushka, located in the headwaters of the Belle River. The name means: "The Wind in the Trees, Sounds Like Waves on the Shore." They say a great valley filled with giant beech trees attracts millions of nesting passenger pigeons. That's where the squab you had for dinner came from."

"Apologies, but I still don't understand. What does that have to do with the Miami leader?" pressed Henri.

Lieutenant DeMarre leaned forward. "You see, the Tutelo have been going up there every spring for the past few years. At first, they collect nesting birds and eggs, then switch to the squab. While all this is happening, their arrow makers go northwest a few miles to the Peiconigowink River—the River of Flint. There's an ancient quarry located there that contains chert stones. The Tutelo are known to produce the finest arrowheads and arrows. Those chert points have a bull's eye in the stone. Other tribes pay dearly for a Tutelo arrow. They say you can't miss when using them.

"Well," continued Lieutenant DeMarre. "The coureurs des bois that set up this post had no use for arrows. But when they heard that the headwaters of the Belle River could produce freshwater mussels and squab, they were more than willing to trade. The Tutelo wanted rum, and the French wanted mussels and squab. So, the fur traders provided the Tutelo with two half-barrows containing rock salt. They told the Tutelo to bring back the barrows full of mussels and cleaned squabs covered in rock salt, and they would receive one gallon of rum per half-barrow."

"Okay ..." Henri said, still not understanding the connection. "What does that have to do with the Miami?"

Lieutenant DeMarre scowled; he didn't take kindly to being rushed. "Well, a few days ago, one of their men fell from the trees and died. So, the group at Mudwayaushka brought him back for burial in one of those hills over there." The lieutenant pointed at two large mounds on the Michigan shoreline.

"The men at the post told me they hear the Tutelo singing and drumming by firelight some nights on those hills. They are there for two or three days and then gone. Anyway, when they came this time with their dead, they brought the squab and mussels you ate."

Henri looked at the lieutenant without saying a word. He suddenly felt guilty. The price of enjoying that splendid dinner was the corruption of a nation of people.

Lieutenant DeMarre was clearly confused by Henri's sudden loss of interest. "Don't you want to know how that tall Miami was involved in all this?"

Henri pushed aside his dismay and forced himself to focus on the conversation. "Yes. Please continue."

The lieutenant took a deep breath and rolled on. "Well, I told you the Miami were on the island a couple of days ago, and the Tutelo showed up. If I knew they had arrived, I would've sent them away. But the men at the post knew exactly why they were here, and when they saw what the Tutelo had brought, they quickly made the trade. I would never have known if it hadn't been for the incident."

Henri cocked his head. "What incident?"

"The one I've been trying to tell you about," snapped Lieutenant DeMarre. "Before the Tutelo could leave, that tall Miami approached their canoes. He was yelling at the Tutelo men. My interpreter said it was about trespassing on sacred grounds. It was difficult for him to understand. But the Tutelo must have understood because one of them pulled a knife. Within seconds, the tall Miami had the Tutelo man on the ground with a knife pointed at his throat. If my guard hadn't fired a shot in the air, alerting the soldiers and me, there would've been bloodshed. When I arrived, I told the tall man to back off and asked the Tutelo to leave. They knew we only allowed one group on the island at a time—for this very reason!

"The men at the post had warned me about that tall fellow. They call him the Ranger. They tell me he showed up shortly after they opened the post. Now and then they trade with him, mostly for tobacco. Then he disappears. One of our interpreters said he was once a great war chief for the Miami tribe. He was famous for his attacks on the raiding Iroquois. Supposedly, he married one of the Miami chief's daughters. But after his wife and child died during childbirth, he's roamed this area ever since. He must have joined that Miami trading party before they came onto the island."

Henri sat there thinking about the sad story of the Tutelo and the Ranger—a tribe of men destroyed by rum, and a man undone by a broken heart. Henri decided he needed to talk to both.

The next day, Lieutenant DeMarre called a meeting of the soldiers, engagés, and coureurs des bois. "Men, it's time to head back to Montreal." All the men let out a cheer. "We'll carry our rich bounty on our backs to our canoes at the Neutral's camp on Lake Ontario. Then, we'll paddle to the Montreal Rapids and make the portage. If we are lucky, God willing, a ship will be waiting to take us home."

"We'll leave in three days," continued the lieutenant.

"However, before we leave, I want everything packed into one-hundred-pound bundles. The soldiers will carry food and military supplies. Each engagé is responsible for one bundle. I estimate we'll have eleven bundles of fur. That leaves two engagés available to carry the trade goods we promised the Neutrals watching our canoes. If we pick up more pelts at the Neutrals or along the north shore and get all this back to Montreal, you boys will go down in the history books.

"Coureurs des bois and soldiers, you must have your guns ready. Word of this large fur transfer must have spread throughout the area. The English are willing to pay rogue trappers and their Indigenous guides handsomely for stolen French furs. I want our sergeant, Jean Plattier, and the Huron guides in front. Jean Tiberge and I will guard the rear. We'll stop every half mile for a short break. Everyone must stay close together. If we spread out too thin, we will be vulnerable to attack. We'll bid farewell to our Black Robes friends and their two coureurs des bois as they take their canoe and head north to the Soo."

After the meeting, Henri told the lieutenant he had decided to cross the river and talk to the Tutelo. The lieutenant shook his head. "After all I told you about that wild bunch, you are still determined to save souls. Very well. I won't stand in the way of you and the Lord. But take Adrien Jolliet with you. At least one of you will have a functioning musket."

"You knew?"

Lieutenant DeMarre smiled. "I knew the minute I saw you carrying those worthless-looking pieces under your raincoats back in Quebec. I suspect the governor-general knew as well. I imagine he didn't want a scene at the dock in front of all the townspeople. However, I must admit what Pierre has done with that old musketoon is impressive. What about your weapon, Henri? Does it turn water into wine?"

Henri dashed to his tent and brought out his rifle with the attached bayonet crucifix. "I call it my peace rifle," Henri said.

The lieutenant laughed. "Henri, it fits you well!"

● ● ●

It turned out that Lieutenant DeMarre had good reason to worry. At that moment, four independent French fur trappers had just entered the Detroit area. In 1664, after the English drove the Dutch out of the Hudson Valley, these trappers had moved north to a small French settlement on the shores of Lake Champlain. They were well known for supplying Dutch guns to the Iroquois.

In the eyes of the French military, they were considered traitors. Within a few weeks, a French patrol had captured and sentenced them to hang. While waiting for their execution, their luck suddenly changed. Unknown to the French, an English captain had sent an Iroquois raiding party to test the strength of the French military in the area. They attacked the settlement, killing the soldiers.

The Iroquois raiders recognized the imprisoned French gun traders and took them to the English captain. Unimpressed with these four turncoats, he arranged to have them tried as French loyalists and Dutch spies. The leader of the four men, Antoine, offered to cut a deal. If the captain set them free, they would agree to interfere with the French fur trade in every way possible. The English captain wanted information on the western Great Lakes region, so, he instructed the trappers to seek out western tribes that disliked the French, trade them guns for furs, and undercut any French fur-trading contracts that were in place. The four men agreed to the terms and headed for Michigan.

While in the area, the French trappers had heard of the large fur cache accumulating at the Detroit Trading Post. They were smart enough to know they could not successfully attack the military convoy on the move—they would face too many guns at the ready. Knowing the Tutelo men's taste for rum, they devised a plan to ally with the Tutelo and attack the post at night when most would be sleeping. If successful, the scoundrels would take the guns and furs, and the Tutelo could have the rum.

Their ill-conceived plan fell apart when the trappers reached the Tutelo camp near the Belle Isle Post. They found only five Chippewa women there; the Tutelo men were gone. The women told the rogue trappers that their men were at the mound site where they had buried the fallen warrior from Mudwayaushka. They assured the trappers that the men would not tolerate their ceremony being disturbed.

Tutelo tradition requires that the men take turns staying at the grave of the newly buried for three days and three nights. They believed the deceased spirit doesn't willingly leave its hold on this world, and so the men must shake turtle rattles and beat drums to drive the lingering spirit into the spirit world. If they fail to do this, the dead person's life-form will crawl out of the grave and wander the land in the form of a box turtle.

Speaking in broken Algonquian, the rogue trappers questioned the women about what they had seen when they visited the Island Trading Post. The women informed them they had seen many soldiers with guns, other men working around the camp, and two Black Robes.

"Sounds like they have us outgunned, my friends," Antoine said. "We need to scrap the mission. Worse yet, those scumbag soldiers brought Black Robes with them. Black Robes are nothing but trouble. I bet they are here to end the rum and gun trade. Those bible bangers will put us out of business if they get their way. Screw them all. We might as well return to our camp and get drunk on the rum we've been saving to prime the Tutelo for war. Nothing good is going to come from this deadbeat group of harlots."

As the four got up to leave, the one with a scarred face slashed holes in the women's fishnets out of spite, and Antoine kicked down a tripod holding the soup kettle over the fire. Laughing, he said, "Lick the soup off the rocks like the dogs you are!"

• • •

Later that afternoon, Henri and Adrien crossed the river and approached the Tutelo camp. When the women saw them coming, they pulled their flint knives from their belts and formed a defensive circle. Adrien and Henri stopped and laid down their rifles. Using the Algonquian language, Adrien said: "Fear not; we come in peace, and we mean you no harm." Henri, speaking in Siouan, repeated the same message. The women looked surprised and seemed a little less tense.

Morningstar, the oldest of the five women, spoke first. "You, Black Robe, how do you speak the language of our people?"

"I come from the land of their birth," replied Henri. "I'm here to tell them about the ones they left behind. Where are your men? I need to talk to them."

Morningstar lowered her knife to her side and stepped forward. "Like I told your trapping friends earlier today, they're not here." Adrien and Henri exchanged questioning looks.

Henri spoke again, this time in Algonquian. "We haven't sent anyone. We are the first of our group to set foot on this side of the river. Who were these men? Were they from the island post?"

"No! We've seen them at our Chippewa camp on the Saginaw River," Morningstar said. That's where the five of us grew up. Those men trade with whiskey and rum. They ruin lives."

Henri looked upset and said: "That's why I've come. I want to stop the rum trade and help those affected by it. We've brought you gifts."

Adrien reached into his pack and pulled out two copper trade kettles. The women looked pleasantly surprised. Then Henri revealed five necklaces adorned with solid-silver beavers. Their eyes lit up with delight as Henri handed them out. The conversation became more cordial after that.

"Yesah is the leader of our clan," Morningstar said. "He told me the Tutelo people were once a great nation out east. They fought with the Mohicans against the Mohawk and lost. Their warriors are now just a fraction of their original strength."

"How did the Tutelo end up here?" Henri asked.

"Yesah said they divided their numbers into three clans. Each set off in a different direction. Yesah's clan, the Turtle people, wandered around, trading with the Dutch and English whenever possible. They were not prepared for the corrupting force of rum. It changed them.

"Eventually," continued Morningstar, "the Oneida Iroquois incorporated them into their tribe."

"Yes, I know," Henri said. "I spent time with their women and children there. But why did they leave?"

"Yesah said the men realized that the women and children were better off with the Oneida, but the men couldn't live under the Oneida rule. So, they left and wandered west. Everywhere they tried to settle, one tribe after another forced them to leave.

They fought numerous battles. Their numbers were down to just thirty warriors.

"Then they found the thumb area of Michigan," Morningstar said proudly. "That was once the land of the Kickapoo. However, the Kickapoo had long ago disappeared, driven out by my people. We Chippewa ended our southern expansion and settled in the Saginaw Valley, leaving the river basins of the Belle, Upper Flint, and Black Rivers as no-man's lands. The Tutelo settled there. We traded with the Tutelo and lived side by side in peace. Eventually, the Tutelo wanted wives, so our chief made the trade."

"What do you mean, traded for wives?"

"We Chippewa have been fighting the raiding Iroquois parties for a long time," Morningstar said. "Many of our warriors have died in battle. They left widowed women. A woman without a husband to support her is a drain on the tribe. When tribes have too many women, they often trade women for things of value."

"What could be of such value to trade away the women of a tribe?" Henri asked.

"Guns! The Tutelo have guns to trade. When they win a battle, they collect the guns from their dead enemies. But the Tutelo don't use guns—they hide behind trees and shoot five or six arrows in the time it takes to reload a gun."

"So, are you officially married to one of them?" Henri asked.

The sparkle in Morningstar's eyes seemed to dull as she looked away. "Not anymore. It was my husband, Shater, who fell from the tree. He was kind to me."

A bit embarrassed for prying, Henri said, "I'm sorry for your loss. We'll return tomorrow when your men come back. I hope to set up a mission here. There are things we can do to help your people."

Henri started to leave, then turned back. "A few days ago, while you traded at the post, the one they call the Ranger started a fight. What was that about?"

Morningstar lowered her head. "The Miami warrior was mad at Yesah's brother, Tenron. Tenron drinks too much rum and says dumb things."

"What did the Ranger say to start the fight?"

"The man you call the Ranger has been in our camp many

times. He understands the Tutelo people have a long history of building burial mounds back east. The Ranger welcomed them and granted them the use of his ancestral land for their sacred ceremonies. All the Ranger asked was that they don't dig into the mounds and disturb the bones of his ancestors. 'Build your turtle-shell grave mounds next to ours,' he said. Then our dead can co-exist in peace."

Morningstar, choking back tears, continued. "When we brought Shater's body back from Mudwayaushka, Yesah stayed at the flint quarry with six men to continue their work. Tenron told the Tutelo burial party to bury Shater on the forbidden ancestral mound. When the Ranger heard of this, he informed Tenron that they must immediately remove the body. He wanted it reburied at the base of the hill as agreed. If not, there would be trouble.

"Tenron told the Ranger that all his people were dead because they were weak and didn't know how to fight. The Ranger didn't take kindly to those words."

Henri was shocked. It wasn't the Ranger that caused the trouble. The Ranger had bent over backward to work with the Tutelo. It was Tenron who had betrayed his trust.

• • •

Dusk had settled in, long past when Adrien and Henri had promised to return to the post. They quickly packed up their things and headed back to the canoe. Meanwhile, the four disgruntled trappers had finished off the last of their rum and were getting angrier by the minute.

Antoine, the leader, was tall with a head like a boulder. His deep brown eyes peered out from under his dirty fur cap. His yellowing teeth and graying beard gave away his age. It had been a while since he had seen a bath.

Slurring his words, Antoine spoke slowly. "Those worthless women, who do they think they are? They were mouthy for not having their men around to protect them. I should have knocked their heads together. Especially the one that talked too much."

One man in the group whose face sported a large horizontal scar said, "We should've done more than bash their heads." The four drunken men all howled.

"Well, why not?" Antoine said. "There's no one there to stop us." He turned to Scarface and ordered: "Bring bells and ribbons. We'll try it their way. If they don't cooperate, we'll take what we want!"

When the women saw the deplorable men staggering their way, they again drew their knives and formed a defensive circle. Antoine walked up to Morningstar, shaking ribbons and bells. "We've come here to trade!" he said in the most disarming voice he could muster.

Morningstar looked Antoine straight in the eyes. "We aren't interested in your bells. Go tinkle them somewhere else."

Her beaver necklace caught Antoine's eye as he leaned down to lick her neck.

Morningstar kneed Antoine in the groin and slashed upward with her knife. With surprising reflexes, Antoine dodged the blade and seized her by the back of the neck—a knife pressed against her throat. "Tell your scum friends to put down their knives and give the men what they want," he slurred, breath ragged. "Or you will be the first to die."

Morningstar's body trembled as she whimpered. "Tell me you will then go away."

With a smirking grin, Antoine hissed. "With pleasure!"

Suddenly, there was a hard thump followed by a gurgling sound. A black arrow had pierced Antoine's back and was now protruding out of his chest. Antoine's face was twisted in a grimace of surprise as his body began to shake, then collapsed.

Just then, the Ranger charged in from the shadows, stone war hammer raised. The club connected squarely with Scarface's jaw, hurling him into the dirt. The Ranger turned on the other two men as they frantically reached for their guns. He kicked one of them in the ribs, sending him sprawling.

As the Ranger turned on the fourth trapper, the terrified man found his pistol. He swung wildly and fired. The lead ball struck the Ranger, knocking him off his feet. As the Ranger tried to stand, the butt of a pistol slammed down on the back of his head—he crumpled, unconscious.

The two men stood dazed. Their leader lay dead, and one of

them was screaming with a broken jaw. "What do we do now?" shouted the man holding his ribs.

The trapper with the empty pistol hesitated, then snapped, "We need to get out of here … fast. That shot will have this area crawling with Indians. Leave no witnesses. Grab your knife and kill them all. Then we run."

A groan rose from the Ranger. "Wait, that one's still alive. Kill him first." The trappers moved in—but froze at the distinctive *click* of a flintlock cocking. Adrien Jolliet stood at the firelight's edge, pointing his rifle at the two men. He had heard the shot and came running.

"Drop your weapons, or I will split your head like a lemon," Adrien said.

"Hello, friend," the trapper with the empty pistol said. "Let's not be hasty. You only have one shot, and my friend here is incredibly good with his throwing knife. If you shoot me, he most certainly will kill you."

The trappers' hearts sank when yet another voice emerged from the darkness. "Hello, my friend. He is not alone. One wrong move from either of you will result in both your souls burning in the fires of hell tonight." Henri stepped into the firelight, rifle raised, its bayonet cross removed.

Henri stared down the barrel at the men. "Drop your weapons and take your whining friend. Run and pray the Tutelo warriors don't find you. They won't be so kind." The two men hesitated for only a second, then dropped everything, hoisted their broken-jaw companion, and vanished into the night.

Adrien gathered the weapons the trappers left behind and walked to the dead body lying on the ground. In Antoine's belt sash were a pistol and a French Biscayne axe. Adrien picked them up, admiring their quality. "These will make excellent replacements for the ones I gave to the Shawnee."

• • •

Adrien stood guard in case the trappers returned while Henri approached the shell-shocked women who were huddled in terror.

129

"Where is the Miami warrior that came to our aid?" Morningstar shouted.

"He's over there," one of the women pointed. "I think he's still alive."

Henri ran to a tall man lying face down, bleeding profusely from his left side. "Adrien, come quick. Help me get him closer to the fire so I can see how badly he's hurt."

The two men carried the Ranger, who was still dazed from the blow to his head. Adrien carefully rolled the man over so Henri could assess the seriousness of the wound. The Ranger came to, reached up, and grabbed Adrien by the neck.

"No!" screamed Morningstar. "These men are here to help. They saved all our lives." The Ranger let go and collapsed backward. Henri asked Adrien to fetch his pack containing his medical supplies. He carefully opened the Ranger's blood-soaked shirt. The lead ball had cut along his left side and passed through the fleshy part of his left arm. Both wounds were concerning but, with treatment, were not life-threatening.

When Adrien returned with the pack, Henri took out the bottle of wound lotion. He cleaned and treated the wound on the side and wrapped it in clean dressings. Henri asked Adrien to help remove the Ranger's shirt so he could dress the arm wound. As they slid the shirt over his shoulders, two tattoos appeared. They were images of a white peace pipe over a black bear.

"Who is this man?" Henri muttered.

"He's a Mascouten peace chief," came a voice from behind them. "His name is Nokee."

Henri and Adrien spun around, and there stood the Tutelo clan leader, Yesah. Behind him were twenty warriors with their bows at half-drawn.

"More importantly, who are you?" Yesah asked, carefully approaching. "Lie, and it will be the last lie you tell! Did you come from the trading post?"

Morningstar spoke first. "Yes, they're from the post, but these men saved our lives. Four fur trappers came down from the north. We've seen them before at our camp on the Saginaw River. They came here to rape and kill us, and they would've succeeded if Nokee and these two hadn't shown up."

Yesah turned to his second in command. "Take ten warriors and go quickly to the place on the river where we saw smoke earlier today. If they've left their weapons here, they will head for their camp to get resupplied before they leave. Catch them and bring them back to me. If they resist, their heads will do!"

Speaking in Siouan, Henri stopped the Tutelo in their tracks. "Great Chief, have your warriors take my friend with them. We were supposed to be back at the post before dark. They'll have heard the shot and will send out a search party. If the two groups cross paths, my friend can call out to the men from the post. He should be able to prevent an unattended conflict."

Yesah, seeing the logic behind Henri's words, promised Adrien that Henri would be safe. So, Adrien grabbed his flintlock, told Henri he would return with more medical supplies in the morning, and left with the warriors.

Yesah walked over to the dead fur trapper with Nokee's distinctive black arrow sticking out of his back. "Nokee, my friend, you must be getting old. You let four fat Frenchmen get the best of you? I thought you didn't get involved in other people's business."

Then Yesah, in a more serious tone, said, "Tenron was a fool to go against my orders and bury Shater on top of your mound. After it happened, one of my warriors brought the news to me. I came immediately and had Shater's remains removed and reburied as you requested. I put Tenron in charge of the three-day vigil, which must start over. That should give him time to think about what he did."

Nokee half smiled at Yesah. "You are a man of your word. I know what you say is true. I have been watching your people for three days. When you finished the reburial, I left the mound site and heard the women screaming as I passed. My hatred of the French caused me to become careless."

Yesah turned to Henri. "How do you speak our language?"

Henri told Yesah how he had spent time with the Tutelo women and children in New York.

Yesah's expression softened, his voice slow and steady. "You must understand. We were in a crisis. When the Iroquois captured us, our people were sick and dying. The Iroquois gave us two choices: join them or die a torturous death. We had no choice but to join. The Iroquois were kind and helpful to my people, but my warriors couldn't live with their lifelong enemy. We left in the dark so the women and children couldn't follow. They most certainly would've been found and killed by the Iroquois. There's no going back for them now."

Yesah noticed the pile of weapons left by the trappers. There were three flintlocks, one pistol, and two metal knives. "Nokee, there are fine pieces here. You saved our women. The spoils of battle go to the victor."

Nokee shook his head. "No, that honor doesn't belong to me. The Black Robe is your hero. The weapons belong to him."

"No! No!" Henri said, horrified. "I've no use for weapons of war. Give them to someone else."

"I'll take them," Morningstar said. "I have a score to settle with those trappers. Those guns might help me accomplish that." Morningstar placed one of the metal knives in her leggings and the pistol in her shoulder bag. The rest she piled next to her belongings.

# Morningstar

Two hours later, the Tutelo search party returned to camp empty-handed. They had located the campsite of the degenerates, but the trappers had cleared out everything and were gone. Tracks in the sand showed they had dragged a canoe to the Detroit River and paddled away. The Tutelo reported that Adrien had seen the post's search party torches in the distance and went on to join them. Henri was pleased that Adrien had made it back to the post safely. Finally, things were beginning to settle down.

Henri sat beside Nokee. "Did you build the mounds?"

Nokee looked intently at Henri. "I've met Black Robes before. They come here claiming good intentions, but soon, they teach our children to turn away from their ancestral training. They convert them to the way of the White man."

Henri was momentarily silent, then said: "Not all Frenchmen are the same. There are evil ones, like the one that lies dead over there, and there are good ones, like my three traveling partners. We're here to watch and learn. We want to record the tribal traditions and religious practices we encounter, safeguarding them to ensure they are not lost forever. We want to help where we can. Like the Tutelo, we want to co-exist in peace. I heard you tell Yesah that you hate the French. Why's that?"

Nokee looked deep into Henri's eyes. "They killed my father, for starters. However, I sense the sincerity in your words, Black Robe. You saved my life, and I'm indebted to you. So, if you wish, I'll tell you the story of my people. When no one remembers their story, the souls of our departed fade away.

"My villagers didn't build the original mounds," Nokee said. "Tionontati, our village spiritual leader, told me our ancestors built the original mounds a hundred generations ago. They buried their dead with bird stones, flint points, scrapers, tools, bowls, pipes, shell beads, and food to aid their spirits in the afterlife. It was important to provide everything they needed on their journey. They sprinkled red ocher powder on the graves before covering them with Mother Earth.

"For as long as anyone can remember, we continued to cremate our chiefs and spiritual leaders on the tops of those mounds. Most of our deceased ended up on raised scaffolds in the fields around the mound sites. Then, two years later, we would clean their bones and place them in leather bags. Every fall, we buried those bags at the base of the mounds. However, none of that is possible anymore. My people no longer live in this land. At the end of the forever war, the Chippewa, Ottawa, and Potawatomi allied and drove the last of my people out."

Realizing the importance of this conversation, Henri asked, "Where are your people now?"

Nokee sighed. "I don't know. They're most likely dead. The Miami told me they moved to the other side of Lake Michigan. That was fifteen summers ago."

Taking a moment to sit quietly, Henri began to put together just how important this information was. *There's much to learn about these people, and if their history is not recorded, it could be lost forever.*

• • •

Morningstar helped Henri care for Nokee throughout the night. As much as Nokee felt indebted to the Black Robe, Morningstar felt the same way toward Nokee. Henri and Morningstar cleaned Nokee's wounds every two hours and changed the dressings. Henri still had some dried hemp roots and wintergreen leaves from the Seneca village, which he gave to Morningstar to make a pain-killing tea for Nokee. The tea seemed to help. As Nokee drifted in and out of sleep, he shared fragments of his people's history. When Nokee dozed off, Henri would record that history in his journal.

As a boy, Tionontati would tell us stories of ancient times. He was a fourth-degree Midewiwin, a storyteller gifted with supernatural powers, capable of healing the critically sick. Tionontati told us we were the last remnant of a once-great nation that ruled this land for thousands of years. They had countless warriors, built great cities, and created hundreds of burial mounds.

Tionontati told me the story of the Confederation of the Yam-Ko-Desh, which consisted of four tribes: the Fox, Kickapoo, Sauk, and Mascouten. The Fox tribe lived in the upper portion of the Lower Peninsula, mostly north of the Manistee and Au Sable Rivers. They were fearless warriors known as the Defenders of the Northern Realm and kept the Ojibwa at bay. They painted their faces red and shaved their heads, except for a tall strip down the middle. It made their already tall bodies look larger when facing their foe. For thousands of years, they repelled all invaders.

The Kickapoo were marshland dwellers living in the Saginaw River Valley and Michigan's thumb. They thrived on marsh plants and animals, freshwater mussels, and fish from Lake Huron. They were shorter than the Fox and Sauk and covered their faces and shaven heads with tattoos. They relied heavily on the protection of the Fox.

The Sauk were the largest tribe in the Yam-Ko-Des Confederation. They were the prairie people. They controlled all the uplands south of the land of the Fox, from Lake Michigan across the Grand River basin down to Detroit. The Sauk were tall like the Fox and dressed similarly. However, they tattooed dark circles around their eyes and mouths and shaved their heads except for a red-dyed strip in the center, which stood straight up. They traded with the Huron, resulting in the Sauk being the first tribe of the Yam-Ko-Desh to contract European diseases. They died by the thousands from smallpox. For the few that remained, their open-land fighting tactics with spears and long shields were no match for the Chippewa in the forever war.

The next morning, as Morningstar tended to Nokee's wounds, Henri sat nearby with his pen in hand. "Tell me more about the forever war," Henri said, excited to learn more. Nokee, exhausted but restless, was happy to tell another story before falling back asleep.

Tionontati told me how a thousand summers ago, a new danger emerged from the north. The bow and arrow developed in the east, and its use spread west. When it reached the Ojibwa in the Upper Peninsula, they had a new weapon to confront the Fox in the northern portion of Michigamme. The Ojibwa crossed the straits and attacked the Fox. The Ojibwa rained deadly arrows on the spear-throwing Fox and inflicted heavy casualties. The Fox had to fall back and yield ground. The Sauk came to the aid of the Fox and fought tirelessly. But the bow and arrow carriers won more battles than they lost. The Fox eventually acquired the bow and arrow and regained some ground. However, the northern tip of the peninsula remained in possession of the Ojibwa, which became known as the Chippewa tribe.

The war lasted for many generations, with neither side making much progress. Then, thirty summers ago, the Fox launched a major offensive and drove the Chippewa back across the straits. The Ojibwa joined the Chippewa in the fight. But the Ojibwa had obtained guns from the French at the Soo. Once again, the Fox warriors were ill-equipped against this new weaponry and lost battle after battle. The Ojibwa chased the Fox west across the Upper Peninsula. The Fox tribe now lives in Wisconsin.

With the Fox no longer there, the Chippewa and Ottawa poured into the Lower Peninsula and fought the Sauk. The Sauk warriors were overrun. With overwhelming numbers and the power of the gun, the Chippewa and Ottawa drove the dwindling Sauk further south.

"And what about you, Nokee?" Henri asked. "What about your tribe, your people, your story?" By now, Nokee's eyes were drooping, his voice so soft that Henri had to lean in to listen.

I'm from the Mascouten tribe. We were the farmers of the Confederation. Our tribe was the smallest in numbers. Each spring, we would burn the prairie grass and plant our crops. My village grew corn, squash, sunflowers, and beans in raised garden beds. We traded freely with all. We were excellent marksmen and often fought beside the Sauk with our bows. When the Sauk Nation fell, their few survivors moved southwest. They joined the Mascouten at our last stronghold, near Paw-Paw Lake. There, we came under attack by the alliance of the Ottawa, Potawatomi, and Chippewa.

I was sixteen when I saw the French trapper shoot down my father. My people had just defeated the Ottawa warriors in a brilliant ambush battle. Being a petulant youth, I didn't follow my father's orders. The Ottawa took me and six other young warriors prisoner. My father died trying to save us. Our capturers brought us to the Chippewa Grand River fishing camp at Grand Rapids. We were certain to die. Then, Tionontati, the Shadow Walker, slipped into the Chippewa camp and freed us. Tionontati, my mother, and the six warriors escaped downriver in canoes.

> Tionontati sent me upriver on a quest to travel the Great Circle and see the ancestral mounds. When I reached the Miami tribe, my people had left without me. Over time, I became a Miami. When my wife and child died, I became no one. I have wandered ever since. I assume Tionontati, my mother, and the six warriors that went downriver all perished. No one has ever heard from them since. From that point on, you know the story of the flight of my people. And you now know how I ended up here.

Henri began to ask another question but was met by the sound of soft snoring. Nokee was fast asleep.

In one of Nokee's lucid moments, Morningstar asked, "Did you say you were at the Chippewa summer camp at Grand Rapids? I was there when Chief Twakanha held a council meeting with the Ottawa and Potawatomi chiefs. I was only fifteen. They had brought prisoners with them, but somehow, the prisoners escaped. Is it possible you were one of those prisoners?"

"Yes, I was one of them," Nokee said, looking up at the stars. "I wish I would've perished with Tionontati and the others."

Morningstar shook her head. "How do you know they perished? No one knows what happened to them. Chief Twakanha looked for them for weeks but never found them."

Nokee sat up, now fully alert. "That's the first encouraging word I've heard of their whereabouts in almost fifteen years. It looks like fate had a reason for us to meet."

Morningstar smiled shyly. "Yes, the spirits must've had something in mind."

Nokee half smiled and said, "After my wife and our first child died in childbirth, I stopped caring about anything."

"I feel your pain," Morningstar said. "I just lost my second husband, and now I'm alone."

• • •

Later, while watching over Nokee and reviewing his notes, Henri noticed he had underlined two things: that Nokee's tribe had built hundreds of burial mounds, and the existence of a Miami tribe. "Did I write this down correctly?" Henri asked. "Did you say your ancestors had built hundreds of burial mounds? And these Miami people, where are they located?"

Nokee, still a little dazed from his head injury, gave Henri a puzzled look. "What are those strange black marks you make? What is their purpose?"

"These lines record history. By writing this, others will know what we have discovered. This valuable information will live on forever."

"Tell me how," Nokee asked, his eyes flickering with interest.

Henri opened his journal and read Nokee a few paragraphs of what he had just written.

Nokee looked amazed. "The story of my people is held in those lines. ... My people pass our history down to our children through stories. Since I'm the last of my kind in this land, I fear my people's stories will be lost when I'm gone. When that happens, the souls of my ancestors turn to dust."

"I can help you with that," Henri said. "When our journals reach our homeland, thousands of people will read your story. The existence of your people will be known forever."

*I'll have to think about this*, thought Nokee. *If only Tionontati were here—he could tell the Black Robe so much more. Morningstar says Tionontati's group may still be alive. I'm not so sure. However, I'll share what I remember with this Black Robe. He may be my ancestors' best hope.*

"Yes, I did tell you that my ancestors built hundreds of burial mounds, and the Miami tribe is just south of the original territory of the Yam-Ko-Desh," Nokee said. "It's all on my map. Hand me my shoulder bag, and I'll show you."

Henri looked around and couldn't find anything that looked like a bag: "It's not here," he said.

Nokee's eyes widened in panic. "I must have lost it when I fell."

Henri took a lit stick from the fire and walked over to where they had found Nokee. On the ground lay a worn woven shoulder bag—the lead ball that struck Nokee had severed its carrying strap. Henri brought it back and handed it to Nokee, who pulled out a two-foot square piece of leather with a faded map on one side.

Henri was immediately struck by the map's astonishing detail. It showed Indigenous trails, rivers, mound sites, campsites, and the boundaries of the Fox, Kickapoo, Sauk, and Mascouten territories. No French geographer had yet produced anything that could compare with this. Henri looked at the Detroit River section. Henri pointed at two circles near the Belle Isle Post.

"Are these the mounds you can see from the post?"

Nokee nodded yes. Henri traced his finger up the Belle River to a bird symbol. "Is this the passenger pigeon rookery at Mudwayaushka?" Again, Nokee nodded.

Then Henri's finger drifted to the center of the map that had an unfamiliar symbol. "What is this?"

"That is the Pine Lake burial site; it was the center of the Sauk Nation," Nokee said. Henri asked if he could copy the map to his journal. Nokee agreed, and Henri eagerly went to work, his mind racing with possibilities.

By the time Henri finished, Nokee was sound asleep. Henri pulled two blankets from his pack, covered Nokee with one, and curled up by the fire with the other. Both men slept the rest of the night, not waking until after dawn. They awoke with the delightful smell of something cooking. Morningstar had made cornmeal wraps stuffed with scrambled duck eggs, diced wild onions, chives, and shredded sandhill crane breast meat. They finished their breakfast with a cup of raspberry tea, sweetened with maple sugar. While they slept, Morningstar had repaired the stitching on the strap of Nokee's shoulder bag. Nokee and Henri complimented Morningstar on her excellent breakfast. Henri noticed that Morningstar appeared particularly pleased with Nokee's response.

Morningstar told the two men the Tutelo had removed the dead body. Henri would later find out they had taken the body to the trapper's abandoned campsite. They put Antoine's head on a pole and left his decapitated body for the scavengers to eat. If the rogue trappers returned, they would most certainly get the message.

Around mid-morning, Adrien, Pierre, Thomas, and the platoon medic arrived. The medic brought a supply of gauze, bandage wraps, an arm sling, and more wound lotion. He also had a bottle mixed with rum and opium and a metal rod.

After examining Nokee's side and arm, the medic said flatly, "Give him two ounces of rum and opium. He's going to need it for pain. I must cauterize that wound in his side."

Henri cringed at the thought of giving an Indigenous person any amount of rum, much less opium. He had seen too much damage come from these things. However, the medic insisted Nokee would need it. "Even with the medicine," he explained, "we will have to hold him down."

Henri watched as the medic placed the metal rod in the fire to heat. He turned to Nokee and explained that they needed to burn the wound to prevent infection.

"My people make a wound poultice of goldenseal, blue cohosh, and balsamroot to apply to deep cuts," Nokee said. "Then we stitch the wound together with thorns."

"I trust the power of your medicines," Henri said. "But the medic says your wound is showing streaks of red, a sure sign of infection. There's no time to gather those herbs. We must treat that wound now."

Henri gave Nokee the two ounces of rum and opium. "Drink this. It will ease the pain from the burning metal. We will still have to hold you down."

Nokee drank the liquid and smiled. "No one needs to hold down a Mascouten warrior. We've learned to overcome pain."

Surprisingly, Nokee was true to his word. When the medic applied the glowing poker to the wound, Nokee lay quietly without moving a muscle. During the procedure, Morningstar disappeared. When she returned, she had the herbs and roots Nokee had suggested for the poultice. As the medic worked his craft, Morningstar ground the herbs in a stone bowl and mixed the powder into rendered beaver fat to make a salve.

The medic, glancing at Morningstar, turned to Henri. "Don't apply anything to that wound for eight hours. We want all the heat to come out first. You can lightly cover it with one layer of gauze to keep the flies off, but I don't want anything sticking to those wounds. After that, you can apply that Indigenous poultice if you wish. I've heard positive reports of the healing knowledge of the Indigenous people.

"If that shot had hit one inch to the right," continued the medic, "it would have destroyed his kidney. One inch to the left, and he would've lost that arm. He is lucky. Now, can someone escort me back to my canoe? I have packing to do. The squad heads back east in two days."

Henri still had a couple of ideas he wanted to discuss with Pierre and Adrien, so he asked Thomas to escort the medic back. Henri glanced at Nokee, who was asleep from the rum and opium concoction.

Then, in hushed tones, Henri told Pierre and Adrien what Nokee had revealed to him last night. "Nokee has a map of an ancient culture that used to live here. No one knows anything about these people—there's no record of their existence. And yet, they were here for thousands of years, built hundreds of burial mounds, and created great cities. I made a copy of Nokee's map in my journal. Look, it's all here."

Henri opened his journal to the map. Pierre, knowing Henri better than anyone, looked at Henri suspiciously. "What does that have to do with us?"

Henri stared at Pierre with a surprised look. "Don't you remember what Father Marquette told us? He said to get to know the people, learn their culture, and study their religious practices. Nokee may be the last of his kind. The history of a whole nation is disappearing. We must see these sites and record this information in *The Jesuit Relations*."

Pierre shot Adrien a grin before turning back to Henri. "This ought to be good. What scheme do you have in mind this time, Henri?"

"Well," Henri said. "Adrien and Thomas must complete their job for the fur company. They should take the canoe and continue up the Lake Huron shoreline as planned. They can contact the Chippewa villages that now control that shoreline area. They can do some trading and set up some future trade deals. The other half of the military platoon should still be in Sault Ste. Marie. Adrien and Thomas can report their findings, and we will join them when we finish our detour."

"What detour?" asked Pierre.

"The one I showed you on the map!" Henri said. "Nokee was sixteen when he did a vision quest and traveled the Great Circle from the Grand to the St. Joseph River. Nokee ended up somewhere south and stayed with the Miami tribe. He told me the Potawatomi and Ottawa live somewhere to the west. We can visit them as well."

141

"Henri, did Nokee agree to this plan?" asked Pierre.

Henri looked a little sheepish. "Well, not exactly. Nokee said he was indebted to us, told me the story of his people, and showed me the map. He wants to keep the story of his people alive! When Nokee is feeling better, I'll convince him to guide us. We must see and record these ancient mounds and visit the Pine Lake Ceremonial Center. Then, we will travel south and meet the Miami tribe where Nokee has been living. Besides, Pierre, you are a geographer. Your maps will go down in history."

Pierre shook his head. "That sounds intriguing. However, you have a lot of work to do to shore up your plan. You have two days to arrange this with Nokee, or we'll get in that canoe and head north."

• • •

Henri agreed to stay with the Tutelo and care for Nokee while his partners returned to the post and began packing. Adrien and Thomas packed their canoe for the journey north, and Pierre separated the Jesuit's supplies in case Henri pulled off his plan. Pierre retrieved the second half of the trade goods the military crew had transported to Detroit. He especially wanted to bring the two remaining copper cauldrons with them. If they were meeting new tribes, he wanted a special gift to present.

Meanwhile, Henri and Morningstar focused on helping Nokee recover. While Henri changed bandages and administered medications, Morningstar washed and stitched Nokee's buckskin shirt and prepared food for the two men. Yesah told Henri that the Tutelo would return to Mudwayaushka and the quarry in three days. If Nokee could walk, he was welcome to travel with them. Henri saw this invitation as an opportunity to put his plan into action.

"Yesah, please encourage Nokee to stay with the Tutelo for a while," requested Henri. "If he does, we Black Robes will travel with you and tend to Nokee's needs."

The next day, Yesah approached Nokee and explained that the Tutelo would soon be moving on. He thanked Nokee for saving the Chippewa women and encouraged Nokee to stay until he was well. He explained that the Black Robes had agreed to continue their healing care if he did.

"Will Morningstar be traveling with you?" Nokee asked. He knew that when a woman lost her husband, she reserved the right to choose her new path.

Yesah turned to Morningstar. "What do you choose to do?"

Morningstar smiled at Nokee. "This man saved my life. I'll go where he goes."

Nokee paused for a moment, then said, "I'll travel with the Tutelo to Mudwayaushka. I want to see that ancient quarry."

Two days later, Nokee was up and moving—slowly, but steadily. Henri put Nokee's arm in a sling as the medic had suggested. Adrien, Thomas, and Pierre showed up and reported that the soldiers at the post had moved on. Henri smiled when he noticed Pierre had brought two full packs. *Pierre must have anticipated that I would find a way*, Henri thought.

Henri sat down with his three traveling partners and filled them in on his plan. "It's all arranged," Henri said. "Adrien and Thomas will continue by canoe up the Lake Huron shoreline. Morningstar told me of a large Chippewa camp upstream on the Saginaw River, and it would be wise for both of you to stop there and negotiate future trade deals."

Pierre stood there shaking his head with his mouth open and said: "So the plan is for the two of us to walk to the Soo from here?"

"Well, maybe at first," Henri said with a thoughtful look. "I've not worked out all the details yet. However, we'll do God's work along the way and pray that he provides us the means to make the journey."

Pierre chuckled. "Why, Henri, I always thought you were conservative. You always said to stick to the plan and not make waves. You always wanted to proceed carefully. Now, here we are, and I'm the one calling your plan ludicrous. I'm wondering whether your plan is too dangerous to undertake, and what will happen if we get into trouble. I'm concerned no one will come to our aid if we do."

Pierre and Henri stared at each other for a long moment, then Pierre laughed and said, "What was I thinking? I've always claimed to be the adventurous one. Well, this is our greatest adventure. I'm all in! Where are we going next?"

"The Tutelo tribe leaves for Mudwayaushka tomorrow," Henri said. "We'll go with them, visiting whatever places on Nokee's map that we can. Nokee also mentioned something about seeing that ancient quarry."

Adrien and Thomas spent the day with the two Black Robes, reviewing the essential supplies the Jesuits would need. They laid everything out in neat rows, double-checking that all items were there.

As they finished their preparations, Adrien gave Pierre a troubled look. "Pierre, I want you to consider something. It was admirable how Henri pulled off that bluff with those deplorable men, but bluffing does not always work. It would be nice if you had a little firepower when needed."

Adrien held up the dead trapper's pistol.

Pierre shot a quick side glance at Henri, who looked like he was about to say something, but Pierre cut him off. "Thank you, Adrien, but no thanks. The Lord has gotten us this far. I figure he must have a special plan for us. We'll put our faith in him." Henri smiled and said nothing.

Adrien noticed Morningstar's interest sharpen when the conversation turned to the pistol. She leaned in, examining the gun. Adrien dismissed it as simple curiosity—after all, Morningstar now had a similar weapon in her possession.

While the four men concentrated on packing, Adrien suddenly sensed movement behind him. Spinning around, he found Morningstar pointing a pistol straight at him. Adrien instinctively reached for the gun tucked in his belt sash. But before he could draw, Morningstar lowered her pistol.

"Show me. Show me how this works," Morningstar said, quietly. Adrien breathed a sigh of relief as he released his grip on his pistol.

"First lesson—never point a gun at something you don't intend to kill," Adrien said, his voice tense. "Second, that's the gun that shot Nokee. It's not even loaded. Come over here and sit down. I'll tell you about that pistol. You need to know what they can and cannot do."

Morningstar sat down, and Adrien laid the two pistols side by side. "These guns are English Dog Lock Pistols," said Adrien. "It's apparent they are twin sisters. My best guess is they were an aristocrat dueling set, and those rogues picked them up in a trade with the English or Dutch fur traders. Look at them closely. They have heavy sixteen-inch-long cylindrical barrels to reduce recoil. Note the fine-finished walnut pistol stocks, the bluing on their barrels, and curved hand grips with solid silver butt plates. Commoners don't carry this weapon—certainly not runners of the woods. With the correct charge of black powder and a .62 caliber ball seated in a cloth wad rammed down the barrel, you can kill a man out to thirty yards. But that takes practice. These heavy pistols are only accurate if you rest them solidly on something. Here, let me show you how they work."

Henri reached into his pack and handed Morningstar the extra powder horn he had been carrying and the last bag of round copper balls. He hesitated and said: "With the musketoon blown up and all the metal crosses given away, I've no more use for these. I pray you use these to save lives, not take them."

Adrien looked at the copper balls. "Perfect match. They're .62 caliber. Now, Morningstar, watch me closely. Your life may depend on knowing how to do this correctly."

Morningstar moved closer and concentrated on every move he made. Adrien showed her how to load the exact amount of powder down the barrel. Then, he pulled a handful of cloth patches from his pocket and gave them to her. He took one of the copper balls, wrapped it in a single patch, and slid it into the mouth of the barrel. Adrien withdrew the ramrod beneath the pistol and gently pushed the projectile down the barrel.

"Here. Do you see this line marked on the end of this ramrod? That ramrod mark must be in line with the mouth of the barrel every time. It indicates the round ball is seated completely down the barrel. If you don't standardize your amount of powder and ball placement, your shot distance and accuracy vary. Remember: you only have one shot!"

Adrien replaced the ramrod and primed the frizzen. He half-cocked the pistol and said: "Mine's ready to go. Let us see you do the same with yours."

Morningstar carefully picked up her pistol and methodically reproduced Adrien's moves. When she finished, everyone looked at her with amazement. "I'm ready," she said as she rose to put her pistol in her shoulder bag.

"Not so fast!" said Adrien. "That was extremely impressive. But you forgot to half cock your pistol. If you fall or drop the gun, it could accidentally discharge. Besides, you haven't shot it yet. Rest your pistol on this tree limb, and we'll see how good your aim is."

Morningstar approached the branch slowly. Adrien had set up a split log at twenty yards. He instructed her to aim at the center, take a deep breath, let half of it out, and squeeze the trigger; don't pull it. Morningstar did as he instructed. There was a *crack* and a puff of smoke, and everyone piled in to see where the shot had landed. The hole was just an inch off-center. All watching cheered. Nokee nodded at Yesah with a big grin.

Morningstar looked at Adrien. "I missed my mark. Next time, I'll not flinch." She reloaded her pistol, half-cocked it, and stuffed it into her bag.

# Long Way Around

Adrien and Thomas spent the night with Henri and Pierre at the Tutelo camp. They laughed and joked about the past six weeks they had spent together. Through the laughter, a sense of quiet sadness permeated their voices—the sadness that comes with the inevitable parting of companions. After breakfast, Adrien and Thomas said goodbye, returned to their canoe, and set off up the Detroit River. Without the two other paddlers aboard to share the burden, their upstream progress was slow against the strong current. Soon, they entered Lake St. Clair, and their pace quickened, only to slow again when they reached the St. Clair River. They slogged along for the next forty miles until they entered the open waters of Lake Huron. There, they raised their sail, and the journey became more comfortable.

Meanwhile, Tenron—Shater's closest friend—and his five warriors returned from their three-day vigil at Shater's reburial. Tenron was surprised to see Nokee was there. He was even more astonished that Morningstar was cozying up to Nokee. He didn't hide his disapproval, fixing them with a cold glare. Yesah, ignoring Tenron's grumblings, announced they would leave for Mudwayaushka that morning. Everyone got ready to break camp.

In addition to all the traditional gear women carry, Morningstar had sewed together a leather carrying case for her three newly acquired flintlocks. As the group headed north along the Shoreline Trail, Morningstar seemed to struggle with the gun sling draped over her shoulder. Nokee offered to help, but Morningstar insisted it was not a burden she was interested in sharing. After traveling forty miles, they reached the Belle River and made camp for the night. They rose early the next morning and continued northwest along the Belle River Trail. After another forty-mile day, they reached the split where Belle River divided into its north and south branches. Tired and hungry, they spent the second night at the fork.

In the morning, they continued upstream along the south branch of the Belle River. In about ten miles, they entered a wide-open valley. Beech trees became more numerous as the river gradually narrowed—first to a stream, then to a small creek. Soft cooing filled the air as they approached the nesting area.

Henri stopped when he saw a male passenger pigeon—the first he'd ever seen—sitting on a low branch twenty yards away. He nudged Morningstar and said, "I would love to have one of those birds up close so I could properly sketch it in my journal."

"You shall have your wish," Morningstar said.

Without hesitation, she pulled out her pistol, leaned it on a branch, and fired. The shot sent thousands of pigeons airborne from the beech trees up ahead, and the swirling cloud of birds darkened the sky. The group laughed and cheered as Morningstar walked over, picked up the dead bird, and strolled back to Henri.

"Is this one close enough?"

"I wish old-dead-eye Adrien could have seen that shot," Pierre said.

As the group proceeded up the valley, walking through the open forest shaded by the massive blue bark beech, they were assaulted by the smell of ammonia. The forest floor was white with countless years of pigeon droppings. When they reached the valley's center, their journey ended at a cedar-lined spring, the birthplace of the south branch of the Belle River. Nokee stopped and looked carefully at the spring. Someone had clearly dug it out and enlarged it long ago.

Nokee picked up a chunk of reddish-brown material lying on the ground and handed it to Henri. "This is red rock," he said. "My people dig this out of the ground and heat it in the fire to make our red-ocher powder. This site with the spring and the birds must have been a very sacred place."

Yesah pointed to the ridge top protruding into the valley. "There, on Pigeon Point, is where we camp tonight. Welcome to Mudwayaushka."

• • •

Miles away, to the north, Adrien and Thomas had reached the mouth of the Saginaw River. Suddenly, out of nowhere, a group of angry Chippewa warriors armed with flintlocks appeared on the riverbank. They ordered the two men ashore, and with firearms pointed at them, Adrien and Thomas didn't dare argue. As the two fur traders slid their canoe onto the beach with their hands up, they were immediately yanked out and thrown to the ground.

Jibewas, now the war chief for the Saginaw River Chippewa tribe, ordered their hands tied. He approached the Frenchmen, grabbed them by their chins, and examined their faces. "Where's the rest of your group?"

Adrien, stunned by the unusual treatment they were receiving, replied, "We left our traveling partners in Detroit. They're heading to Mudwayaushka with Nokee, Morningstar, and the Tutelo tribe."

Jibewas's grip on Adrien's jaw tightened. "Tell me how you know Morningstar. If you lie, I'll cut out your tongue."

Adrien quickly recounted how they had saved the Chippewa women from rape and murder by four deplorable Frenchmen while the Tutelo were away.

"Nokee killed one of them, and the other three got away," Thomas added.

Jibewas released his grip on Adrien. "What did these Frenchmen look like?"

"It was dark," Adrien said. "But one of them had a scar across his face and left with a broken jaw. Nokee landed a good one on him."

"We'll take the Frenchmen to Chief Twakanha," Jibewas yelled to his men. "Put them in my canoe. Twakanha will decide what to do with them." He then pointed at two of his men. "Bring their canoe and see that no one disturbs their belongings."

Chief Twakanha's village was a half-day paddle upstream, where the Tittabawassee and the Cass Rivers joined the Saginaw. When the canoes arrived, the inhabitants ran to the river to see if Jibewas had captured the perpetrators. Jibewas stepped from his canoe and went straight to Chief Twakanha for private counsel.

Chief Twakanha approached Adrien and Thomas, their hands

still tied. He called for the three women who had lost their husbands. "Are these the men you saw on the beach?"

The three women looked closely and shook their heads. Dawn, the oldest woman in the group, spoke up. "No. The men on the beach were older and fatter."

Chief Twakanha ordered the two Frenchmen to be cut free. "There has been a misunderstanding. Jibewas thought you were the men that killed three of our men two days ago while they were fishing in the bay. You are not them. They are evil men who trade in rum. Jibewas told me you killed their leader in Detroit—that's good. When I find the rest, I will finish the job."

"We stopped here to tell you that the trading post in Detroit is open and well-supplied," Adrien said. "We're on our way to Sault Ste. Marie. We'll warn the villages we see along the way of the danger these three men present."

"I will do the same when we move to our fishing and hunting camp at the Grand Rapids," Twakanha said. "We trade with the Potawatomi and Ottawa people. Those disgraceful men will have no haven in the Lower Peninsula. Now, eat and smoke with us. We can talk trade."

Adrien and Thomas spent the night in the village. In the morning, they informed Chief Twakanha that they would return to this area next spring with trade canoes heading south to Detroit. Chief Twakanha was pleased with the arrangement. After saying their goodbyes, Adrien and Thomas boarded their canoes, headed down the Saginaw River, and then turned north toward Sault Ste. Marie.

• • •

Back at Mudwayaushka, the Tutelo had set up camp on top of Pigeon Point. The atmosphere was carnival-like, with the men smoking kinnikinnick and drinking rum. The first nesting period was over, and the squabs were now fully feathered and capable of limited flight. The men climbed high into the trees, shaking the branches to coax the young birds to fly. Most chicks were old enough to fly to another tree, but the younger ones would flutter down to the ground. Henri, Pierre, and Nokee howled as they watched the Chippewa women chase down the rook chicks as they hit the ground. They feasted on roasted young squeakers strung on sticks over the fire that night.

After dinner, Yesah found Nokee and took him aside. "Tomorrow, seven of our best craftsmen and I will return to the flint quarry. You are welcome to come along if you wish. The trip takes us northwest up the Saginaw Trail until we reach the Peiconigowink—the River of Flint. Deep in the river cut, we find the chert stone. The death of Shater has put us a week behind in our flint knapping and arrow production. We must finish our work and reach the mouth of the Flint River in time to intercept the Chippewa. They will travel up the Shiawassee River, moving their people west to their Grand Rapids fishing camp. The plan is to trade arrowheads and arrows for smoked fish and duck meat. But we cannot know what they will offer. They are clever traders, and they remember every deal they have made. Cheat them once, and they do not forget."

Yesah left Nokee to enjoy the evening and walked over to Tenron. "I'll leave you in charge of everyone here. When the nesting season ends, take our people back down the Saginaw Trail. When you reach the Shoreline Trail, send them north to our summer camp on the Black River. I know your taste for rum. Fill your barrels with squab and mussels and head straight for Detroit. When you satisfy your thirst, join us on the Black River."

As the festivities began to wind down, Morningstar held a private counsel with Nokee. "If Yesah is going to meet the people of my village at the mouth of the Flint River, I wish to go with him. My siblings will be traveling with my father, Chief Twakanha. I would like to see all of them one last time."

"What? Chief Twakanha is your father?" Nokee felt a deep ache rise within him—one he had thought long buried. "Is he still alive? You heard what Yesah said: cheat a Chippewa, and they never forget. I cheated him out of my death!"

"Yes, my father is alive ... but he is old. If he remembers you, he remembers you as a boy, not an adult. Besides, you dress like a Miami. We have been at peace with the Miami people for years. No one will recognize you." Nokee looked up to the stars for answers. He would need time to think about what he had just heard.

Tenron, seeing their conversation, staggered up to Morningstar.

He swayed back and forth from too much kinnikinnick and rum. "Why do you spend so much time with that Mascouten?" he said, slurring his words. "You should be in mourning. Instead, you run around like a female cougar looking to mate." When Morningstar slapped Tenron, he shoved her to the ground.

Nokee, with his left arm still in a sling, was on Tenron in a second. Tenron pulled his knife, and Nokee did the same with his right arm. As the two circled, they heard the cocking of a flintlock. Morningstar was aiming her pistol directly at Tenron.

"Would you shoot your husband's best friend?"

Morningstar's eyes were as sharp and cold as blades. "Like the Frenchman in Detroit said just before he died ... 'I'll do it with pleasure!'"

Yesah grabbed Tenron by the neck, dragged him away, and told him to sleep it off. Tenron, visibly humiliated, stumbled away. Henri and Pierre halted their daily entries in their journals and ran over to see if Morningstar was okay.

"What just happened?" asked Henri.

"Tenron thinks I am getting too attached to Nokee."

"Well, are you?" Henri asked, grinning.

"Don't make me slap you too!" she said with a smile, equal parts mischievous and dangerous. "Nokee told me the four of us are leaving with Yesah's team at first light for the quarry. After that, Yesah plans to wait for the Chippewa, where the Flint River joins the Shiawassee River. I hope to get Nokee to travel there with Yesah."

Henri opened his journal and studied the map he had copied from Nokee. He focused on the route to the quarry and then north on the Flint River to reach the Shiawassee River. Henri made a show of slowly stroking his chin, as though he was in deep contemplation.

"What's the matter?" Morningstar asked.

"Oh, nothing. I had hoped I could get Nokee to take us to the Pine Lake Center and continue south to meet his Miami tribe."

Pierre jumped into the conversation. "Henri, I told you to get that worked out before we began this adventure. Now we have no choice but to go with the flow and be flexible."

Morningstar studied Henri's map. She traced her finger up

the Shiawassee River to where it was possible to portage into the Maple River. Halfway down the Maple, the river intersected the Marsh Trail to Pine Lake. From there, the Grand River continued south to the St. Joseph River. The Miami village on the St. Joseph River was due west from there.

She looked at the two Black Robes and said, "I may have found a way for both of us to get what we desire—leave this to me. There's something at the Miami camp that I need to investigate. Now get some sleep—tomorrow will be a long day!"

• • •

The flint-knapping team was gone before the sun rose. Even with that early start, they did not arrive at the quarry until just before dark. In the fading light of the day, Henri and Pierre were disappointed at what they saw. It looked more like an excavation site than a quarry. There were no walls of exposed rock formations. Instead, it appeared as though someone was searching for buried treasure.

Hundreds of dirt piles covered the flood plain, and flakes of light brown to medium gray pieces of stone covered the river edge. Henri picked up one of the flakes. It had a waxy, chalk-like texture and was extremely sharp. The quarry extended downriver as far as the two men could see. Henri sketched a picture in his journal, and Pierre charted the location. Then, exhausted from their long walk, they hastily ate dinner and went to sleep.

The next day, the group got straight to work. Everyone knew their tasks. Two men were the seekers. They searched and dug for the rounded chunks of chert stone along the riverbanks. Another was the striker. He would strike the chert chunks with a sturdy hammerstone, breaking them in half. Each of the halves now had a flat surface with sharp edges. A fourth man was the flaker. He hit the flat surface of each half with a section of elk antler to knock off large chert flakes. Two men were the pressure knappers. Using deer antler tips, they applied pressure on the edges of the large chert flakes, causing long pieces to pop off. By working on both sides, they shaped and sharpened the point. The final phase of point production went to Yesah, the notcher. Using a copper needle and a small piece of sandstone, he carved out the notches at the base of the arrowhead. The points were then ready to be bound to the arrow shaft.

Finally, there was the shaft maker. His job was to locate the arrow bush plant and cut straight stems the length of his outstretched arm and pointed index finger—roughly thirty inches. He stripped the bark and smoothed the shafts with a sandstone shafter. He then slowly dried them by hanging them over the fire, turning them frequently to ensure they dried perfectly straight. The arrow shafts were split in front for arrowhead attachment and slit three times in the back, evenly spaced, for feather placement. In the final phase, the shaft maker inserted square-cut turkey feathers into the three rear slits of the shaft using a copper needle. Then he sealed the connection with pine pitch.

Nokee volunteered to be the meat provider. He provided rabbits, grouse, sandhill cranes, and deer, but never meat from a bear. When they asked for bear meat, he would refuse, vowing to never kill his spirit animal. But the truth was, his dreams were still haunted by the death moans of the great bear he'd killed all those years ago. Morningstar and Pierre agreed to cook, and Henri gathered the firewood. The team worked from sunrise to sunset crafting arrows. The labor was hard but satisfying, and the effort bonded them together.

One evening after dinner, Morningstar found Nokee alone by the fire and sat down beside him. "Nokee, are you aware that Henri wants to visit the Miami tribe?"

"Yes. Henri expressed interest in seeing the Miami, Potawatomi, and Ottawa tribes when we were in Detroit. He was interested in the history of the mounds built by my ancestors." Nokee gazed into the fire, the flame flickering in his eyes. "Do you think I said too much? My head was spinning from that medicine he gave me. I need to understand why he wants to know these things."

"No, I don't think you said too much," Morningstar said. "I heard what those marks on their papers say. They let other people know what has happened. Perhaps they will keep the stories of your people alive. Tribal lands and people are changing so fast. I heard him say that if they get these stories back to the other side of the great saltwater sea, the histories of our people will be told forever. Others will know who lived here."

"*I* know who lived here!" Nokee said indignantly.

"Of course, Nokee. I know you do! But who will remember when you are gone? The Black Robes and their paper may keep your people's memories alive."

Nokee pulled his gaze away from the fire and looked up to the night sky. "What you say makes sense. However, the Black Robes will have to wait. I have decided to go with Yesah to meet the Chippewa." He turned to look into Morningstar's eyes. "I want to help you return to your family. When I was a boy, I ran and hid from Twakanha. As a man, I run and hide from no one. If he still wants a fight, he'll get one."

Morningstar thanked Nokee but slyly added, "There is a path that might lead all of us to find the answers we are seeking. The Black Robes told me they plan to go to the other side of Lake Michigan next spring. They want to look for your people. We should go with them."

"If you and the Black Robes want to go there, I'll go with you. There is nothing that holds me here. But know this—my past life is over. I won't be chasing childhood dreams." Morningstar nodded in understanding. But she knew his words betrayed him. He *was* running from something; he just didn't know it yet.

At the end of the week, the group headed down the Flint River. On the way to the river mouth, they passed three mound sites shown on Nokee's map. Yesah and his men waited patiently while Nokee, Morningstar, and the Black Robes entered the mound sites. Each site contained five to ten mounds. The average size mound was about thirty feet in diameter and between six to ten feet tall. Nokee commented that these are all traditional dome-shaped mounds.

Henri could sense the weight of history in this sacred place and tried to temper his excitement with respect as he sketched the site. "Are there other types of mounds?"

"These are the type of mounds I grew up knowing," Nokee said. "But I found another type when I traveled around the Great Circle. I saw chamber mounds mixed in with traditional ones. I marked the chamber mounds on my map. I wanted to ask

Tionontati if these were a different group of people who lived with my ancestors, or if our traditions changed over time. ... But I never got the chance."

• • •

Two days later, the group reached the mouth of the Flint River, where it emptied into the Shiawassee. They set up camp and waited for Chief Twakanha's group to arrive. The spawning run of yellow perch had just begun. The Chippewa women had salvaged a section of the fishnets that the rogue trappers had destroyed in Detroit. The women sang as they strung a short piece of gill net at the mouth of the Flint River. That evening, they feasted on fat-bellied yellow perch, ripening blackberries, and Pierre's cornbread muffins.

They had arrived at the Shiawassee River just in time. On their second day, Chippewa cargo canoes appeared in the morning mist. Chief Twakanha's village was on the move. Jibewas's canoe led the way. He raised his hand, and the convoy came to a halt. Jibewas broke away from the group and proceeded upstream slowly. Yesah, who had waited for this moment, raised two hands above his head, holding an *opwaagan*—a peace pipe.

"What business do you have with the Chippewa?" Jibewas called out.

"We're here to smoke peace and talk trade," Yesah answered. Jibewas, satisfied with the appropriate greeting protocol, moved his canoe forward. As the craft slid into shore, Jibewas hopped out. The two men approached each other and locked arms in a long embrace. Over the past few years, they had become good friends.

"Yesah, you sly trader, did you bring straight arrows this time?"

"Only if you brought freshly smoked fish, Jibewas!" They both laughed.

"Where is she?" Jibewas asked, glancing around. Just then, Morningstar stepped out from behind the Tutelo warriors. She ran to him, wrapped her arms around Jibewas, and kissed him on his cheek.

"How have you been, my dear brother?"

"Excellent, my dear sister. Now, where is he? Father will demand to see him immediately."

The hairs on the back of Nokee's neck stood on end. Every imaginable thought raced through his mind. *Had Morningstar betrayed him? Was this all a setup? Chief Twakanha was her father, the Chippewa leader who had captured him fifteen years ago was her brother. Had his feelings for Morningstar made him careless again*? He felt trapped, like an animal in a snare. His hand slid to his knife. He was prepared to fight.

Morningstar took two steps back and put her hand in her shoulder bag, caressing her pistol grip. "Who are you looking for?"

"You know who—the Miami warrior in your group," Jibewas said. "Your fur trader friends told us that Nokee would travel with you. Father has heard of the legendary battles Nokee led against the Iroquois. Twakanha wants to honor him with a great feast and hear about his battles." Morningstar let out the breath she hadn't realized she was holding and slowly withdrew her hand from her gun.

With adrenalin pulsing through his veins, Nokee stepped forward. "I'm the one you are looking for!"

"Nokee is a big fellow," Jibewas said, looking him up and down. "Welcome. We are honored to have such a famous *ogichidaa*—warrior—visit our village."

Nokee stood dazed. *How can they know my name and not know who I am? Think*, he told himself. *Jibewas was the one who delivered me and the six Mascouten warriors to Chief Twakanha's camp at Grand Rapids. However, I don't think he ever asked me my name. He always referred to his captured prize as the son of Mahtowa. Morningstar was right—they don't know who I am!*

Jibewas motioned for the convoy to continue upstream before turning to face his sister. "Morningstar, I heard about Shater. I'm sorry. I hate to tell you this, but I have more sad news. Our sister Dawn lost her husband this week."

"No!" Morningstar said. "What happened?"

"Those trappers that attacked you in Detroit came here and shot Dawn's husband and two other men."

Morningstar's knees buckled as if from a gut punch. "Where is she? I must go to her!"

"She's in the last canoe. The three women are traveling

together. They are still mourning." Morningstar took off in a sprint downriver.

Chief Twakanha stepped from his canoe. He looked much older than Nokee remembered. In Nokee's nightmares, Twakanha had always appeared as a fearsome warrior. Now, he just looked like a grandfather. The chief greeted Yesah and his warriors first, then rejoiced at the sight of the returning Chippewa women. At last, he turned to Nokee. "So, I finally meet the legendary Miami warrior! Tales of your countless victories against the Iroquois have warmed my winter lodge on the coldest of winter nights. Welcome, Nokee. We'll camp here tonight, smoke, feast, and exchange stories."

Then, Chief Twakanha turned to address Henri and Pierre. "We've not seen Black Robes in these parts for years. Are you just passing through, or do you plan to stay in the area?"

Pierre stepped forward. "We are heading to Sault Ste. Marie. But we intend to visit many tribes and help wherever we can be of use."

Chief Twakanha slyly grinned at the two of them. "What type of help do you think we need?"

Henri reacted without taking time to think. He reached into his pack and pulled out the fourth copper cauldron. "Hopefully, we can help with useful items like this, as well as French medicines."

Twakanha looked thrilled with the kettle. And even more so when Henri pulled out the confit pot. "You Black Robes bring fine gifts. I know there are both bad and good among the French. I hope you are the latter."

Pierre jumped in. "I've made some fine French foods in those kettles we gave to other chiefs. I can do the same for you if you wish." Chief Twakanha seemed interested.

While the Chippewa set up their temporary shelters, Chief Twakanha and his clan leaders talked trade with the Tutelo. The Chippewa were impressed by the fine craftsmanship of the arrows and points. Yesah was pleased with the smoked fish and duck meat he received in return.

Meanwhile, Morningstar had returned from her visit with her sister. Approaching her father, she said, "My chief, I've talked to the women and heard of their encounter with those despicable men. They told me you and our fur-trapping friends are spreading word of the evil these men bring. If you should capture them, I have something for you."

Morningstar walked over to her belongings and returned with one of her muskets. "Here is one of their flintlocks. If you find them, shoot them with this weapon. Please do this for all the pain they have caused our Chippewa women." Twakanha took the rifle and nodded.

That evening, Pierre talked Chief Twakanha into letting him make dinner in the cauldron. He made deep-fried perch and hush puppies. With a new supply of ingredients from the Detroit post, he prepared a blackberry cobbler for dessert.

After dinner, Chief Twakanha took Morningstar aside. "You're now a free woman. Will you be traveling with us to Grand Rapids? Your sister needs you during this most challenging time."

"I want to be with her," Morningstar said. "They all need time to recover from what has happened. However, Nokee saved my life. He has wandered too long and needs to return to his people. If you would allow it, I've thought of a way to accomplish both. If Nokee, the Black Robes, and I travel upstream with you for a while, we could eventually break away and turn south. That would allow me time with the women while still taking Nokee in the direction of his people."

In the morning, the Tutelo said their goodbyes. The four Chippewa women cried, and the Tutelo men thanked their traveling friends for their help at the quarry. Yesah embraced Nokee. "Nokee, my friend, thank you for saving our women in Detroit. We'll watch over the land of your ancestors in your absence. If our paths cross again, you will always be welcome in our camp." With that, Yesah spun around and headed southeast for the Black River.

Chief Twakanha turned to Morningstar and said, "You and your friends are welcome to join us. Nokee and the Black Robes can ride in my canoe. You can travel with your sister and the other mourning women."

Henri seemed thrilled, Pierre appeared neutral, and Nokee thought it was a bad idea. "Nokee," Morningstar said. "There's nothing to worry about. Twakanha thinks you are the best thing to have come to his village in a long time. He'll spend the entire trip telling stories. All you need to do is act interested, and we travel with ease." Nokee lowered his head and reluctantly agreed to the plan.

# Pine Lake

Within an hour of the Tutelo leaving, the Chippewa convoy was on the move. They traveled the rest of the day up the Shiawassee River and spent the night at the Maple River portage, a tributary of the Grand River. All day long, Chief Twakanha did most of the talking. At the end of every story of battle, he would turn to Nokee and say: "Of course, a great warrior like you already knows this!" That evening, Chief Twakanha kept Nokee up most of the night. He wanted to hear every detail of the great battles Nokee had led against the Iroquois.

Nokee was exhausted the next morning as they paddled downstream on the Maple. Again, Chief Twakanha dominated the conversation. Nokee, half in a stupor, just nodded along to every story.

"Nokee, where did you learn your incredible ambushing skills?" Twakanha asked.

Without any thought, Nokee blurted out, "At the Battle on the Kalamazoo Ridge."

Chief Twakanha spun around, almost upsetting the canoe. "You were at the Battle on the Kalamazoo Ridge?"

Nokee, realizing he had just blown his cover, quickly responded: "Everyone knows about that Battle. The Miami warriors have studied that event in great detail."

Nokee looked down at the water and kept paddling. He tried not to notice Twakanha's penetrating stare. When they stopped for their midday meal, Nokee asked Morningstar to help him gather firewood. He quietly whispered to her what had happened.

Morningstar looked concerned. "Nokee, we need to get out of here before he asks any more questions. You continue gathering wood, and I'll figure a way out of this."

Morningstar returned to camp and found Twakanha sitting and talking to Jibewas. As she approached, the conversation paused.

"Hello, my chief," Morningstar said. "Our group has decided to take the Marsh Trail south to the Ottawa village on the Red Cedar at Okemos. I hope to trade my two muskets for two canoes. We can then paddle up the Grand River and portage into the St. Joseph River. From there, it will be an easy downstream journey to the Miami Camp at Three Rivers."

Chief Twakanha nodded agreeably, and Morningstar walked away. But rather than leaving, she hid by a nearby bush, eavesdropping on the conversation.

"See, do you think they would take him to an Ottawa camp if what you think is true?" Jibewas said. "Mascoutens hate Ottawa. Besides, that battle was fifteen years ago. He would have been a young boy."

"Maybe he was one of those boys you captured?" Twakanha asked.

"With all due respect, my chief, those boys probably drowned in the river, or we would've found them. You know they're land travelers. They don't know the front of a canoe from the back."

"You are probably right," Chief Twakanha said. "I just want to be sure they are not taking me for a fool."

A short time later, the convoy reached the Marsh Trail. Morningstar hugged her sister and consoled the other women as the canoes pulled over to let out their traveling guest. Henri and Pierre were tense, having witnessed the conversation in the canoe. They acted even friendlier than usual, thanking everyone—especially Chief Twakanha. Nokee kept busy gathering their gear while trying not to make eye contact with the Chief. But he knew the Chief was paying attention to his every move.

Waving goodbye to the villagers, the four travelers headed south. As soon as they got out of earshot, Morningstar turned to the others and relayed what Jibewas had said to Chief Twakanha.

"How dare he say I've fallen in love," she snapped, clearly frustrated. "That is pure nonsense."

With that, she quickened her pace and walked ahead, leaving Nokee speechless. Henri and Pierre exchanged amused glances and hustled to keep up, doing their best to hide the widening grins on their faces. By mid-afternoon, they reached the Looking Glass River crossing. Henri found the river pleasant and suggested they spend the night there. Morningstar insisted they move on. She thought they should get as far away from Twakanha as possible. They crossed the river, and before sunset, they reached Pine Lake.

As they circled the west side of the lake, they found lodges but no people. The shelters were in disrepair, clearly abandoned for some time. Stunned, Morningstar insisted that the Ottawa villagers were in this area a few years ago, when her people traded with them. Disappointed, the group moved on. They spent the night on the south ridge of Pine Lake—the same place Nokee had visited fifteen years prior when he was on the run.

That night, as they sat around the fire, they reflected on their encounter with Chief Twakanha. Though the chief had appeared satisfied with their cover story, they all agreed that the only way to guarantee Nokee's safety was to avoid any future contact with Twakanha. The conversation changed directions when Henri expressed interest in seeing the Pine Lake mounds.

"Henri," Nokee said, "the boulder-line trail that leads to that site is only a couple hundred paces from here. I'll take you to that mound center in the morning, but I must stress the religious importance of that place—nothing can be disturbed.

"The Dark Forces still watch over these areas," added Nokee. "Even the Chippewa and Ottawa refuse to go near these sites." Morningstar nodded in agreement.

"To give you an idea of how sacred these places are to my ancestors," Nokee continued, lowering his voice, "I'll tell you a story. Each winter, on frigid winter nights, Tionontati would assemble the children around him in his warm, comfortable lodge. He would look into each child's eyes and say: 'You must never forget that you are descendants of a Great Nation! My grandfather told me this story, as other grandfathers have done for countless generations. Someday, you must pass this on to your grandchildren so they can pass it on to theirs.'"

Henri listened intently and recorded much of it in his journal.

> Pine Lake was the center of the Sauk Nation—the capital of the most fearless warriors of the ancient Yam-Ko-Desh. Now, if you could travel back countless years to the Pine Lake village on an early fall day, you would have seen the shoreline dotted with cooking fires of the various clans. Families dispersed during the summer would have returned for winter and the Interment Day of the Dead. All would be busy setting nets and traps to catch, smoke, and dry as many migrating ducks and geese as possible.
>
> The Interment Day of the Dead is a sacred time for those who have lost loved ones. The cremated bone fragments and ashes of the deceased are ready in leather burial bags. The mourning families are busy carefully crafting grave goods. These items are essential for the departing souls in their final journey into the afterlife. Carriers of these burial bags will hold a special place in the ceremonial procession that is about to begin; they will walk at the head of the line, just behind the chiefs, clan leaders, and priests.
>
> Over many years, numerous changes have taken place at the Burial-Mound Center. The spiritual leaders had to learn how to cut and shape boulders to create their structures, alters, and stone effigies at the burial site. This effort required modifying rocks with simple stone tools. They had to develop methods of heating boulders with fire and splitting them along natural fracture lines. Their stone artists and priests continued to develop their techniques and talents. They became experts at carving birds and other animal images on rocks and boulders and painting them with vivid colors to enhance their effect. Then, there was the effort of moving hundreds of large boulders to line the ceremonial trail from Pine Lake to the burial site.
>
> Were you here to witness it, you would have seen a peace chief who was quite pleased with the report he had just received from his ceremonial chief and priests. The mound site was ready, the night sky was clear, and the alignment of the sun was in place. The time of the Changing Leaves Moon had arrived. This peace chief's mound was the tallest of the six mounds, a testament to his long life. Each succeeding peace chief starts a new mound to honor their reign.
>
> Chief White Heron ordered everyone to prepare for the nighttime procession. As the sun disappears over the horizon, the ceremonial chief turns to Chief White Heron, and the camp goes silent. White Heron raises his hands to the west and begins the age-old chant honoring the souls of the ancestors. The priests join in,

followed by the entire village chanting the song of the dead. They light torches and lined up, two by two, behind the chiefs, priests, and mourning families, followed by the different clans. They slowly proceed eastward, down the boulder-lined Pine Lake trail, singing and chanting the ancient burial songs.

The chiefs, priests, and mourning families continue to the top of the ceremonial mound and take their places. The clans follow with baskets of food and drink and assemble at the mound's base. They feast and tell stories honoring the recent dead while waiting for the moon to rise. There will be no sleep this night. They will dance, sing, drum, blow panpipes, and shake turtle-shell rattles until dawn. Then, in an ever-increasing tempo, they will celebrate the first rays of the sun, signaling the beginning of the Interment Day of the Dead.

As the sun rises in the east, the celebration peaks as a sunbeam pierces the hole in the rock and shines directly on the center altar. The priests wildly chant songs honoring the life-giving sun and the spirits of the dead. The procession reassembles and heads northeast to the mound built in honor of Chief White Heron's reign.

The ceremonial chief begins the burial chants. Each family representative carries their burial bags to a preselected site on the mound. They carefully place their cremation bag in Mother Earth. The remaining mourning family members follow, placing their handcrafted burial items next to each bag. The priests sprinkle the graves with red-ocher powder. Then, the remaining villagers approach the graves with their hands full of dirt, and the ceremony quietly ends.

Everyone will rest for the day because tomorrow, the hard work begins. Their mobile shelters, used during the summer, must be strengthened to withstand the heavy winter snow. But the most honored task is to be selected for the mound-building team. That team will carry hundreds of baskets of dirt to recap and pack the burial mound for next year's Interment Day of the Dead. Then, the ground will freeze, and all work on the mound will end for another year. As the cold winds began to blow, the people must be ready to hunker down for the long winter ahead. One last celebration occurs during the shortest daylight period of the year, the time of the Little Spirit Moon. On that day, all the village members will gather at the ceremonial mound to dance, sing, and plead with the sun to return from its southerly retreat.

Nokee paused and looked at the night mist settling in on the lake. Then, in a slightly quivering voice, Nokee said, "Tionontati always ended by saying: 'We must never let this story die. Each of you must remember!

"I fear that soon there will be no grandchildren to hear the story ..." Nokee said, his voice trailing off. Morningstar turned away so they wouldn't see the tears in her eyes.

Though entranced by the story, the group drifted off to sleep in a somber mood.

• • •

After breakfast, they followed the boulder-lined trail to the Pine Lake Mound Center. It had been fifteen years since Nokee visited the site and twenty-five years since the Midewiwin had maintained it. Nokee looked shocked. Red cedar, pine, and aspen had taken over the site.

"Why the look of concern, Nokee?" Henri asked.

"Because soon, the trees will grow taller than the mounds. Then the forest will swallow up this area like it never existed."

Henri gave Nokee a comforting smile. "That's why we are here. Pierre and I will map and record what we see so that these mounds and the story of the people who built them will remain forever. We'll stay as long as it takes. Show us what you can remember and leave the rest to us."

Nokee led them first to the ceremonial mound. The altars still stood proud, but a white pine had grown up to shade the stones. Nokee explained how this tree would interfere with the seasonal alignments of the sun.

Using an axe borrowed from Pierre, Nokee cut down the obstructing tree. Next, they visited the bubbling spring. Alders filled in much of the spring, but past offerings could still be seen glittering at the bottom. Henri sketched the spring and the location of the surrounding mounds. The last thing they visited that day was the chambered mound. A wolf family had dug a den under the boulder that sealed the chamber. The ground had collapsed, tilting the stone sideways, leaving the tomb half-open. Pierre wanted to look inside, but Nokee refused to let him.

"You mustn't dare!" Nokee said. "The Dark Forces will curse you with unmeasurable bad luck. Please, Pierre—some things are best left alone."

Henri and Pierre paced around the area for two more days. They mapped out connecting trails, streams, lakes, and rivers.

Pierre continued to hound Nokee for permission to look in the open chamber tomb—Nokee would not relent.

That night, they sat on the ceremonial mound and watched the moon rise. Henri thought about what Nokee had said about the different types of mounds and asked, "How did the practice of mound building first get started?"

As Nokee began, Henri grabbed his journal again and started writing.

> Tionontati told me that after the founding of the Confederation of the Yam-Ko-Desh, it continued to grow, both in area and population. Over time, we spread south into the land your French call "Ohio." We met a talented group of hunters, farmers, and fishermen. They were master craftsmen and long-distance traders famous for their polished siltstone platform pipes and animal figures. Our traders were dazzled by the many items these people made from copper, obsidian, mica, and exotic shells. Our leaders marveled at the tall, well-built burial mounds, some as high as seventy feet. Those strangers embraced lavishing the dead with gifts for their journey into the afterlife. When our leaders brought back these ideas, we adopted them into our culture.
>
> We started building mounds, but we created them on existing hills and ridges. The whole community would participate in the construction, and the burial mounds would be used by all—not just village leaders. The Confederation lasted for countless generations. During that time, we built hundreds of villages and burial mound centers. But Tionontati told me nothing about these chambered mounds!

The evening before they were ready to move on, Pierre made one final appeal. "Nokee, I understand your hesitation about disturbing the site, and I respect that. However, Henri and I feel the chambered mound is the missing link to this story. It was the last mound built before they abandoned the site. That mound holds secrets that might help us understand what happened. If I can take a torch and look inside, I promise not to touch anything."

Morningstar persuaded Nokee to consider that this information might help explain why the era of the mound builders had ended. Nokee reluctantly conceded and allowed Pierre to take a quick look—but not before warning, "Remember what I told you about the curse of the grave guardians. Don't touch or disturb anything!"

Pierre fashioned a tightly wound grass torch and smeared it with bear grease. As he approached the chambered mound, the sun dipped below the trees. The tomb was pitch black. He rattled a long stick inside the opening, wanting to make sure no animals—or ghosts—were lurking within. All the dire warnings from Nokee had put his nerves on edge.

Pierre inhaled, lit the torch, and peered inside. The flame pushed back the darkness, revealing three or four log-lined beds containing skeletal remains. The bodies appeared to be adults in various stages of decay, suggesting they had been buried at different times. Clay pots, pipes, and tools were arranged throughout the chamber. Some of the crafted items glowed in the torchlight, their copper or silver surfaces catching the flickering of the flames. As Pierre withdrew his torch from the tomb, he noticed a pile of sharp stones—likely spear points—near the entrance. He instinctively reached to pick one up, but as he did, a gust of wind blew out his torch. Pierre pulled his hand back, a chill creeping up his spine as he remembered Nokee's warning. Pierre slowly walked away, locking what he saw into memory.

When Pierre got back to camp, Nokee insisted Pierre tell him precisely what he saw. Pierre happily obliged, impressing everyone with his photographic memory. As Pierre mentioned the pile of spear points, Nokee stopped him. "Where were those spear points you saw?"

"They were just inside the door," Pierre replied. "I almost brought you one, but I decided not to."

"This is what I feared. Fifteen years ago, while fleeing the Chippewa, I dreamt about something lurking inside one of those chamber mounds. In the dream, I saw what you just described, along with six spear points lying next to the door. Think, Pierre, how many points did you see?"

Pierre thought for a moment. "I count six."

"What did they look like?"

Pierre fumbled in his pack and brought out a deck of cards. He shuffled the deck and flipped over the top card—it was an ace of spades. Nokee cringed when he looked at the symbol. "What stopped you from picking it up?"

"When I reached for one of the points, I pulled the torch back, and when I did, the wind blew it out. I was then reminded of your warning not to disturb anything, so I backed up and walked away."

"This is what I feared would happen—you may have just woken the Dark Forces. The grave guardians that watch over the mounds may have just put the death curse on us all. We must take corrective action."

Nokee told Morningstar and Henri to look away. "You mustn't see what I'm about to give Pierre." Morningstar immediately turned away. Henri followed suit—though not before flashing a grin at Pierre.

Nokee reached into his shoulder bag and pulled out the medicine pouch. He brought out the point he had found under the large stone obelisk fifteen years ago. "This is what you saw?"

"Exactly," Pierre replied.

"Medicine bag items, seen by another, no longer provide protective power for their owner," Nokee said. "But if you accept it as yours, that power transfers to you. You must now take this to the open tomb and toss it in. Hopefully, the Dark Forces will accept it. That may break the death curse they've placed upon you."

Pierre put the point in his pocket and began to say, as a Christian, he did not believe in this superstition, but Henri spoke up first. "We respect and honor your ancestors. Pierre most certainly will follow your instructions." Henri leaned over to Pierre and whispered, "Syncretism."

Pierre returned to the gravesite alone. The sky was clear and the moon full. It was easy to maneuver through the night. When he reached the open grave, he pulled the point out of his pocket and prepared to toss it in. Its waxy, chalky surface glinted in the moonlight in the palm of his hand. It was a fine piece of craftsmanship. *This point will make a fine souvenir of our trip*, Pierre thought. He slid it back into his pocket. As he turned away, a lone wolf howled in the distance. He felt a cold touch on the back of his neck but dismissed it as the chill of the evening air.

• • •

The following morning, the group returned to Pine Lake and headed south on the Marsh Trail. After a few miles of hiking, they reached what had once been the Ottawa village of Okemos on the

Red Cedar River. Like the Pine Lake settlement, there was not a soul to be found. The Ottawa, being middle-men traders, had figured out that the center of the Michigan Peninsula was predominantly uninhabited. Tribes crisscrossed the area on well-trodden trails, but all the permanent villages were located on the flooded river mouths along the Great Lakes. Trading occurred in a north and south direction along the Great Lakes, not east and west across the peninsula.

Pierre turned to Henri. "So much for catching a canoe ride to the Soo. We walk from here, I suppose."

"Not so fast," Morningstar shouted, exiting one of the abandoned lodges. "Look what I've found."

When the three men went over to where Morningstar was standing, they saw she had found a *cannot*, an eighteen-foot, six-person canoe that the Ottawa had left behind. Henri and Pierre remarked that it looked terrible and was in complete disrepair.

"No," Morningstar said, "you're mistaken. The split cedar framing is in excellent condition. Look at the sturdy end pieces, the floor planking, and the well-spaced ribbing. Even the thwart spreaders, double-laced gunwales, and cedar seats are solid. We've found a fantastic canoe. All it needs is a new strip of *wigwaas*—white birch—around the bottom. The top half of this canoe is in great shape. With your help, we can have this on the water in a week."

Henri and Pierre exchanged glances with Nokee. "Do you know how to rebuild a canoe?" Nokee shook his head.

"I do!" Morningstar said cheerfully. "In the Chippewa camp where I grew up, the men provided the materials, and the women built the canoes. If you bring me what I need, I can do this."

"Riding in a canoe beats walking any day in my book," Pierre said. "How do we start?"

"The first thing we need is a long, wide piece of birch bark, preferably in one section. With that, we can stitch one long seam on both sides. On the Marsh Trail this morning, I noticed a huge white birch mostly cut down by a beaver. With Pierre's axe, we could finish the job quickly. With a tree that size, we should be able to create a perfect outer bottom wrap. July is late for harvesting birch bark because the sap flow has slowed. ... However, if you drop it in the shallow water, the wet, soft bark should come off in one piece."

She turned to Nokee and said, "I need you to shoot a young buck while we are gone. We'll need a good deal of animal fat to make the sealant. Remember—a buck, not a doe! The season of fawning and milk-producing has drained the doe's fat reserves. We can enjoy the meat as we make the necessary repairs this week. The three of us will cut down that tree and try to get a continuous piece of bark for the bottom of this canoe."

Pierre's axe quickly brought down the tree the following morning. It fell into the shallow water as planned, and the upper branches kept the trunk suspended off the bottom, making their work easier. Pierre used his ax to make a circular cut in the bark around the top and bottom of an eighteen-foot section. Then, he cut a straight line down the center of the log.

Morningstar looked pleased with the work so far. "We'll let the tree lay in the warm backwater for a day. The bark will accept water and soften. Now, the real work begins."

Pierre, already sweating profusely, looked dejected. "You must be kidding. What could be harder than this?"

"Now, we go into the swamp and find the black-spruce roots," she said, smiling. "We'll spend the rest of the day pulling roots to make the stitching. We'll need a lot of it."

When they returned to camp, Nokee had a young buck skinned and cut up. The smell of smoked jerky filled the air, and fresh meat strips hung ready for cooking. He also had a large bowl of deer fat sitting in the shade.

"How was your day?" Nokee asked with a smirk. "I had this buck down and skinned an hour after you left. I have been sitting by the river enjoying a good smoke ever since."

"Well, that's just great!" snapped Morningstar. "Because you'll be up most of the night stripping these roots in half as soon as we soften them in hot water. Your job from now on is to oversee the production of the stitching material." Henri and Pierre turned away so Nokee couldn't see them giggle.

Nokee sat there, feeling a little miffed, but after a good meal,

171

he came around. Despite what Morningstar had said earlier, they all worked as a team that night. They stripped the outer skin off the roots, then spit them down the center using a knife, creating long strips.

On day two, all four were back at the fallen birch tree. Nokee used his small copper celt for woodworking, and Pierre had his axe. With those simple tools and an extra set of hands, they peeled the bark off in one continuous piece. They had the bark rolled up and back at camp by midday.

At sunrise on the third day, Morningstar announced she was going into the woods to collect spruce pitch and asked if anyone wanted to go along. Nokee informed her that the three men would stay in camp to fish for brook trout. Morningstar gave him a nasty look as she stomped off.

Nokee yelled to her as she was about to disappear into the forest. "Besides, I need to stay here and oversee the soaking of the stitching material." She turned and snarled something inaudible. He suddenly felt childish for having made such a snide remark.

Morningstar moved slowly from tree to tree, collecting tiny amounts of resin with her knife. It was a beautiful day, and the work was pleasant. A little time to herself turned out to be exactly what she needed. When she returned to camp that afternoon with her basket full of spruce pitch, she smiled at the fine batch of fresh trout. The atmosphere around the fire was relaxed and carefree that night.

Day four was more relaxed than the previous ones as they finished turning the remainder of the deer meat into jerky. Morningstar told everyone to enjoy the downtime—tomorrow would be busy, and everyone's help would be needed.

The morning of the fifth day was hot and humid, the air still heavy from the previous night's rain. Working around a fire wouldn't be pleasant, but they would have to do just that for the rest of the day. Morningstar had already removed the damaged bottom half of the canoe. The four of them stretched the new strip of bark over the bottom and slowly flipped the canoe right-side up.

With her knife, Morningstar carefully cut the excess bark off both sides of the new strip, leaving a half-inch overlap with the top section. They removed the stitching strips from the river and placed them into the cauldron of hot water. Working in pairs, Henri held the bark tight as Nokee used his awl and drilled small holes through the overlapping bark. Each hole had to be spaced a half inch apart along both sides. Pierre worked the inside as Morningstar threaded stitching into the holes from the outside. Back and forth went the spruce-root stitch, forming a tightly bonded seam. When both sides were bonded, they stopped for something to eat.

Afterward, Morningstar slowly melted the spruce pitch over the coals in one of the trade kettles. Spruce pitch is highly flammable and will catch fire if heated too quickly. When all the resin had melted, Morningstar strained the liquid through a piece of grass mat into a second trade kettle. She put the kettle on the coals and started adding deer fat. She would mix in a little, then check the mixer with a dried cattail leaf. If the cattail leaf cracked when she flexed it, the mixer was not pliable enough, and more fat was required. When the mixer was at the correct consistency, she added a small handful of wood ash to give the sealant a rich, dark color.

With a split piece of cedar, she applied the sealant to the canoe stitching. As the sticky material started to cool, she told the men to press the coating with their fingers, ensuring it filled in tightly around the holes. They placed the sealant kettle back in the coals and took a break. When the side stitching had hardened, they carefully turned the canoe over and applied sealant anywhere there were knotholes or cracks. When finished, they stood back, examining their work. The three men congratulated Morningstar on what she had accomplished. Morningstar blushed modestly, but inside, she was beaming with pride.

"Tomorrow," Morningstar said, "we assess our craft on the river, and if all goes as planned, on day seven, we glide across the water."

# Facing the Enemy Within

The canoe proved to be flawless. It was sturdy, had no leaks, and slid effortlessly across the water. They spent the day packing the refurbished Ottawa canoe and polishing the fire-blackened cauldron in the river using sand. They reloaded the cornmeal and confit pot back into the used copper cauldron and shoved off.

On day seven, just as Morningstar had predicted, they floated down the Red Cedar and turned upstream on the Grand River. After forty miles of river travel, they reached the upper rapids and set up camp. Before darkness fell, they visited the nearby mound site. Henri noted that there were no chamber mounds present—only traditional ones. The visit only intensified his desire for answers: why were chamber mounds present at some locations and not others?

After three more days of paddling, they portaged into the Upper St. Joseph River and spent their last night camped on a bluff. On July 10, they arrived at the Miami camp at Three Rivers. Chief Myamick was ecstatic to see Nokee and welcomed his traveling partners. Myamick had heard about the trouble that had taken place while the Miami trading team was in Detroit and was desperate to know if those Tutelo men were still causing Nokee problems. Nokee explained that everything was fine, and that it was through the Tutelo that he met Morningstar and the two Black Robes. Chief Myamick requested no more details, much to the relief of the new arrivals. Some things are best left unsaid.

Henri and Pierre gave the copper cauldron and confit pot to Chief Myamick, and surprisingly, Morningstar gifted him one of her muskets. The chief was pleased with the gifts and provided them with comfortable lodging.

Before Nokee could escape to his quarters, Myamick stopped him. "Is the Chippewa woman your wife, and will you stay with us for a while?" All five of the chief's daughters leaned forward to hear the answer to the first question.

"No, she's not, and our destination is the rapids at the Soo. However, I would be happy to spend a little time with the people who've done so much for me."

"You're welcome to come and go as you please, but I insist you stay at least through the Festival of the Green Corn. You know it's a special time for our unmarried men."

The festival of the Green Corn always begins on the first full moon after the corn ripens, usually around mid-August. The festival celebrates the season of plenty and thanksgiving. It's a time for celebration, dancing, and feasting. It's also a time for forgiveness, spiritual renewal, purification, rekindling relationships, and healing. Henri pleaded with his fellow travelers to stay so he could journal the event. Pierre and Morningstar readily agreed; both were weary from the unrelenting work and travel. Nokee's mind told him they should keep moving, but Morningstar appealed to his heart, convincing him to stay.

Everyone in the village was excited to have Nokee back. He had left so abruptly after his wife's death during childbirth. The chief assumed that Nokee would eventually marry one of his remaining daughters. The daughters now saw their chance to fuss and fawn over Nokee, hoping to capture his heart. Wherever Nokee went, at least one of the daughters would show up. They brought him food, blankets, and drinks.

"Morningstar, why don't you step in and say something?" Henri asked, watching one of the chief's daughters present Nokee with gifts.

She smiled and coolly stated, "Nokee must decide which path he wants to follow."

During their month-long stay, Henri made many entries in his journal that described the people of the Miami Nation. He wrote:

> The Miami live in well-maintained and neatly rowed dome-shaped wigwams. They grow extensive fields of corn, squash, sunflowers,

and beans. Their children are lavished with gifts and have little responsibility. They run freely with little supervision, spending their days playing with the dogs. They're attractive people. The women have long, well-kept hair, often adorned with flowers and beads. Their lean bodies support knee-length skirts and colorful leggings.

The men tattoo their muscular bodies with lines across their faces and cheeks and wear breechcloths of varying colors. They shave their heads except for a strip in the middle, where they often attach a red-dyed porcupine-hair roach worn as a headdress. During ceremonial celebrations, both sexes paint their faces red and put on full-length, colorful costumes that they proudly display.

Like the Tutelo, the Miami braves were exceptionally good with their bows and arrows and loved to bet on competitions. They've taken to Pierre with his magic tricks and cups and ball game for obvious reasons.

By mid-August, the moon was full, and it was time for the seven-day Ceremony of the Green Corn to begin. During the first three days, the married men offered prayers, performed dances, and undertook periods of fasting. The women set up the ceremonial dancing square. They established four fires on the outside edges of the area, each aligned with the four cardinal directions, and one communal cooking fire in the middle of the square. The women gathered the remainder of last year's corn, beans, and squash for consumption at the opening evening meal on the third day. Bear meat is a mandatory requirement at that meal. The Miami people have a unique custom. The first and last meals of the festival must include bear meat. However, they must acquire the meat in a certain way. When they locate a female bear den in the spring, they kill the mother and take her cubs. The cubs are raised and fattened for two years. Then, at the time of the Green Corn Festival, they're slaughtered and eaten.

The slaughtering of the bears was a solemn ceremony. Even still, it was something Nokee avoided. The death cry of a bear always caused him to have terrible nightmares—even watching others eat bear meat caused him to feel uneasy and was something he refrained from. When he lived with the Miami tribe, he always found an excuse to be elsewhere during the ceremony, going off to hunt for food or fight the Iroquois. Chief Myamick was not ignorant of the reasons behind Nokee's convenient absences and was accepting of it. He knew all too well of Nokee's troubled past. His daughter had told him of Nokee's frequent nightmares. The death of Nokee's wife and child had only worsened his ailment.

• • •

During the festival, unmarried men in the village were encouraged to undertake a dream quest to help them discover their purpose in life and begin thinking about marriage. Chief Myamick had convinced Nokee to join the group this year. He felt Nokee was at a pivotal point in his life. His confusion put him at risk of being possessed by a *wendigo*—spirits that pray on troubled minds. Once they enter your body, the victim refuses to eat and develops an insatiable hunger for human flesh. Nokee's refusal to eat bear meat led some to wonder if the evil spirit had taken hold of him.

On the fourth day of the festival, the dream quests began. The unmarried men headed for the sweat lodges. They fasted for two days and smoked kinnikinnick to start the purification process. On their sixth day, they ate and drank a sacred mixture of psychedelic mushrooms, moonflowers, poppies, and morning glory seeds to induce hallucinations. Then, each participant set off on their own. Some went to a sacred site chosen by the elders, while others sought out places that held special personal significance.

Nokee already knew the place he must go. He headed north up the Rocky River, then west until he reached the Kalamazoo moraine. It was on top of that moraine that his world had turned upside down fifteen years ago. This was the only place where a correction could take place. Nokee arrived in the dark, exhausted and hungry. He laid down on his back and looked up at the countless stars. In a matter of minutes, he was fast asleep.

He dreamt he was in a cave, sitting by a fire with an ancient shaman wrapped in a blanket. A pot of stew bubbled over the fire. Nokee stared at the food with an insatiable hunger. It was in a cauldron, like the ones that Henri and Pierre had given to the Chippewa and Miami chiefs.

"I'm here to assist you on your quest," the old man said. "But first, you should eat. I know how hungry you are. One taste of this stew and everything you desire will be possible." Nokee looked at the boiling mixture. As each bubble popped into the air, Nokee thought he could hear the mournful sound made by a dying bear.

"What type of meat is in that stew?"

"It is bear meat," the shaman replied.

"No! No, thank you. I don't eat bear meat."

"But this isn't just any meat. It fills your greatest needs!"

"I already have what I need," Nokee replied.

"Ah, you think you do, but you are at a pivotal point. Three paths lie before you. Which one will you choose?"

Suddenly, three longhouses appeared before Nokee, preventing him from exiting the cave. "Whichever one you choose to pass through will be where you'll remain for the rest of your days. There's no going back. Come, look inside, and see what each has to offer."

Nokee peered into the first lodge and saw nothing but blackness. Then, the great bear he had slain when he was fourteen appeared. It was lying on the ground, crying out in pain.

Nokee heard the shaman's voice carry on the wind like a whisper. "You see. Lodge number one is your past. You think you hear the torturous whine of a dying bear. But what you're hearing are the death cries of your people. You saw your friends paddling away on the Great Lake as you sank deeper into the water. However, you know it was not you that sank. It was them. They're gone, and you'll never see them again. And what about how the rest of your tribe left you? You heard they live on the other side of the Big Lake. But your mind says that isn't true.

"I know they met an Iroquois raiding party in the land of the Illini," the old shaman continued. "What chance do you think your battered warriors, with their women and children, had against an army of a thousand Iroquois? Deep down, you know they've passed into the spirit world. You can join them now. Here, taste the stew and pass through the first lodge. You will never be bothered by these thoughts again. You can live the free life of a ranger. No one will tie you down. You'll have no worries, no cares. Everything will revolve around you. Just one bite of stew, and it's all yours! What do you say?"

"No," Nokee growled. "Those are just evil thoughts. You have no proof. My heart says they are alive."

"Well then, what about lodge two?"

When Nokee looked into the second lodge, Chief Myamick and his daughters appeared before him. "You know how much Chief Myamick loves you," the shaman whispered. "He wants you to stay and live as a Miami. You're a war hero in the eyes of everyone in the tribe. You see how his daughters adore you ... you could have any of them for your wife. They are all stunning, don't you agree? One bite of the stew, and that path is open to you."

"No," Nokee replied. "I had that life, and I was never happy."

"Oh, you stubborn, foolish man! The future is hard to predict. The thoughts and dreams you see there are like the wind. They blow one way and then change directions. There's no way to know how things will end. Are you willing to give up all I've offered for an uncertain future with those Frenchmen? Remember that it was a Frenchman that killed your father! And what about that Chippewa woman? How can you trust her? She might be trying to lure you away from the Miami, to have you captured and killed by the Chippewa."

"That is ridiculous! She was the one that helped me get away from Chief Twakanha just a few weeks ago."

"So, you think! I was there in the shadows when she talked to Chief Twakanha. She plans to get you to follow her north to meet the Ottawa at their trading camp. She has probably already arranged with Chief Twakanha to deliver you when the Potawatomi, Ottawa, and Chippewa rendezvous at their fall trading session. It would be quite a victory for Chief Twakanha to finish the job he started so many years ago. You still have time to rethink your other paths. The past and present are easy to deliver—I can guarantee the results!"

Nokee's head swam in a storm of emotions. How did this shaman know so much? What he said made sense—but is this all a trick? Nokee stared into the third lodge. Suddenly, a vision appeared in the dark interior. Tionontati was gesturing for Nokee to follow him.

Tionontati spoke softly. "Gitchee Manito, the Great Spirit of the Midewiwin Order, came to me. He told me you must undertake a great journey before being accepted as chief of our tribe. You're to travel the Great Circle, visit the sacred places, listen to the guiding voices of the spirits, and find your way back to your people. You'll receive help from unexpected people and places along the way. Trust your heart. When you finally return to your people, you'll be recognized, and there'll be immense joy."

The darkness peeled away, revealing Nokee's mother standing next to Tionontati. She extended her arms, and a young boy named Illiniwek ran up to her. While they embraced, a second woman entered the vision. She had her back to Nokee, but he could see she was younger. As the scene began to fade, she turned toward Nokee and smiled. It was Morningstar.

Sensing the shaman behind him, Nokee spun around. "I know my chosen path. I will walk into the future. Tionontati has shown me the way. I must complete my journey around the Big Lake. I'll go there and look for my people. I know they are alive. I've done the things that the Great Spirit requested. I've been to the sacred places and listened to their guiding voices. Now, it's time to fulfill my birthright. Help has come from unexpected people—the Black Robes, Morningstar, the Tutelo. I must trust my heart. Morningstar is the one I want to be with."

"Indeed," the shaman said, "but be aware. You may have seen your journey end, but there will always be unseen pitfalls. Consider yourself warned. Now, sit down and eat with me. Like you, I have an insatiable hunger and can't eat alone."

"Sorry, but I told you I don't eat bear meat. I must be on my way."

Nokee got up from the fire and suddenly felt an unseasonable chill and smelled a foul stench in the air. The cauldron began to shake and glow. As the light increased, Nokee could see the pot didn't contain bear meat. Human body parts lazily floated around inside. At that moment, the shaman's body transformed into an emaciated headless form. Nokee recognized it immediately: it was Antoine. His ash-gray body smelled of decaying flesh, and strips of decomposing skin hung from his bones. A horned wolf's head grew from the flesh of his neck. It was a wendigo, a cannibal, craver of human flesh.

Wendigo spirits possess victims who live lives of gluttony, greed, and excess. People that are never satisfied. Those that hurt, rape, kill, and consume everything they encounter are prime targets. The trapper Antoine was a perfect host. The first thing a wendigo desires is to seek out the one they most despise, and for Antoine, that was Nokee. If Antoine could get Nokee to eat the human stew, Nokee would also become a wendigo, and Antoine would then turn his revenge on Henri and Morningstar.

In a flash, the wendigo slashed at him with his razor-sharp claws. Nokee ducked and drew his knife—he saw a beating heart through the open arrow hole in its chest. The creature seemed to radiate cold. Nokee roared, slashing open its chest and ripping out its frozen heart. His hands burned as he tossed the pulsating organ into the fire. The rotting body collapsed, and the wendigo spirit sank back into the underworld. Nokee ran through the entryway of the third lodge as it began to fade away. On the other side, he was greeted by darkness. His knees gave out and he collapsed, falling backward into unconsciousness.

When he came to, dawn was breaking. Nokee shook his head, unsure of what had just happened. It had felt so real—could it really have been a dream? Nokee decided it didn't matter. He now knew what he had to do. He backtracked down the moraine and headed for the sweat lodge where all the young men were regrouping. Everyone was bathing, applying body paints, and dressing in their finest dancing outfits for the Dance of the Green Corn.

After cleaning up, Nokee went to the preparation lodge to get dressed. When he emerged, he wore only a loincloth. He applied red paint to his entire body except for the black circles around his eyes and mouth. He shaved his head except for a strip in the middle, which stood straight up with the aid of red-dyed bear grease. He held a shield in his left hand and a spear in his right. He tucked a stone war club into his belt, and the copper crescent-moon that once belonged to his father hung across his chest.

As the men paraded into the village, all eyes were on the towering stranger. The five sisters almost fainted. Morningstar stood tall as she marveled at the transformation. Chief Myamick appeared stunned as he ran up to Nokee. "Mahtowa, you have returned from the grave!"

"No, I'm Nokee, son of Mahtowa, son of Manomin—peace chief of the Mascouten and Sauk tribes. Last night, I fought the wendigo and cut out his heart. But before his death, he showed me my destiny. I now know my path. I'm ready to return to my people."

Nokee turned to Morningstar. "Last night, I saw Tionontati in my dream. He called for me to make the journey around the Big Lake. My people are waiting there for me. I want you to go with me."

"Nokee, you know I have already agreed to do that," Morningstar said.

"No, you don't understand. I want you to go as my wife—if you will have me!" Nokee said, gazing deeply into her eyes.

Morningstar threw her arms around Nokee. "Yes."

The crowd let out a great cheer. "A double celebration tonight. The spirits have spoken!" announced Chief Myamick.

The five sisters recovered quickly from what had just happened. They grabbed Morningstar and said: "Come with us," as they pulled her away, "we need to get you ready for your wedding!"

Henri sat down and recorded the Celebration of the Green Corn in his journal:

> The village shaman began the ceremony as the full moon rose. The villagers placed bowls of corn, beans, squash, and sunflowers around the ceremonial fire. The heart of the second sacrificed bear hung over the flames. The shaman began the purification and renewal process with cleansing songs, and the villagers quickly joined in. A female leader began the Stomp Dance. She moved in a counterclockwise motion. She shuffled and stomped with rattles and shells tied to her leggings as she called out short verses of thanksgiving and prayers.
>
> A male leader followed her with a turtle-shell rattle, calling out the appropriate responses. Then, village members join the line dance in a female-male-female-male procession. Children were encouraged to join in. Each time they completed a full circle, the female leader changed to a new chant. The male leader answered with a new response. After four times around, they took a short break, then started up again with another caller and response partner. Over the next hour, they cycled through four sets of callers. The Stomp Dance ended, and the wedding ceremony and great feast began.

• • •

The five sisters had been busy getting Morningstar ready. She wore a white doeskin knee-length skirt, doeskin moccasins, a shell-bead necklace, and a freshwater pearl headband. She looked beautiful. Nokee stood tall and proud, handsomely dressed in a long turkey feather robe. Both held a single eagle feather in their left hand, symbolizing strength.

Chief Myamick began the wedding ceremony by presenting an elm-wood bucket of water. He asked Morningstar to give Nokee her eagle feather. She washed her hands in the bucket and said, "I wash away the past loves I've known, and I'm now committed only to the one that stands before me." She did so with a joyful heart.

Nokee handed Morningstar the two eagle feathers, symbolizing their new union, and repeated the same hand washing and vow. The chief directed the couple to sit on their buffalo wedding blanket in front of the central fire. Hunting and skinning buffalo requires the effort of the entire village, and all married couples receive a buffalo wedding blanket as a show of support from the entire community. Then, Chief Myamick lit a small two-handled clay incense pot filled with cedar shavings and dried spices. The two handles symbolize two coming together as one.

As the smoke drifted upward, carrying their marital intentions to the heavens, Chief Myamick said in a strong, clear voice:

*Together, you shall feel no rain, for you'll be shelter for each other.*

*You shall feel no cold, for together, you'll be each other's warmth.*

*You shall feel no loneliness, for together, you'll be companionship for each other.*

When Myamick finished, the village shaman brought out four bowls. He gave two bowls of cornbread to Morningstar and two bowls of stew to Nokee. He instructed Morningstar to give Nokee a bowl of cornbread and repeat the words: "With this bowl, I promise I'll prepare and cook the meals for you and our family."

Then the shaman asked Nokee to hand Morningstar one bowl of stew and repeat the words: "With this bowl, I promise to provide you and our family with fresh meat, so the bowl will never be empty." Nokee's eyes never left hers as he repeated the phrase.

"Now eat what you've shared, and your union will be complete."

A hush fell over the crowd. Everyone knew the stew contained bear meat from the second ceremonial bear. Nokee took a bite of the cornbread, smiled at Morningstar, and swallowed a spoonful of stew. The crowd cheered. At that moment, Morningstar knew the nightmares were over, and though the future was uncertain, Nokee had overcome his troubled past. She placed her silver beaver necklace around Nokee's neck, and Nokee placed his father's silver bear necklace around hers.

Chief Myamick ended the marriage ceremony with these words: "Go now and seal your wedding vow. If you both return to this village happy in four days, I'll declare your marriage official and bless your days upon Mother Earth to be good and long. Now let the feast and celebration begin!"

After a fine late-night dinner, the villagers filled the newlyweds' Ottawa canoe with gifts and food for their four-day retreat. Henri and Pierre gave them a four-cup French kettle with a spun brass body, hand-rolled copper lugs and hand-rolled rivets. Morningstar was thrilled with all the gifts they'd received. She thanked everyone, and then, with tears streaming down her face, she turned to Henri and Pierre and hugged both.

As Morningstar and Nokee paddled away, Henri and Pierre smiled at each other, thanking the Lord for allowing them to be instruments of peace and comfort and asking Him to bless this new union with years of happiness.

It was late when the newlyweds left the village. They traveled a short distance downstream and camped on a hill overlooking the mouth of the Rocky River. Finally, with a full moon above and a buffalo robe beneath them, they spent their first night truly together. Morningstar had no idea what Nokee was planning or where he was taking her. But honestly, she didn't care. Her first two marriages weren't of her choosing and were short-lived. This one was a dream come true, and she was in love.

In the morning, they enjoyed a leisurely breakfast as the sun rose. Then, Nokee laid out his plan. "There's a place I need to show you. You must understand my past. From there, we can plan our future together."

After two days of much needed relaxation, they hid their canoe and belongings in the woods. Then, with their buffalo blanket and two leather supply bags, they hiked the Grand Rapids Trail north until they reached the St. Joseph Trail.

Nokee looked to the setting sun, then pointed to the top of the

Kalamazoo moraine. "This is where it all started. That's where my father died—where I became chief. If there's one place where the spirits will offer us guidance, it will be on top of that hill. That's where we will spend our third night."

Sitting on top of the moraine, Nokee took Morningstar through the events of that infamous day so many years ago. How his father planned their defense. Where the Sauk spearmen hid and the Mascouten archers knelt. His eyes lit up as he explained how his father had drawn the Ottawa into the trap and defeated their enemy. Then he told Morningstar how he had disobeyed his father's orders, resulting in his father's death and the capture of him and six Mascouten youths. After he finished the story, Nokee and Morningstar sat there for a long time. Neither said a word.

Then Morningstar broke the silence. "I have something that I must share. The night you and your young braves showed up in our fishing camp, I cheered the capture of our blood enemy. I looked forward to the killing of those seven men. I reveled at the news that the Mascouten and Sauk were gone. I couldn't wait to see the head of the Mascouten peace chief on a post and for the ravens to feast on his eyes. That head was yours. Now, I sit here ashamed. I should've told you this before."

Nokee put his arm around Morningstar. "We were young, and we knew nothing about the suffering and evil of war. We have both been through so much since then. We did not meet by chance—the great spirits had a plan for us. Think about it: a Mascouten peace chief representing the past, a Chippewa princess representing the present, and two French Black Robes representing the future. We are destined to be a delegation of peace for the Great Lakes tribes."

"That sounds incredible, but how do we make it happen?" Morningstar asked.

"I know the Miami will leave on a trading mission on the next full moon. Their trade canoes head downstream to the mouth of the St. Joseph River to join the Potawatomi. There, they travel up the shoreline of Lake Michigan to trade with the Ottawa. We can travel with them as a delegation of peace."

Morningstar nodded in agreement. "I know the Ottawa traders go north from there to the rendezvous at Michilimackinac.

Our Ojibwa brothers from the Upper Peninsula come down to meet them. We can then cross over to the other side with the Ottawa and continue north with the Black Robes to their trading post at Sault Ste. Marie."

"Now we have a plan," Nokee said. "Now, let us get some sleep and see if Chief Myamick will go along with it."

In the middle of the night, Morningstar suddenly jolted awake.

"What is wrong?" Nokee asked, only half awake.

"I just had a dream. You were there with an older woman and a white-haired shaman. The woman extended her arms as a young boy ran to her. While they embraced, a second woman entered. As my dream faded, the second woman turned toward you and smiled. I was that woman, and the boy was our son!"

Nokee smiled. "I had that same dream the night I fought the wendigo. The boy's name is Illiniwek, the shaman is Tionontati, and the older woman is my mother. The Great Spirits have spoken and blessed our plan. Let us pack up and head back to Three Rivers. We don't want Chief Myamick to think we have reconsidered our wedding vows." With a deep sense of purpose, they joyfully started packing for the return trip.

Chief Myamick was pleased when he saw them returning. He declared their marriage official and blessed their days to be good and long. He was thrilled with the peace delegation plan joining together the past, present, and future. Myamick knew the world that had existed was changing. His people would have to adapt or perish. He decided he would travel with the trading party to the Potawatomi camp and vowed to do everything he could to get this peace alliance off to a good start. But Myamick knew one person would not be thrilled with the idea. That person was Chief Twakanha of the Saginaw Chippewa.

# Peace Delegation

Henri and Pierre were ecstatic about the plan. Being part of a peace delegation to unite the tribes was a dream come true. Henri whispered to Pierre, "Once again, the Lord has provided a way forward, without a single musket shot fired."

Pierre grinned. "Henri, I should never have doubted you!"

As the corn moon waned, the Miami trading team and peace delegation set off downriver, heading to the Potawatomi camp at the mouth of the St. Joseph River. Chief Myamick had become good friends with Winamac, the Potawatomi chief, after the two tribes had allied against the invading Iroquois. Chief Winamac knew the Miami people were mostly land travelers. Their canoes were dugout trees, adequate for river transportation but poorly designed for voyages on the Great Lakes. So, early in their friendship, Chief Winamac offered his Great Lakes canoes to help the Miami tribe transport their trade items north to the Ottawa camp. The Ottawa had become the middlemen in the trade market between the tribes of the Upper and Lower Peninsulas. All the villages in southern Michigan knew that the Ottawa camp at the mouth of the Pine River, located along Lake Michigan's shoreline, was where the best deals were made.

As the convoy moved along, Henri took note of the trade items the Miami traders had brought. There were baskets of corn, dried nuts, roots, berries, and jerky meats. Decoratively designed clay pots filled with sunflower seeds, strings of freshwater pearls, brightly colored stone-carved effigies, and bundles of buffalo blankets and robes filled the lot.

Henri turned to Pierre. "Don't the various tribes already have many of these things?"

"I suppose so," Pierre said. "But it's also about the exchange of ideas and technology. Who knows, maybe we will see something out there that's new, even to us. I can't wait to see what the other tribes offer."

In two days, the convoy arrived at Chief Winamac's camp on the river mouth. An extensive palisade of tightly bound logs fortified the village. The front gates were open, and Henri and Pierre peered in to see lines of dome-shaped wigwams covered with bark and cattail mats. The Potawatomi people seemed very friendly, waving at the canoes as they slid onto the shore. Everyone was busy at work. Pierre pointed out a group of men setting fish nets at the mouth of the river. But Henri was more interested in the women and children tending the massive fields of corn, squash, and sunflowers.

Henri sat in the shade and watched all the activities as the formal greetings and pipe smoking took place. He noted in his journal:

> The Potawatomi, like the Miami, wear more clothing than most of the tribes we have encountered. The men dress in leather shirts, waist belts, and multicolored breechcloths. Most have added leggings and moccasins to their outfits. The women wear leather skirts tastefully decorated with paint and porcupine quills. Both sexes tie feathers in their long black hair. I have seen ear spools and nose rings in both men and women, but the women also like to paint their faces red.

• • •

It was now time to introduce the peace delegation to Chief Winamac and his council. "Standing before you are the voices of the past, present, and future," Chief Myamick said in a loud voice. "Listen to their counsel.

"First, I present Nokee, a Mascouten-Sauk peace chief. He is a reminder of our brutal past. For years, the Chippewa, Ottawa, and Potawatomi fought to destroy the last remnants of the mound builders. At the same time, the Miami people fought to defend them. I wish the fearless Sauk warriors were here today to fight the Iroquois. How often, my friends, have you wished for more warriors during battles?

"But there's hope. Nokee is on his way to the other side of the Big Lake, where his people have settled. The bond between his four ancestral tribes is still strong. If Nokee can convince them to join the Illinois in our fight against the Iroquois, we would get much-needed help from those western allies.

"Next, I present Morningstar, a Chippewa princess. She represents our current situation. Her father, Chief Twakanha, is now old and has grown tired of sending warriors to die in battles with an enemy that he thinks is far away. He fails to see that if the Neutrals, Miami, and Potawatomi fall, the Chippewa and Ottawa villages are next in line to suffer the Iroquois raids.

"But there's hope. Jibewas is Chief Twakanha's war chief. He is also Twakanha's son and a brother of Morningstar. If Morningstar can get Jibewas to bring Twakanha to the Ottawa camp, we can try to rekindle the Alliance of the Three Fires. That alliance would produce thousands of new warriors to battle the Iroquois.

"Finally, I present the future, the Black Robes. The French signed a treaty with the Iroquois, but it only applied to the Christian tribes. Yet there's hope. The Black Robes are here to teach us about their Christian God. They tell us, if we become Christians, we have the protection of their God and the protection of the French soldiers."

After a pause, Chief Winamac said, "After our evening meal together, I will hear what the peace delegation has to say, and then I will decide."

Henri, Pierre, Nokee, and Morningstar nodded at Chief Winamac as they backed away. They needed to hold a private council to process what Chief Myamick had just laid out.

Nokee spoke first. "Myamick has promised that I'll try to unite the four tribes of my ancestors. I'm to convince them to take up arms against the Iroquois. How is that possible if I don't know where my people are, much less if they will recognize me as their leader? Even if they do, how will I convince the other tribes to follow me?"

Then Morningstar spoke softly, tears in her eyes: "Chief Myamick wants my brother and me to convince our father to join this new peace movement. You saw how suspicious Chief Twakanha was of Nokee. Wait until he hears that the peace delegation contains a Mascouten-Sauk peace chief named Nokee. His rage will be immeasurable."

Pierre looked on with a troubled expression. "What am I supposed to do at the dinner tonight? My musketoon is gone. Even if I had it, it seems silly to tell them that if they get baptized and wear the metal cross, our soldiers will come to protect them. As far as I can determine, we're in an uncharted area, and I doubt soldiers will be coming this way for quite some time. What have we gotten ourselves into?"

Henri—the last to speak—cleared his throat and stepped forward. "My brothers and sister of this unorthodox peace movement. Pierre and I didn't know this place existed a year ago. You two were blood enemies—and now you are married. There's no logical reason we're in this situation ... except one. God wanted this to happen. He has a plan and a guiding hand that steers us through this difficult journey. Trust in God, and he'll show us the way!"

Pierre couldn't help but smile. "Henri, you have such strong and unbending faith. You have been right all along the way. However, I hope God sends us a sign before I present our idea tonight to five hundred skeptical Potawatomi."

Just as Pierre finished speaking, there was a big commotion at the mouth of the river. When the peace delegation peered out of the wooded area where they had taken private counsel, they saw three voyageur canoes pulling into shore. Each canoe contained two coureurs des bois and six Indigenous paddlers.

"Those fur traders are traveling with Ottawa from the north," Morningstar whispered.

In the lead canoe stood a tall Frenchman. His right hand held up a long peace pipe, his left, a musket. As the tall, striking figure stepped ashore, he called out, "As I promised last year, Nicolas Perrot, the gun trader, has returned!"

By the time the peace delegation approached, Perrot's men had already come ashore and arranged an impressive display of over one hundred firearms. Henri and Pierre jolted to a halt, dumbfounded. As Perrot offered ten guns to Chief Winamac for his pile of furs, Henri lost his temper and began yelling at Nicolas Perrot, using words that would have made his superiors in Paris blush. Pierre grabbed Henri to prevent him from hitting Perrot over the head with his peace rifle.

"Calm down, Henri," Pierre said. "Everyone is watching. We're here to represent a peace delegation, for God's sake! Let's hear him out and find out who sent him."

Nicolas Perrot was taken aback by Henri's reaction. Contrary to Henri's beliefs, Perrot felt his work overlapped closely with theirs, and he hoped to join the Black Robes in their peace effort.

When Henri settled down, Nicolas Perrot told the two Black Robes about his travels with Father Allouez throughout northern Wisconsin. He told them he had been with Father Allouez when the priest founded the St. Esprit Mission for the displaced Ottawa and Huron people on Chequamegon Bay, along the shore of Lake Superior. Perrot also claimed to have accompanied Allouez on a visit to a Siouan-speaking tribe, the Winnebago, at Lake Winnebago. He went on to explain how he became the guns-for-fur trader sanctioned by the French military. Starting in Green Bay the previous spring, he had traveled south around Lake Michigan, arming the western tribes along the way.

"The attacks on the Illinois tribes to the south have been increasing," Perrot said. "They'll need more guns to defend themselves. A strong defense is the only way to bring peace to that region."

Perrot noticed Nokee standing behind them. He leaned closer to Henri and Pierre. "Before I left Father Allouez, a band of roving Sauk and Fox warriors showed up at the mission in Chequamegon Bay. Both Father Allouez and I thought those two tribes would be difficult to convert. It will require significant effort to convince the Fox and Sauk to become part of your peace movement."

Unlike Henri, Pierre was thrilled that Nicolas Perrot knew the area around Green Bay. The peace delegation planned to visit that side of the Big Lake next spring, and Perrot's contacts with the western tribes could ensure a smooth introduction to the people there.

Henri wanted nothing to do with the gun trader. "We've made it this far without guns, and we've left no unnecessary deaths in our wake. You said so yourself."

"Yes, that's true—and I understand your concerns," Pierre said. "But what is the harm in talking to this man? You said that God always provides us with a way to get things done. Maybe meeting Nicolas Perrot is part of his plan." Henri performed the sign of the cross and begrudgingly agreed to the meeting.

Tension hung thick in the air when they sat down with Perrot. Henri stared cooly at the man across from him. Pierre tried to break the ice. "I would love you to join our peace mission, Perrot, but my partner has grave reservations."

Nicolas Perrot stood and extended his hand, but Henri refused to shake it. Nodding, Perrot sat back down and pulled his chair closer to Henri. "I understand your concerns about having a gun trafficker traveling with your peace delegation. But you need to know a few things about me that might change your mind. The Jesuits in France raised me. I benefited from learning their caring ways and their respect for human life.

"I have lived with the tribes on the western side of Lake Michigan for the past six years. I have seen the destruction the Iroquois are doing to the Illinois villages to the south. They'll not stop there. I pray for peace daily, but peace will not come until the Iroquois know the Great Lakes tribes have sufficient arms to repel them. I need to show you a letter I received before I left Montreal last spring. It might be the best way to explain my intentions."

Perrot handed Henri the letter, and Henri slowly read it aloud:

Dear Mr. Perrot,

On behalf of King Louis the 14th and a grateful French Nation, we wish to congratulate you on your exemplary work in bringing peace and stability to the tribes of the western Great Lakes. Your exploratory efforts and diplomatic skills have exceeded all expectations. Many have noted your assistance to our Jesuits during their attempts to establish missions and spread our Catholic faith!

As you know, our treaty of 1666 with the Iroquois Confederation had one major flaw. When the Iroquois promised to stop attacking Christian tribes, they took that literally. They keep moving their raiding parties further west to attack the tribes not yet aware of our Christian values. The Iroquois attacks on the Illinois tribes have been relentless, and if they succeed there, we fear they will turn their efforts north to the woodland tribes. The northern tribes armed with bows and arrows will be no match against the gun-toting Iroquois.

Your efforts to trade guns for furs have gone a long way in reestablishing a balance of power. We believe that sufficient deterrents can prevent a full-scale war.

In addition, we humbly request that you take note of strategic locations for establishing military forts. We can have all the soldiers in the world in Quebec, but if we can't get them to a conflict in time, our promise of defending the Christian tribes will be meaningless. Also, you should be aware that we are currently working on a proximation confirming the appropriation of all territories west of the Great Lakes, including those yet to be discovered. That entire area will become the property of France. Having a well-armed Native population allied with France would be extremely helpful if England or Spain decided to challenge our claim.

In the name of your King, please continue your good works.

Governor-General Daniel de Rémy, Quebec City, New France

---

Henri was moved by the letter. In the back of his head, he could hear the words of Father Agard, their eighth-grade teacher. "The Dutch and the English traded guns for furs, and the French didn't. That mistake completely offset the balance of power, resulting in countless deaths."

Henri realized there was truth to Nicolas and Pierre's perspective. *What are we trying to accomplish?* he wondered. *We can baptize the people, promise them missions, and tell them they're under the protection of the French. However, if we know our military is a thousand miles away, and they'll not arrive in time, we are lying to them. At the same time, if we hinder their ability to defend themselves, we commit a most grievous sin. Assuming guns can stabilize the region, I must accept that God may have sent Nicolas Perrot to us at this critical juncture.*

Henri stood up, walked over to Nicolas Perrot, and shook his hand. "I accept your explanation and sense your sincerity in wanting to help the Indigenous people of the Great Lakes area. I welcome you as the newest member of our peace delegation. May God guide our efforts."

"Amen," Nicolas said.

Pierre let out a cheer. Morningstar and Nokee sat there quietly, deep in thought.

• • •

Pierre turned to Nicolas Perrot and asked if he would assist them with the presentation they had to deliver to the tribal council that evening. Perrot quickly agreed to do so. After everyone got up and left, Pierre sat there thinking about what he would say that evening. His carnival routine, magic tricks, and fireworks show seemed out of place when so much was at stake.

After the evening meal, Pierre and Henri rose to address the villagers. Standing before Chief Myamick, Chief Winamac, and Winamac's clan leaders, Pierre began, "It is an honor to speak tonight to the chiefs and members of the free and independent Potawatomi Nation. We Black Robes, members of the peace delegation, are here to present a plan that could bring full and lasting peace with the Iroquois."

Pierre could see the skeptical looks on their faces, but he continued. Pierre reached into his pack and pulled out a series of trade items. "You've met our fur traders. They brought you items made of iron, copper, and silver."

Pierre handed a trade axe to Chief Myamick, Chief Winamac, the village war chief, and the village shaman. He passed out three small copper trade kettles to three clan leaders and small solid-silver crescent-moon necklaces to the remaining four. Pierre smiled and nodded at the wife of Chief Winamac and the wives of his seven clan leaders. He then gave each of them a packet of *rassades*—glass beads and colored ribbons.

"Some of you have met our Black Robes," continued Pierre. "We bring news of an all-powerful God and promise that our French soldiers will protect you if you join our Christian family. We provide new medicines, tools, and technology. We start missions to care for the suffering and displaced tribes. But, like the fur traders, we haven't yet brought you peace.

"That is about to change. Our great chief, King Louis the 14th, from the other side of the great saltwater sea, has decided to unite the Great Lakes tribes and end the Iroquois raids. The French will continue to bring you the things you desire, but without peace, those things mean nothing. What good are missions, medicines, and fancy trade items if the Iroquois overrun your villages and kill your people?"

"Our great chief realizes that the French made mistakes with our Indigenous allies. Our fur traders bartered with axes, kettles, and knives, while the Dutch and English traders supplied the Iroquois with guns. The balance of power has been upended. Our great chief has decided that must change. He has already built military forts and missions along the St. Lawrence River. He wants to do the same in the Great Lakes area. He now sends fur traders like Nicolas Perrot to trade guns for furs with tribes allied with the French. He doesn't want to start a war. He wants to end one by restoring that balance.

"Henri and I have been sent to the Great Lakes area to look for tribes willing to join our growing Christian movement. We already have a list of numerous tribes receptive to our Christian ways. Our king promised he would send soldiers to those tribes first. There, they'll build forts to protect our Indigenous allies. Nicolas Perrot has told me he has already requested a military fort at Detroit, Michilimackinac, Sault Ste. Marie, and Green Bay. He also told me he would like to locate one near this village to protect the southern Lake Michigan tribes. Isn't that so, Nicolas?"

Nicolas Perrot stood up. "That's true, Pierre. This village would be an excellent location for stationing soldiers to help the Potawatomi and Miami defend against the Iroquois." Nicolas held two fingers up and motioned to one of his coureurs des bois. The man quickly ran to one of their voyageur canoes and brought back two muskets. Perrot handed one to Chief Winamac and one to Chief Myamick.

"As I travel up the lakeshore with the peace delegation," Perrot said, "I'll continue to trade guns for furs. In addition, I promise to give every chief joining our Christian Peace Coalition twenty muskets." The chiefs nodded, and the crowd cheered.

Morningstar stood up, holding up the musket she had acquired from the deplorable trappers in Detroit. "As a representative of the great Chippewa Nation, I'll do everything in my power to rekindle the Alliance of the Three Fires. I'll explain to the Chippewa Council why we must stand together. An alliance of thousands of Chippewa, Ottawa, Potawatomi, and Miami warriors will be a massive deterrent. Not even the boldest Iroquois force would dare to approach any village in the Lower Peninsula."

Morningstar then handed Chief Winamac her last musket. "Here's the first of the many Chippewa guns that will soon come to your aid." Again, the crowd cheered.

Finally, Nokee stood up and turned to the crowd. "I'm the son of a Sauk peace chief; my mother was the daughter of a Mascouten peace chief. Peace is in my blood. Yet, I fought many battles against the Iroquois. I know the death and the destruction the Iroquois bring. Therefore, when I return to my people on the other side of Lake Michigan, I will call a Great Council with the four tribes of my ancestors. With Nicolas Perrot's promise of many guns and a new alliance with the Illinois tribes, we'll drive the Iroquois out of the western Great Lakes for good."

With that, everyone was on their feet. Drums and war chants roared, and a war dance began to form. Chief Winamac raised his musket high and silenced the crowd. "Before I commit the Potawatomi to this alliance and war, I need a private counsel with Chief Myamick in my lodge." He turned to Nicolas Perrot. "Gun trader, how many of your people live on the other side of the great saltwater sea?"

Nicolas stood up and waved his arm at the night sky. "As many as the stars in the heavens, my great chief!"

"And how many will come to this land?" Winamac asked.

"Over time, they'll come by the thousands."

"I see." With that, Chief Winamac and Chief Myamick disappeared into Winamac's lodge. The crowd sat down to wait for Winamac's decision.

Sitting on bearskin rugs, Chief Winamac spoke first. "Our job as chiefs has always been to look after our people. Our forefathers taught us that our decisions must reflect the needs of the present and the needs of the next seven generations. However, so much has changed in one generation. It's impossible to see into the future. Our way of life has changed. My warriors spend more time trapping trade beavers than caring for their families.

"The Black Robes have promised us new medicines. But they were the ones that brought the diseases that killed our people. The White man's rum has destroyed many tribes. The fur trader promised more guns and soldiers to fight off the Iroquois. However, the Iroquois are only a problem because the White Man gave too many guns to the Iroquois in the first place. Now, they tell us to unite our tribes against the Iroquois and English. They say that will bring peace to the Great Lakes area and allow their fur trade to go uninterrupted. Tell me why I should support this effort."

Chief Myamick folded his hands and took a moment to gather his thoughts. At last, he said, "All you say is true. The life we knew has changed and will never be the same. But life under the rule of the Iroquois and their English allies would be far worse. My people have traded with the French fur traders for years. We have seen the kindness and care of the Black Robes. If the words of Nicolas Perrot are true, that the White men with guns will come by the thousands, would you rather have the French or the English as your neighbors? I choose to side with the French!"

"Your counsel is wise," Chief Winamac said. "Like you, my experience with the French has been mostly pleasant. I'm not familiar with Englishmen. However, if the Iroquois are their friends, the Potawatomi will have nothing to do with them. If the Chippewa join the cause, the Potawatomi will do the same."

"Winamac, my friend, there is one more thing we must speak of. Nokee's past holds a secret that will complicate things."

"No need to say it! I know of Nokee's earlier contact with the Chippewa," Winamac said.

"Then you understand the difficulty this will cause with Chief Twakanha?"

Chief Winamac closed his eyes as if remembering a troubling scene from the past. "Yes."

# The Great Council

When the two chiefs emerged from Winamac's lodge, Winamac announced that the Potawatomi people should prepare for war. A mighty roar rose from the crowd. The drums and war chants returned, and the dance continued through the night.

In the morning, Chief Winamac sent out his best runners to inform Chief Twakanha that a multi-tribal war council would occur. The message they were to deliver to Twakanha was simple:

*Nokee, a Mascouten-Sauk prophet, devised a plan to unite the tribes against the raiding Iroquois. A Great War Council will convene at the Ottawa trading village on Pine River on the next full moon. Input from the Chippewa delegation is essential to restore the old alliance.*

Everyone was exhausted after the all-night celebration. Despite that, Chief Winamac insisted there would be no rest until the trade fleet was ready. Winamac knew it would take his group three days to reach the Ottawa camp. He needed to arrive well ahead of the Chippewa delegation. Winamac and Myamick had to have the buy-in of the Ottawa chief before Twakanha arrived.

The following morning, eleven Great Lakes canoes commanded by Winamac, Myamick, and Nicolas Perrot paddled north. At the front of the group was a six-person canoe sporting a white sail. Everyone knew that any chance of uniting a Great Lakes fighting force rested in their hands. As they passed the mouth of the Paw-Paw River, Nokee longed to stop and show his friends where he had grown up. But it had been almost fifteen years since his people had lived there. What would be the point? The buildings burned down long ago, the raised crop beds were overgrown, and the memory of his people was erased. With his head down, he paddled on.

They spent their first night at a Potawatomi village at the mouth of the Kalamazoo River. The villagers added another trade canoe to the group. That evening, Nokee took Henri and Pierre up the Kalamazoo River to visit another mound site shown on his map. Both traditional and chamber mounds were present at that location.

On day two, they passed Ottawa villages on the Grand and Muskegon Rivers, and more trade canoes joined the convoy. They spent the second night at White Lake. Nokee and his peace delegation visited two mound sites on the White River. Curiously, this site only had traditional mounds.

On the afternoon of the third day, they arrived at Chief Atowas's village, located on the flooded river mouth of the Pine River. Eighteen canoes loaded with trade goods, guns, and a promise of lasting peace pulled onto the shore. The Ottawa village was the largest settlement the Jesuits had seen in the Great Lakes area. Henri counted over a hundred dome-shaped, bark-covered lodges along the shoreline. He estimated the village population to be over two thousand.

Nicolas Perrot gave Chief Atowas two French-style tomahawks, each with three-inch forged blades and rough-sanded hickory handles for a solid grip. They were perfectly balanced for throwing and were deadly at short range. Chief Atowas smiled and gave one to his young son, Pontiwas. Perrot also presented the chief with two small French brass kettles. Both were built with cast iron hanging handles and held about a quart of liquid. Chief Atowas was so pleased with his gifts that he returned the favor, gifting Nicolas two full-length elk blankets.

While the men in the trade canoes unloaded their wares, the peace delegation, including Nicolas Perrot, sat quietly watching the activities. Henri wrote in his journal:

> The Ottawa people are very friendly and welcoming. The Potawatomi and Ottawa languages and manner of dress are remarkably similar. The men have long black hair, wear breechcloths in summer, and tattoo their faces. They add soft, tanned animal skin shirts, leggings, and moccasins in the fall. The women wear colorfully designed dresses, leggings, and moccasins.

The men carry shields, bows, arrows, and clubs and appear skilled at using them. Archery contests seem to be a daily ritual. Both sexes love to gamble. The Miami warriors urged Pierre to show the Ottawa his cups and ball game. Pierre did, and he was a big hit again!

I'm surprised at how organized the trading process is. The new arrivals unload their trade items in neatly divided piles. No trading takes place on the first day; it's like a show-and-tell session. The Ottawa traders walk up and down the visitor's display, perusing the items and asking questions. The new arrivals promote their products and secretly try to make side deals.

When the Ottawa traders finished assessing the visitors' offers, it was time to present the Ottawa inventory. Not since the vendor booths at the Paris Carnival had I seen anything like it. They had twelve open-ended lodges that held everything imaginable. Each lodge had a different theme: food, medicine, clothing, furs, household goods, tools, jewelry, tobacco and pipes, musical instruments, weapons and knives, and canoes.

But the lodge that caught most eyes was the last one, which held spirit items. It contained various types of flint, iron, copper, silver, and a smattering of gold. Pierre was fascinated with a colorful conglomerate that they had shaped into round balls, hearts, and bird heads. The stone contained chunks of jasper, chert, and quartz. Pierre named it "puddingstone" because it reminded him of the French rice pudding containing grapes, cherries, and raisins. Undoubtedly, Pine Lake Ottawa village was the trade center of choice for the Upper Great Lakes.

While the trading was in full swing, Chief Winamac, Chief Myamick, and Chief Atowas headed for Atowas's lodge to hold private counsel. Once inside, Atowas welcomed them with open arms. "Come in, brothers of the old alliance. We shall smoke, share food, and drink while we relive the battles we fought to drive the Iroquois from our lands."

"That's exactly why we're here, my old friend," Chief Winamac said. "The Iroquois are back and in greater numbers than before. They've been attacking the Illinois tribes all summer. Recently, they attacked a Kiskakon village on the Kankakee River, just south of our territory."

"Rest assured," Chief Myamick said, "we're also here to trade! We have every intention of keeping that relationship strong. But what if our forces to the south begin to weaken? The Iroquois have set their sights on the Potawatomi. If the Potawatomi fell, do you think the Iroquois raiders would come in peace to seek fair trade? If we lose our Potawatomi allies, the Miami people don't have the numbers to repel the growing Iroquois forces.

"However, we are also here to assure lasting peace," Myamick continued. "We have brought a four-part peace delegation with a plan to make that happen. The first part is Nicolas Perrot, the gun trader. He is traveling with your Ottawa brothers from the north. He promises the support of the French military and twenty muskets to every chief that joins the alliance.

"The second part is the Black Robes and their missions. You know the kindness and care they have shown your people to the north. With each new mission they start, a fort and soldiers soon follow to defend that area.

"The third part is Morningstar, a Chippewa woman. You know Chief Twakanha and the challenging times we have shared with him. He is old and tired of war, but we are sure we can convince the Chippewa to rejoin the alliance. The hard part is getting Twakanha to attend the Great Council. However, Morningstar is his daughter. She has assured us Chief Twakanha will come.

"The fourth and last part is Nokee, the peace prophet. You know him from ten years past when he led the Miami, Potawatomi, Chippewa, and Ottawa warriors in battles against the Iroquois. His brilliant battle strategies saved many lives. However, you probably don't know that Nokee is the son of Mahtowa. He was one of the youths you delivered to Twakanha for torture at Grand Rapids. He escaped Twakanha's grip and now comes before you as the peace chief of the Mascouten-Sauk tribe."

Atowas was furious. "Why did you bring him here? How could you? The Chippewa have been at war with the Yam-Ko-Desh for countless generations—and they don't let go of bitter feelings easily. I can't risk alienating the Chippewa!"

"I know," Chief Winamac said. "I was there and saw his hatred of the Mascouten youth. But Twakanha isn't a fool. Nokee says he can unite the tribes on the other side of the Big Lake to fight the Iroquois. The French assure us that the Iroquois know they won't survive being caught between multiple armies. They will flee back east to their homeland."

"Good luck convincing Twakanha," Chief Atowas said. "If you can persuade him to let go of the past and join the alliance, the Ottawa will join."

"That's all we ask of you," Chief Winamac said. "Now, let's smoke and enjoy the evening. Tomorrow, we shall trade."

In the morning, the trading began. Nicolas Perrot traded ten muskets to Chief Atowas for a fine pile of fur. The other traders moved from one lodge to the next, and the community was alive with the sights and sounds of lively bartering. The peace delegation wandered through the crowd throughout the day, enjoying the festival atmosphere. It appeared that the peace movement was off to a good start.

• • •

Things weren't going smoothly at the Chippewa camp in Grand Rapids. When Chief Twakanha received the message, he was furious. Jibewas entered his lodge to the sound of enraged shouting.

"I knew there was something wrong with that lying Mascouten. How dare he come into my camp and thumb his nose at me. A peace prophet! I should've killed him the minute I suspected something. Assemble a team of our best warriors and intercept him before he gets to the War Council. Bring me his head."

"Father, the full moon is in five days. If this so-called peace prophet travels with Chief Winamac, they will go by Big Lake canoes, which are likely already there. Besides, killing him without knowing what Chief Winamac is up to would likely start a war with the Potawatomi. That's the last thing we need with the Iroquois barking at our door."

Chief Twakanha scowled but could not deny the truth of Jibewas's words. "If Chief Winamac wants to rekindle the Alliance of the Three Fires, he thinks the Iroquois will strike there first. The distant war with the Illinois tribes has caused the Iroquois supply lines to grow thin. They'll not try to attack the peninsula from the west. The attack on the River Raisin has exposed their plan. They'll try to conquer the Neutrals first and take Detroit. They can launch multiple raids on our Chippewa villages along the Lake Huron shoreline if they establish a base there. If Chief Winamac wants to ally with us to fight the Iroquois, I'll welcome that with a smile."

"But what about Nokee?" Jibewas asked.

"Ah yes, the Mascouten peace prophet. I want him dead. If I can't convince the War Council to kill him and erase the Mascouten-Sauk name for good, we'll have to arrange for an accident. Things have a way of happening, you know. Now, quickly assemble our Chippewa war delegation. It will take us three days to get there. I don't want to keep the great peace prophet waiting."

• • •

While the council chiefs waited for the Chippewa delegation to arrive, the four members of the peace delegation took their canoe and headed east on Pine Lake. Henri was interested in a mound site at the head of the lake, and Pierre wanted to map the river that flowed into it.

After spending a good portion of the morning examining the mounds, they paddled upstream. Pierre wrote in his journal:

> This river is one of the prettiest places we have seen. Towering white pines and blazing red maples lined the sand and gravel stream banks. Crystal-clear spring-fed water feeds the stream year-round. As we proceed upstream, giant rainbow trout scatter, splashing up the shallow riffles and then dashing under brushy cover in the deep pools. Tributary streams run black with spawning brook trout, and wild game abounds at every turn in the river. I can't wait to tell Father Marquette that the Ottawa camp would be an excellent location for a mission. In his honor, I will label this river the River Marquette. He will get a kick out of that.

At midday, the peace team slid their canoe onto the riverbank to enjoy a relaxing meal of cornbread, elk jerky, and fresh wintergreen tea. Morningstar lit a small fire to warm things up. Suddenly, Nokee stood with a concerned look. "I smell smoke!"

"Of course," ribbed Henri. "How do you think she will heat the tea?"

"Be quiet. It's coming from upstream."

"Me too," Morningstar said. "Do you think it could be the Chippewa delegation?"

"Why would they be out here?" Henri asked, his face tense with fear.

"When I was still with the Chippewa," Morningstar said, "my people would often trade extra smoked fish and bear meat with the Ottawa before leaving the Grand Rapids site. We canoed down the Grand River when we had substantial amounts, then followed the shoreline up to the Ottawa camp. With light cargo, we often took the land route. That took us north on the Grand River Trail, then west along Pine River. We mustn't let them see us. If they find Nokee away from the Ottawa village, it will bring certain death to us all!"

"Wait," Nokee said. "You three find a place to hide. I'm going to see who's out there."

"I'm going with you," Morningstar said.

"No! I need you here. If I'm pursued or captured, I need you to get the Black Robes to the Soo. Promise me you'll do that. Make sure their journals are delivered there."

With that, Nokee disappeared into the shadows. The rest of the team retreated from the riverside to wait for his return. After a long, tense wait, Henri leaned over to Morningstar. "Do you think they saw him?"

Before she could answer, a deep voice behind them said, "Yes, and they have invited us to eat."

Henri and Pierre almost jumped out of their skin. Morningstar slowly turned around. "Nokee, that's not funny! What did you see?"

Nokee stepped out of the brush, grinning. "It's just a group of Ottawa women smoking grayling. They have invited us to taste the fruits of their labor. That's if you three trembling rabbits aren't too afraid to leave your rabbit hole."

Henri and Pierre were fascinated with what they saw at the Ottawa fishing site. Six Ottawa women had set nets in a large pool beneath a series of rapids. As the spawning rainbow trout released their eggs and milt in the upstream gravel beds, hungry graylings swarmed below, snatching up every stray egg that drifted into the pool. The women had caught hundreds of these graylings and soaked them in a salt-water brine overnight. They hung the fish on sassafras branches and smoked them in makeshift smokehouses along the riverbank.

The Black Robes had never seen a fish like this. They had

blue-gray bodies with freckled black spots and large scales. Although the fish averaged about twelve inches long, they were round and fat like a loaf of French bread. What set them apart from other fish was their large sail-like dorsal fin.

Pierre watched the women peel back the bark-covering on their smokehouses and fill their baskets with the now golden-brown smoked fish. They explained how Chief Atowas planned to incorporate this special treat into the feast for the visiting traders and members of the Great Council. They proudly told the peace team that one of these fish, rolled in a cornmeal wrap, was highly favored by traveling warriors.

"One fish wrap provides an adequate meal for one man," the group's leader said. She handed each member of the peace delegation a smoked fish. Pierre was delighted with its hickory-smoked smell and flavor. The white, flaky flesh was firm, not soft and greasy like the smoked Great Lakes whitefish and chubs he had tried before.

As the Ottawa women finished packing, the peace delegation decided it would be best if they headed back to camp with the women. They didn't want to tempt fate and chance running into the arriving Chippewa delegation.

When they arrived at the Ottawa village, they saw two Chippewa cargo canoes pulled up along the shore. The Chippewa had taken the water route down the Grand River. Standing next to Chiefs Atowas, Winamac, and Myamick were Chief Twakanha and his war chief, Jibewas. To everyone's surprise, Chief Twakanha waved at the peace delegation members as he and Jibewas headed toward them.

"Hello again, my friends," Twakanha said. "I hear you've been remarkably busy since we parted ways. My fellow chiefs have told me you want to reunite our tribes and drive the Iroquois from our lands. Nothing would please me more. Tomorrow, we'll trade with our Ottawa brothers. Then, when the moon is full, the Great Council will consider your plan. The Chippewa look forward to that presentation. But I must warn you. I've many questions." Then Twakanha walked away, and Jibewas remained behind to talk to Morningstar.

"What was that all about?" Pierre whispered to Henri. "There was no sincerity or love in that conversation. I fear that Twakanha is aware of Nokee's history. ... Nokee better watch his back."

Jibewas spent a long time with his sister. They spoke of many things, enjoying each other's company late into the evening. They laughed over the joyous time they had shared as children and wondered how life had grown so complicated as they grew older. At the end of the conversation, Morningstar took Jibewas aside and whispered in his ear.

"Brother, I need to tell you something. Nokee and I are married now!"

His reaction surprised her. It was not the congratulatory look she was expecting.

"What's the matter, dear brother?"

"You know this will upset Father," Jibewas said, shaking his head.

"Yes, but I hoped you would talk to him. You two are so close. Tell him I love and fully trust Nokee. He should trust him, too. Assure him that Nokee will deliver the warriors he promises."

"I can't guarantee anything. You remember how Father reacted when you refused to marry our previous war chief after the death of your first husband. He traded you to the Tutelo." Jibewas left without saying another word.

When Jibewas located his father, Twakanha had deliberately set up his shelters at a noticeable distance from the others. Secrecy would be critical to his plan. "My Chief," Jibewas said. "Nokee plans to travel to the other side of the Big Lake and unite the remaining tribes of the Yam-Ko-Desh. Then he will ally with the Illinois tribes and fight the Iroquois."

Twakanha's nostrils flared as he smashed his fist into the lodge pole of their temporary shelter. "The members of the council are being played for fools. Do they believe that a force like that would stop there? Once the Iroquois are out of the way, the Yam-Ko-Desh will turn north into the peninsula. They'll try to reclaim their homeland. We would replace one enemy with another."

"Father, the other members of the council are blinded by their fear of the Iroquois. They're willing to try anything that gives them hope. If we refuse to join the alliance, we jeopardize our people."

"I'm aware of that," Twakanha said. "I'll try convincing the members of the Great Council that we can't trust this Mascouten. I'll explain how our four-tribe alliance will accomplish what we need without his assistance. I'll explain that killing one Mascouten today can prevent us from fighting ten thousand next year. However, if they don't listen, there are other ways."

"Father," Jibewas said, his head down. "Morningstar has married that Mascouten and suspects she is already carrying his child."

Chief Twakanha was devastated, but Jibewas was taken aback as he watched his father's anguish swiftly turn to rage. He grabbed Jibewas by his bear claw necklace and pulled him close. "I want him dead. When you have done that, drag your sister back with you. You'll do this for me or you will no longer be my war chief ... nor my son."

• • •

When the moon shone full, the Great Council began. The rules were simple. War chiefs and village shamans were allowed to accompany their chiefs. Each chief would take as much time as needed to present their point of view and then declare his vote. If anyone voted no, the proposal would fail.

Chief Myamick was the first to speak. "I present this council with two paths. We can dwell on the past or turn to the future. Which direction we take will be decided here today. Nokee is a Mascouten-Sauk peace chief—once your blood enemy. However, he lived with the Miami people for many years and married my oldest daughter. That puts me in a position to tell you why we should trust him now.

"You thought he was a Miami warrior when he led our warriors in successful battles against the murdering Iroquois. Knowing he was a Mascouten, would you have trusted him less? Would you have considered him our enemy? He vows to unite his people on the other side of the Big Lake and join the Illinois tribes in the fight against the Iroquois. Would you turn down an offer of ten thousand additional warriors because of past hatred for a Mascouten?

"Then there's Morningstar, daughter of Twakanha, brother of Jibewas. She represents our future. She has felt the pain of war, lost her first husband in an Iroquois battle, and longs for lasting peace. She believes the eastern alliance of Chippewa, Ottawa, Potawatomi, and Miami can defeat the Iroquois in battle. However, she believes that Nokee's plan to unite the eastern and western tribes will create such a fighting force that there will be no need for war. Her trust in the Mascouten is so great she goes with him as his wife. I trust them both. The Miami delegation votes yes on the alliance."

Next it was Chief Winamac's turn. "The Potawatomi people also look to the future. However, fur traders continue to show up on our shores. They bring things that have changed the way we live. We can argue whether that is bad or good, but the life we once had will never be the same. The days of the bow and spear have come and gone. The weapon of war is now the gun. The French have promised us each twenty muskets today if we ally with them. They say the French will come with guns by the thousands. I see little choice. The Potawatomi delegation votes yes on the alliance."

Then Chief Atowas stood and said, "The Black Robes have learned to live with our Ottawa brothers in the eastern Upper Peninsula. In many trading trips north, I've frequently encountered Black Robes. They speak our language and move freely amongst our people. They offer medical assistance to our sick and feed the displaced Hurons and Algonquins that flood into our land from the east. Of course, they instruct our children about their God. But they do it in a way that includes our spirits, allowing our two cultures to coexist.

"I don't see the Black Robes or fur traders leaving this land. Soon, the French military will follow in substantial numbers. It's time to decide whether the French will be our friends or enemies. Let's not underestimate the power of the French military. The Ottawa delegation votes yes on the alliance."

Chief Twakanha rose to address the council. "I'll begin my discussion with Nokee. Chief Myamick, you say we should trust him because of his past deeds. No one would argue that he's a tremendous warrior. The Chippewa warriors who fought with him say he is unstoppable in battle. They commend his leadership skills and ambushing strategies. I have no doubt that he'll unite the four tribes of the Yam-Ko-Desh and convince them to come to the aid of the Illinois people. The Iroquois will fall under his leadership.

"But think of what happens after they succeed in that effort. Jibewas has reported that the so-called Mascouten peace prophet carries a map of the Lower Peninsula that shows all the land once held by the Yam-Ko-Desh. He has taken the Black Robes to these ancestral burial grounds. The Black Robes draw pictures and make strange symbols of those places on paper. My question is, why? When the Iroquois have fallen, why stop there? Why not use that massive fighting force to retake their lost homeland?

"Chief Winamac, you say the French will come with thousands of guns. That may be true, but I hear other White men say they want our furs. I know nothing about the English or the Spanish, but if they're stronger or join forces against the French, whose side should we choose? We should be careful to whom we promise our allegiance!"

"Chief Atowas, you say the Black Robes have been kind and helpful to your people. They provide food, medicine, and care for the displaced. I don't doubt that is true. However, when you travel alone in new lands, you learn to walk softly to stay alive. When the Frenchmen come in vast numbers, with the support of their military, will the Black Robes continue to care for our people? Or will they turn their attention toward caring only for the French?"

Chief Twakanha sat down. "I raise these issues not to discourage the new alliance but to emphasize its necessity. Many outside forces are threatening our way of life. More than ever, we need to unite if we are to survive. I agree with my daughter that the eastern alliance of Chippewa, Ottawa, Potawatomi, and Miami can defeat the Iroquois in battle. The Chippewa delegation votes yes on the alliance."

Chief Twakanha turned to the other council chiefs. "Now, do we all agree that this talk of backing a western alliance is far too risky? There's only one way to stop a snake from striking: you must cut off its head. Do we kill the Mascouten leader while we have a chance? I call for the vote! The Chippewa vote yes." The other three chiefs weren't ready to vote until they heard from the peace delegation. Twakanha agreed and sent Jibewas to get the five peace team members.

When they arrived, Chief Twakanha was the first to question Nokee. "Nokee, I've heard that you've been visiting your ancestor's burial grounds across the land now ruled by the Chippewa. The French Black Robes are making maps and strange marks on their paper. These are the things spies do when planning an attack. What are your intentions?"

Morningstar gave Jibewas a dirty look as if he had betrayed their private conversation. She was about to speak when Nokee rose and motioned her to wait. "What you say is true. We've been at the sites of my ancestors, not to spy but to pay tribute to their spirits. You know as well as I do that when no one remembers the stories of their people, the souls of those spirits die.

"I'm leaving the Lower Peninsula and most likely will never return. Nicolas Perrot tells me that my people live in vast numbers on the other side of the Big Lake. That's where I'm going and plan to stay. The Black Robes say they can keep the stories of my people alive with those maps and strange marks. Chief Twakanha, you could do that for me. Or are you still afraid to go to those places protected by the Dark Forces?" Nokee sat down, grinning as Chief Twakanha scowled at him.

Chief Winamac stood up and addressed Nicolas Perrot. "Gun trader, you have promised each chief twenty firearms if we ally with the French. How soon will we receive the muskets?"

"Today, if you join as one," Perrot said.

"And will you do the same on the other side of the Big Lake?"

"I already have with the Menominee and Winnebago."

"And with the Sauk, Fox, Mascouten, and Kickapoo?"

"The same if they ally with the French."

"And what about the English and Spanish? Are you strong enough to fight them?"

"We have kept the English out of the St. Lawrence River and Great Lakes area for fifty years," Nicolas Perrot said proudly. "I see no reason we can't keep doing that for the next fifty."

"I've no more questions," Winamac said as he sat down.

Chief Atowas stood up and turned to Henri and Pierre: "I've seen how Black Robes helped my Ottawa brothers in the north.

Will you continue to help my people when the Frenchmen come by the thousands?"

Pierre spoke first. "We come here to do the good works our God expects of us. We do this for Christian and non-Christian tribes. We have missions with the Montagnais, Micmac, Abenaki, Huron, Algonquin, Neutrals, and Ottawa. We've opened a new mission with the Iroquois now that we have a treaty with them.

"The French military promised to place soldiers and forts in Christian tribes first. But we Black Robes are not bound by that rule. Henri and I visited the Neutrals, Seneca, Erie, Shawnee, Miami, Chippewa, and Potawatomi this summer. We plan to visit the Menominee and Winnebago next spring. Then, hopefully, Nokee's tribes and the Illinois people. Like the Ottawa, the reach of the Black Robes is long, and we plan to make it longer."

Then Henri spoke up. "We Black Robes do this work without the aid of guns." Henri held up his peace rifle. "On top of this rifle is a musket bayonet. But instead of a blade, it supports an iron cross."

Henri took off the iron bayonet, handed the cross to Chief Atowas, and said, "Keep this as a promise that the Black Robes will return and build a mission here. And when we do, hang this on the mission door so you know we keep our word. Now, about this rifle. Pierre modified it in Quebec. It doesn't work. It's my walking stick and symbolizes the power of God over guns. From this day forward, the Black Robes go forward with only our God!" Henri grabbed the gun by the barrel and smashed it to the ground, breaking the stock in half.

"I've no more questions," said Atowas as he sat down.

Chief Myamick was the last to speak. "Morningstar, you are a daughter of a Chippewa Chief, and yet you decided to marry this Mascouten. How's that possible?"

"Because he saved my life, for starters. I love him because he's kind, decent, and trustworthy. He'll deliver what he promises or die trying!"

"How do you know that?"

"I knew it the night he fought the wendigo and won."

"A wendigo, you say," Myamick's voice was quiet but firm. "Tell us about that."

A hush fell over the group. Wendigos are spirits of immense power, feared across the nations.

"The wendigo tried to lead Nokee down the paths of certainty, but Nokee chose to accept his future as a Mascouten-Sauk peace chief and claim his birthright, no matter how dangerous that journey may be."

"What caused him to make this choice?"

"He had a vision that he and I would find his people and raise a son."

Chief Myamick, now looking more at the group than at Morningstar, said, "And you believed that to be true?"

"Yes, I had the same dream!"

"Is there anything you would like to add?" Myamick said in closing.

Morningstar paused as if holding something back and said: "Nokee doesn't yet know this, but I believe I'm pregnant. Last night, I had another dream. A spirit came to me and told me to name our son Illiniwek. He'll be a fearless warrior like his father and will lead the people of the Illinois Confederation."

Pierre slapped Nokee on the back and congratulated him. Nokee sat there with a stunned look on his face.

"I've no more questions," Myamick said. "I wish to thank the peace delegation and ask them to leave so the Great Council can decide our next choice of action."

When the peace delegation left the lodge, Twakanha rose to address the group. "I admit, the peace delegation gave a good talk. However, what proof do they present? Stories of wendigos and dreams—I don't believe them. Do we have one shaman here who can verify these stories? I see none backing their claims. He's playing us for a fool. I suggest we kill the Mascouten leader while we have a chance. I again call for the vote! The Chippewa vote yes." The three remaining chiefs cast a resounding "no" vote.

As Twakanha stormed out of the lodge with his delegation, he leaned over to Jibewas and muttered, "They're fools. It's time to set our backup plan in motion."

Chief Atowas declared the Great Council over and announced a feast to celebrate the renewed alliance would occur tomorrow afternoon. Everyone agreed to assist the Ottawa people in preparing food and drink for the celebration. Nicolas Perrot was true to his word and presented each of the four chiefs with twenty muskets.

• • •

In the morning, Jibewas approached Morningstar and led her to a quiet place where there was no risk of being overheard. "My sister, I'm worried about your safety. Father wants to protect our people, but he's only making matters worse. I fear this will be the last time I'll see you—he will ban you and Nokee from ever setting foot in our village again. I'm going to prepare elderberry tea for the celebration. Will you help me? It would mean a lot to spend our last few hours together."

With tears streaming down her cheeks, Morningstar said, "You'll always be my brother. I would be honored to help."

They spent a pleasant morning together collecting ripe elderberries. Jibewas asked her many questions, interested in hearing about her plans for the future. They laughed and told stories while they mashed the elderberries in a wooden bucket with their feet. After adding water, they let the mixture steep. They strained it into a large kettle and placed it on the fire to boil. Everyone knows elderberry tea is delicious, but boiling is necessary to neutralize its deadly cyanide toxin. Jibewas intended to serve the tea cold as a refreshing drink, so they set the kettle in a groundwater spring to cool.

Morningstar left to help Pierre, who had promised to prepare a special treat for the feast. As soon as she was out of sight, Jibewas pulled out a small leather pouch containing a mixture of elderberry leaves, stems, and freshly cut roots. Secretly, he made a second batch of tea and added the mix—this time, he didn't boil it.

As the sun started to set, the celebration began. Still bitter that no one supported his distrust of the peace delegation, Chief Twakanha refused to attend. Jibewas stepped in for his father and joined the three chiefs. Nicolas Perrot and the four other members of the peace delegation sat down with them. Despite Twakanha's objection to Nokee, the alliance of the Great Lakes tribes was a cause for celebration.

Henri bowed his head, made the sign of the cross, and said

grace. Before starting the meal, Pierre offered a wish. "May God and all the spirits that look after this land bless this new alliance. And may the alliance of east and west be so strong that peace comes without bloodshed! Let the feast begin."

For starters, there was burdock root and wild-carrot soup with dried grapes, honey-glazed cornbread, and Chief Atowas's prized smoked grayling. Watercress salad with crushed nuts and cranberries topped with maple syrup vinaigrette followed. Next was roasted bear, elk, deer, or grilled trout with freshwater mussels, wild rice, and mushrooms. For dessert, there was maple candy and Pierre's huckleberry scones. A finer feast was not possible.

At the end of the meal, Jibewas announced he, too, wished to offer a blessing for the new alliance. He asked Morningstar to fetch the kettle from the spring. Then Jibewas took the kettle into his temporary shelter and poured the tea into brightly colored wooden cups. He handed Morningstar a tray with nine cups and asked her to pass them to the men in the group.

When everyone had a drink in hand, Jibewas raised his cup. "Members of the new alliance and prophets of peace. On behalf of the Chippewa Nation, I want to thank all of you for making the Great Lakes tribes safer. To our great chiefs: no longer can the Iroquois pick off one small village at a time, for they shall soon know that an attack on one is an attack on all. To our peace delegation, my hopes and dreams of lasting peace go with you. May you raise a great fighting force in the west and join us in driving the Iroquois from the Great Lakes area forever.

"When it comes to my father," continued Jibewas, "please be patient with him. He has seen many battles and witnessed much change. Those things harden a man and make him suspicious of all things new. I know and love my father. He'll bring the full force of the Chippewa Nation to the defense of the new alliance. I ask the Great Spirit to help him realize that uniting with our brothers in the west will benefit us all." All cheered and downed their drinks.

Then, to everyone's surprise, Twakanha stepped out from behind his son's shelter. "I heard what you said, my son. Your counsel is wise, but I still doubt this peace prophet's sincerity.

However, I'll drink with this Mascouten and ask the Great Spirit to prove my doubts wrong."

Jibewas bowed to his chief. "Father, I would like to join you in that wish. I want all to see how continuing the struggle between the Chippewa and Mascouten will only result in more deaths." He asked Morningstar to bring out the three remaining cups. Jibewas handed one to his father, one to Nokee, and kept the third for himself.

Chief Twakanha raised his cup. "May the Great Spirit protect the righteous and vanquish our enemies." The three men took a long drink.

Twakanha backed up to keep an eye on Nokee and Morningstar. *Look at them standing there smiling*, he thought. *See how they deliberately flaunt their inappropriate union in front of me. Watch now as the Great Spirit vanquishes my enemy.*

"There is something wrong with Jibewas!" someone yelled.

Jibewas was holding his stomach and grasping for breath. Henri and Pierre, standing next to him, grabbed his arms as he stumbled. Jibewas leaned forward and vomited. As they laid him on the ground, Chief Twakanha came running.

"What is happening? What have you done to my son?"

"Nothing," Henri said. "He seems to be reacting to something he ate or drank. Look at him: his pupils have dilated, his skin is clammy, and his breaths are slowed and shallow. Those are signs of poisoning."

"Poisoned! By whom?" Twakanha turned to Morningstar. "It was you. You brought him his last drink. You put something in it to kill him."

"No, no!" Morningstar cried, falling to her knees. "We made the tea together. We boiled it and did everything right. I love my brother and would never do anything to harm him. How can you say these evil things, you wicked man? Your hatred for Nokee has brought this evil on your son."

"Then the poison was intended for me?"

Twakanha whipped around to face the other chiefs. "I told you we couldn't trust this so-called peace delegation. I'm going to get my shaman—he will know how to help my son. We will decide what to do with these traitors when I return."

As Chief Twakanha raced off, Pierre looked at Henri. "Is there nothing you can do for Jibewas?"

"Treatment for cyanide poisoning is tricky," Henri said. "It all depends on how much an individual has taken in. Sodium nitrite can sometimes work, but I have none. ... Wait, there might be a way. Pierre, do you still have some saltpeter in your fireworks kit?"

Pierre nodded.

"Nicolas, you have that barrel of rock salt?" Nicolas nodded yes as well.

"If we mix the potassium nitrate with the sodium chloride and coax Jibewas to drink it, we may be able to slow the poison." The two men ran to their canoe to gather the requested items.

Morningstar sat by Jibewas, holding his hand as her tears rained down on his face. Jibewas, fading in and out of consciousness, squeezed Morningstar's hand. "Sister, this isn't your fault. Father forced me to make a second batch of poisoned tea. I was to serve it to Nokee. If I didn't try to kill Nokee, he would have banished me from the tribe as he did you.

"I saw the love between you and Nokee. I believe in what you are trying to do. When you told me you were carrying a child, I knew I had no choice. It was the only way to end this. I switched the cups. Now go, before he returns. If you don't, he'll kill the four of you." Jibewas's body began to shake in violent seizures. Soon, his heart stopped beating.

Chief Atowas looked at Henri and shook his head. "You heard Jibewas. Twakanha will want the four of you dead, and there is nothing we will be able to do to stop him. If someone kills one of your family members, you are obligated to seek revenge—most tribal wars begin this way. However, this is inter-tribal, between father and daughter. We chiefs have no say in this matter. Your only hope is to run away." Chief Winamac suggested they head south and promised that his Potawatomi villagers would provide them refuge until he returned.

When the rest of the peace team reached the canoes out of breath, they informed Nicolas and Pierre of Jibewas's death and Twakanha's promise. Perrot's men were busy loading for the morning shove-off. "My traders and I head north tomorrow," Nicolas whispered. "Quick, hide your gear in my canoes. Paddle out in the dark, set your sail—tonight, the wind blows from the northeast—abandon your canoe. Swim back and hide in my trading canoes underneath the fur. No one will know the precious cargo I'll be carrying as we head toward the rendezvous at Michilimackinac."

As Nicolas Perrot's canoes pulled away in the morning, Morningstar slowly raised her head to look at the life she was leaving behind. She watched her father load her brother's body into his canoe, cursing the sky as he vowed to hunt down the perpetrators.

"You're wrong, Father," she whispered. "You've always been wrong about your children's kindness and compassion. You saw it as a weakness. I hope you now see how your hatred and lack of compassion has left you weak and alone. I fear where your vengeance will lead you." Morningstar sank slowly back into the pile of furs, trying to push the sorrow from her mind as she buried herself in their softness.

# On to the Soo

The trading team made rapid progress as they traveled up the shoreline, the southwest wind at their backs. The peace delegation kept looking over their shoulders, half-expecting to see Twakanha in pursuit, but there was nothing. Maybe the canoe they set adrift had worked at sending Twakanha on a false trail. Or perhaps he was following them unseen, waiting for them to step ashore before springing his trap. Either way, it was now out of their control. Ultimately, they had no choice but to let the warm October weather, the white sandy beaches, and the whispering white pines put their mind at ease.

As they traveled north, the dunes along the shore grew higher and higher. At sunset, they made camp on a beach along the Leelanau Peninsula. To the east was a massive dune towering hundreds of feet in height. To the west were two islands, the Big and Little Manitous.

Pierre was fascinated by the spectacular size of the dune that rose into the horizon. When he asked how so much sand ended up in one place, the leader of the Ottawa team told Pierre a story, and Pierre recorded it in his journal.

> A long time ago, there was a great fire on the other side of the Big Lake. All the animals were forced into the water to escape the fire. The Great Spirit told a massive mother bear that she and her cubs must swim to the other side of the lake or face certain death. The mother bear pleaded with the Great Spirit, saying they would never reach the other side. He promised her she would. So, they started to swim. The three were about to give up when the mother spotted land. She told her children they were almost there, and she swam on.

But when she reached the shore, she turned around only to see her two children sinking below the waves.

She cried out to the Great Spirit: "You lied to me! You said we would make it!"

"No," answered the Great Spirit, "I said that you would survive. You can now live on and have a chance for many more children."

The mother bear was so distraught that she climbed the dune and lay down watching the shore, waiting for her children to appear. She refused to eat or drink, and over time she perished. The Great Spirit was so upset with what had happened that he scooped up the lake bottom and covered the mother bear with sand. He did the same with the bear cubs, creating two islands.

In the morning, the Ottawa warriors were up well before sunrise, preparing to get underway. "Why do we need to leave so early?" Henri asked.

"The mouth of the Grand Bay is miles wide, and the wind can make that place very dangerous for canoe crossing," one of the warriors said. "The wind is down now. If we wait, we'll have to hug the shoreline around the bay, adding many more miles to our travel."

At the break of dawn, the group rounded the tip of the Leelanau Peninsula. Henri looked south into the bay and saw a large rolling white cloud hovering low over the water. "Is that fog?"

"No! Don't be silly, Henri," Morningstar said. "Those are the great white swans. They gather here each year before they fly south for the winter."

Henri sat in awe as he watched thousands of trumpeter swans lift off, one flock at a time. As they ran across the water, flapping their wings to get airborne, the sound was like rolling thunder. As the swarm of swans drew closer, their high-pitched cries filled the air. It reminded Henri and Pierre of the gleeful crowd laughter at the festival of fools in Paris. As they passed overhead, the sky darkened, and the whoosh of wings roared. It was a breathtaking sight to behold.

After a long day, the Ottawa trading crew pulled into the rocky, windswept shoreline at Michilimackinac. The Ojibwa, led by Chief Waubay, were already there. To the shock of the peace delegation, the Tutelo were with them. Morningstar jumped out and ran to the Chippewa women. The women hugged, laughed, and shed tears of joy when Morningstar told them she had married Nokee.

"How did you get here?" Morningstar asked.

"We came on foot by way of the Mackinac Trail," said Makademin, Morningstar's best friend. "Tenron got into another fight at the Detroit Trading Post, and the Tutelo were banned from the island forever. Yesah decided it was time for us to move on. We stopped when we reached the great crossing at the Straits of Mackinac. Then, a few days ago, Ojibwa from the other side of the straits showed up here. I thought there was going to be a fight at first. And there likely would've been if Chief Waubay hadn't seen Chippewa women with the Tutelo. When Chief Waubay learned we women were from Twakanha's winter camp, everything calmed down.

"The meeting became more interesting when Chief Waubay showed the Tutelo the many types of cherts, flint, and pipestone they had brought to trade. The Tutelo hadn't seen flint of that quality since they left their homeland back east. They traded for some and went right to work. When Chief Waubay saw the arrow points the Tutelo could make, he realized they were master craftsmen. He offered them a winter stay at his village in return for their knapping skills."

Suddenly, a voice called out. "Morningstar, is it true you are the daughter of Chief Twakanha? I bet he wishes he were here with you right now!"

Morningstar froze momentarily, then slowly turned to see Chief Waubay standing behind her. "Yes ... more than you know!"

"Well, how is that old rascal doing? Causing more trouble, I suspect?"

"Same as usual," Morningstar said, forcing a smile.

After exchanging pleasantries and laughter, Chief Waubay headed off to show the new arrivals what he had to trade. A few minutes later, Tenron walked by and yelled, "I see you are still hanging around with that no-good Mascouten."

"At least he's not a troublemaking drunk like you." She did not need to say more—her cold eyes chased him off.

The Ojibwa had brought hundreds of pounds of wild rice, moose jerky, northern furs, and spirit items to trade. In turn, they wanted food items that didn't grow well in the Upper Peninsula. Corn, beans, and squash were high on their list. The Ottawa wanted spirit items. On their list were agates, greenstones, jasper, quartz crystals, float copper, and especially stones with flecks of silver or gold.

Nicolas Perrot traded ten guns to Chief Waubay for a small pile of northern furs and an eight-person canoe, which he gave to the members of the peace delegation. After the goods had exchanged hands, Perrot told Waubay about the peace delegation's plans and the French military's offer to unite the Great Lakes tribes against the Iroquois. Chief Waubay listened intently.

"The French military will supply me with guns if I join the fight against the Iroquois?" Chief Waubay asked. "I've never seen an Iroquois, but I've felt the pain they inflict on others. Our lands are full of Huron and Ottawa refugees who have suffered their wrath. My fight is with the Fox and Sauk to the west. But if you can supply my people with guns and bring the Fox and Sauk into your peace alliance with the French, the Ojibwa will join your alliance."

Nicolas Perrot assured Waubay he could get the guns, and the two smoked and ate together that evening. After the meal, Perrot asked Chief Waubay where they gathered all that shiny copper. Waubay looked at Perrot suspiciously. "We pick most of it up off the ground, but we know of mine shafts made by the people that once lived here. Why do you ask?"

"Just wondering. Why don't the Ottawa collect it on their own?"

"Because they don't control the Keweenaw Peninsula as we do!"

Nicolas Perrot thought to himself, *now I know where to look.* The next day, the same coureurs des bois that had left Quebec City with Henri and Pierre showed up. They had come down from the Soo to finish their fur collections for the year. In addition to what the Ottawa had to trade, the fur traders were after prime northern furs: caribou, moose, wolverine, lynx, sable, fisher, and beaver. They planned to return to the Soo with their canoes fully loaded. From there, the soldiers would escort the fur convoy back to Montreal. Louis Jolliet, Jacques Largillier, and Pierre Porteret planned to spend the winter at the Soo. Adrien Jolliet and Thomas Pajot

Jr. would return with the convoy and bring back a new supply of trade goods next spring.

It was a joyous reunion. Adrien and Thomas thanked the Lord when they saw their two traveling partners had safely made their journeys. They wanted to hear every detail of what had happened since they parted in Detroit.

More than anything, Henri wanted to know about Father Marquette. "Was Marquette still at the Soo?" Henri asked, his voice urgent. "Did Father Dablon start the mission there? Had Father Marquette crossed paths with Bishop Laval? Did the bishop have a new assignment for the three of us?"

They answered, "Yes, yes, yes, and yes," as Henri hounded them for every detail.

Adrien Jolliet and Thomas Pajot Jr. begged Pierre to retell the story of the musketoon blowing up during the fireworks show in Detroit. They laughed and laughed.

Louis Jolliet and Jacques Largillier were highly interested in Pierre's new map. Pierre told Jolliet and Largillier that the peace delegation planned to travel to the other side of the Big Lake next spring.

"I plan on mapping that side of the lake as well," Pierre said.

"That's wonderful news," Louis Jolliet said. "The territory controlled by the Fox tribes to the west interests me the most. Supposedly, a river runs through their land, taking you to a great saltwater sea." Pierre looked interested but admitted he knew nothing about that river.

Henri, who had listened to the conversation, interjected. "Pierre, of course you do! Don't you remember Father Agard telling us that in 1635, Jean Nicolet returned to Quebec to report that he had found the route to China? Nicolet told Champlain how his team had traveled along the north shore of Lake Michigan to Green Bay. It was there that he met the Menominee tribe. They guided him south to a large freshwater lake where the Winnebago lived. The Winnebago knew of a great river to the west that leads to a saltwater ocean. Nicolet claimed he traveled the Fox River to its headwaters and portaged into a larger river. He said he followed it until it grew wide and deep. It was there that Nicolet felt sure the ocean wasn't far away. He returned immediately to

Quebec and told Champlain of his findings. Champlain recorded this in his books but died before he could confirm it."

Nicolas Perrot spoke up. "Jean Nicolet was right. Father Allouez and I spent much time living with the Winnebago. I plan to spend the winter with them after I leave here. They claim that the Fox River is the gateway to the big river, the Misi Sipi. Father Allouez and I attempted to travel up the Fox, but the Fox tribes expect you to pay a sizeable toll to cross their lands. We weren't in a position to pay at that time. But I hope to do some friendly trading with the Fox this winter and establish that relationship."

"The Winnebago told you that route to the sea truly exists?" Jacques Largillier asked. "You understand their language?"

"It's Siouan—I speak that language as well," Henri said. "I learned it from the Tutelo."

Henri waved for Yesah to come over. Communicating in Siouan, Henri asked Yesah if he knew anything about the Siouan speaking Winnebago on the other side of the lake. Yesah replied that he didn't, but said he would like to move his people there.

Also speaking in Siouan, Nicolas said, "I'll be spending the winter with the Winnebago. I'll ask if your people can come and live there. I will return in the spring, stop at Chief Waubay's camp, and tell you about their decision." Yesah was pleased with Perrot's offer.

The fur traders built a huge bonfire that night and broke out the rum and harmonicas. They danced and sang voyageur paddling songs. Unfortunately, with all the festivities, no one noticed Tenron had caught wind of the drinking. He snuck over to their canoes and helped himself to the rum supply.

Hours later, Tenron, in a drunken stupor, staggered back toward the Tutelo camp. He tripped over a sleeping Ojibwa wrapped in a moose-hide blanket on his way. The man jumped up and knocked Tenron down. Tenron produced a knife and slashed the man across his chest, cutting his shirt and drawing blood. In seconds, four other Ojibwa warriors had Tenron pinned. Yesah and Chief Waubay heard the commotion and came running.

"Maiingan, my son, what happened?" asked Chief Waubay. "Are you alright?"

"I'm fine," said Maiingan. "Just a scratch. This fool kicked me while I was sleeping, then attacked me with a knife."

"Tenron, what have you done?" screamed Yesah, as he looked down at Tenron with raging anger. "Do you realize who you attacked? You attacked the son of Waubay. Have you no sense? You've disgraced our people for the last time. I warned you that if I ever caught you in another drunken fight, I would have no choice but to banish you forever. Who gave you the rum?"

Tenron pointed toward the fur traders. Henri, Nokee, and Adrien Jolliet, having heard the shouting, were already on their way over.

"Did you give this man rum?" Waubay yelled as they approached.

Seeing Tenron pinned to the ground, Henri said, "No sir, the head of my order has forbidden the rum trade to the Native people. He despises the practice, and so do I. I've seen too many good men ruined by it."

"Let me check with the men," Adrien said. "I'll see if anyone knows how this could have happened."

As Adrien hurried away, Yesah turned to Waubay. "He attacked your son. The decision on his punishment is your choice. You heard what I would do."

"What's your wish, Maiingan?" Chief Waubay asked.

"I agree with the Black Robe. The White man's rum makes the warriors weak. And there's no honor in killing weak men. Send him away!"

Adrien returned and told Yesah and Waubay that Tenron had gotten into their supplies. He had spilled more rum than he had drunk, which appeared to be a lot. Yesah looked at his brother with pity and sadness in his eyes. "Go before Maiingan changes his mind. Maiingan is an honorable man, and you're not. Gather your belongings and never return. Ever!"

Then, turning to Nokee, Yesah said, "If Tenron shows up again, you have my permission to kill him."

Nokee nodded silently.

• • •

After three days, the rendezvous ended. The entire group crossed the straits safely, stopping at Chief Chamintawaa's Ottawa camp in St. Ignace. Nicolas Perrot transferred all his furs into two voyageur canoes so his eighteen Ottawa paddlers could take them to the Soo for transport to Montreal. He and his six coureurs des bois would take the other lake canoe and head west with Chief Waubay to his winter camp. Perrot and his team would help drop off the Tutelo and continue to Green Bay.

Before the Tutelo headed out for their winter home, Morningstar's friend, Makademin, told Morningstar that she should come to Waubay's camp in the spring to give birth to her child. "No one knows how to deliver babies like the Chippewa," Makademin said. All the Chippewa women laughed; however, Morningstar contemplated the idea seriously.

Chief Atowas's trading team paddled east, carrying food supplies for their Ottawa brothers in the Soo. The peace delegation and Louis Jolliet's coureurs des bois followed closely behind. The Soo-bound team spent the first night on Drummond Island. On day two, they traveled up the St. Marys River, arriving at Neebish Island in Munuscong Bay around mid-afternoon. They found a group of displaced Huron trapping waterfowl for their winter food storage.

The Hurons had developed a unique way of catching waterfowl. They built square cages out of young aspen trees stuck in the shallow water spaced two inches apart. The structure had a cattail roof and a sliding door held up with a stick attached to a rope. When the baited cage filled with ducks and geese, the warrior hiding in the bulrushes would pull on the rope, causing the door to slide shut. The panicking waterfowl would stick their heads out of the opening between the poles, and the men would club them.

The Hurons were using wild rice for bait with limited success. The Ottawa, who had lots of experience trapping birds, traded corn bait to the Huron trappers in exchange for smoked ducks. With the corn, the Hurons were substantially more successful.

The convoy was ready to leave the following morning when one of the Ottawa men heard a cow moose call and a bull answer. Five Ottawa wanted to stay and hunt the moose while the convoy continued upstream. Pierre and Henri sent Nokee and Morningstar with the convoy and offered their eight-person canoe if they could tag along. The moose hunters quickly agreed.

One of the Ottawa warriors stripped off an eighteen-inch-long strip of white birch bark from a tree to make a moose call. He shaped it into a cone, punched holes every two inches, then threaded a leather strip through the holes to hold the funnel together. Equipped with spears, bows, and knives, they set off. As they worked the shallow marsh edge, all eyes scanned the shoreline ahead for moose.

When they reached the spot where they had last heard the bull, the warrior in front used his mouth and the birch cone to make the bawling call of the female moose. They got an immediate response from the bull a short distance away. Quickly, they slipped the canoe into the cattails and headed inland to a small opening with a creek running through it. The warrior made another cow bawl—this time, the reply was closer. Henri and Pierre stayed with the caller as the four other men spread out to the left and right.

After a few minutes, the warrior called again, but the bull only grunted, expecting the cow to come to him. The caller cupped his hand over the bottom of the cone and filled it with water. He slowly poured it out to sound like a cow urinating in the water. He gave one more cow bawl, but the bull wouldn't move. The caller made a bull moose grunt and thrashed the canoe paddle up and down a spruce tree, mimicking the sound of another bull having entered the area.

That was all it took. The bull came charging in, expecting a fight. The four archers sent arrows deep into the beast's chest, but he kept charging. The caller shoved Henri and Pierre aside and dropped to one knee, bracing his spear firmly against the ground. When the thousand-pound bull hit the spear, he jumped, spraying blood everywhere. He crashed to the ground and was dead in seconds. Everyone rushed to the caller, expecting the worst. But luckily, the bull had cleared him in his final leap, and the caller was unharmed. Henri and Pierre seemed to be the ones most shaken. Both promised never to go moose hunting again.

The Ottawa went right to work skinning and quartering the animal. It took two trips with the help of the Hurons to get the meat, hide, and horns back to the Huron camp. They gave the Hurons a hind quarter for helping, and the five Ottawa and two Black Robe deacons set off for the Soo.

# The Long Winter

When the hunting party and their two Jesuit deacons arrived at the Soo, they found the Ottawa traders camped with their Ottawa brothers at Baawitigong, next to the cascading Soo Rapids. The Ottawa traders from the south had exchanged their corn, squash, and beans for smoked whitefish and bear rugs, and the mood in the camp was festive. The women immediately went to work fire-smoking most of the newly acquired moose meat and roasted the rest for a great feast.

The French had set up their camp on the bluff, where they planned to build a fort. They call the area Saulteaux, nicknamed "the Soo." Father Dablon, Father Allouez, and Father Marquette were there with the coureurs des bois, Nokee, and Morningstar.

Henri and Pierre were impressed with the French camp. They found a log trading post and mess hall surrounded by a half-dozen well-built cabins. Off to the side, Fathers Dablon and Marquette had just finished building a small chapel and officially opened their mission. The young Jesuits were grateful for the accommodations, especially when they discovered that the area often receives over two hundred inches of snow in the winter, with bitter Lake Superior winds frequently driving temperatures down to minus twenty degrees.

Father Marquette informed Henri and Pierre that he had intercepted Bishop Laval at Lake Nipissing as the bishop returned to Quebec City. The bishop had agreed to Marquette's new plan, which Marquette would explain in detail tonight. Pierre turned toward Henri and smirked.

"I can't wait to hear about this!" Pierre said, laughing.

"I hope he's not trying to change the bishop's wishes …" Henri said, concerned.

"Don't worry. Father Marquette will twist some arms to get what he wants, but he would never break from a direct order."

"I hope you're right."

Just then, snowflakes began to fall. Though Henri was initially overjoyed, the soldiers, engagés, and coureurs des bois looked to the sky with trepidation. Their pace quickened as they packed to leave. It was a thirty-day trip back to Montreal, and everyone wanted to get as far south as possible before winter set in.

After a quiet dinner, during which the hungry men stuffed themselves, Father Marquette laid out his plan to Henri and Pierre. "When I arrived at the Soo, Allouez and Dablon were about to leave on a mapping adventure. They invited me to accompany them on their expedition along the southern shoreline of Lake Superior. We mapped the section from the Soo to Chequamegon Bay and returned here just a week ago. They plan to continue that effort next spring. They asked me to watch over the Lake Superior mission at La Pointe du St.-Esprit while they were away. Of course, I said yes.

"Now, about your stay here. I'm so pleased that Louis Jolliet, Jacques Largillier, and Pierre Porteret plan to stay with us for the winter. They're great woodsmen and hunters—we should eat well. They told me they plan to head down to Detroit next spring after the soldiers and their fellow coureurs des bois return with fresh trading supplies. They want to revisit the tribes you contacted last summer in the Lower Great Lakes."

"Louis Jolliet was very interested in the maps I had drawn," Pierre said. "He was especially excited to hear that we planned to head to Green Bay. Nicolas Perrot thinks a gateway river through Fox territory takes you to the big river, the Misi Sipi. Louis Jolliet wants us to gather information on that river. Nicolas Perrot said he has never traveled it because the Fox tribe demanded a heavy toll to pass through."

"That's interesting," Marquette said. "If you learn anything about that river, report directly to me. I don't care about finding a new route to China, but if that Big River takes us to unknown tribes and new mission sites, I want to be on that trip. The more information I have, the better chance Jolliet will take me along.

"And your plans to visit the tribes on the other side of the Big Lake fit the bishop's wishes perfectly," Marquette continued. "Because Bishop Laval knew I would be ministering to the tribes around Lake Superior, he requested you travel to the far western edge of Lake Michigan. Go as far as you can. He wants you to contact new tribes, record their customs, and report what you find to Father Dablon and myself at the Soo."

"Is that all that Bishop Laval had to say?" Henri asked. "I thought the bishop already had a list of missions we needed to establish. I thought we came here for that reason—we were meant to be the first. Pierre and I had hoped to start a mission in Green Bay!"

"Yes, and you most likely will," Father Marquette said. "But the bishop knows he can only send a few Jesuits at a time. He needs to know which sites to assign the highest priority and the greatest chance for success. That's why the work you and Pierre are doing is so valuable. Your contacts and assessments of tribal willingness to accept God's word will provide critical information. We must get the work you have already done, your maps, and your journals back to Quebec City. That information must be ready when the fur convoy leaves in the morning. The bishop will be so pleased with what you have already accomplished."

"If that's what Bishop Laval wants," Henri said, "we'll prepare everything tonight and have our records ready for shipment. Isn't that right, Pierre?" Pierre nodded.

The three of them stayed up most of the night sharing their travel stories since they separated at the mouth of the Ottawa River six months ago. According to Henri, Father Marquette and Pierre drank too much rum that night, causing the incident to occur—one that Pierre dismissed as untrue.

Henri recorded the incident in his journal:

> I awoke suddenly, and it was well past first morning light. I looked at Jacques and Pierre, and I could see they could not deliver the documents in their current condition. I hurried down the bluff to where the convoy had packed the canoes yesterday. They were gone. The soldiers, engagés, and Ottawa traders were all gone. The only thing left were tracks in the gravel where they had launched their canoes.

An Ottawa warrior was standing in the rapids spearing whitefish, and he told me the convoy had left a few hours before daybreak. He suspected they were halfway down the St. Marys River by now. I considered chasing after them in our eight-man canoe, then realized it would be nearly impossible for me to paddle that craft back upstream in the heavy current. I returned to our cabin to inform my partners of the unfortunate event. Father Marquette and Nokee were gravely disappointed. I looked at Pierre and shook my head, silently cursing the evils of rum.

• • •

The rest of October proved challenging for the Soo team as they prepared for winter. Morningstar began to suffer from morning sickness but kept busy helping in the mess hall and preserving winter supplies. In her free time, she enjoyed visiting the Ottawa women by the Soo Rapids. This being her first pregnancy, she had lots of questions for them. Nokee kept busy hunting with the men. He specialized in snaring snowshoe hares and beavers under the ice. He even brought back a woodland caribou kill, to everyone's delight.

By November, the snow started to stick to the ground and never let up. At first, the residents in the French camp shoveled trails from the cabins to the mess hall and chapel. Soon, the snowbanks reached their shoulders, giving Louis Jolliet an idea. With help from others, he cut poles and laid them across the top of the banks, then covered them with cedar boughs. From then on, no one had to shovel any more snow as it continued to accumulate on top. The residents effortlessly moved back and forth in their frozen tunnel network for the next four months.

It seemed the only cheerful times in that long, dark winter came from the discussions in the mess hall each night. Gathered around the open fireplace, the residents would take turns talking about the events they had witnessed. Henri, Pierre, and Father Marquette were glad they had not shipped their journals as they read passages that delighted everyone. Stories of the fireworks antics had the crowd roaring. Tales of the puppet shows left the men begging for a performance, which resulted in Henri and Pierre adding the show to their bible school for the Ottawa children. Still, Pierre's maps were what the coureurs des bois found most interesting. They spent days studying and discussing them.

Henri, Pierre, Father Marquette, Nokee, and Morningstar held daily language lessons. Henri taught French to Nokee and Morningstar so they could better understand the French fur traders and soldiers at the trading post. He also taught Siouan to the group so they could carry on a conversation with the Winnebago. Marquette described the variations between Algonquin and Huron. Nokee focused on teaching the differences between Miami, Sauk, Potawatomi, and Ottawa. Morningstar explained the subtle differences between Chippewa, Ojibwa, and Menominee. Pierre taught them Iroquoian so they could communicate with them if captured. By the end of winter, all had a working understanding of the various local Indigenous languages.

Finally, after months of cold and darkness, the end of March arrived, and winter's icy grip began to soften. The people in the Ottawa village sensed it, too. They knew the warming days and cold nights would soon signal the beginning of the maple syrup run. Henri had heard about the sap season but knew little about it. So, he snowshoed to the Ottawa village to see the process firsthand. The women had just finished making dozens of birchbark bowls and drip tubes from hollowed-out elderberry branches to collect the raw sap. Henri asked them to explain the process. One of the Ottawa women told him the Story of the Sap.

Henri recorded the story in his journal:

> Many years ago, sugar would naturally form on the sides of the trees like the pitch on spruce. All we had to do was scrape it off and eat it. It was so delicious and satisfying that the men refused to hunt and grew fat and lazy. Nanabozho, the trickster and guardian of the woods, saw the people sitting around, ignoring all the other food sources he provided for those who foraged. He cast a spell on the sugar maple tree and turned the sugar into a watery sap. To get the sugar, you would now have to collect the sap and concentrate it to make it sweet. The men returned to hunting, and the women took care of the sap run.

The next morning, with the temperature rising above freezing, Henri helped the women gather their gear before they headed up the ridge to where the sugar maple trees grew in abundance. At each mature sugar maple, they stopped on the south side of the tree and removed a four-inch strip of bark. Then, they gouged out a hole at the base of the strip, deep enough to insert the split elderberry tube. The tube started dripping sap almost immediately. A birchbark bowl was placed on the ground in front of every tree to catch the dripping sap. By the end of the day, they had tapped about thirty trees. The sap dripped late into the night until the temperature dipped below freezing.

In the morning, Henri showed up early to help the women carry sturdy elmwood buckets up to the sugar bush. When they reached the tapped maples, the women would toss out the ice layer on top and pour the sugar-concentrated liquid into their buckets. They brought the sap back to camp and poured it into long wooden troughs beside the fire. All day long, the women worked, adding and exchanging fire-heated rocks to keep the sap boiling. Watching the labor-intensive process, Henri thought there must be an easier way.

That night, Henri approached Father Marquette. "Do you still have any copper cauldrons from Quebec?"

"I do," Marquette said. "I've one left. I gave them to chiefs at Allumettes Island, Lake Nipissing, Manitoulin Island, and Drummond Island. When the time is right, I plan to give the last one to Chief Quinousaki here at Baawitigong."

"Well, Jacques, the time is right. However, I don't want to give it to the chief—I want to give it to the women."

"The women!" Marquette said. "You know there are tribal protocols to follow? The chief must be honored first, and he'll demand that you accept something of equal or greater value in return."

"I know. Pierre and I have witnessed that custom of exchange several times already. I plan to give the confit pot to the chief and tell him I'm giving the kettle to the women so they can make syrup and sugar twice as fast for him and his people. If he agrees, I'll gladly exchange the kettle for some of that heavenly smelling syrup the women are making."

Marquette laughed. "Henri, you always have a way of making things happen. Yes, I'll give you the cauldron. God has sent you here for a reason, and you make that fact clearer every day."

The next day, Henri brought the cauldron and made the confit pot presentation to Chief Quinousaki. The chief was pleased with the gift, and as Father Marquette had predicted, he gave Henri a moose blanket in exchange. It was the tanned hide from the kill that Henri and Pierre had witnessed in the fall. Henri thanked the chief and showed the women how to use the kettle to boil the sap. In two days, one of the Ottawa women showed up at the trading post with two quarts of fresh syrup. For the next three weeks, the men at the trading post and their guests feasted on cornbread smothered in the finest syrup they had ever tasted.

• • •

However, not everything was going as well as Henri thought. Morningstar was concerned about her pregnancy. Her morning sickness had continued through her second trimester, and she was depressed and anxious. Her vomiting continued, she experienced a loss of appetite, and she often felt faint. One of the Ottawa women told her these signs meant trouble for the baby. This talk only brought on more depression and anxiety. When Nokee told Henri about these symptoms, Henri looked very concerned and insisted he needed to see Morningstar immediately.

The following morning, Henri and Morningstar sat alone in the chapel and discussed her situation. "Morningstar," Henri began, "I've been praying daily for you and your baby. I know God has brought all of us together for a reason, and he has big plans for you and your child. He'll not let you down. I know that in my heart.

"I spent most of the night reading about your condition in my medical book. It appears we are dealing with three problems. The stomach, the heart, and the head. Although these issues are all connected, let's address each separately.

"First, the stomach. We need to stop the vomiting. You are robbing your body of the fluids and nutrients you need. The same goes for your developing child. We need to determine which foods agree with you and which don't. I want to increase the amount of cooked squash, pumpkin, and fresh fish you eat. Avoid heavy red meat dishes and increase your intake of dried fruits. I'll be brewing ginger tea in the morning to calm your stomach and a mixture of herbal teas in the afternoon to keep you hydrated.

"Second, the heart. I read physician William Harvey's work on blood circulation in the human body. He emphasized that blood movement affects all organs. I assume that applies to your unborn baby. He suggested that too much salt can affect blood flow. I know the mess hall serves a lot of salted pork brought here by our fur traders. I want you to minimize your intake of that dish.

"Lastly, the head. Harvey also suggested that your head is the key place for blood flow. Those fainting moments could have something to do with your blood flow. If we can keep your blood and body hydrated and maintain good flow to your head, that may fix your dizziness. But there is more to the head than physical health. There's also the health of your mind. If you are sick from worry, the rest of your body can become sick. So, what's causing this depression?"

"I'm worried about my baby, Henri. The Ottawa women say I have all the bad signs. They tell me that women who go through this give birth early or deliver a stillborn. I can't let that happen to Nokee. He has seen too much loss and death in his lifetime. I wish to be with Makademin and my Chippewa sisters at Chief Waubay's camp. They would know how to give birth to a difficult child."

Henri paused thoughtfully. "When are you due?"

"It should be around mid-May."

"Good," Henri said. "Let's start with improving your diet. The ice will break up on the river in a couple of weeks. I'll talk to Pierre and Nokee and see if we can get an early start toward Green Bay. You can have your baby at Chief Waubay's camp, and we'll continue from there when you are ready to travel." Henri could already feel the stress draining from Morningstar's body as she hugged him.

"Oh, by the way," Henri said. "I've heard fried fresh liver and spring leeks are good for the blood." Morningstar made a disgusted face and immediately paled at the thought.

"Don't worry," Henri said, chuckling. "We'll try it together."

Morningstar changed her diet and drank her tea as Henri had prescribed. Her health and attitude began to improve almost immediately. Nokee and Pierre agreed to the new departure date and began preparing for the trip.

• • •

On April 15, they said goodbye to their friends, packed their supplies into the eight-person canoe, and headed for the Chippewa camp on Ossawinamakee Lake along the Manistique River.

They spent the first night at the Ottawa camp on Drummond Island, the second night at the Ottawa village in St. Ignace, and the third at the mouth of the Millecoquins River. As they beached their canoe at the Millecoquins, the river ran black with spawning fish.

"What kind of fish are these?" Henri asked.

"They're crappie!" Morningstar said. "The early warm spring has started the run. We must catch some for dinner. Crappies are delicious."

Pierre looked around for something to catch the racing hoards but could not find anything suitable for the job. Thinking quickly, he grabbed one of his wool shirts and tied off the sleeves. With one scoop, Pierre could hardly lift his shirt as it filled with dozens of squirming eight to twelve-inch fish. He dumped his prized catch onto the rocky riverbank. They all laughed as they watched the pregnant woman struggle to keep the flopping fish from returning to the water.

Sitting on the rocks, they cut off the fish's heads and stripped entrails from about thirty fish. Morningstar insisted they keep the female eggs. That night, taking advantage of Pierre's cooking skills, they feasted on lightly battered crappie fillets, fried spawn, and freshly made cornbread. It was a dinner to remember.

They had a favorable wind in the morning and were able to raise their sail. They arrived at Chief Waubay's camp by mid-afternoon. The whole Ojibwa tribe turned out to greet them, the quickest being the Tutelo's Chippewa women, who raced to the head of the line.

Makademin hugged Morningstar and couldn't resist rubbing her belly. "Look at the size of your baby! It most certainly is a boy."

"Of course it is," Morningstar said, with a smile. "His name is Illiniwek. The Great Spirit foretold us of his coming."

"Ah," Makademin said. "Together, we'll be delivering a prophet!"

The rest of April was pleasant for everyone. The warming spring winds melted off the winter snowcap, even in the dark recesses of the spruce forest. Soon, the first spring flowers and plants emerged, and the spring harvest was underway. Daily fresh salads made from leaves of wild dandelion, garlic, chickweed, and plantain, tossed with maple syrup vinegar, were devoured by all. Sliced burdock and dandelion root, fried with fiddlehead ferns, morel mushrooms, and rabbit, were served on a bed of wild rice. Young shoots from daylilies, cattail, and burdock were grilled and relished. Stinging nettle leaves made a surprisingly good hot tea, and roasted dandelion root made an excellent coffee substitute. It was a time of plenty.

On May 1, the spring supply convoy arrived at the Soo. Adrien Jolliet, Jean Plattier, Jean Tiberge, and Pierre Moreau were with them. Adrien immediately told his brother Louis that he and his team had encountered La Salle the explorer with Ottawa hunters on the Ottawa River last October.

"He's claiming he discovered the route to the Mississippi by way of the Ohio River," Adrien said. "He didn't look very healthy, and many are questioning his story." Louis just shook his head.

The arriving coureurs des bois demanded a little rest; however, Louis Jolliet, Jacques Largillier, and Pierre Porteret were anxious to get underway. In less than a week, Louis Jolliet had the canoes loaded, and the seven were off heading down the eastern shoreline of Lake Huron. They planned on retracing the same route Adrien and Thomas had taken the previous summer.

• • •

At the Ojibwa camp, Makademin and Morningstar had built a small, round birthing hut near the river. They covered the shelter with sweet-smelling cedar boughs and placed cattail mats on the floor. The Ojibwa and Chippewa tradition allowed the mother-to-be to have one midwife assist in the birthing. Of course, Morningstar chose her dear friend Makademin. It was her responsibility to ensure that Morningstar stuck to the spiritual leader's diet, restricted her activities, and refrained from doing anything to offend the spirits watching over the fetus's health.

By mid-May, Morningstar felt that the time had come. The

women in the village gathered to chant birthing songs that made the baby uncomfortable in the womb and want to come out. They gave Morningstar a medicinal drink made from the roots of black cherry and golden seal to induce labor. On May 18, 1669, Morningstar's first contractions started, and they quickly headed for the birthing hut.

Morningstar's labor was painful but mercifully short. When the time came, she squatted for the delivery, and the newborn dropped on the cattail mat at her feet. Makademin picked up the baby, shook it, and said, "Illiniwek, welcome to this world. You'll do remarkable things." Illiniwek wailed, and Morningstar cried.

Makademin wiped the baby down with cloth and water she had brought along. Then she tied off the umbilical cord and cut it free with a knife. Following tribal tradition, Makademin helped bring Morningstar and the baby to the river where they bathed. Afterward, Morningstar and Illiniwek were wrapped in blankets while Makademin buried the placenta under the floor mat. That was important, because if men saw menstrual blood or the placenta, it was said to make them weak. All three stayed in the birthing hut for one day until the baby was nursing well. Then, they set the birthing hut on fire and returned to the village.

That evening, a festive celebration in the village welcomed the new arrival. Nokee carried his son above his head, showing him to everyone. If anyone called the adorable baby Little Bear, Nokee would quickly correct them.

"His name is Illiniwek. The Great Spirit told us of his coming in a dream."

Nokee, enthralled with showing off his son around the village, lost track of time. It became necessary for Morningstar to search the crowd to retrieve her son. She smiled when she saw the joy in Nokee's eyes and said, "Nokee, it's time for him to nurse and get some sleep."

The Chippewa women crafted a beautifully decorated cradleboard that Morningstar used to carry Illiniwek on her back. At first, she was permitted two days of light work, but by the end of the week, she was performing her regular duties of collecting firewood, foraging for food, making pottery, and cooking.

Difficult as it was, Morningstar took motherhood in stride,

moving through camp with a constant smile. All signs of her earlier depression had vanished. That was until Nicolas Perrot suddenly showed up with his coureurs des bois returning from Green Bay. Standing in the bow of his canoe with a musket in one hand and a peace pipe in the other, he slowly approached the shore. Perrot jumped out of the canoe and ran to Henri and Pierre when he saw them in the crowd.

"Henri," Perrot shouted. "You must go quickly to Green Bay. *Coqueluche*—the flu—has broken out in the Menominee village. Tribal members are dying daily! They asked me to bring Father Allouez, whom they love and trust. I told them I would return with Allouez and two other Black Robes, but I don't think you should wait. Go now, and I'll go to the Soo to get Allouez. We'll meet you at the Menominee village as soon as possible."

As Henri ran off to prepare, Nicolas Perrot took Pierre aside. "I've laid the groundwork for your peace effort. The word is that there is a Mascouten tribe living with the Sauk at the headwater of the Fox River. Perhaps that is the group that Nokee is seeking, but I cannot be sure. It's best not to get his hopes up, but I wanted you to know. I will bring more guns to trade with the Fox. That should give you the necessary access to get through their territory."

# Green Bay

"What caused the flu outbreak?" Henri asked after returning with his things.

"As best as I can figure," Nicolas Perrot said, "it was brought into camp by those three French trappers seeking sexual favors. I heard they were crude and rough. The Menominee women wanted nothing to do with them. Supposedly, the one with a scar across his face pulled a knife and threatened to kill one of the women if she didn't give him what he wanted. One of the men heard the struggle and tried to intervene, but they shot and killed him. The trappers ran off before more help could arrive."

Shocked, Henri turned to Nokee and said, "You don't think it could be those fellows from Detroit, do you?"

"Did the scar-faced man have a broken jaw?" Nokee asked.

"Yes. In fact, the women called him 'crooked face.'"

"I'm going with Henri and Pierre," Nokee said. "I have a score to settle with those men."

"I'm going too," Morningstar said, stepping into view.

"No," Henri said. "Native Americans have little or no resistance to this European flu. It could kill all three of you in a matter of days. Let Pierre and I go to the Menominee camp alone. We've been through this sickness before. We'll gather information about those rotten scoundrels when we reach the Menominee camp, and after the illness passes, you can go after them if you wish."

"I'm not afraid of the sickness," Nokee said. "I'm going with you."

"Calm down, Nokee," Nicolas Perrot said. "I've worked out a plan to keep you and the Tutelo together and safe. The Winnebago chief has agreed to take in the Tutelo. I'll ask Chief Waubay, our Ojibwa host, if his warriors can take you to the Sturgeon River Ottawa camp on the eastern side of Green Bay. You can safely wait there for my return. I doubt those rogues will show their faces again.

"After I deliver these furs to the military convoy at the Soo, I'll get my new supply of guns to trade with the western tribes, grab Father Allouez, and head for the Ottawa camp on the Sturgeon River. I'll pick up Morningstar and Illiniwek on the way. The whole trip should take two weeks at most. Henri and Pierre should have everything cleaned up over there by then. Isn't that right, Henri?"

"I hope so," Henri said. "However, no one from any tribe should go anywhere near that Menominee camp until we have things under control."

"I agree," Nokee said. "Morningstar and Illiniwek should stay here. I'll go with the Tutelo and wait at the Ottawa camp, as Perrot has requested. But if those trappers show up, I'm not sitting around."

"Understood," Henri said. Morningstar, clearly unhappy with the arrangements, walked away.

That night, Henri took out his two medical books, *The Treatment of Common Ailments* and his fifty-year-old copy of *The Medicinal Plants of Canada*, published by Louis Hébert. He read about the influenza pandemic that hit France in 1510. A French physician who worked at that time described the outbreak as, "A rheumatic affliction of the head ... with constriction of the heart and lungs." Symptoms were fever, heaviness in the head, and intense coughing.

However, the treatment of the ailments wasn't well defined. They reported that bloodletting and purgation were not effective. Chest rubs of earthy clay-bole armoniac and tonics of oily linctus or pectoral troches showed poor results. Some doctors felt the boiling of plant leaves or roots showed some promise. Henri put down the medical book and picked up Louis Hébert's plant book.

Henri knew that juniper berries and spearmint leaves boiled in water could improve breathing. He had also seen how the boiled extraction of hemp root and wintergreen leaves could ease the pain. But he was looking for more help in treating the flu. The medical book implied that the 1510 influenza pandemic in France mostly killed young and old. However, he remembered that Father Agard had said that the 1636 flu at Quebec killed thousands of Algonquins of all ages. Most of the deaths in various tribes occurred within the first two weeks of the disease's arrival. Since Henri and Pierre would be the first on-site, they needed a recovery plan well before Father Allouez arrived. Henri spent most of the night reading about the medicinal healing effects of various plants.

While Nicolas Perrot was preparing his canoe to head to the Soo, Nicolas handed Pierre a calumet peace pipe. "Show this to the chiefs at Green Bay. They'll recognize it as mine. Tell them I'm on my way with Father Allouez, and you'll be helping the Menominee until we arrive. That should win their cooperation."

Pierre thanked Nicolas and handed him a promissory note signed by Father Marquette, guaranteeing payment by the Catholic Church in Montreal. "We left the Soo before the spring convoy arrived," Pierre said. "We need a resupply of salted pork, salt, pepper, mixed spices, cornmeal, flour, lard, and tobacco. I would greatly appreciate it if you would acquire those items for us."

"Add gingerroot, honey, extra salt, and lemons to that list if you can," Henri shouted.

As Nicolas Perrot paddled away in his canoe, he yelled, "Good luck, my friends. It's best to stay away from the Fox tribe controlling the Fox River until I return. The Fox don't like the French or Ojibwa—they'll make you pay a sizable toll to travel through their land!" The peace delegation could hear him laughing as his canoe disappeared into the mist.

Chief Waubay readied two Great Lakes canoes to transport the Tutelo, their wives, and eight of his warriors to Green Bay. Henri, Pierre, and Nokee added four Ojibwa paddlers to their eight-man canoe, and the convoy was off. The Ojibwa were to return with the canoes immediately after delivering their passengers. In two days, they reached the Ottawa camp on the Sturgeon River. Pierre held up the calumet as instructed, and the Ottawa welcomed them with open arms.

Nicolas Perrot had used Chief Kawachewan's Ottawa village for the past two years as his home base for trading guns for furs along the western side of Lake Michigan. When the Black Robes had the flu under control in the Menominee camp, Perrot planned to hire Kawachewan's Ottawa warriors. They were to take the peace delegation and Tutelo up the Lower Fox River to Lake Winnebago to meet the Winnebago people.

• • •

As the Tutelo and Nokee settled in, the two Black Robes crossed Green Bay to tend to the flu-stricken Menominee. They approached the village with Pierre in front, holding up the calumet. The welcome they received was overwhelming. Everyone ran to the shoreline with Chief Malomimis in the lead. Henri was stunned that there was no attempt to separate the sick from the healthy. Pierre and Henri introduced themselves and explained that Father Allouez and Nicolas Perrot were coming soon.

"We've come here to slow down the spread of the disease and start the recovery process," Henri said.

"Father Allouez has been coming to us for the past four years," Chief Malomimis said. "He has done many things to help my people, but we need his help now more than ever. We have tried everything to break the curse of the Serpent Spirit, but nothing seems to work. When Perrot told me he was sending Black Robes ahead of Father Allouez, my medicine men were not pleased. They insisted that I don't allow you to come here. They said it would enrage the Dark Forces, and the Serpent Spirit would bring more death. When I demanded they cooperate with you, they refused, and I was forced to banish them. We've lost fifteen people in twenty days. We need the Black Robes' magic medicine. Please, help me save my people."

"I believe we can," Henri said. "I don't believe this is the curse of the Serpent Spirit. It came from those fur trappers you chased away. White men brought this disease here, but I believe that White men's medicine should be able to fix it. However, I'll need the cooperation of all your people."

"You have my word," Chief Malomimis said. "I'll see that you get whatever you need. Where do you want to start?"

Pierre was amazed to see the speed at which Henri took control of the situation. Up to this point, Pierre was the one who did most of the talking, made the presentations, and won the support of the people. But this time, it was all Henri. The first thing Henri asked for was a tour of the village. Chief Malomimis pointed out the people who were currently sick. Then Henri wanted to inspect the availability of the larger structures, such as the meeting hall, council center, and sweat lodge. After a few minutes of thought, Henri laid out his plan.

"First, we need to separate the sick from the healthy," Henri said. "I want the sick children, their mothers, and all sick women brought to the meeting hall. The sick men are to go to the council center. If a family has a sick member, I want the rest of that family quarantined in their hut for five days. If quarantined family members show signs of sickness, bring them to our treatment centers immediately. I'll oversee the men, and Pierre will care for the women and children. The sweat lodge will remain closed to all who are not sick. I'll use it for daily treatments of those with breathing complications using *nookwezigan*." (Smudge pots containing mullein leaves.)

"The only way this will work," Henri continued, "is if we set up a community cooking and medicine prep center operated by non-sick villagers. We'll need men to provide meat from fish, mussels, and birds. The women can prepare the soups and tonics. Those sick with stomach problems should avoid heavy red meat meals until they are well. Leave all prepared foods and medicines at the doors of the sick. I don't want non-sick people entering any of those quarantined shelters. Adults who have recovered from the sickness can help Pierre and me in the centers. They most likely won't get sick again. This effort will be hard on everyone. However, if we do this for a week to ten days, I think we can beat this."

Chief Malomimis agreed to the plan and assembled his clan leaders to explain the details.

After being given their directions, the crowd gave a supportive cheer and immediately broke into various assigned groups. Twelve tribal flu survivors went with Henri and Pierre to the sickness centers to support the seriously ill. The women began acquiring the necessary roots and leaves and set up the cooking and brewing fires. The men brought in dozens of grouse and started grilling sturgeon steaks. Henri and Pierre began serving hot teas and warm grouse broth as fast as the children could deliver it.

At the same time, the support staff in the sickness centers kept replacing heated rocks in the vapor buckets. The centers and sweat lodge soon filled with the aromatic scent of juniper berries and spearmint leaves, easing the wheezing breaths and allowing the sick to sleep. On the first day, they lost two tribal members, one young and one old. Henri was heartbroken but told everyone that those patients were too far gone when treatment started. Henri insisted that the people should not lose heart.

"Keep doing what we're doing," Henri said. "Each day will get better, trust me!"

That night, Henri wrote in his journal:

> The Menominee people are lighter skinned and less interested in combat than other Indigenous people we have met. They wear more clothes than the Ojibwa. Women wear dresses adorned with layers of beads and shells. Men are tall and well-built, wearing decorative leggings, moccasins, thigh-length cloths, and shoulder vests covering their bodies. Their hair is tied up and heavily feathered. They say they are a neutral nation and don't take sides. That must be true, because I saw Ojibwa and Winnebago canoes pass the camp without concern for fighting to break out. Surrounding tribes refer to the Menominee as the rice traders, supported by the massive rice beds that grow in the bay. The Menominee language is a blend of the tribes around them. It is Algonquian based, but I hear Sauk and occasionally Siouan words mixed in.

The next day, many of the sick showed signs of improvement. On day four, most individuals who were seriously ill were up and moving around. The number of new infections was drastically down. On day six, a celebration broke out around the center fire with songs of thanks and joyous dancing. Henri had won the gratitude and respect of the Menominee village, but Pierre had won their hearts.

"How do you always do it?" Henri asked Pierre as they sat around the fire, surrounded by the sounds of joyous celebration.

"Well, your medical skills heal the bodies of the little ones," laughed Pierre, "but my puppets, magic tricks, and laughter heal their souls. I guess a happy soul wants to keep on living!"

• • •

On day eight, Nicolas Perrot's three trading canoes slid onto the shore of the Menominee camp without Father Allouez.

Henri was aghast. "Where's Father Allouez?"

"Please tell me you brought the things we need," Pierre said.

"Yes, I brought your supplies. I left Pierre's items with Nokee and Morningstar at the Ottawa camp. Here are the things that Henri requested."

Nicolas handed Henri a package. "Now, as to the whereabouts of Father Allouez. ... It's a long story, but I'll try to make it brief. When I arrived at the Soo, Fathers Allouez, Dablon, and Marquette had already left for Chequamegon Bay. However, while I was there, Tenron and six of Twakanha's warriors showed up."

"Tenron!" Henri said, with a disgusted look. "What did he want?"

"Well, he was at Baawitigong, the Ottawa camp at the Soo. His group demanded Chief Quinousaki turn over Morningstar and Nokee by order of Chief Twakanha. When I heard Tenron's group was there, I thought it best to stay out of sight. I didn't want them to know I was around. I did hear Chief Quinousaki say that he doesn't take orders from a Chippewa chief. He said he didn't know where those two had gone, and besides, it was none of his business. He told them to ask the French.

"I knew the men at the post liked to talk. For a few furs, they'll tell you anything. It was only a matter of time until Tenron appeared at the post. So, we packed up immediately, hired our Ottawa paddlers, and our three voyageur canoes left in the middle of the night. The plan was to grab Morningstar and Illiniwek and head directly to Green Bay. When we got to the Ojibwa camp, I thanked Chief Waubay for everything he had done and explained why I couldn't stay—not even for one night.

"Waubay told me I was right to hurry. Unlike Chief Quinousaki, Chief Waubay said he must comply with Ojibwa and Chippewa laws. If Tenron and Twakanha's warriors demand the return of one of their tribal members, he has no choice. He would have to turn Morningstar and Illiniwek over to them. He told us to leave while we had the chance.

"In three days," Perrot continued, "we were at the Sturgeon

River Ottawa camp. We dropped off Morningstar and Illiniwek and headed across the bay. And now, we are here. What can we do to help?"

"Things are much better today than a week ago," Henri said. "We seem to have the disease under control."

"The credit goes to Henri," Pierre said. "He put forth an incredible effort."

"We all put forth the effort," Henri corrected, embarrassed by all the praise.

"Like it or not, your fame is spreading," Nicolas Perrot said. "The Ottawa villagers at Sturgeon River call you the Black Magic gods."

"Great," Henri mumbled, smiling at Pierre. "The truth is this was my time to shine. Pierre has always been the leader. Ever since we were kids, he was the ambitious one, the first in line, the one to take charge. I followed him, and he got me into—but more importantly, out of—more trouble than I care to tell you. But this time, I felt God had placed me here for a reason. Those many experiences we've had over the past few years had prepared me for this moment. I pray I didn't disappoint Him!"

"You shouldn't worry about that," said Nicolas Perrot. "When both of your lives are over, I'm sure the good Lord will have a place at his table for both of you."

"To tell you the truth," Henri said, "the best thing you and your men can do is to get in your canoes and return to the Ottawa camp. Wait there for one week. If no outbreaks occur over the next three days, we will leave. We will quarantine for four days to ensure we are not carrying the sickness. Then we can all get together and head for the Winnebago camp. We will leave instructions for the Menominee in case of a flare-up."

"That makes sense to me," Perrot said. "That'll give me time to make arrangements with Chief Kawachewan. Remember, we promised the Eastern Peace Conference that the gun trafficker would return next summer with more guns to trade."

Henri and Pierre nodded, returned the calumet peace pipe to Perrot, and said goodbye as Nicolas Perrot's crew paddled away. For the next three days, there were no new infections. Henri and Pierre continued to serve gingerroot tea with honey for sensitive stomachs, hemp root with wintergreen leaf tea for headaches, and saltwater gargles for sore throats. He insisted that everyone drink boiled lemon water for general good health. When all seemed well, Henri left dietary instructions with Chief Malomimis, and he and Pierre got ready to move a half mile down the bay.

"Come for us if you need us," Henri said as they pushed out their canoe. "We'll be there for four days. Afterward, you can find us at the Winnebago camp."

They set up their camp along the shoreline, and there were no reports of any new sickness in the Menominee camp. Luckily, the two of them also seemed to have avoided catching the flu. Henri took long walks along the shore while Pierre worked on his map.

On day four, Pierre was confident to announce that it was finally "finished."

"Yes," Henri said. "And I couldn't have done this without you. I thank the Lord every day for your presence. You saved a lot of lives."

"You mean, together, we saved a lot of lives. Thank you for that, but that isn't what I meant. I meant I finished the map of our journey. Do you want to see it?"

"Of course I do. Let me see what you have."

Pierre handed Henri the map. "This is incredible! You put this together from just your notes?"

"Oh no! I had lots of input. Father Marquette, the Jolliet brothers, Father Allouez, and Father Dablon ... and, of course, you, have all had a part in its creation. I'm proud of the notes we took along the way. Think about it. Lake Ontario and Lake Erie, from Detroit to Saginaw Bay, across the mainland to the Potawatomi camp, and up the Lake Michigan shoreline. Our canoe trip to the Soo, our travel around the northern shoreline of Lake Michigan to Green Bay ... it's all on this map."

"But how did you create this section that runs south of here?"

"Well, that was the tricky part," Pierre said. "Some of that is straight from Nicolas Perrot. He knows this area well. Some of it is from the information I got from the Menominee. And yes, some of it is from Old Agard's stories about Jean Nicolet."

"Jean Nicolet's river must be the Misi Sipi River," Pierre said. "The Menominee men told us that the 'Great River' runs south from there for many moons. Also, there's something I haven't told you or Nokee. Back at Chief Waubay's camp, Nicolas Perrot said Sauk and Mascoutens are living at the headwaters of that Fox River. He thought they might be Nokee's people. That's where we ought to go next. As you said, God seems to be steering us through this journey for a reason. Maybe we are here to help Nokee get back to his people. Nokee is the key to making this peace plan work. I feel it in my heart. We need to get Nokee there, then return to the Soo to tell Marquette that this 'Great River' does exist!"

"Well then, now we know where we will head," Henri said.

As Henri turned and began to leave, Pierre stopped him. "One more thing, Henri. I know your apprehension about the gun trade. But I feel meeting up with Nicolas Perrot was also part of God's plan. He knows the Fox, and he can get us through their territory. We will need Nicolas if we're to arrange a meeting with those people. I don't think we can do this alone. Before he leaves, ask for his help. He thinks more of you than you know."

They packed their gear and crossed the bay to join the others at the Ottawa camp on the Sturgeon River. Nicolas Perrot had successfully made the desired arrangements with Chief Kawachewan. The Ottawa chief prepared two Great Lakes canoes to take the Tutelo to the Winnebago camp. Chief Kawachewan decided to go with them. Nicolas Perrot's trading team was eager to get underway, but everyone was waiting for the arrival of the two Black Robes.

The Tutelo woke up early the following morning and were excited to find a place they could call home. But just before they shoved off, two Menominee braves showed up in a canoe asking for the Black Robes. A young girl was showing signs that she had the flu. Henri agreed to return to the Menominee village without a moment's hesitation.

However, Pierre stepped in. "No, Henri. I'll go. You taught Chief Malomimis and me what to do. We know the drill. Besides, the peace delegation is supposed to show up with the Tutelo. It will not look very official if neither of us is there!" Before Henri could speak, Pierre read his mind. "You speak Siouan—you should be the one to go." Pierre chuckled as he loaded his gear into the Menominee canoe, and with the two warriors, they shoved off.

Pierre turned around as they paddled into the distance. "I'll see you in less than a week! I'm sure Chief Malomimis will provide me a ride to the Winnebago camp." And with that, he was gone.

• • •

With a favorable northwest wind and the use of the canoe sails, the Tutelo convoy glided south to the end of the bay, then paddled ten miles up the Lower Fox River to the first rapids. There, they had their first encounter with the Winnebago. Six men and six women were creating rock fences in the rapids to guide the spawning sturgeon into pools so they could spear them. The Winnebago knew the Tutelo were coming and welcomed them with friendly greetings. Although Tutelo and Winnebago spoke the Siouan language, Henri could discern slight differences in the dialects. However, the Tutelo were so thrilled to have others to converse with they jumped into the water and started helping with the rock structures.

Soon, the Tutelo and Winnebago were spearing sturgeons and chasing down the splashing giants. One by one, they hauled the fish ashore, cut them into thick steaks, and collected the females' eggs in wooden buckets. The women went right to work, fire-smoking the chunks of meat. The peace delegation laughed as they watched the men wrestle the monstrous fish. By nightfall, they had caught six sturgeons, the largest being nine feet long and weighing almost three hundred pounds.

That night, they sat down to grilled sturgeon steaks, wild rice, cornmeal cakes, salted pork with poke greens, wild onions, crushed hazelnuts, and corn coffee with maple sugar. The Winnebago and Tutelo laughed as they watched the Frenchmen rave over caviar on flatbread. A bowl full of sturgeon eggs seemed so much easier to consume.

After dinner, Henri asked one of the Winnebago men, "How far away is your village?"

"Puant is the name of our main village on Lake Winnebago. It is a half-day paddle south from here. It's where the Upper Fox

River drains into the center of Lake Winnebago. We'll take you there tomorrow to see Chief Hoocak. He has been expecting your arrival."

Henri thought about the Menominee camp to the north and the Winnebago camp to the south. *They're about equal distance from these rapids*, he thought. *I'll tell Pierre to mark this spot on his map. It's the perfect place to start our mission to serve both tribes. I'll ask Pierre to label this place on his map* De Pere, *which means "Rapids of the Fathers." Father Allouez and Father Marquette should get a kick out of that.*

They spent the second day at the rapids helping the Winnebago smoke the rest of the sturgeon meat. On the third day, they packed up a couple hundred pounds of smoked sturgeon steaks and six buckets of fish eggs and were off to Puant to meet Chief Hoocak. Henri noted in his journal that Lake Winnebago seemed more massive than Pierre's map had indicated. It appeared to be as long and wide as Leelanau Bay in Michigan. He described the shoreline as being a continuous forest of massive white pines.

They arrived at Chief Hoocak's camp by midday to a warm and friendly welcome. An enjoyable afternoon filled with festive food, drink, talk, and trade was underway. The Tutelo fit in perfectly with the Winnebago, and everyone seemed happy with the merging of the two tribes.

Henri wrote in his journal:

> The Winnebago speak Siouan and are an exciting blend of people. They tell me they are in contact with other western Siouan tribes when they go on buffalo hunts in the fall. However, their habits are similar to woodland Algonquian.
>
> Their acceptance of Nokee's appearance makes me believe they have direct contact with the Sauk and Fox. They are well-dressed and good-natured people like the Menominee. I can see why the two tribes get along so well. Now more than ever, I am convinced that the De Pere location would be an excellent site for a mission. I do hope Pierre and I can start one there.
>
> Many of their dwellings are house-like with steeply sloping roofs. I assume that is to shed the abundant winter snow. However, they also build longhouses like the Algonquians. The difference is the Winnebago people use bark roofing and grass mat walls rather than all bark.

> They hunt, fish, and gather wild fruits and nuts but are predominately farmers growing corn, squash, beans, and tobacco. And like the Ottawa and Menominee, they are middle-men traders. Their pottery is the finest we have seen. I am sure they are desirable items in the trade industry.
>
> Chief Hoocak is a member of the Thunderbird clan and comes from a long line of peace chiefs. I have also met Bear, Wolf, Elk, Deer, and Snake clan members. Their religious practices seem in line with Nokee's beliefs. That is not surprising considering their proximity to their Sauk and Fox neighbors. One slight difference is they call their creator Earthmaker rather than Gitchee Manito. However, both refer to the supernatural power of manito in all things.

Chief Hoocak found an empty shelter for his guests, and together they went to bed tired but happy. In the middle of the night, Henri suddenly screamed, sitting up drenched in cold sweat.

"What's wrong?" Nokee asked. "Is it the sickness?"

"No ... I had a bad dream. Pierre was calling out, and I could not reach him. But it's just a dream. I need to quit worrying about Pierre. He knows how to handle himself."

Nokee shook his head. "Dreams are powerful things. You shouldn't take them so lightly."

"Henri is right," Nicolas Perrot said, sitting up and rubbing his eyes. "He's just dreaming. Both of you shut up and get some sleep. Don't make me come over there and knock your heads together."

Nokee smiled at Henri and whispered, "I would like to see him try!" Feeling calmer, Henri chuckled softly and drifted back to sleep.

• • •

On the morning of the fourth day, the Ottawa and fur traders began preparing to head back north when suddenly Chief Hoocak approached them. He appeared very upset and was concerned he or his people had done something to offend their guests.

"Why are you leaving so soon?" Chief Hoocak said. "In three days, it will be the Strawberry Moon, the beginning of summer. It's a day of great celebration and the night of the Buffalo Dance. It's a spiritual event that assures a healthy buffalo calving season. You must stay and dance with us."

Understanding the significance of the Winnebago event, both groups agreed to stay. Henri suddenly recalled Pierre's words: "Nicolas Perrot is the key to getting us through the territory of the Fox. We need him to arrange a meeting with those people. I don't think we can do this alone. Before he leaves, ask for his help." Henri approached Perrot.

"Nicolas, you told Pierre and I that you and Father Allouez have met the Fox. And you told us you were heading to the Soo to get guns to trade with them."

"That's all true, Henri, but what's your point?"

"My point is you also told Pierre that Nokee's people might be at the headwaters of the Fox River, and we'll have to get by the Fox to get there. You're here with your voyageur canoes full of guns. Since we have three days before the Great Celebration, why don't we try to meet the Fox while we wait?"

"Henri," Nicolas said. "That's what I like about you. You always go straight to the issue at hand. However, you need to understand a few things. First, I said Nokee's people might be there. When and if you ever get there, you may find Sauk and Mascoutens, but they may know nothing of Nokee or his lost tribe.

"Second, you don't find the Fox. They find you! They are nomads. They go where they find food and comfort—they have no permanent villages. That way, their enemies never know where to look. And other than the Sauk, they consider everyone else their enemy.

"Third, you forgot to mention I told you we promised the Eastern Peace Conference that the gun traffickers would return to their Lake Michigan camps next summer with more guns to trade.

"And fourth, I had hoped to use these three days to counsel with Chief Kawachewan and Chief Hoocak. They must understand that we're here to seek allies for the French. If they join the alliance like the Ojibwa to the north, they'll receive many guns and the protection of the French soldiers."

Not a bit deterred, Henri said, "You also said that you are part of this peace delegation. You said the contribution you can make to the group is to provide guns so we can continue to spread our mission of peace. Well, without guns, it looks like our peace mission stops here. The success or failure of the peace delegation now falls on your shoulders."

Smiling, Nicolas Perrot said, "The Lord couldn't have picked two better peace soldiers than you and Pierre. After the Great Celebration, I'll give you two days. If we encounter the Fox, and I suspect we will, I can at least provide the guns to gain you a safe passage. And who knows, with you and God on our side, maybe we can talk peace with the Fox."

• • •

On the afternoon of the fifth day, someone spotted a fleet of canoes heading for the Winnebago village. There were seven in total: six smaller canoes surrounding a much larger vessel belonging to the peace chief. Nicolas Perrot took out his telescope and reported that all canoes displayed white banners, and the paddlers had white-painted faces.

"That's a death procession," Chief Hoocak said. "It's the announcement of a fallen leader. Something must have happened to the Menominee chief."

"Can you see Pierre?" asked Henri.

"No," Nicolas Perrot said. "But I remember Pierre saying he would be gone for about a week. Maybe the flu killed Chief Malomimis, and Pierre had to stay on to help."

"I should've gone with him," Henri said, kicking the dirt. "I feared this would happen."

"Calm down," Nokee said. "We should wait and see what they have to say."

A large crowd gathered at the shore as the seven canoes glided in. A crowd had formed, and they let out a collective gasp as Chief Malomimis stepped out of the canoe dressed in a white spirit robe and carrying a six-foot wooden cross. Chief Hoocak signaled the crowd to step back as the death procession assembled. Chief Malomimis led the group, with two men carrying a woven basket. They were followed by twenty paddlers, in neat rows of four, carrying their white banners. As the procession came up the hill, Chief Hoocak and Chief Kawachewan stepped forward to greet them.

The crowd went silent as Chief Malomimis spoke. "We come

here bearing tragic news. The Black Robe you call Pierre, one of the saviors of the Menominee people, has passed into the spirit world, and we're here to honor his memory!"

A low, guttural moan escaped Henri. "No, no ..." he whimpered. "I told you. I should've been with him!" Then, Henri fainted and collapsed.

# Recovering from the Loss

"Wake up, Henri," Nokee said, gently shaking him. "Chief Malomimis needs to talk to you."

"Is this a dream?" Henri asked.

"No, sadly not. Pierre is dead, and the Menominee have come here to inform us of his passing and celebrate his life. But first, he needs you to understand how it happened."

"Was it the flu? He shouldn't have died of the flu. Not that fast anyway."

"No, Henri, it was not the flu. It was murder!"

"Murdered!" Henri gasped, sitting up. "By whom, and why?"

"That's what chief Malomimis wants to explain to you."

Henri, Nokee, Morningstar, and Nicolas Perrot approached the Menominee Chief. Henri tried to pull himself together for the sake of his friends, who were as upset as he was.

"Who murdered our dear traveling companion?" Henri asked, holding back his anger. "Was it those Frenchmen that brought the flu to the Menominee?"

"Oh, no," said Chief Malomimis. "That I could understand. But it was two of our villagers. We are looking for them. When we catch them, I'm certain the tribal council will sentence them to death."

"Did you say two of your people?" Henri blurted out. "I can't believe it! After everything we did to help them! How could they possibly do this to Pierre? Everyone loved him! Tell me, when and where did this happen?"

"It happened on the third night that Pierre was with us. When everyone was asleep."

"The third night!" screamed Henri, turning to Nokee. "That was the night I dreamt Pierre called to me."

The two Menominee clan leaders, holding the basket, looked at Chief Malomimis. "Your two souls must be closely intertwined," Chief Malomimis said. "Only fourth-degree *Midewiwins* can call out from the dead. You Black Robes must truly have powerful black magic."

Henri ignored the comment. "Who is responsible for this?"

"Do you remember that I had to banish two members of our medicine society for disputing my orders?"

"Yes, but the rest of the medicine men worked side by side with us to save the people."

"That is true. That's why the whole tribe was shocked when the murder took place. You may not know this, but all Menominee medicine men come from the Snake clan. They have power over all serpents. Those two felt we had slighted the Serpent Spirit. They were certain more death would come to our people if they didn't rid our village of the evil black-robe magic.

"Pierre worked tirelessly for three days to save the young girl. His efforts were successful, but he needed rest. I showed him an empty wigwam where he could sleep and quarantine for a few days. That night, the banished medicine men snuck into camp and placed a bag of timber rattlers inside his resting area. It was a chilly night, so the snakes crawled out and curled up next to Pierre's warm body. When Pierre rolled over in the night, he was bit multiple times. We tried to save him, but the poison was too much and too strong."

Henri's knees buckled, and Nokee grabbed him to keep him from falling again. "Pierre hated snakes," Henri whimpered. "It must have been terrifying for him." Henri closed his eyes and prayed. "Lord, please take him straight to heaven. The man suffered an unbearable death."

"Where is his body?" Nicolas Perrot asked.

"In our tradition, we bury the body before the sun sets the next day," Malomimis said. "We wrapped Pierre in our finest woven blankets and buried him on the bluff where our fallen chiefs lie. We laid his body on the ground and built a dirt mound over him. Everyone in the tribe brought a river stone to lay on his grave. That way, we will always remember how many lives the Black Robes saved. Father Allouez said he wants to build a chapel up there to watch over our ancestors' spirits. We thought Pierre would like that. It's also our tradition to burn the wigwam of the deceased along with their possessions."

"Did you burn his journal and maps? They meant everything to Pierre!" Henri said, again raising his voice.

"No, Black Robe Henri. That's why we are here. We believe that if you don't burn the deceased possessions, the soul of the departed will not leave. They will linger and haunt the village seeking revenge."

Chief Malomimis motioned his two clan leaders to come forth with the basket. Henri hesitated before looking in, fearing what might be inside. But what he saw brought tears and a sigh of relief. The basket held Pierre's pack, gear, and Pierre's neatly folded black robe. And on top of the pile was Pierre's journal, tightly bound with his vow cross.

Henri broke down again. He was ashamed for having felt joy at recovering the documents. He wanted to run away and pray for the salvation of his soul.

"Henri, my Black Robe friend," Chief Malomimis said. "I must ask you one more thing. Because we didn't burn Pierre's possessions, we need your permission to perform the Ghost Dance so his spirit can pass into the next world."

Henri felt a sense of rage and wanted to tell them to go away. They have caused enough grief. But then he heard a voice in the back of his head. It was Pierre repeating one word: "SYNCRETISM." Henri knew what he had to do.

"It would be an honor to all of us if you would," Henri said.

Chief Hoocak granted the Menominee the use of his central-fire dancing area. Chief Malomimis ordered two of his men to bring the dry firewood. The basket was placed near the fire, and the six-foot cross was planted next to it, such that it stood straight up. Henri, Nokee, Morningstar, and Nicolas Perrot were directed to sit next to the basket. They then handed Pierre's journal, pack, and vow cross to Henri. Finally, to the surprise of the peace delegation, they draped Pierre's black robe over the cross, making it look like he was standing there.

Chief Malomimis led the procession with twenty men forming a tight circle around the peace delegation and the central fire. His two clan leaders worked the drums. Each person put their hand on the shoulder of the one in front to show group unity and not allow the spirit to break free. Shuffling and stepping to the drums, they moved counterclockwise around the circle.

Chief Malomimis led the chant. "Come forth, Pierre."

The Menominee warriors responded, "And rise to join the spirits of our brothers."

After three rounds, Chief Malomimis stopped so a second larger circle could form outside of the first. The Tutelo, Ottawa, and Nicolas Perrot's men joined the dance. After three more rounds of chanting, the Winnebago villagers stepped in, creating a third ring so all the village men, women, and children were involved. The dance went on nonstop for almost an hour. Chief Malomimis even got Henri, Nokee, Morningstar, and Nicolas Perrot to hold hands and dance around the basket with them.

It was a breathtaking sight; the whole experience seemed to draw the grief and suffering out of the peace delegation. Henri heard chants in Siouan, Menominee, French, Chippewa, Ottawa, and Sauk dialects. Henri smiled as he thought how proud Pierre would be, knowing that his death had peacefully brought all these different people together. His death was not in vain.

Chief Malomimis stopped the dance and called out to Henri. "It is time." One of the drummers presented Henri with a burning torch and instructed him to light the basket on fire. The circle dance started again until the robe disappeared, and the burning cross collapsed. The crowd cheered and yelled. "Now go and rise to the heavens!" Suddenly, it was over.

Nicolas Perrot, feeling the sense of cooperation amongst the tribes, asked for a council meeting with the three chiefs. The rest of the peace delegation returned to their wigwam to figure out what to do next. Henri sat clutching Pierre's journal and reciting quiet prayers. Morningstar was fussing with Illiniwek, who seemed a little colicky. And like all new mothers, she worried he could be coming down with something more serious. Nokee sat quietly by Henri, waiting for him to speak.

Finally, the prayers stopped, and Henri looked up. "It

should've been me. I was the one who told them that I knew how to fix things. But all I did was utilize the plants and medicines they have used for hundreds, maybe thousands of years. Their medicine men mixed most of the remedies. Chief Malomimis wouldn't have banished those two if I stayed out of the way."

"Don't talk like that," Nokee said. "Chief Malomimis and the villagers don't feel that way. They wouldn't be here if they did. You heard Chief Malomimis: everyone in the village placed a stone on Pierre's grave so they could always remember how many lives the two of you saved."

"I pray what you say is true," Henri said, his head hanging down. "Still, it should've been me. Pierre wasn't to blame. ... Nokee, I must tell you something. I felt joy when I saw Pierre's journal. Can you imagine that? My thoughts were on preserving paper over the loss of my friend. I'm ashamed."

"I don't believe that for a minute," Nokee said. "You two were inseparable. And I was happy to see the journal as well—so much of my people's history is in the two of your writings. Pierre would want us to carry on. We will miss Pierre's joyful spirit. It would bring me great comfort to see his final resting place. We'll go there tomorrow."

"Yes," Henri said. "We need to see Pierre's grave."

Henri clutched Pierre's journal as his eyes filled with tears. "He was so talented, you know. Pierre had a photographic memory. He could map every detail he had seen at the end of the day. Would you like to see the map of the Upper Great Lakes he just finished?"

"Yes, that would please me greatly," Nokee said with a smile.

Henri flipped the journal over to pull the map out of the back sleeve, and something fell out and hit the floor. Henri picked it up and looked at it inquisitively. "Is this what I think it is? Is this the blade you gave Pierre at Pine Lake?"

Nokee pulled his hand back. "I dare not touch it. There's only one way to know. Turn it over and tell me what you see."

Henri slowly turned the spear blade over. "I see a carved *N*."

"Yes, that is the one," Nokee said, his hands covering his face. "That stone carries a deadly curse. I was only sixteen and fleeing from the Chippewa when I picked it up. I thought it was placed there by my ancestors—I thought it would bring me luck. But it didn't. I now know that is the mark of Nanabozho, the trickster and shape changer. Pierre became part of that curse when he failed to toss it in the grave. That curse is now on you!"

"Nokee," Henri said, putting his hand on Nokee's shoulder. "Pierre and I don't believe in curses or the evil of the Dark Forces. Our God chooses the time and place when he wants to call one of his children back home. He decided it was time for Pierre."

"Well, you better start believing now. After I picked up that blade, the Chippewa and Ottawa pursued me for weeks. When I arrived at the Miami camp, my tribe had abandoned me. I waited for Tionontati's return, and he never showed up. The war with the Iroquois broke out, and I fought endless battles. When I thought things had settled down, I married, only to have my first wife and child die in childbirth. I wandered for months and ended up in Detroit."

Morningstar came over to calm her husband. Nokee looked up and said, "Shortly after your husband fell from the tree, Tenron deliberately buried Shater in the mound of my ancestors. I saw you with the Tutelo at the trading post and thought you were beautiful. Tenron saw me looking at you on the island and started the fight. I'm afraid I passed this curse on to you as well.

"It wasn't just by chance that I showed up at your camp in Detroit," Nokee continued. "I was coming to see if you wanted to leave the Tutelo. Those trappers happened to show up first. Then there was that fight with Tenron at Mudwayaushka, when Chief Twakanha turned on me in the canoe, the battle with the wendigo, and the tragic death of your brother. ... If that isn't proof enough, Tenron reappeared at the rendezvous, you had a difficult pregnancy, and Tenron forced you to flee Chief Waubay's camp. It's all tied to that stone. Now, the death of Pierre. That stone is cursed, I tell you. All near it will suffer until we get rid of or destroy it."

Nokee emptied his tobacco pouch and asked Henri to drop the point in the leather bag. He told Morningstar to spend the night with the Winnebago women. The evil in the stone may already be affecting the health of little Illiniwek. Nokee left to find a flat rock to tie to the pouch. The plan was for Henri to drop it in the deepest part of Lake Winnebago as they headed toward Pierre's grave in the morning.

Henri sat there shaking his head, thinking. *Nokee is ridiculous. All those things that happened were just coincidental. They are part of the risk we took when we decided to undertake this journey. Pierre didn't believe in the curse. He chose to keep this point for a reason. Who am I to deny him that?*

Henri removed the spear point from the tobacco pouch and placed it back in the sleeve of Pierre's journal. He picked up a small flat stone and dropped it in the pouch. *I'll let Nokee have his victory*, he thought. *This one's between you and me, Pierre. No one needs to know.*

Nokee came back with the flat rock and some cord. "Here, tie this around the pouch, and you can drop it in the lake tomorrow when we leave. I don't dare touch it. It has come to you, and you must be the one to get rid of it."

"What do you need to get rid of, and who is leaving?" Nicolas Perrot asked as he stood at the open door. "You aren't throwing away Pierre's journal, are you?"

"Heavens no," Henri said. "Pierre had a spear point that Nokee is convinced is causing all the trouble we are experiencing. We are going to Pierre's grave tomorrow, and Nokee wants me to drop the point in the lake. I was hoping you would go with us."

"That's a splendid idea. I think it will do all of us some good. I'm sorry, Henri, for the loss of Pierre. He was a splendid fellow with the heart of an angel. God wanted him back sooner than we wanted."

Nicolas turned to Nokee. "Planning on getting rid of that spear point must have worked. Just minutes ago, the three chiefs agreed to the alliance with the French. I'll provide each of them with ten guns, powder, and lead. It looks like the mission of the peace delegation is back on track."

As the three men prepared to leave in the morning, Morningstar approached Nokee. "I wish I could go with you, but I'll need to stay with Illiniwek. He seemed to get better after we moved to the other wigwam, but I don't want to take any chances." Nokee looked at Henri and grinned.

"Nokee, would you be upset if I asked you to place the bear necklace you gave me on Pierre's grave? It's the most precious item I own, and I want the love in it to pass on to Pierre."

"I think that is a perfect gift. I'll do the same with the one you gave me. He was a dear friend to us all!"

• • •

The following day, they set out early with one of the Menominee clan leaders. As they neared one of the deepest parts of the lake, they dropped the pouch containing the fake stone into the water. Nicolas Perrot winked at Henri, and they moved on. The group arrived at the Menominee village around noon to a cheering crowd.

"I told you they considered you a hero," Nokee said with a smile. "They'll be singing songs about you for a hundred years."

The clan leader told the Menominee villagers that Chief Malomimis had stayed for another night to celebrate the Buffalo Dance with the Winnebago. He described how the Ghost Dance had drawn out Pierre's soul and sent it to the spirit world and explained that Black Robe Henri had come to see Pierre's grave and count the stones to see how many lives they had saved. The crowd cheered again and led the peace delegation up the hill to the graves of their ancestors.

When they reached the top of the bluff, Henri saw ten well-kept grass mounds. The mounds were three to four feet tall and about ten feet around. *If a Chief lives approximately thirty years*, Henri thought, *these people have been here for hundreds of years.*

Off to the side, Henri saw a fresh dirt mound covered with hundreds of stones. His eyes filled with tears as he approached the grave. The crowd was quiet as Henri said a series of Our Fathers, first in Algonquian, then in French, and finally in Latin.

Then, sensing they were waiting for Henri's reaction to the pile of stones, he gestured like he was counting each one. Each time he counted ten more, he would flash his ten fingers, and the crowd would roar. He repeated these gestures twenty or more times until everyone was laughing and cheering.

Henri remembered what Pierre had said: "Medicine is important, but laughter heals souls."

Nicolas Perrot had brought a four-foot cross, which he pounded into the ground at the head of Pierre's mound. Nokee placed the two necklaces around the cross, and Nicolas Perrot added a black beaded rosary he had received from Father Allouez. Henri said more prayers and tearfully placed Pierre's vow cross with the rest of the items. Returning to the village, Henri spent time talking to the people. They thanked and praised him for everything he and Pierre had done. It brought Henri some sense of closure.

Then, a young child, guided by her parents, approached Henri. They gently pushed her forward, and in a soft, clear voice, she said: "Merci, Mon Ami."

Henri looked stunned. Then her parents, speaking in Algonquian, said, "Your friend taught her that just before he died. She is the one he saved!"

Tears welled up in Henri's eyes. "*Merci, Mon Cher Petit, Merci beaucoup.*" Then, speaking in Algonquian so all could hear, he said, "That is the greatest gift anyone has ever given me!"

• • •

While the three men were on their way back, a group of Winnebago women approached Morningstar. They were going upriver to empty their walleye traps for the Buffalo Dance Celebration feast, and they asked her to come along. At first, she was reluctant, but they assured her that the older women would take loving care of Illiniwek.

The women paddled upriver until they entered a large lake the French called Lake Butte des Morts. The French named it after the tall hill on the north side of the lake, which had been used for burials by the Menominee and Winnebago for countless generations. At the far end of the lake, they entered the Upper Fox River and the western boundary of the Winnebago territory. The women had set their traps there because the hungry walleye came out of the deep waters of the lake at night and entered the river to feed on the abundant minnows. The women's traps were filled with lively fish. The women gleefully stripped down to keep their clothing dry and waded in with baskets to retrieve the fish.

They had just dropped off a load of fish to the younger girls on the bank and were returning to the traps when a voice called out from the other side of the river. "Hey, ladies, we are here to trade!" To Morningstar's horror, she looked over to see the three rogue trappers standing on the bank, shaking beads and ringing bells.

Morningstar squatted low in the water, hiding behind the women. "Splash playfully and draw their attention as you wade upstream toward them. But don't get too close. I have a plan!"

Morningstar took a deep breath, dove underwater, and swam back to shore as the women seductively splashed and slowly moved toward the men. Morningstar was confident she was undetected as she slid in behind a large boulder where she had placed her clothes. But she had underestimated the men's depravity. They quickly grew tired of the display and raised their muskets, demanding the women come ashore.

Crooked Face grabbed the first woman he could reach and put a knife to her throat. "No one has to die if you give us what we want."

Morningstar reached into her shoulder bag and pulled out the pistol she had been carrying for over a year. She braced it across the boulder as Adrien's words echoed in her mind: "With the correct charge of black powder and a .62 caliber ball seated in a cloth wad rammed down the barrel, you can kill a man out to thirty yards. But that takes practice. This pistol is heavy and accurate only if you steady it on a good rest."

Morningstar estimated the distance to Crooked Face to be about forty paces. The lead ball would most likely drop at that distance, so she steadied her pistol on the boulder. She lined the sights up at the top of his head and waited. Morningstar made a cardinal bird call to catch the eye of Aashvi, the woman with the knife at her throat. When Aashvi saw the other two men set down their guns, she slowly tilted her head to the side, and Morningstar fired. The ball caught Crooked Face between the eyes. She saw his silhouette collapse into the dark water. The sound of the shot echoed off the rocks, causing the two remaining men to think they were under fire from multiple fronts. They grabbed their muskets and ran off, heading upriver.

• • •

When Nokee, Henri, and Perrot returned from the Menominee village, they were enraged by news of the attack. As they interviewed the women for all possible details—what happened, what the men looked like—Morningstar told the men to settle down.

"Crooked Face is dead. Here's his musket," she said, handing it to Nokee. "We left his ugly carcass where it fell. Let the carrion-eaters feast on his flesh. The other two are now in the territory of the Fox tribe."

"Tomorrow," Nicolas Perrot said, "we'll go after them. Henri, you may now get your wish to meet the Fox. We better be prepared for that!" Nokee nodded in agreement.

# Reunited

As the peace delegation readied their gear for the trip up the Fox River, Nicolas Perrot went over to talk to his gun-trading team. He told them to leave without him if he didn't return in four days—he would catch up with them in St. Ignace in the fall.

Nicolas Perrot then told the three chiefs that he and the peace delegation would spend the night enjoying the celebration and dance, but they would leave in the morning. They hoped to chase down those two trappers and maybe set up a peace meeting with the Fox. Chief Hoocak offered to send ten of his finest warriors, and Chief Malomimis did the same.

Nicolas Perrot thanked them but turned down the offer. "We want this to look like a peace delegation, not an invading army. If we do meet up with the Fox tribe, I want to offer them the same deal I presented to you. If they join our alliance of Great Lakes tribes, the French military will also supply them with guns."

"Well then," Chief Hoocak said, "I'll offer you one warrior. His name is Banabou—he is my son. He has traded with the Fox tribe and can verify that I've joined your alliance."

"I'll send one of my clan leaders," Chief Malomimis said. "His name is Omano. He can verify that I've done the same."

The Ottawa Chief, Kawachewan, joined in. "I'll give you two of my lightest, well-built, four-person canoes. There will be many portages on the Upper Fox River. I pray the river spirits will be kind to you. The Fox people dislike the Ojibwa, and the Ojibwa are Ottawa's closest ally. It would be best not to mention the Ottawa in your dealings with the Fox."

"We will graciously accept your offers," Nicolas Perrot said with a smile. "Now let's enjoy the rest of the day, and tonight we celebrate the Buffalo Dance."

At sundown, the celebration began. Henri described the event in his journal:

> The process began early in the day when the Winnebago women emptied the last of their corn, beans, squash, and wild rice from their underground winter storage pits. They began preparing every conceivable meat, fish, and vegetable dish you could think of. There was fresh grilled deer, elk, turkey, baked walleye, steamed mussels, and smoked sturgeon. The sides consisted of roasted squash, salad with crushed nuts and dried cranberries, and frybread. Rabbit stew with duck potatoes and mushrooms, prairie chicken and wild rice soup, boiled duck eggs, cornmeal pudding, and sassafras-root tea were available. And, of course, Chief Hoocak's favorite, chilled sturgeon eggs.
>
> After the Great Feast, the crowd gathered around the central fire. Twenty men and twenty women disappeared into the meeting house to prepare for the Buffalo Dance. Shortly afterward, twenty women emerged wearing buffalo head masks with horns. A long strip of hide with the hair and tail attached ran down their backs, dragging on the ground. They danced around the fire twice like a herd of buffalo cows slowly grazing on the prairie grass. On the third round, five evenly spaced women dropped to their knees, crawling behind the women dancing in front of them, symbolizing five newborn calves. On round four, five more women dropped and crawled, insinuating every adult buffalo cow had given birth to twins. The crowd cheered and beat drums, knowing the buffalo herds would be plentiful on their fall hunt.
>
> The women slowly returned to the meeting house, and twenty men, wearing buffalo head masks and hides, sprinted to the fire. As they raced around the central fire, they were chased by twenty women carrying torches, acting like they were setting the prairie on fire. Five archers came screaming out of the crowd with bows and leather-blunted arrows and shot five running buffalo men. Five women ran out, dragged the fallen buffalo men to the side, and acted like they were cutting them up. The archers shot five more buffalo men and five more women with knives butchered them. This scene repeated until all the buffalo men were on the ground, skinned and butchered.

As the first part of the dance ended, the crowd roared and everyone jumped up, forming four circles around the dancing buffalo men and women until everyone was dancing to the drums. Henri joined the dance, but he had one last trick he wanted to pull off to honor his best friend. Every time the crowd made a full circle, Henri would step one ring closer to the fire. After four rounds, he was in the first ring, next to the dancing buffalo men and women.

Earlier, Henri had gone through Pierre's pack and found the six small tins in the wooden box labeled fireworks stars. He put the tins in the pockets of his black robe. As the crowd began to slow down, Henri made his move.

On the next round, he yelled, "May the yellow prairie grass grow long and fatten the buffalo herds!" Then Henri threw sodium stars into the fire. The fire crackled, and yellow flames filled the air.

"Fatten the buffalo," responded the crowd.

On the second round, Henri yelled, "May the blue skies turn dark and bring rain to the grass." He threw in copper stars, which flashed blue.

"Rain for the grass," responded the crowd.

On the third round, Henri yelled, "May the flames of fire drive the buffalo to your hunter's spears." He threw in strontium stars, which flashed red.

"Drive the buffalo," responded the crowd.

On the fourth round, Henri yelled, "May the stars in the heavens watch over the herd." He threw in aluminum stars, which flashed white.

"Watch over the buffalo," responded the crowd.

On the fifth round, Henri yelled, "May the setting sun guide the way for your fallen warriors." He threw in calcium stars, which flashed orange.

"Guide the fallen," responded the crowd.

And on the sixth and final round, Henri yelled, "May the grass be forever green on the graves of your ancestors." He threw in barium stars, which crackled and flashed green. The crowd roared, danced in a frenzy, and finally, out of breath, stopped for a break. When the group started up again, they danced late into the night until a pouring rain sent everyone scurrying for cover.

• • •

In the morning, two canoes headed upriver. Nicolas Perrot, Banabou, and Omano were in the lead canoe carrying three wooden boxes of guns and a large woven basket with a lid. Nokee, Henri, Morningstar, and Illiniwek followed with enough provisions to last a month. They entered Lake Butte des Morts, and Morningstar pointed out the large hill from which the lake derived its name. At the other end, they turned south and entered the Upper Fox River.

The men wanted to see Crooked Face's body, but when Morningstar pointed to where he fell, they found nothing. "You're sure it was here?" Nicolas Perrot asked. "Maybe you were a little upstream."

"It was right there," she insisted. "I can still smell the rotting fish guts on the other side of the river."

They all got out and looked for blood, but last night's rain had washed everything away. "Maybe Crooked Face wasn't dead," Nicolas said. "Maybe the other two came back and got his body. They might be watching us right now. We better keep our guard up!"

"He's dead, I assure you," Morningstar said, "and I doubt those two lowlifes will return. They ran like scared rabbits."

"I've seen Morningstar shoot," Henri said. "I doubt she missed her mark."

Just then, there was a whistle from the sandbar willows, and Banabou was waving them over. He pointed to a pile of leaves and brush. "He's in there, half-eaten. Judging from the tracks, a male mountain lion dragged him over there. They always cover their kill so the vultures don't find it before they return for a second meal."

"Well, Crooked Face is history," Nokee said. "Let's go get the other two."

Cautiously, they traveled the next ten miles up the Fox River until it widened into a large marsh created by a tall beaver dam. As they pulled their canoes out to portage around the dam, twenty Fox braves with bows drawn stepped out of the trees. Everyone froze.

"I am Pemoussa, a Fox war chief. What brings a mixed bag of trespassers into the Land of the Fox?"

"We come in peace," Banabou replied. "We seek counsel with your peace chief, the great Meskwaki."

"I can arrange that," Pemoussa said, waving his warriors to stand down. "But first, is your group prepared to pay the required toll for trespassing on Fox territory? The two Frenchmen that came before you weren't, so we extracted it from them." Pemoussa pointed to the side, and the heads of the French trappers, swarming with flies, were on poles. Henri felt sick.

"Good," said a voice behind Banabou as Morningstar approached the front. "I killed their leader for trying to rape a group of Winnebago women two days ago. I killed him with this!" She slowly pulled the pistol out of her bag and handed it to Pemoussa. "I've no more use for it."

Pemoussa looked at Banabou. "You brought an Ojibwa woman with you? You know what we think of the Ojibwa."

"I'm Chippewa," Morningstar said proudly. "Daughter of Chief Twakanha, ruler of the Saginaw Valley!"

"Saginaw Valley, you say," Pemoussa said. "Our ancestors knew that area all too well. My people fought with our Sauk brothers to defend that land until we grew tired of fighting the Chippewa and Ojibwa for it."

"Then they fought beside my father," Nokee said, stepping forward and displaying the markings of a peace chief on both arms. "Chief Mahtowa, Sauk Peace Chief of the Grand River Band was my father. He died in battle. Morningstar is my wife, and she goes where I go. I gift you this rifle as well, taken from the trapper she killed. We are here to offer you lasting peace if you are willing to unite with the rest of the Great Lakes tribes."

"And how does a son of a fallen peace chief have the ability to make such an offer?" Pemoussa asked.

"He does it with the backing of the French military," Nicolas Perrot said. "I'm here to provide Chief Meskwaki with many guns if he wishes to join the alliance."

"Banabou, did your father join this alliance?" Pemoussa asked.

"Yes, he did, and so did Chief Malomimis of the Menominee. Malomimis sent one of his clan leaders, Omano, to verify this." Omano nodded.

Then Henri stepped forward. "Take these as well. Here is the trade axe and metal knife of my Black Robe friend. He died because those three trappers brought a deadly disease into the Menominee village. Pierre was a man of peace. May Pierre's peace and happiness come to you through these items."

"Who is this black-robed spirit?" Pemoussa asked. "Why is he here?"

"He's a powerful shaman," Banabou replied. "He can heal the sick and has magical powers over fire."

"Come," Pemoussa said, ordering his men to ready their canoes. "We'll take you to Chief Meskwaki. He will decide the fate of your mission."

They traveled up the Fox River for a day and a half until they reached Puckaway Lake. It was there, on an island in the middle of the lake, that they found Chief Meskwaki's camp. To their surprise, the Sauk Chief Keokuk was with him.

Pemoussa explained to the chiefs that the Frenchman promised to bring many guns. "The other three claimed to present an offer of peace," Pemoussa said. "And Banabou told me the Black Robe has power over fire."

Chief Meskwaki approached Banabou and Omano. "Brothers of trade, who are these strangers you bring to my village? You know the Fox tribe guards our location from strangers with our very lives."

"My father has known the Frenchman Perrot for many years," Banabou said. "He welcomes him and his Black Robe friend Allouez. They care for our sick."

"Nicolas Perrot was the one that brought the two Black Robes to our village," Omano said. "We were dying from the flu sickness. Black Robe Henri and his friend saved our people with their black magic. But first, before we seek counsel, our chiefs offer gifts." He nodded to Banabou to fetch the basket from the canoe.

Omano lifted the lid and pulled out a full-length white and gray caribou coat with a hood. He gave it to Chief Keokuk. "It will keep you warm and dry in the heaviest rains."

Then Banabou reached into the basket and lifted a large, beautifully decorated clay vase. Handing it to Chief Meskwaki, he said, "It will keep your wild rice fresh and dry for months."

The two chiefs were thrilled with the gifts and thanked Omano and Banabou. Chief Meskwaki turned to Nicolas Perrot. "I remember when you and Black Robe Allouez tried to enter the territory of the Fox. You had nothing to offer but this."

Chief Meskwaki pulled from his medicine bag a black beaded rosary like the one Nicolas Perrot had hung on the cross at Pierre's grave. "Black Robe Allouez told me this would bring me peace, and it has—until recently." With a frown, he nodded at Chief Keokuk. "The Sauk chief tells me there is much trouble brewing throughout the lands of the woodland tribes, and I know that the Fox people have few friends! However, I've heard many good things about Allouez since he was here. I wish I hadn't been so hasty at sending him away. Maybe the Black Robe with you can bring back the magic in these beads?"

"Well, Great Chief," Nicolas said, "You must ask the Black Robe that question. I likewise remember you, but I have more to offer this time. We bring you an offer of lasting peace and the firearms to ensure it endures."

Nicolas Perrot motioned to Banabou and Omano to retrieve two boxes from the canoe, each containing ten French military muskets.

"One box is for you, Chief Meskwaki, and the other is for Chief Keokuk. I have a twenty-pound bag of lead balls and a full keg of powder for each of you."

Both chiefs looked pleasantly surprised. "Why is the Frenchman so generous?" Chief Meskwaki wondered aloud.

"I have offered the same deal to all the Great Lakes tribes I've visited. And I promise more guns to all that join the alliance. The tribes to the south are under constant attack by the Iroquois, and the Ojibwa Chief Waubay says he is experiencing raids from the Dakota Sioux from the west. When a Great Lakes tribe allies with the French military, they become an unstoppable force."

"You have given guns to the Ojibwa to the north? You know they're our blood enemy!"

"Not anymore," Nicolas Perrot said. "By joining the alliance, they've agreed not to attack alliance tribes."

"You will bring us more guns if we do the same?" Sauk Chief Keokuk asked.

"Yes, I'll return next year with more guns and the chance to trade furs with the French. We provide many useful items to those that trade with us."

"Frenchman, your timing is good," Keokuk said. "I'm here to convince Chief Meskwaki that we must ally and prepare for war. The Iroquois have been raiding our southern border. The Kickapoo tribe is stirring up trouble with the Dakota Sioux to the west. Those Kickapoo people are an unruly bunch. They moved in here some years ago, and they have taken to stealing Sioux horses. It is only a matter of time until the Sioux declare war on the western woodland tribes!"

"Did you say there are Kickapoo here?" Nokee asked. "Where did they come from, and how long have they been here?"

"They say they came from the other side of the Big Lake," Chief Keokuk said. "From the land of my ancestors. Who are you to ask, peace chief with no tribe?"

"My name is Nokee! I'm the son of Mahtowa. He was the last Sauk chief to die defending the land you once called home. My tribe came this way following a group of Kickapoo many years ago. I hope to find them."

"And who would be the current leader of that tribe?"

"His name is Muskuta. He was my father's war chief."

"Then old Tionontati was right!" Chief Keokuk said. "He told me their true chief would return someday!"

"Tionontati is alive?" Nokee asked. "Was there a woman with him? Did he find the rest of our tribe?"

"He's alive, but Tionontati is incredibly old and frail. There's an older woman who takes care of him—I don't know her name. Yes, all your people are there. They live near our southern border, at the portage between the headwaters of the Fox and the Wisconsin Rivers. On the route to the Great River, the Misi Sipi. I'll take you there."

Nicolas Perrot's ears perked up at the news that they were on the same route traveled by Jean Nicolet in 1634. Chief Keokuk had just confirmed the route to the Mississippi.

Henri missed the significance of what had just happened—his focus was on Nokee. Henri put his hand on Nokee's shoulder.

"Congratulations Nokee. You've found your tribe. We did it. The peace delegation is well on the way to completing our mission."

"I'm afraid the three of you will have to do that without me," Nicolas Perrot said. "Banabou, Omano, and I will head back in the morning. If I leave now, I can catch my fur-trading crew before they head out. After you find Nokee's people, what will you do next?"

"Well," Henri said, "I haven't thought that far ahead. I'll probably head back to the Menominee village. I still want to set up a mission at the De Pere Rapids. Nicolas, my dear friend, are you certain you will return to Green Bay in the spring?"

"Yes. God willing, I'll be back next year with another load of guns."

"Then I need you to do me a favor. When you see Father Allouez and Father Marquette, tell them the news about Pierre and that I'll spend the winter with the Menominee. I want to start ministering to them and the Winnebago people right away. Ask Father Allouez to accompany you to the Menominee camp next spring before returning to his Chequamegon Bay mission. I need his approval for that site at De Pere. Oh, and most importantly, make sure you tell Father Marquette that Jean Nicolet was right. The way to the Misi Sipi, the Big River, is the Fox River through Lake Winnebago."

"You have my word. I'll do both," Nicolas said, giving a nod and a smile.

Chief Meskwaki called his war chief, Pemoussa, to his side. "Stay with them. Find out which tribes joined this alliance with the French. Note their numbers and strength, then report back to me. Chief Keokuk has been telling stories that a Great Uniter would come someday. He could easily fall prey to a false prophet drummed up by the French."

That night, Henri wrote in his journal:

> The Sauk and Fox in Wisconsin are fearless warriors. They are the defenders of the north, spending most of their time keeping the Ojibwa and French at bay. They paint their faces red with fire-heated hematite. They shave their heads, except for a tall strip down the middle, which makes their already tall bodies look even more prominent when facing their foe.

> The Fox speak the same dialect as the Sauk, but they talk much faster. It is like they are nervous. Maybe that is because they have enemies on all sides of their territory. The Fox tribe disliked the French because our fur traders traded guns to the Ojibwa, not them. We seem to have alleviated that concern through the help of Nicolas Perrot. However, their sincerity remains a question.

In the morning, Nicolas, Banabou, and Omano headed downriver, and Chief Keokuk, Pemoussa, and the remnants of the peace delegation headed upstream. Just before nightfall, they reached Chief Keokuk's camp on Packwaukee Island in the middle of the Upper Fox River.

As they landed, Chief Keokuk approached Nokee. "Peace chief of the Grand River Sauk, I want to show you something."

Keokuk took Nokee, Henri, and Pemoussa to the top of a long ridge and showed them a group of effigy mounds. There were five animal-like figures, each three to five feet tall, with the longest measuring about one hundred feet. But their images were striking. They saw a bear, deer, buffalo, turtle, and bird. The largest was the thunderbird mound, its wings outstretched.

"Who created these?" Henri asked after sketching the images in his journal.

"I don't know," said Chief Keokuk. "Our stories tell us they were here when the first Sauk and Fox arrived." Pemoussa nodded in agreement. "Tionontati has an idea, but no one knows for sure."

"I must ask Tionontati about these," Henri said.

"Well, you better hurry. Tionontati is old and near death. But he claims the Gitchee Manito told him he would not die until his rightful chief returned. We should arrive at their camp in a half-day."

Looking at Nokee, Keokuk said, "If you are who you say, you may be what brings about Tionontati's death." Nokee returned to camp without saying a word, deep in thought.

# The Chosen One

In the morning, Chief Keokuk approached the peace delegation's wigwam with troubling news. "Word has spread that the Chief of Legends has arrived. Our stories tell us that this Chosen One will come at a time of great trouble. He will be invincible, wielding the power of the sky and the Dark Forces below. His offspring will unite the tribes.

"War is coming at us from multiple fronts," Keokuk continued. "The strangers are changing the way we live. Our people need a savior now more than ever. Your arrival with a sky wife named Morningstar, a Black Robe figure that heals the unhealable and has power over fire, and a child whose father claims he's here to unite the tribes, you can see why people are hopeful."

Nokee shook his head. "Stories get told and retold. In each telling, the main character always gets bigger and more powerful. I, like my father, am just a man. I want them to accept or reject me for what I am."

"I'm afraid it's not that simple," Keokuk said. "Yesterday, when we were at the effigy mounds, two of my warriors traveled south to your tribe and spread the word of your arrival. All your people are expecting a grand entrance, and for some reason, fate has chosen me to be the one that delivers you. If you are the Chosen One, your arrival must happen a certain way. Legend says you'll appear from the east, walking on water in a cloud of smoke and fire. The stories we tell our children are what keep our people together. If our stories are untrue, our history is a lie.

"Therefore, I've ordered my people to assemble the finest clothing we can produce for you and Morningstar. Tonight, there is a full moon. We'll travel then. There is a bend where the river turns west, just before reaching your village. Tionontati picked that location to watch the eastern morning sky for your arrival. We'll wait there until dawn. That way, we can approach from the east, in the morning mist, with the rising sun at your back. That's how the prophecy says it will happen."

Chief Keokuk looked at Henri, a questioning expression on his face. "Black Robe, Pemoussa told Chief Meskwaki and me that you have power over fire. Is that true?"

"No, that's not true," Henri said solemnly. "It was my friend who died at the Menominee camp. He knew how to light up the sky with fire. I only borrowed a few of his tricks at the Buffalo Dance. I wish he were here. He could help with your grand entrance plan."

"I wish the same," Keokuk said. "Very well. I need a private counsel with Nokee in my lodge. I must be certain he's truly the promised one."

As Chief Keokuk walked away, Nokee sat down beside Henri and Morningstar, his head in his hands. "What have we gotten ourselves into? They think I'm a god. How am I supposed to live up to that? What am I supposed to say in private counsel to convince Chief Keokuk that I'm the one he is supposed to deliver?"

"Don't worry, Nokee!" Morningstar said. "That should be easy—you *are* the one they are expecting. Tionontati and Muskuta are alive. The woman taking care of Tionontati is most likely your mother. Tionontati foretold this day would come years ago. Your people know who you are. What more do you need to prove?"

"She's right, Nokee," Henri said. "Since we met, I've believed that a higher force has guided us on this journey. Too many things have fallen into place for this to be by chance. You can't quit now. If you do, everything we've been through was for nothing. Pierre's death will have been in vain. Be the savior you are. I know you will exceed all their expectations."

"Thanks for the vote of confidence," Nokee said as he stood up. "I guess I'll go over and talk to Keokuk. I hope the first test isn't walking on water."

When Nokee reached Chief Keokuk's lodge, he paused at the door, considering his situation. *What could Keokuk possibly want?*

he thought. *Why do I have to prove myself to anyone? I know who I am and what my purpose is. It's Tionontati who should be asking questions, not the delivery service. I don't need this!*

As Nokee started to turn away, a strange yet vaguely familiar voice echoed around him, as if it came from everywhere and nowhere. "Where are you going? I'm here to assist you in your quest. But first, you should eat. I know how hungry you are. One taste of this stew and everything you desire will be possible."

"I've heard these words before," Nokee said as he whipped open the door, expecting to see the wendigo. But all he saw was Chief Keokuk smoking his pipe next to a fresh pot of stew and two bowls.

"What's the matter, Nokee? You look like you have seen a ghost."

Nokee sat down, visibly shaken. "I heard those same words the night I fought the wendigo."

"Wendigos are potent spirits," Keokuk said. "Only the purest of souls can defeat one. What did he want?"

"He showed me three paths. They represented the past, present, and future. He told me I must choose one. Whichever path I chose would be the one I would follow for the rest of my days. There was no going back."

"And which one did you choose?"

"I chose the future."

"Why?"

"Because Tionontati had a dream where the Great Spirit, Gitchee Manito, came to him. The spirit told him I would undertake a great journey before being accepted as chief of my tribe. I would travel the Great Circle, visit sacred places, listen to the guiding voices, and find my way back. If I did this, I would receive help from unexpected people and places along the way—and I have. 'Trust your heart,' he said, and I found Morningstar. He said when I finally returned to my people, I would be recognized, and there would be much joy. Now, I sit with you as you prepare to deliver me to my people and fulfill the prophecy. Why do you question my authenticity?"

"I no longer do. Those are the same words Tionontati used

when he predicted your coming. You are the Chosen One, and your son will become the Great Uniter. I'm at your service."

"I was hoping I would be the one that unites the tribes and brings about the defeat of the Iroquois raiders."

"You most certainly will play a major role in your son's development, but the prophecy says that task will fall on his shoulders."

When Nokee returned to his wigwam, he found Henri anxiously waiting for him. "What did he say?"

"He told me he now believes I'm the Chosen One, and Illiniwek will be the Great Uniter. He said we should all get some rest because we are to gather at the meeting house tonight when the full moon is directly overhead. At that point, they'll dress us for our grand entrance."

"Wow, this is getting crazy," Henri said.

"I agree," Nokee said, shaking his head.

While Morningstar and Nokee rested, Henri went to see Chief Keokuk. Entering Keokuk's lodge, Henri said, "I have an idea that might help you with your unveiling. However, I will need some things from you to make it work."

Chief Keokuk listened and agreed to provide Henri with what he needed. Henri insisted everyone had to be in on the plan for it to work. Keokuk promised that his warriors would be ready. Henri left to inform Nokee and Morningstar and help them prepare for Keokuk's shock-and-awe presentation.

• • •

Later that night, ten two-person canoes led the way, their path lit by a full moon high in the sky. Trailing them was a ceremonial canoe, with six Sauk paddlers and Chief Keokuk and Pemoussa seated comfortably in the middle. Last in the procession was the peace delegation in their Ottawa canoe.

Traveling quietly through the night, they reached the western bend in the river and waited for dawn. When the morning sky started to glow red, they lit a torch in each canoe and headed upstream to Nokee's waiting tribe. The ten lead canoes slid onto the bank at the village, leaving an opening in the center. The villagers cheered as the warriors jumped ashore, drums beating as they called out, "The Chosen One has arrived."

Chief Keokuk slid his canoe into the center opening, followed by the peace delegation. As he stepped out, he announced, "The heavens have heard our cries. I present to you Morningstar. She holds in her hands the offspring of the Chosen One. The child that will become the Great Uniter."

Morningstar stood up wearing a long white doeskin dress, delicately designed with embroidered patterns. Her long sleeves, fringed on the ends, hung loosely over her arms. Carefully braided feathers highlighted her long black hair, and a white pearl necklace hung elegantly around her slender neck. Her eyes shined like the moon as she smiled and held up Illiniwek for all to see. The crowd roared with excitement.

It was now time for Henri to put his plan into motion. While Nokee and Morningstar had been sleeping the afternoon before, Henri had assembled his pyrotechnic display. From Chief Keokuk, he had obtained a small wooden bowl with a lid, a cup of black powder, and a long wooden canoe-shaped trough used to concentrate maple syrup by the fire. Henri placed the black powder in the small bowl and added the last of Pierre's firework stars. He then twisted all the remaining fuses into one two-foot-long wick and inserted one end in the bowl. He tightly replaced the lid, flipped the bowl over in the trough, and prepared for the Grand Entrance.

"The Dark Forces have heard our cries," Chief Keokuk continued. "I present to you the Black Robe. He heals the unhealable and has power over fire."

Chief Keokuk paused while Henri lifted the tiny canoe-shaped trough for all to see and set it down in the water. Lighting the fuse with one of the torches, he gently pushed the little canoe into the current and nodded to Keokuk.

"I now give you the Chosen One," said Keokuk. "The one the prophecy said would come at a time of great trouble. I present Nokee. He wields the power of the sky and the Dark Forces below."

Suddenly, there was a thunderous bang, a bellow of smoke, and the contents in the bowl shot into the air, followed by the cracking blurts of orange, yellow, green, red, white, and blue. The villagers dropped to their knees as a tall, muscular figure rose from the canoe. Nokee emerged from the billowing smoke, his legs so obscured that he appeared to be walking on water. A decorated shield lined with ermine tails hung from one arm. He held a feather-dressed spear in his right hand and a shiny metal tomahawk in his left. Red paint covered his face and shaven head, except for a tall rooster-tail strip supporting a single eagle feather. He wore a heavily decorated sleeveless tunic, grizzly bear necklace, red breechcloth, buckskin leggings, black bear-furred shin guards decorated with porcupine quills, and elk hide moccasins. He was a breathtaking sight to behold. But what caught the eyes of the crowd, however, was a copper crescent-moon hanging across his chest, once worn by his father.

In a deep voice, Nokee bellowed, "I am Nokee, son of Mahtowa, son of Manomin. I've walked through fire to get here, but that journey wouldn't have been possible without the help of my wife, Morningstar, and my Black Robe friend, Henri. Welcome them as though they were our own."

With that, the women rushed to Morningstar to introduce themselves and fuss over Illiniwek. The younger shaman gathered around Henri, asking questions about his medicine and how he controlled fire. Then, the crowd parted and went silent as Muskuta, the acting chief, slowly approached Nokee. In his hand, he held the chief's staff.

There was a long pause as Muskuta looked Nokee up and down. "This was your father's staff. It came to me when your father died in battle. It can only belong to one man at a time. I now return it to its rightful owner. Welcome back, my chief!" The crowd broke out into a rousing cheer.

Nokee hugged Muskuta and thanked him for his many years of service. Then, looking up, Nokee saw a tired-looking man of many years standing next to a bark-covered wigwam, with a middle-aged woman holding tightly onto his arm.

"Excuse me, Muskuta," Nokee said as he laid all his weaponry on the ground. "There's someone I must see."

As Nokee approached the wigwam, a hush fell over the crowd once more. Wrapping his arms around Tionontati, tears flowed from Nokee's eyes. It felt like twenty years of pain, worry, and doubt were draining from his body.

When he finally found the strength to speak, Nokee said, "I've done the things you asked. I've visited the sacred places and listened to their voices. You foretold of my coming. I now return to you."

"Nokee, you've done what the spirits asked," Tionontati said. "Your people have recognized you. You are now ready to be chief. What's all this smoke and yelling about?"

"Well," whispered Nokee. "Chief Keokuk told us this is how the prophecy said it must happen. He said it was the only way the people would recognize me and listen to what I have to say."

"Well, let me give you some friendly advice, my new chief. The fastest way to spread a story is to whisper it to someone. Yelling goes about as far as a thrown stone."

"I'll remember that, my old friend," Nokee replied with a smile.

Turning to Manomin, Nokee hugged her and said, "Mother, I missed you so much."

"Nokee, look into my eyes," Manomin demanded. She stared for a moment, then said, "I see the strength and determination of your father. You'll make a great chief. Welcome back, my son. I never doubted that you would return."

After a day of fine food and celebration, all the villagers gathered around the central fire as Nokee told his story. To the thrill of the old warriors, he retold how his father had defeated the Ottawa in the now famous ambush battle on top of the Kalamazoo ridge. The children winced when he described how he and the other young warriors were about to be tied to posts and killed. They cheered when Nokee told them how Tionontati had freed them. The young shaman listened with great interest as Nokee described the Great Circle and the burial mound centers he had visited. All the women smiled and shed tears as he talked about his first wife, how she and their son had died during childbirth, and how he had found his new love when he met Morningstar.

The clan leaders showed great interest as Nokee described the numerous items they could gain by trading with the French trappers. The young warriors flooded Nokee with questions as he told how his peace delegation had united the Michigan tribes by promising many guns and assistance from the French soldiers.

"Will the Frenchman be giving us guns?" Muskuta asked in a

loud voice. "The only guns we ever got from the French were the ones we took from them when they shot your father." The crowd went deadly silent.

"I'm aware of who shot my father," Nokee said. "I've met some despicable Frenchmen, and I assure you those men can no longer cause harm. I've also met some exceptionally good Frenchmen, like my Black Robe friend," pointing at Henri. "He and his Black Robe companion have saved many people on the brink of death in neighboring tribes. Henri will bring his Black Robe medicine to our people as well. Then there's our good French friend, Nicolas Perrot. He promises the support of the French Army."

Nokee lowered his voice, whispering to Muskuta, "Nicolas Perrot has sent you ten muskets. They are in a box in my canoe. He promises many more if we ally with the French." The clan leaders behind Muskuta exchanged glances, and a murmur rippled through the crowd. Nokee looked up and winked at Tionontati.

• • •

Chief Keokuk and his warriors returned to their village the following morning, feeling they had done their part. However, Pemoussa, the Fox War Chief, stayed. By mid-afternoon of the second day, a group of Sauk clan leaders from neighboring villages showed up to hear the stories. The Fox leaders arrived the following day, and the day after that, the Kickapoo. Word of the Chosen One's power to obtain guns had spread like wildfire across the land.

Tionontati and Manomin sat with Nokee every day as he retold his story. Tionontati would add a bit here and there, and Manomin would nod in agreement at points in the story she was familiar with. As Nokee sat with the constant stream of visitors, Morningstar trained the Sauk warriors to load and fire their new muskets. By the end of the week, their aim had greatly improved. But not all the news was good. Tionontati was tired, and Manomin informed everyone that he wouldn't be attending the next day's session. Henri was preparing to check on Tionontati when a commotion broke out at the edge of the village. A group of Kaskaskian warriors, holding up peace pipes, were requesting to see Nokee and the Black Robe.

Henri and Nokee jumped up and hurried to meet them. Henri found their speech somewhat Algonquin-like, but difficult to understand. Luckily, Nokee had traded with the Kaskaskians when he lived with the Miami and could understand their language. The Kaskaskians reported they had just come from a trading post on Chequamegon Bay at the La Pointe du St.-Esprit Mission. When Henri asked if they had met another Black Robe there, they reported they had spent a month with a Black Robe named Marquette. He was highly interested in learning their language and wanted to visit them at their village on the Illinois River.

While returning home from Chequamegon Bay, the Kaskaskian warriors had stopped at the Kickapoo village, where the Wisconsin River emptied into the Misi Sipi. The Kickapoo had told them about the prophet and Black Robe who were bringing guns to tribes in need. The Kaskaskian tribes were under frequent attack from the Iroquois to the east, and the stories of a Great Uniter—someone who could bring the tribes of the Illinois Nation together as one—filled them with hope.

They reported that unity was urgently needed, as the Iroquois were targeting one tribe at a time while the others looked on indifferently. If the tribes were to confederate, they could become a powerful defensive force. But until that happened, they needed guns. They had come to see if they could get in on the French gun trade.

Nokee saw this as the opportunity he had been looking for. He sat with the warriors and told them the peace delegation's story: how they had united the Miami, Chippewa, Ottawa, and Potawatomi to fight against the Iroquois on the eastern side of the Big Lake; how the Fox and Sauk had just joined the alliance with the French and promised to stop attacking other woodland tribes; and how the peace delegation planned to visit the Sioux to explore if peace could be re-established. Nokee promised to visit the Kaskaskia soon, and Henri gave the group leader his last two trade axes.

After the visiting warriors left the village satisfied and hopeful about their request, Nokee and Henri agreed that things were finally back on track.

"You see, Henri," Nokee said, "after we got rid of that cursed spear point, things turned around. No more trouble from the Dark Forces."

Henri wanted to tell Nokee he didn't believe in superstitious Dark Forces. He hadn't thrown the spear point into the lake—he only pretended to, hoping to calm Nokee. He wanted to show Nokee that the stone was still in his possession. If anything was guiding their journey, Henri believed it was the hand of the Lord. But in the back of his head, he heard Pierre's voice: "SYNCRETISM. You believe the angels are protecting you. Nokee refers to them as good spirits. They are pretty much the same. SYNCRETISM!"

Suddenly, Manomin came running, panic in her voice. "There's something wrong with Tionontati!" she screamed. "I can't seem to wake him!"

# Tionontati the Storyteller

Henri and Nokee followed Manomin back to the wigwam, where they found Tionontati's condition worsening by the minute. Henri gently shook Tionontati to try to get a response. At first, there was nothing. Nokee sighed, remembering the words of Chief Keokuk: "Tionontati claims the Gitchee Manito told him he'll not die until his rightful chief returns. If you're who you say, by showing up, you may bring about Tionontati's death."

Slowly, Tionontati opened his eyes, and the room fell silent—everyone let out a deep breath. "So, the famous Black Robe has come to save an old medicine man from the fingers of death," Tionontati whispered. "I'll not die lying down. There's still fight in this old warrior."

"Well, there will certainly be no fighting today," Henri said. "Let me look at you." Henri listened to Tionontati's chest and checked his breathing. He felt his pulse and examined his legs.

"Tionontati's heart and pulse are weak," Henri said. "His breathing is labored, and there is swelling in his lower legs. This man's heart is failing. What has he been eating?"

"Well," Manomin said, "Morningstar has been feeding him that salted pork you brought. He seems to like that a lot."

"There'll be no more of that," Henri said firmly. "We need to treat this differently than we did the flu. This man isn't dehydrated; he is retaining fluids, drowning his heart and lungs. We need to draw some of this fluid out. Manomin, have Morningstar bring me my pack."

When Morningstar returned, Henri pulled out his book on medicinal plants. The symptoms of heart failure were shortness of breath, swollen ankles, and a weak pulse. A tea made from the leaves of the foxglove plant was the suggested treatment. It was supposed to strengthen the heartbeat and encourage the kidneys to eliminate excess fluid. However, there was an ominous footnote to the treatment: Administer only one cup per eight hours. All parts of the plant are highly toxic.

"We need to elevate his legs to reduce swelling and raise his head to ease his breathing," Henri said. "Morningstar, have the villagers help you find the foxglove leaves and make the tea. Manomin, you'll need to find us a bowl for a bedpan. He will do a lot of urinating where he lies until he has the strength to get up and walk."

The first twenty-four hours were terrifying for everyone. They started a vapor bucket of juniper berries and spearmint leaves to ease Tionontati's wheezing. By morning, he had taken two treatments of foxglove tea. His urine output went up, and his leg swelling started to go down. They limited his liquid intake to tiny amounts of herbal tea and served him fresh blackberries and boiled beans. On day three, they increased Tionontati's food intake to small portions of boiled grouse or crane breast served on beans or wild rice. On day five, Tionontati was standing and taking short walks.

Everyone in the village remarked that Tionontati had robbed the death spirit of his victory. Henri's fame continued to spread, and the talk around the village was about how anything was possible with the magic of the Black Robe. Henri warned everyone that Tionontati's recovery would take time, and there was no guarantee that he wouldn't slip back into the shadows of death.

"However, don't worry," Henri told them. "I'll stay with him for his recovery, no matter how long it takes."

The villagers laughed at Henri's concerns. "The Black Robe's magic has power over death. Tionontati will be back telling stories in no time!"

By the end of the week, Tionontati's recovery seemed inevitable, and Nokee began visiting surrounding villages to spread his plan of uniting the nations. He went north to the Fox and the Sauk villages, then southwest to talk to the Kickapoo. Next, he decided to head southeast to see the Kaskaskia village along the Upper Illinois River.

During Nokee's absence, Henri was true to his word, staying tirelessly at Tionontati's side. Together, they would talk for hours. Henri would explain the Roman Catholic belief in one God, which consists of three parts: the Father, Son, and Holy Spirit. Henri told Tionontati that the Black Robes had been sent to the Indigenous people to teach them about the God of all gods, show them the way to heaven, and to bring them to conversion and baptism. He told Tionontati that if his people believed these things, then the God of all gods would welcome them to his mighty kingdom in the sky.

Henri stressed that there was no beginning or ending to the life of his Christian God. "Our God sent down his only son to teach us the way to heaven," Henri said. "He provides help through the power of the holy spirit."

Tionontati listened with interest and smiled. Then, it was Tionontati's turn to share his people's belief in creation and the various spirits that ruled over forces of light and dark. Tionontati was still weak and needed frequent rest periods. When Tionontati dosed off, Henri would write down what he had heard.

As best as Henri could recall, the story went something like this:

> My people also have a creator consisting of three parts. At first, there was only a swirling life force called Manitou. However, nature requires balance, and nothing stays nothing for long. So, nothing split in two, and two great spirits arose. Aasha Mannittoo took shape to do good, and Otshee Mannittoo to do evil. Aasha created the sun, sky, and water. Then, Otshee created the moon, stars, and land.
>
> Each morning, Aasha would find the sun and push it out of the darkness into the center of the sky. But the burning ball was hot and heavy, and eventually, Aasha had to let it fall slowly back into darkness. Aasha loved the light so much that he started collecting Otshee's stars and hid them inside the moon to brighten the night. In twenty-eight days, the moon was full. However, Otshee hated the light. So, for the next twenty-eight days, Otshee took his stars out of the moon and threw them back into the night sky. To this day, Aasha and Otshee's struggle with the moon continues.
>
> Aasha Mannittoo decided to populate the first world with strange creatures. Giant animals filled the land and swam in the

sea. Otshee Mannittoo found the world too crowded. He rained fire down from the sky, destroying most of the animals. That is why we find animal shapes and bones burned into the rocks.

Aasha Mannittoo created a second world and populated it with fireproof giant stone people who would care for the remaining animals. Then, Otshee created the Great Ice to crush the stone people. The stone giants would push the ice back during the day, and Otshee would replenish the Great Ice at night. Aasha poured all his energy into the sun to melt the ice during the day. At the same time, Otshee poured all his energy into the Great Ice to freeze the stone people during the night, making their bodies crack and grow weak.

Eventually, Aasha's sun won, and the Great Ice melted. However, the stone people were beyond repair. They crumbled, and their stones spread across the land. The second world came to an end. To this day, pieces of the stone people still contain the spirit of Manitou. My people seek out those stones as a powerful source of energy—especially the red ones, which represent the stone people's blood, and white ones, which represent their souls.

Finally, Aasha Mannittoo and Otshee Mannittoo called a truce and agreed to create a third world consisting of three layers: The Sky World, ruled by Aasha; the Underworld, ruled by Otshee; and the Middle World composed of equal portions of land and water. The upper and lower worlds shared equal power, flipping back and forth as day became night and night became day. Deities created by both Mannittoo would oversee the Middle World. The Mannittoo put deities in charge of the weather, plants, animals, land, water, fire, sky, and heavenly bodies.

Aasha created the sun god, the great protector, the guardian of fertility and birth, the peacemaker, the creator of fair-weather, and numerous animal deities ruled by the thunderbird. Then Otshee created the moon keeper, the destroyer, the death bearer, the war maker, the storm starter, and numerous animal deities ruled by Nanabozho, the trickster and transformer. All deities had the gift of traveling between the different worlds whenever they pleased.

However, the struggle between the Mannittoo continued. For every beneficial tree, plant, bird, mammal, or fish that Aasha Mannittoo created, Otshee Mannittoo would make one that was harmful. If Aasha Mannittoo made a honeybee, Otshee Mannittoo would make a stinging wasp. If Aasha Mannittoo made a delicious fruit, Otshee Mannittoo would create a poisonous one. If Aasha Mannittoo made a buffalo, Otshee Mannittoo would make a cougar to eat its calves. And on and on it went until the third layer became filled with equal amounts of good and evil.

But things did not stay balanced for long. The deities became sick and weak. They started fighting amongst themselves. You see, deities crave attention and will perish without it. However, the trees, plants, birds, mammals, and fish did not know how to provide that needed attention. So, Aasha Mannittoo created men to attend to the deities' needs, and Otshee Mannittoo created women to ensure that men did so. The world was once again in balance.

• • •

"That story is fascinating," Henri said excitedly when Tionontati woke from his nap. "In fact, it reminded me that there is one more thing about the Christian creation story I forgot to tell you. Our God created two forces that oversee the behavior of men and women. On the side of good are the angels that guide, guard, and enlighten the human soul, and on the side of evil is the Devil that deceives, denigrates, and darkens the soul with evil thoughts. Do your deities work in this manner?"

"Yes," said Tionontati. "But deities are not all good or all bad. They require tribute, or they will bring you harm. For example, the Thunderbird soars in the sky, watching over his deities to ensure they do good. He delivers the rain and makes the land green. But if men fail to pay him homage, he sends down flashes of lightning from his beak and beats his wings to create the thunder. Then there is Nanabozho. He roams the night in various animal forms. His purpose is to encourage his deities to spread suffering and pain. They thrive on want, misfortune, and death. However, if one shows Nanabozho the respect he craves, he will tell the Dark Forces to leave you alone."

For days, Henri and Tionontati continued their discussions. On one of those days, Henri directed his questions toward the history of Tionontati's people. "Nokee told me the Confederation of the Yam-Ko-Desh consisted of four nations, or tribes: the Fox, Kickapoo, Sauk, and Mascouten.

"Yes," replied Tionontati. "But to understand how that came to be, we must go back much further into the past."

Henri grabbed his pen and began to write:

When the Mannittoo created the first men and women, they placed them in the grasslands far south of the Great Ice. They existed in small family groups. Eventually, different family groups, or clans, joined together and formed bands. These bands were widespread and had little contact with each other as they hunted the remaining giant animals. But as the ice animals began to move north, following the emerging grasses and willows, the hunters pursued them. As the bands entered the peninsula of Michigamme, contacts became more frequent, and bands joined to form a tribe.

The first Great Ice to melt from Michigamme was a thinner sheet from Saginaw Bay, and the hunters followed the animals to the edge of the bay. Over time, the world warmed, and the spruce replaced the grasses and willows. The great ice animals lost their food source and soon perished.

But then came the migrating caribou herds. Life became easy for the people of Saginaw Bay. With spring and fall migrations of caribou, abundant supplies of numerous fish species and mussels in the bay, swarms of waterfowl, and their choice of marshland plants and animals, the people forgot about the Mannittoo and their deities. The deities again grew sick and weak. That infuriated the Mannittoo to the point that they decided to destroy man by creating a Great Flood.

"Did you say a Great Flood?" asked Henri, putting down his pen. "We believe our Christian God created a great flood. It destroyed the sinners and non-believers. Noah and his family gathered all the animals in a great ark and had to start the world over again."

"Yes, yes," said Tionontati. "The Mannittoo decided to destroy the people!"

Henri picked up his pen when Tionontati started again:

The Mannittoo devised a plan to purge the world of people. Aasha poured his energy into the sun and dried up all the land. The spruce and pine withered and died, and the Thunderbird set the forest and prairie ablaze with lightning. The people fled into the waters of Saginaw Bay to survive the fire. While the Thunderbird was busy scorching the land, Otshee went north to the great ice dams that held back the melting ice water. With his fingers, Otshee cut holes in the dam and sent torrents of water into the Bay, drowning the people.

However, the night before the Great Flood, Nanabozho knew of a group of people who had been faithful to the deities, and he led them around the fire to reach higher ground. When the flood occurred, those who had remained loyal lived.

"Why would Nanabozho do that?" Henri asked.

"Because, as I said, deities are both bad and good. Nanabozho wanted to take care of those faithful to him, and he knew that deities don't survive without people paying homage to them. After the flood, the Thunderbird poured down the rain and put out the fires. It became a much different environment than exists today. Clear rivers and streams crossed vast prairies with glacial lakes and pothole wetlands. The prairies to the south were so open my people called the area 'Maskoutenich,' the treeless land. Yet between the prairies were scattered uplands of massive oak, hickory, walnut, butternut, beech, and sweet chestnut. And the lowlands were choked with impenetrable ancient cedars and mixed spruce forests.

"To the north, oak, hickory, maple, and tall pines filled the forest. Eventually, the surviving people split up. One group went north into the forest and became the Fox. One stayed in the Saginaw Bay wetland area and became the Kickapoo. Another moved into the prairie and became the Sauk. A small group went southwest and became the Mascouten, the farmers."

"Okay," Henri said. "That explains the four tribes. But how did they become the Yam-Ko-Desh?"

Tionontati started again, and Henri continued to write:

> Although the survivors went separate ways, they had learned the lesson of not paying attention to the deities. They remained linked by a common Algonquian language, social structure, religious beliefs, and an ancestral connection to the Saginaw Bay area. They stay connected through trade. The Mascouten tribe grew early forms of squash, gourds, and sunflowers. The Fox tribe was known for their excellent moose and woodland caribou meat. Kickapoo produced smoked whitefish, sturgeon, and lake trout. The Sauk specialized in raising warriors. Together, they became the Confederation of the Yam-Ko-Desh.

• • •

Henri spent many evenings going over the entries he had made in his journal. One day, he again raised the issue of building the burial mounds. "Nokee said that your people didn't build the original mounds. He said your ancestors started building them a hundred generations ago. But he wasn't sure how the practice of mound building ended."

### Henri grabbed his journal again and started writing.

It never really ended. It just went through a series of changes. As I said, we built hundreds of villages and burial mound centers for countless years. Then, a new group of mound builders showed up in Michigamme. They first appeared in the St. Joseph River. They were from the Illinois Moundbuilders and called themselves Havana.

    No one knew if they were direct descendants of the Ohio people from whom we had initially learned about the mound-building culture, but their craftsmanship was even more exquisite. They had beautifully decorated pots and pipes, shark and grizzly-bear teeth necklaces, copper spear points and silver breastplates, colorful woven textiles, shiny bird figurines, and powerful spirit stones delicately etched with bird petroglyphs on them. Once again, they dazzled our leaders, and we readily accepted the Havana people.

    The Havanas were river floodplain farmers. At first, they set up their centers along the St. Joseph River. However, our leaders encouraged them to move into our centers along the Kalamazoo, Grand, and Muskegon Rivers. In addition to their fine artwork, what made these new people so attractive was their sustainable food source. They brought squash, beans, tobacco, and corn that could sustain an entire village throughout the long winter.

    The Mascouten in that area were the farmers of the Yam-Ko-Desh and welcomed the newcomers with open arms. The Havana taught the Mascouten to build raised garden beds aligned with the seasons and the heavenly bodies. For many generations, the two co-existed and intermarried. The Havana were shorter people with round faces, and over time, the two tribes began to look alike. When the Havana culture reached the Upper Grand River, it crossed over and spread into the Saginaw River basin. The Kickapoo fishermen welcomed the newcomer farmers, and the comingling process repeated.

    The Sauk and the Fox accepted the presence of Havana and benefited from trading with them. But they never modified their culture or lived in Havana villages. That is because the price of joining their lifestyle was the acceptance that the village chief had to be a Havana. Havana chiefs considered themselves direct descendants of the Sun God, and they demanded a hereditary rank above all others. They established a distinctive class system that set up a division of labor. There were laborers, traders, artists, and warriors with little chance of advancing from one class to the next.

    But the hardest thing for the people to accept was that the mounds were to be built only for the ruling family. Havana laborers worked tirelessly to create wood and stone-lined inner chambers covered with thousands of baskets of dirt to heights of thirty or more feet. Artists would work year-round, making extensive grave goods to be ready when the chief died. A large boulder was placed in front of the chamber to gain access when needed. Some mounds contained one chief and his wife. Others held multiple generations.

The controversy surrounding single royal family burial mounds became a cultural issue with the Kickapoo. They refused to build only chamber mounds. Eventually, the Havana leaders sent warriors to the Saginaw area to force the laborers to comply. At that point, the Sauk and Fox had had enough. They attacked the Havana warriors and drove them back west. The Sauk and Fox freed the Kickapoo villages. Then, one after another, they attacked the Havana centers and chased the Havana out of Michigamme. Stories tell that the Havana people settled in central Wisconsin and that they are the people who created the effigy mounds that are there today.

"Wow," Henri said as he put down his pen. "That explains the chambered mounds on the rivers flowing to Lake Michigan. That's why there are only traditional mounds in the Saginaw Bay area. Did the tribes of the Yam-Ko-Desh ever reunite?"

"No," said Tionontati sadly. "After many years of Havana rule, the tribes had developed different lifestyles. However, they continued to trade together and united to fight the Chippewa and Ottawa in the forever war."

• • •

"The story of your people is now complete," Henri said. "It's all here in my journal. When Father Allouez and Nicolas Perrot return in the spring, I'll transfer Pierre's and my journals to them. They'll see that this story gets back to France. Your story will be published in *The Jesuit Relations* for all the world to know and remember."

"That's good, my friend," Tionontati said. "Because my ability to keep the stories alive grows weaker daily."

"Nonsense," Henri said. "You're getting stronger. I think you'll be telling stories for years to come. However, there's one more thing I need to discuss with you. And that's Nokee's obsession with the curse of the Dark Forces."

"Yes, please tell me about that," Tionontati said with a deep frown.

Henri undid the binding on Pierre's journal and handed the spear point to Tionontati.

"Where did you get this?" Tionontati asked as he dropped the point to the floor. "This is a Havana blade. Nothing good can come from having this in your possession."

"That's what Nokee says, but he didn't think that when he found it. The night you left him at the Chippewa Grand River camp, he ran south and spent the night at a mound site. It had a large boulder in the center area, and he found the point buried there."

"I know that site," nodded Tionontati. "It was one of the Havana centers."

"Yes," Henri said. "There were chambered mounds there. Nokee claimed the curse on that point plagued him until he gave it to Pierre to get rid of."

"Was Pierre the one that died from the snake bites? Why did Nokee give him the point?"

"Yes, that was Pierre. After we met Nokee, he took us to the Pine Lake Burial Center. The chamber mound there had fallen open, and Pierre looked inside. Nokee told Pierre he had a dream that matched what Pierre had seen in the chamber mound. Nokee said it was a dire warning from the Grave Guardians. He gave Pierre the point he had found at Grand Rapids so Pierre could toss it into the grave opening to appease the Dark Forces."

"Then why is the point here?"

"Because Pierre didn't do that. He placed the point into the sleeve of his journal."

"Has anyone else touched this stone?" Tionontati asked, his face showing deep concern.

"Only you and me. After Pierre's murder, Chief Malomimis gave Pierre's journal to me. When I opened the journal, the point fell out. Nokee refused to touch it. He told me to throw it into Lake Winnebago. But I didn't. I put it back in Pierre's journal and forgot about it until now."

"This is very serious," Tionontati said. "The Dark Forces' powers are strong. If they think you have wronged them, they'll not rest. Does Nokee know you still have this?"

"No, he thinks I threw it into Lake Winnebago."

"Good—don't tell him. But you had better find a way to get rid of this thing. Until you do, both of our lives are in great peril!"

Just then, there was a loud commotion outside the wigwam. The villagers were gathering because a worked-up Peoria chief had just arrived. Chief Echohawk had come seeking counsel with the Mascouten, Sauk, and Fox to see if they could influence the Kickapoo.

"The Kickapoo are stirring up trouble with the Dakota Sioux," Echohawk said. "If someone doesn't stop them, there will soon be a full-scale war."

# Kickapoo and the Dakota Sioux

Sakenuk was the name of Chief Echohawk's Peoria village, located on Rock Island at the mouth of the Rock River, where it emptied into the Misi Sipi River. A band of Dakota Sioux had arrived to ask if his people knew who was killing the tatanka before the agreed-upon hunting season. The Dakota Sioux scouts had found ten adult bison skinned and butchered in early September. In the same area were the remains of six orphaned calves killed by cougars.

Generations ago, the tribes had agreed that no one nation would own the bison herds of the prairie. So, they established a rule that during the calving season, no hunting would occur until the October full moon. That would ensure the summer calves were old enough to survive without their mothers.

Chief Echohawk assured the Sioux that it wasn't his people who broke with the traditions, and that he would try to find out who had done this. Echohawk sent messengers to other Peoria villages on the Misi Sipi. Days later, word came that they had found a second group of butchered tatanka. The arrows and spears left at the site bore the markings of the Kickapoo.

Nokee assured Echohawk that the Sauk, Fox, and Mascouten weren't involved in this violation. If the Kickapoo were at fault, he would do everything possible to correct the situation. Nokee and Chief Echohawk grabbed a canoe and paddled down the Wisconsin River to the Kickapoo village located at the confluence of the Wisconsin and Misi Sipi Rivers. However, only the women, children, and elderly were present, and they were in dire straits. Wildfire had destroyed their meager crops, and they had moved their village to the western side of the Great River. The men had gone off to hunt for food.

Nokee and Chief Echohawk informed the villagers that the Dakota Sioux had threatened war if the Kickapoo continued hunting the tatanka before the agreed-upon time. "If food is the issue," Nokee said, "the Sauk, Fox, Mascouten, and Peoria will gladly provide you with what you need until the fall bison harvest. We'll return within ten days with sufficient supplies to carry the Kickapoo tribe until the full moon in October."

Nokee and Chief Echohawk headed up the Wisconsin River, made the two-mile portage into the Upper Fox River, and returned to Nokee's camp in record time. As the word spread that the Kickapoo required help, supplies started pouring into Nokee's village. The Fox sent wild rice, the Sauk provided smoked fish and elk meat, and the Mascouten supplied corn, squash, and beans.

In a couple of days, five overflowing canoes were heading down the Wisconsin River. Not sure what they might encounter, Nokee had ten of his Sauk warriors armed with muskets paddle the five canoes. Nokee led the procession in an eight-person canoe with Morningstar, Baby Illiniwek, Henri, Chief Echohawk, Pemoussa, and Tionontati. Tionontati had demanded to be part of the peace delegation and refused to be left behind.

When the supply convoy reached the Kickapoo camp, the men had returned, and the smell of fresh smoked meat filled the air. The peace delegation delivered the desperately needed supplies and requested immediate counsel with Kiakiak, the village chief.

"We left a message with your villagers," Nokee said angrily. "Didn't you get it? The Peoria village was threatened that if the killing of the tatanka continued, there'd be blood to pay. That little bit of meat you are smoking may have started a war that could draw in the entire woodland tribes."

"Settle down," Kiakiak said. "We didn't kill more tatanka. We tried, but a Dakota Sioux scouting party ran us off."

"Then what's that fresh meat the women are preparing?" Chief Echohawk said, pointing at the cooking fires.

"It's horse meat." Kiakiak laughed coldly as he gestured toward a makeshift corral holding five horses.

"You caught five wild horses?" Nokee asked, surprised.

"Six, actually," Kiakiak said. "We stole them from the hunting party that ran us off. We have been feasting on one of their horses for two days. It tastes better than tatanka."

Chief Echohawk lowered his head and sighed. "This is worse than I thought. The Sioux love their horses more than their women. They'll not let this pass. This village is in grave danger. Chief Kiakiak, you must order your people to pack up what they can and move to the other side of the Misi Sipi. They can hide in the forest along the Wisconsin River. There's no time to waste. The Nation of the Dakota Sioux is vast in size. They can assemble a thousand warriors in short order. I'm surprised some of them aren't already here."

"Last I checked, I was the chief of this village," Kiakiak said indignantly. "However, maybe you are right. I'll have my people break camp and load the canoes. In the morning, we will cross after we finish smoking the rest of the horse meat. Besides, the day is almost over, and we haven't seen any sign of the Dakota yet."

The Kickapoo villagers slowly began packing their belongings with little urgency. Nokee and Chief Echohawk encouraged them to hurry, but it seemed to fall on deaf ears. Nokee looked around the camp, assessing how their defenses would hold up to an attack. They were in a terrible location. They had their backs to the river and were at the bottom of a parallel-running ridge. If an attack occurred, it would come from above. The only advantage he could see was the tall prairie grass surrounding the village. Nokee sent two of his warriors to the top of the ridge to watch for any movement.

• • •

As the sun was about to set, Nokee's scouts came running back. They'd seen fifty horse riders approaching from the west, and they appeared to be wearing war paint. Instinctively, Nokee took charge of the situation. He ordered Kiakiak to send the women and children to the canoes. They were to leave with whatever they had loaded. Surprisingly, Kiakiak responded favorably and ordered an immediate evacuation.

"How many archers do you have in this village?" Nokee asked as he tried to formulate a plan.

"We've about forty," replied Kiakiak.

"I want twenty of your warriors standing shoulder to shoulder behind our peace delegation. The Dakota Sioux must think they have us outnumbered. I'll need the rest of your archers to accompany my warriors with muskets."

Within minutes, Nokee had a fifty-man army assembled in front of him. Chief Kiakiak and his twenty archers lined up behind Nokee. With muskets and bows, the remaining thirty warriors hustled out front to the sides, half to the left, half to the right. They were to hide in the tall grass and not attack until Nokee raised his spear. Nokee was still hoping for a peaceful settlement. But if it came to blows, at least they'd have the element of surprise. Chief Echohawk reminded Nokee that the Dakota Sioux favored attacks using horses.

"We must do something that disrupts their attack plan!" Nokee said. "Kiakiak, tie a tanned bison hide on each horse. Then, bring the five horses to where the Dakota Sioux can see them."

Kiakiak started to resist, but Nokee cut him off. "You got everyone into this mess. You had better hope that you can get us out of it!"

As the Dakota Sioux warriors topped the ridge, Chief Echohawk took a deep breath. "This doesn't look good. The Dakota Sioux Confederation consists of four tribes: Mdewakanton, Wahpeton, Wahpekute, and Sisseton. These are the Sisseton. They like to attack with the sun at their backs. Showing up at this moment is intentional. I'm afraid a fight is inevitable."

"We must give peace a chance, no matter how unlikely it may be," Nokee said. "I want our entire peace delegation lined up in front. Chief Echohawk will be on my right side, and Tionontati and Henri will be on my left. Pemoussa, you don't have to be part of this fight if you don't want to."

"I stand with you," Pemoussa said. "My people don't care much for the Sioux."

"And I stand with you, too," came a voice from the back.

Spinning around, Nokee saw Morningstar standing there with her bow. "Morningstar, you shouldn't be here. You should be with Illiniwek."

"Illiniwek is halfway across the river by now," Morningstar said indignantly. The Kickapoo women will take diligent care of him. I'm as much a part of the peace delegation as you are. I told you I would go where you went. If this is your last stand, I stand with you!" Nokee could see the conviction in her eyes as she stepped up next to Henri.

Six Sioux riders broke from the group and slowly approached. Chief Echohawk leaned over to Nokee. "The one in the center is Bdote, Chief Mahpiyawa's oldest son. To his right is Wakan, Bdote's younger brother. Watch out for Wakan. He is the hothead in the group. We need to choose our words carefully. Let me address them first."

Nokee handed Chief Echohawk his peace pipe, who took it and held it high above his head. "Welcome, Bdote, son of Mahpiyawa. We're here as a peace delegation, to right a wrong."

"And we are here to catch horse thieves," Wakan said bluntly.

Bdote raised his hand to silence his brother. "Does a peace delegation always have twenty archers standing behind them?"

"When fifty warriors approach your village wearing war paint, it's best to determine their intentions," Echohawk countered.

"Fair enough," Bdote said. "But as my brother said, we are here to catch a horse thief. I see you have my horses. How do you explain that?"

Nokee stepped forward. "I'm Nokee, Chief of the Sauk and Mascouten tribes that live at the headwaters of the Fox River. I'm the leader of the peace delegation that has come to unite the Great Lakes tribes against the raiding Iroquois from the east. The Kickapoo are our brothers, and they have wronged you. They've violated the tatanka hunting rules and have taken your horses. We're here to make that right." Nokee motioned to bring the five horses forward.

"There were six, and I only count five," Bdote said.

"Yes," Nokee nodded. "One of the horses died in the process. The Kickapoo people have included a tanned bison blanket with each horse. They hope that will compensate you for your loss.

We don't condone their behavior, but I ask you to look across the Great River where their village once stood. See how it was burned to the ground by wildfire. They lost everything. Their people were starving. We have provided them with new provisions, and they promise there will be no more early hunting."

"What you say makes sense. But why take our horses? The one missing belonged to my brother Wakan."

Nokee swallowed hard, took a deep breath, and said: "They saw how fast and well-trained your horses were. They thought it would help them run down elk or bison. Now that they have taken care of their dire needs, they wish to return them to you."

"They are not only thieves, but liars!" Wakan yelled.

Bdote again raised his hand to quiet his brother. "Tell me about this peace delegation. I see a Sauk, Fox, a Peoria chief, a Mascouten shaman, and an Ojibwa woman."

"Chippewa," Morningstar corrected.

"And I see you travel with a French Black Robe. ... We have no use for the French. They poison our men with their rum and steal our women. I suggest you send them away before they do the same to you. Are there other tribes in this peace delegation?" Bdote asked.

"Yes," Nokee said. "On the other side of Lake Michigan, the Chippewa, Ottawa, Potawatomi, and Miami have joined the peace delegation to defeat the Iroquois."

"Our quarrel isn't with the Iroquois," Bdote said. "However, we have heard of the attacks on the Illinois tribes. I'll accept the horses and your explanation. It'll be up to my father to decide if this matter ends."

As Bdote's delegation turned and rode away with the five horses, Wakan spun around to fling one last barb. "You killed my horse. Someone must pay!"

He charged at Nokee and threw his spear. In a flash, Tionontati stepped in front of Nokee and took the full force of the spear to his chest. Nokee grabbed Tionontati as he collapsed. Morningstar drew her bow and sent an arrow into Wakan's left shoulder as he retreated.

As Wakan slumped forward, riding off, Chief Kiakiak yelled: "*Philamayaye*—thank you—the horse meat tasted great!"

Henri ran to Tionontati, but there was no healing to be done. Tionontati slowly opened his eyes, and a soft voice escaped his lips. "I told you there was one more fight in this old warrior."

Tionontati's eyes faded, his head fell backward, and he quietly passed into the spirit world. Nokee wanted to sit down and weep, but there was no time.

"Warriors, ready yourself," Nokee said. "War is upon us. Kiakiak, you need to spread your archers twenty paces apart. Have them kneel in the grass. The peace delegation will stand tall in the middle. We need to draw the charge directly at us. Tell your warriors not to shoot until I raise my spear. Henri, you have no weapon. You best get out of the way."

Henri refused. "I'll stand with Morningstar. God has placed me here, at this moment, for a reason. I'll not question his intentions."

On the ridge, the Dakota Sioux had formed into three groups. As Nokee had anticipated, they prepared to charge twenty riders directly at the twenty Kickapoo archers. The other two groups, each containing fifteen Dakota riders, would flank the archers on the left and right and circle in from behind.

As Bdote launched the frontal attack, Nokee steadied his men. "Hold your fire and wait until I raise my spear."

Nokee could feel the fear in the Kickapoo archers as the horses thundered closer. He insisted they wait until the enemy was in range. When Bdote's warriors were fifty paces out, Nokee raised his spear, and Nokee's entire fighting force rose from the grass and fired. A barrage of arrows, musket balls, and smoke filled the air, sending horses and riders into a panic. As the horses circled in a state of confusion, the Kickapoo archers picked off one rider after another. Bdote spun around, ignoring the chaos, and charged. Just as he was about to release his spear at Nokee, Pemoussa raised his musket and fired. It was the same musket he had taken from the two trespassing Detroit trappers after he killed them. Pemoussa's aim was true, and Bdote was dead before he hit the ground.

The Dakota Sioux tried to regroup in the center. However, the Sauk had reloaded and killed another six Dakota warriors. In a matter of minutes, the Dakota Sioux had lost the battle and were retreating. But as the smoke began to clear, a lone rider emerged. He drew his bow and aimed at Morningstar. Henri shoved her to the ground as Nokee took the rider out with his spear.

"Are you okay, Morningstar?" Nokee yelled over the chaos.

"I'm fine," Morningstar said as she raced toward Nokee. "Henri saved my life. I didn't see that last rider coming. Henri pushed me down just in time."

"Pemoussa saved me as well," Nokee said. "That was close. How many men did we lose?"

"Two Sauk, three Kickapoo, and Tionontati," Pemoussa said. "We have three Kickapoo wounded, but their injuries appear minor."

"And how many did the Dakota lose?"

"The Kickapoo tell me they've counted twenty-one, including Bdote."

"That's almost half the Dakota force," Nokee said. "The loss of their leader and possibly his brother will devastate them. I don't think they will be coming back soon."

"I wouldn't count on that," Chief Echohawk said. "They'll be back when it gets dark. They never leave their dead for long."

"Then we should get everyone to the other side of the river. Do it now!" Nokee commanded. "Where's Henri? I need him to check on our three wounded. Has anyone seen him?"

"He's over here," yelled one of the Kickapoo archers. "I think he's wounded."

Morningstar and Nokee found Henri lying face down in the tall grass.

"Are you all right, Henri?" Morningstar asked, fear in her eyes.

"I don't think so. I can't feel my legs. However, I'm glad you are okay. I thought that rider had you."

"You saved my life," Morningstar said, tears streaming down her face. "Now we'll save yours."

Nokee knelt and examined the wound. The arrow had nicked Henri's spine as it passed through his back and exited his lower left side. He was lying in a puddle of blood. Nokee froze for a moment, feeling helpless without the guiding voice of Tionontati.

*We won the battle and yet we lost so much*, thought Nokee. Everyone was looking at him, waiting for his next move.

Scanning the faces of his men and Morningstar, he looked up and saw a dozen Kickapoo canoes approaching from the other shore. The women had returned to their canoes and were coming to evacuate their brave warriors. Suddenly, a tremendous inner strength filled Nokee as he stood up.

"Pemoussa, help me carry Henri to the canoes," Nokee said. "The rest of you gather the dead. We move to the other side of the river. Tomorrow, on top of that bluff, we will bury and pay tribute to our fallen warriors. We must let Dakota know we aren't afraid. If the Nation of the Dakota Sioux wants war, they will have it." The warriors let out a loud war cry as they jumped into action.

• • •

It was dark by the time everyone was safely on the other side. Nokee sent his remaining Sauk warriors with muskets to watch the river. If there were any signs of the Dakota attempting to cross, they were to fire a shot in the air. Morningstar and the village shaman tended to Henri's needs while Nokee called for an immediate council meeting. Everyone agreed it was not safe for them to stay where they were. However, they needed to inform the villages along the Misi Sipi that war with the Dakota had begun.

The Dakota negotiating team had seen a Black Robe and representatives from the Sauk, Fox, Mascouten, Chippewa, and Kickapoo tribes. From this point on, all the woodland tribes and their French allies would now be considered their enemy. Chief Echohawk feared his presence at the battle would add his Peoria villages to that list.

Nokee had to produce a plan fast. He turned to the Kickapoo chief, Kiakiak, and said: "See what you have started. Whatever happens, you must play a big part in correcting this. There are many tribes we must warn. That means we must split up."

Nokee called for his Sauk warriors to bring the two muskets from the fallen warriors. He handed one to Kiakiak and his war chief and said, "Take these. My men will teach you how to use them. I want you and your archers to accompany my Sauk warriors as they head north, up the Misi Sipi, to warn the river villages. Here's my peace pipe. It belonged to my father. It'll signal your intentions and guarantee safe passage."

"When you reach the St. Croix River, you can take it northeast into Ojibwa territory. It will not be long before the Ojibwa scouts will intercept you. Tell them war is coming and ask them to contact the two Black Robes working in their territory. Like it or not, the Black Robes are now part of this fight. Have them inform the Black Robes that Pierre is dead and Henri is wounded. Then, return downriver and meet me at Chief Echohawk's camp on Rock Island. Do you understand?"

"Yes," Chief Kiakiak said. "But who will look after my people?"

"I'll have Morningstar and Pemoussa escort them up the Wisconsin River to our village at the headwaters of the Fox. Pemoussa can continue north to warn other Sauk and Fox villages. Go now, under cover of darkness. Full-scale war will soon be upon us!"

"And what is your role in all this?" Chief Kiakiak asked, his voice dripping with sarcasm.

"I will travel south on the Misi Sipi with Chief Echohawk," Nokee said. "We'll inform the Peoria villages along the river of the possibility of an attack and encourage them to move inland, away from the river, to avoid detection. You had better do the same as you head north! When you return, I'll take you and your warriors to the Grand Village of the Kaskaskia to rejoin your people. Does everyone understand the plan?" All heads around the council meeting nodded yes.

After the council ended, Nokee went directly to Morningstar. "You must prepare our people to move our camp as soon as possible. They will be terrified when they learn that Tionontati is dead, Henri is wounded, and the Dakota Sioux are coming for them. Find the three Mascoutens who traveled with me to the Kaskaskian village on the Illinois River. They'll guide our people there. You'll be welcomed and safe until I can join you."

"What makes you think the Dakota Sioux can find our village?" Morningstar said with a puzzled look. "I thought they were prairie people, more familiar with horses than canoes."

"They are. But unfortunately, during our talk with the Dakota negotiating team, I told them exactly where our village is. If Chief Echohawk is right, they'll consult with the other Sioux tribes. Within a few weeks, they will assemble a thousand warriors and be ready to fight. With the death of Chief Mahpiyawa's oldest son—and possibly Wakan, too—it will not take much effort for Mahpiyawa to convince the council to attack our village. They'll eventually cross the river and come after us."

"He is right, Morningstar," Chief Echohawk said. "Chief Mahpiyawa will not let this go. He'll be certain all the woodland tribes are involved in this fight. He now sees Nokee as their leader. What better place to attack than Nokee's village? He can defeat the Sauk, Mascouten, and Kickapoo in one fell swoop."

# Preparing for War

The Kickapoo and Sauk warriors reached the northern part of the St. Croix River five days later. They had warned dozens of river villages along the way to prepare for the impending war and to move away from the river. Just as Nokee had predicted, a well-armed Ojibwa force quickly intercepted them. Kalwahnee, the leader of the Ojibwa group, demanded to know why they had entered Ojibwa territory unannounced. Chief Kiakiak informed Kalwahnee of the great battle they had won against the invading Dakota Sioux. He explained how the Dakota had retreated and were probably sitting around their camp licking their wounds. However, he had been sent here by Nokee, the Great Uniter, to warn them that the Dakota would most likely seek revenge on other woodland tribes.

"They already have," Kalwahnee replied. "Two days ago, the Dakota Sioux attacked one of our villages on Lake Superior. It was a small scouting party looking to capture two Black Robes known to be in the area. Luckily, the Black Robes were away from the village at the time of the attack. The villagers repelled the Dakota using the guns they had received from the French.

"Did you say his name is Nokee?" Kalwahnee asked. "We've heard of a Great Uniter by that name. He spent the spring with Chief Waubay. Waubay told us that through Nokee's efforts, the Fox and Sauk are no longer our enemies."

"Yes, that's true. Nokee is a powerful chief. He united the tribes and supplied them with guns to fight the Iroquois. He does so with the backing of the French military. Now, we need those guns to fend off the raiding Dakota Sioux. Nokee wants you to tell the Black Robes they are in great danger. They need to clear out before full-scale war begins. One of their Black Robes, Pierre, is already dead. He died at the Menominee camp at Green Bay." Kiakiak deliberately withheld mention of Henri's injury, fearing it would make his successful battle story sound less impressive.

"You must tell both Black Robes that the Dakota Sioux have vowed to eliminate them and kill all who live at their missions," Kiakiak insisted. "They must leave now!"

With the message delivered, Chief Kiakiak and his team turned around and headed back downriver. They hoped to reach Nokee at Chief Echohawk's village before total war broke out. By now, Chief Kiakiak was feeling guilty about what he had done. His blatant disregard for the tatanka hunting rules had put all the other woodland tribes in danger. He called over his war chief and informed him that he was handing over his position as chief. He knew he had disgraced his people.

"When we reach the mouth of the Wisconsin River," Kiakiak said, "I'll take one of the canoes and head upstream. If war comes to the Sauk and Fox Nations, I'll fight with them. Only if I fight well can I restore my honor. Only then will I be able to return honorably to our people!"

After Chief Kiakiak and his warriors left, the Ojibwa force doubled their pace as they headed toward the camp that had come under attack. By the time they arrived, Father Allouez and Father Dablon had returned. Both were stunned by the news of Pierre's death. Immediately, they started packing for their return trip to the Lake Superior mission. The two missionaries were gravely concerned about Father Marquette and the Ottawa and Huron refugees at La Pointe du St.-Esprit in Chequamegon Bay. The residents there, totally unaware of what was coming, would be an easy target for the Dakota Sioux.

In three days, the two Black Robes were back at the Chequamegon Bay mission. Father Marquette was devastated by the news of Pierre's death. Not only had he lost a dear friend, but his vision of the three of them starting new Upper Great Lakes missions was falling apart. He wanted more information about the death of Pierre and was concerned about Henri's whereabouts. Unfortunately, Father Allouez and Father Dablon had very few details to report. Marquette insisted that a trip to the Menominee village to find out what happened was necessary.

Father Allouez and Father Dablon argued that it was a bad idea due to the pending war. They both thought it best for Marquette to stay and focus on evacuating the Ottawa and Huron villagers at the mission. They needed to get everyone safely to Sault Ste. Marie, hundreds of miles away. The best route would be by canoe along the Lake Superior shoreline. Father Marquette reluctantly agreed. He and the other two priests worked tirelessly for the next two days. However, word of Father Marquette's desire to go to Green Bay circulated throughout the camp.

On the morning of the third day, Marquette got the break he was praying for. A small group of Ottawa traders approached the three priests. They had come to the mission to trade corn and squash for northern fur and were about to head back to Chief Kawachewan's village on the Sturgeon River at Green Bay. They offered to take Marquette with them.

The plan was to travel with the convoy as it headed east on the Big Lake. When the convoy reached the Ontonagon River, the Ottawa traders would break off from the group and turn south. Father Allouez and Father Dablon were reluctant to let Marquette go. However, they gave in to Marquette's request on the condition that he promise to get the information he sought and then head immediately east to the Ottawa village at St. Ignace.

• • •

Father Marquette and his guides traveled up the Ontonagon River to its headwaters. They hid their canoes under spruce boughs and traveled south on foot, following Duck Creek to the Land of the Lakes. Then, they turned east until they reached the canoes the Ottawa traders had left at the Brule River. Paddling downstream, they entered the Menominee River and arrived at Chief Malomimis's village in less than a week. The Ottawa traders dropped off Marquette, then crossed the bay, heading for their Sturgeon River village.

Chief Malomimis greeted Marquette at the water's edge. "Welcome, Black Robe. You're the fourth of your kind to visit our camp. I assume you have come to join the council to discuss the impending war with the Dakota."

"I have come to find out what happened to Pierre and ask if anyone knows the whereabouts of his partner Henri," Marquette responded. "But I would be glad to join your council. After all, this war will affect all of us."

"The Black Robes saved our village from the flu," Malomimis said. "They saved hundreds of villagers. Pierre is a hero in the eyes of my people. He lies buried on that hill next to our ancestors. I'll take you to his grave and tell you the whole story, but first, I want you to meet the rest of the council."

As Marquette entered the meeting house, he was surprised at the number of chiefs there. Chief Malomimis pointed to each as he introduced them: "To the right is the Ojibwa chief, Waubay, from Ossawinamakee Lake along the Manistique River. He told me the peace delegation spent the spring with him before coming here."

"Did Morningstar have her baby there?" Marquette asked.

"Yes, she had a fine, healthy boy," said Waubay with a smile. "She named him Illiniwek. I was sorry to hear of Pierre's death. He was truly kind to the children."

"Thank you," Marquette said, smiling back at Waubay. "Morningstar knew from the start her baby would be a boy. And yes, Pierre was always great with kids. I hope to find out more about his death."

"You will," Chief Malomimis said. "To the left of Waubay is Chief Kawachewan, the Ottawa chief from the Sturgeon River. It was his traders with whom you were traveling. The Black Robes also spent time at his camp when Nicolas Perrot brought the peace delegation to Green Bay."

"My people have had a strong relationship with the French for the past five years," said Kawachewan. "We welcomed your Black Robes friends sent by Nicolas Perrot. I agree with Waubay. The children loved Pierre with all his tricks and stories. His death saddened our entire village."

"Then it's true that both Black Robes spent time here?" Marquette asked, feeling like he was getting somewhere. "Is Henri still in the area?"

"To answer that," replied Malomimis, "we'll turn to the Winnebago chief, Hoocak, sitting over there on the far left. He was the last to see Henri before he entered the territory of the Fox."

"That's true," Chief Hoocak said. "Nicolas Perrot and the peace delegation traveled up the Fox River to counsel with the Fox tribe. Malomimis and I sent two of our best warriors, Banabou and Omano. When our men returned with Nicolas Perrot, they said the peace delegation had successfully brought the Fox and Sauk tribes into the French alliance. We heard the peace delegation continued upstream, trying to find Nokee's tribe."

"Do you think Henri is still alive?" Marquette asked.

"Probably," said Chief Hoocak. "Rumors of a Great Uniter visiting tribes and promising guns have reached us. I suspect they are referring to Nokee. Nicolas Perrot said Henri planned on wintering with the Menominee. But no one has reported seeing the Black Robe yet."

Chief Malomimis nodded at Marquette and said, "Now that you have met the council members, let us explain why we are all here. Before your arrival, we discussed whether the Ottawa, Menominee, and Winnebago tribes could remain neutral in this war. The Menominee and Winnebago have strong ties to the Dakota Sioux. The Menominee and Winnebago tribes are neutral traders, dealing with all the tribes equally. We take no side.

"However, the Ottawa Nation has established close ties with the French. Chief Kawachewan, on the other side of the bay, has many French guns and could be extremely helpful to the Ojibwa in this upcoming war. That's why Chief Waubay is here. He wants Chief Kawachewan to send his warriors north to join the fight. Chief Kawachewan would do so if the Menominee and Winnebago agreed to protect his village if it comes under attack. However, if we say yes, we will no longer maintain our neutral status."

After taking a moment to think, Father Marquette said, "I believe it may be possible that the Menominee and Winnebago could remain neutral due to your ties with the Dakota. I highly doubt that will be the case with Chief Kawachewan. I just came from the mission on Chequamegon Bay. The Black Robes there have evacuated the Ottawa and Huron villagers because the

Dakota have vowed to kill all Frenchmen and any who associate with them. The Dakota must know of the French ties with the Sturgeon River village. That alone would make the Ottawa village a prime target."

Father Marquette scratched his chin thoughtfully. "My superiors insisted that I don't stay here long. I plan to head for the Ottawa camp at St. Ignace. I know Chamintawaa, the Ottawa chief there. He would gladly welcome Chief Kawachewan's people to spend the winter. They would be safe under the protection of the French soldiers."

Chief Waubay looked at Chief Kawachewan, waiting for his response. Kawachewan sat quietly, then said, "The ties between the Ottawa and the Ojibwa have been strong for generations. We have fought together in many battles. We'll honor Chief Waubay's request and stand together and fight. Black Robe, take my people with you and see they remain safe."

After the council meeting, Chief Malomimis took Father Marquette to the top of the hill to see Pierre's grave. A wooden cross still supported a black rosary, beaver and bear necklaces, and Pierre's vow cross. Chief Malomimis bowed his head and explained the whole story. He told how Henri and Pierre had saved the village from the flu, how the two of them left, and the sickness returned. He explained how Pierre returned and saved the sick little girl, only to be murdered. Father Marquette spent three hours praying for Pierre's soul. Then, he left to evacuate the entire Sturgeon River Ottawa village to their temporary home at St. Ignace.

• • •

When they arrived at St. Ignace, Chief Chamintawaa welcomed the new arrivals, and to Marquette's delight, Nicolas Perrot was there. He had made his gun trading voyage around Lake Michigan and was waiting for the Soo fur convoy to come down the St. Marys River. Perrot planned to join them as they made their way back to Quebec.

The two of them sat for hours talking on the lakeshore. Father Marquette wanted to hear every detail about where Henri had been since Pierre's death. Tears came to his eyes when Perrot told him about the Menominee's celebration of Pierre's life. He laughed at Henri using Pierre's fireworks during the Buffalo Dance and smiled at how the peace delegation had convinced the Fox and Sauk tribes to join the alliance. Marquette cringed at Morningstar's encounter with the Detroit trappers. However, Father Marquette almost fell off the boulder he sat on when Nicolas Perrot told him that the Sauk chief had confirmed the existence of the passage to the Great River.

"Louis Jolliet will want to explore that route," Marquette said. "If that passage can show me the way to the Kaskaskians, I must be part of that expedition."

Father Marquette told Nicolas Perrot about a group of traveling Kaskaskia-Illinois people he had met last summer at Chequamegon Bay. He found them gentle and civilized and longed to visit them in their homeland.

Marquette opened his journal and read Perrot a short section:

> The Kaskaskians say they live far south along a great river that runs to the ocean. I take this news as evidence of the Misi Sipi and possible side tributaries that could take you to the West Coast and maybe China. They also tell me of a Siouan tribe, the Puants, that live on the shores of a great body of water south of Green Bay. You must pass through the Puants, Fox, and Sauk territory to reach the Great River.

"Exactly, said Nicolas Perrot. "The Puants are the Winnebago. They are the gatekeepers to the Misi Sipi."

"Do you think Henri is okay?" Marquette asked, still concerned about Henri's whereabouts.

"The last I saw Henri, he was with the peace delegation at the Fox village. Henri planned to return and spend the winter with the Menominee once they found Nokee's people. He wants me to bring Father Allouez back with me next spring. Henri found a perfect place for a mission between the Menominee and the Winnebago. He calls the place 'De Pere'—the Rapids of the Fathers."

"That's comforting news ... but Henri was not at the Menominee village when I arrived. With the war starting, I fear for his safety."

"Don't worry, Father. Henri knows how to take care of himself. Father Allouez and I will find him next spring. You can count on that."

A week later, the fall fur convoy from the Soo arrived at St. Ignace, with Father Allouez and Father Dablon among them. They had stopped at Munuscong Bay to pick up the Hurons. They feared that a small, isolated band would be an easy target for the Dakota Sioux if they pushed that far east.

Half of the military escort had remained in the Soo to defend the post and protect the Chequamegon Bay refugees now living with Chief Quinousaki at Baawitigong. The other half of the soldiers would stay at Chief Chamintawaa's village in St. Ignace. The coureurs des bois would paddle on, transporting the fur cargo to Quebec.

Nicolas Perrot saw how the new arrivals from Green Bay had spread out along the shoreline. Being well acquainted with military operations, he could see there was no way to set up a proper defense to protect everyone. The newly arrived Hurons only made matters worse. He approached the lieutenant in charge and suggested they move all the villagers to Mackinac Island. The people would be safer there, and it would be easily defendable.

They discussed the idea with Chief Chamintawaa, and he quickly agreed. Chief Chamintawaa had also been approached by the Ojibwa chief, Waubay, requesting men for the war. Like Chief Kawachewan, Chief Chamintawaa feared that there would be no one to protect his people if he sent away his warriors. The Mackinac Island winter camp would alleviate that problem.

The three Black Robes agreed that Father Dablon and Father Marquette would spend the winter on Mackinac Island with the refugees. Father Allouez would return to Quebec City to inform the bishop and the governor-general of what happened. Father Allouez was still determined to return to Green Bay with Nicolas Perrot next spring to look for Henri.

If the war to push the Dakota back went well, Father Dablon would return to the Soo. Maybe Father Marquette could go back to Chequamegon Bay. Either way, Father Allouez needed to ask the bishop for additional Black Robes due to the loss of Pierre and Henri's unknown whereabouts.

When Marquette heard of this plan, the wheels in his mind began turning. He sat down and wrote two letters. The first one was to Louis Jolliet, stating that Nicolas Perrot had confirmed the route to the Mississippi. He requested that Jolliet begin preparations for their joint exploration down the Great River. The second one was to Bishop Laval.

Marquette wrote:

Dear Bishop Laval,

We are all devastated by the loss of Pierre. He was a faithful and dedicated servant of the Lord. He will be impossible to replace, but we must try.

If you are reading this, Father Allouez has made it back safely. Thank God for that. He has told you of our need for two additional priests. I humbly ask that you consider Father Druillettes from Trois-Rivieres as one of them. Before we left the Quebec area, he stated he longed to return to the remote missions. He is such a seasoned field Jesuit. His expertise is needed now more than ever.

Father Dablon and I are spending the winter on Mackinac Island with the Ottawa and Huron refugees. This intersecting location is traveled by all that pass through the Upper Great Lakes. It is a perfect location to promote our Catholic faith. Next spring, if conditions warrant it, Father Dablon will return to the Soo, and Father Allouez will travel to Green Bay to find Henri. Allouez and Henri hope to start a mission there.

With your blessing, I wish to stay at St. Ignace and open a new mission here. Father Dablon has expressed a desire to retire when possible. Father Druillettes could take his place at the Soo, and the second requested priest could take over the mission at Chequamegon Bay for Father Allouez. Thank you for considering these thoughts. It is through the grace of God that we will persevere.

Your humble servant,

Father Jacques Marquette

---

Sealing the letters, Marquette and Perrot headed straight for Father Allouez, who was packing his canoe. Marquette handed the letters to Allouez as Nicolas Perrot stood quietly waiting to see Father Allouez's reaction.

"Do you mind telling me what's in the letter to the bishop?" Father Allouez asked.

"Not at all. I'm asking the bishop for permission to start a mission here at St. Ignace. It's the perfect location."

Father Allouez grinned. "I agree. I should've considered this place from the start. If the bishop asks for my opinion, I'll tell him you are more than ready for the task. It has always been your dream, and I can think of no finer priest to do the job." Marquette smiled, and his hopes soared.

• • •

Meanwhile, in the land of the Fox and Sauk, the war with the Dakota raged on. The Council of the Dakota Sioux had agreed with Chief Mahpiyawa's request to go to war and immediately sent small raiding parties to attack the villages along the Misi Sipi. But, when the Dakota arrived, they found the villages empty. The villagers had heeded earlier warnings and moved east into the woodlands. The Dakota warriors pursued them—but each time they did, the Sauk and Fox, with superior knowledge of the territory, inflicted heavy casualties on the invaders.

Kiakiak, the disgraced Kickapoo chief, moved to the east bank of the Misi Sipi and patrolled for signs of the smaller invading war parties. He promised the Sauk and Fox chiefs that he would be their eyes and ears, and quickly became known as a reliable scout, alerting them whenever the Dakota crossed into their land.

After a while, the Dakota Council saw the futility of this approach. They granted Chief Mahpiyawa's request for a full-scale attack against Nokee's village on the Upper Fox River. However, unbeknownst to the Dakota Sioux, the villagers had already been evacuated to the Kaskaskian village on the Illinois River. That is, all except one. While Kiakiak watch for a southern invasion up the Wisconsin River, he spotted a massive force of Dakota horsemen gathered on the west bank of the Misi Sipi. They had found a suitable crossing near the mouth of the Wisconsin River, but recent rains had temporarily swollen the crossing area.

Kiakiak hurried back to the Sauk and Fox, alerting them of the impending attack. Kiakiak, who had studied the area around Nokee's abandoned camp, devised a plan. If the war party approached from the south, the horses would have no problem maneuvering through the open pine forest along the Wisconsin River. But when they reached the two-mile portage through the swamp to reach Nokee's village, they would have to leave their horses behind and proceed on foot. The narrow pathways through the area would force the Dakota to stretch their forces into long, thin lines, making them very vulnerable to attack.

The Sauk and Fox knew of many scattered islands in that swamp where they could station their warriors. It was a perfect setting for an ambush. When the time came, this proved devastating to the Dakota forces. The attack came from all sides, scattering the Dakota into the swamp with the Sauk and Fox warriors in close pursuit. Only a third of the Dakota forces made it out, and they retreated in disgrace. The war between the Dakota Sioux and the woodland tribes was over, though the Dakota vowed to seek revenge if they ever caught a Sauk, Fox, or Kickapoo in the open prairie. Kiakiak had fought fearlessly in the battle. Despite being wounded many times, he wouldn't quit. In the eyes of the Sauk and the Fox, Chief Kiakiak's honor was restored.

# Father Allouez

In May of 1670, ten voyageur canoes left Montreal destined for the Soo. The Jolliet brothers manned three with their coureurs des bois and engagés. Three canoes held Nicolas Perrot and his team, packed with muskets for his gun trade. The rest carried a company of fifty soldiers sent to strengthen the French defenses at the Soo. In the last military canoe sat Jesuit priests: Fathers Allouez, Druillettes, and Andre. Father Marquette had gotten his wish.

The soldiers headed north up the St. Marys River toward the Soo with Father Druillettes and Father Andre. Father Druillettes would manage the Soo Mission, and Father Andre, with twenty soldiers, would head for the Holy Spirit Mission at Chequamegon Bay. Father Marquette and Father Dablon would stay behind with the refugees. Their charge was to start up the St. Ignace Mission, fulfilling a dream Marquette had longed for since he was a young man.

The Jolliet brothers and their three canoes headed south down the Lake Huron shoreline, trading for fur. One of Nicolas Perrot's gun-trading canoes headed down the other side of the Michigamme Peninsula, a second took the route down the western shoreline of Lake Michigan, and a third carrying Nicolas Perrot and Father Allouez headed for Green Bay to find Henri.

Nicolas Perrot and his trading team set up a trading post at the Winnebago camp on Lake Winnebago, then he and Father Allouez continued up the Fox River, alone. In three weeks, they arrived at Nokee's abandoned camp and pulled their canoe onto the shore. It was an eerie, surreal feeling. Nothing moved; not even a bird flushed from the trees. The dome-shaped wigwams were still standing. They looked like they needed some repair from the heavy winter snow, and the grass had grown long. But it felt like someone might return any minute to reclaim their village.

As they unloaded their canoe and turned it over to empty the afternoon rain, they heard a voice behind them. "Back away from your canoe and show your hands." Slowly, they turned to see a French musket protruding from the shadows of one of the huts, pointing directly at them.

"What brings a fur trader and a Black Robe to these parts?" the voice asked. "No one lives here anymore."

"We are seeking information on our Black Robe friend, Henri," responded Father Allouez. "My name is Allouez, and this is Nicolas Perrot, the gun trader. Chief Keokuk told us that a Kickapoo Chief named Kiakiak is known to visit this site. He said Kiakiak might be able to help us."

The musket lowered, and a figure in the shadows rose. Softly, the voice said: "My name is Kiakiak. Not chief! That title now belongs to another. And yes, I know where your friend is, and I can take you there. But you aren't going to like what you find."

Slowly, a hunched-over figure emerged from the wigwam using the musket as a crutch. "Don't worry," Kiakiak said. "I've run out of powder, and I'm afraid my fighting days are over."

As Kiakiak stepped into the sunlight, you could see his left arm hung loosely to his side, and his right leg had a limp. Scars ran across his face, and he was missing part of an ear. This was a man who had seen many fights. Kiakiak looked the two of them over and ordered them to sit down, for he had much to discuss.

Father Allouez looked visibly upset that this stranger was telling him what to do. Refusing to sit, he said, "We don't have time to waste. If you know where our friend is, come out with it!"

"He's dead!" Kiakiak said. "Now sit down, and I'll tell you about it."

Nicolas Perrot grabbed Allouez as it appeared he was about to collapse. "I don't believe him," Father Allouez said.

"Please sit, Father," Perrot said. "We need to hear what the man has to say."

They sat by the canoe, and Kiakiak began: "I bear responsibility for that man and the death of many others. We may have won the battle with the Dakota, but I lost the battle with myself."

Kiakiak then went on to tell them the whole story. He told them how he had started the war with the early killing of the tatanka, the stealing of the horses, and the death of the Dakota chief's son. He went on about the battle, how the Dakota had killed Tionontati, and how Henri was wounded. He told them that Nokee sent him and his warriors north that night to warn the northern river villages and the two Black Robes. Then, sadly, he told them how he had given up his chief position and returned to this camp to help the Sauk and the Fox fight the war.

"When I arrived here after leaving my warriors, I found Morningstar getting ready to move Nokee's people to the Grand Village of the Kaskaskia.. She told me the rest of the story."

*The morning after the battle, scouts reported that no one had attempted to cross the river, though they had heard horses during the night. The assumption was that the Dakota had returned to retrieve their dead. Nokee had just ordered the villagers to gather enough wood to build six funeral pyres on the bluff when Morningstar came running.*

*"Henri is coughing up blood," she said, out of breath. "You must come quickly. I don't understand—he was doing fine. We've stopped the bleeding, and he can move his legs."*

*Nokee knelt beside Henri and placed a hand on his abdomen. It was hard and distended. "No form of black magic will fix this," he said gravely. "He's bleeding inside." Morningstar began to speak, but Nokee shook his head. He took Henri's hand.*

*Holding back tears, Nokee said, "Henri, you have been a dear friend. We could never have made it this far without your unbreakable faith in the quest. Your God will surely welcome you into his kingdom in the sky. We will be forever thankful for what you have done."*

*As Henri's eyes began to glaze, he looked upward and whispered, "Is that you, Pierre? I'm glad I found you." Then, with a long, shuddering breath, Henri slipped away.*

*Nokee held Henri tightly as Morningstar wrapped her arms around his shoulders. Together, they wept uncontrollably. With* two members of the peace delegation dead and full-scale war at their doorstep, they both knew the peace mission had failed.

Nokee ordered a seventh wood pile assembled. One after another, the seven bodies were carefully laid out. The villagers lined up to say farewell and added grave goods next to the bodies of the deceased. Tionontati received his walking staff and many other items he would need in the spirit world. Nokee added a shield and spear beside Tionontati, an honor usually reserved for warriors. But Nokee knew that no warrior had ever contributed more to the tribe's protection than Tionontati.

Morningstar meticulously placed personal items belonging to Henri around his body. However, she deliberately held back his vow cross. Nokee added the two leather-bound journals he had removed from Henri's pack to the pile, but Morningstar quickly pulled them back.

Nokee was confused. "Why would you deny him his books? You know they meant everything to him. The chance of those stories ever making it to their homeland died with our two Black Robe friends. Those books carry a dark curse. We should destroy them."

"No, Nokee, that's not true. Our friends died doing good, not evil. You heard Nicolas Perrot promise to return with more guns. You heard Henri ask him to bring Father Allouez back with him. More Black Robes will come. We'll give them these journals, and they will tell your story."

"Your optimism is beautiful," Nokee said. "However, my dream died with Henri. If the Black Robes come looking, we'll no longer be here. Keep those journals if you wish, but beware their dark powers. That curse could have ended here." With a heavy heart, Nokee lowered his head and lit the fires.

When the fires were out, they mounded dirt on each grave. Morningstar carefully placed a wooden stick cross at the head of the mound containing Henri's ashes. She lovingly hung his vow cross over it, marking the spot where the greatest peacemaker she had ever known would forever lie.

"Morningstar was right," Kiakiak said, blinking his eyes after coming back to reality from his memories. "Another Black Robe has come. Unfortunately, Morningstar is gone, and I don't know the fate of those journals."

Father Allouez and Nicolas Perrot sat there awhile, trying to absorb what they had just heard. "I want to see his grave," Father Allouez said. Kiakiak agreed to take them there. The next day, they made the portage into the Wisconsin River, traveled to its mouth, and climbed the bluff to see the graves. The land had recovered from the wildfire. The prairie grass was thick and ablaze with wildflowers. At the top, seven grass strips stood taller than the rest. Kiakiak pointed to the mound closest to the river. Father Allouez parted the grass and found the wooden cross, a weathered vow cross still hanging from it. Both men knelt to pray. They wept.

As they packed up for the return trip, Kiakiak told them he would stay behind. "I've done everything possible to correct my mistakes. I hope the spirits that lie here can now rest in peace. And yet, there's still one person for whom I must seek forgiveness. I must apologize to the Peoria chief, Echohawk. Please take me to the other side of the Great River, where I can head south to find his village."

"I don't think that's a good idea," Nicolas Perrot said. "The Fox chief, Meskwaki, told us the war is over, but no woodland tribesmen are safe from attack on the open prairie."

"I fear nothing," Kiakiak said. "They've broken my body and my spirit. What more can they do to me? Please take me to the other side."

Nicolas Perrot and Father Allouez ferried Kiakiak across the river, then turned their canoe around to begin their return trip.

• • •

In October of 1671, the returning fur convoys arrived in Quebec City. The governor-general immediately summoned Louis and Adrien Jolliet to his office. Governor-General Daniel de Rémy and his royal intendant, Jean Talon, were waiting to greet them.

"Gentlemen, I imagine you must be exhausted from your lengthy journey, and I don't wish to detain you, but this news can't wait. As you may or may not know, France is experiencing serious financial problems. Inflation is running wild, and grain is five times what it was just a few years ago. Workers' wages have stagnated, and the standard of living for rural peasants has diminished due to back-to-back bad harvests. Demands for social reforms are mounting daily. At the same time, our young king is spending enormous sums of money to rebuild Versailles. We are in desperate need of more revenue.

"Why am I telling you this?" continued the governor-general. "Because the minister of finances, Jean-Baptiste Colbert, has created a new taxation system. Henceforth you are required to pay a percentage of your income, not a set rate based on your occupation. If you make more, you pay more. Already, this is causing problems in the grain industry. The farmers are asking why they should work harder to produce more if they get taxed more when they do."

"In all due respect, sir," interrupted Louis Jolliet. "What does this have to do with us?"

"That's what I'm trying to tell you, Louis. The same rules will apply to New France and the fur industry. The rate for the fur harvest is fifty percent."

"What?" screamed Louis Jolliet. "Fifty percent of the profit … that is insanity."

"No, Louis. It's fifty percent of the take. Since the French Government provided all the guns you used in your trade, they want half of the take. And it starts today!"

"That'll be the end of the fur trade," screamed Louis, pulling at his hair. "It takes almost fifty percent of the take to purchase the provisions and pay the coureurs des bois and engagés. The rest goes to the investors. Who will finance an adventure if there's no return?"

"I understand," said the governor-general. "I'll argue that point in a letter to the minister of finances and try to get an exemption for the fur industry. But I'm afraid I must instruct the military to confiscate half of all the fur you brought back today. I promise I'll fight for you and the people of New France. Fur is the backbone of our economy. I'll argue that only furs bought through the trading of guns should be taxed, and this should be a one-time tax. It may cost me my governorship, which is up for renewal next year, but I'll fight for you. You have my word!"

Louis Jolliet stood silently, head tilted down. Rémy continued, "I know this ruling will temporarily put you out of business.

But if you are still interested, I can arrange that commission for you and your men to explore the Mississippi."

Louis Jolliet looked up. "I accept your offer!"

# Mississippi River

That fall, Louis Jolliet went right to work planning the Mississippi adventure. He knew that no fur trading teams would be heading afield until next spring due to the taxation assessment. None of the usual investors would be interested in funding a trip until they were sure the government had lifted the fur tax. His regular crew of five coureurs des bois would be looking for work, so he planned on hiring them before they looked elsewhere. Adrien Jolliet and Thomas Pajot Jr. would remain in Quebec City and manage the fur business while lobbying for change.

Louis planned on loading a twenty-man voyageur canoe with enough supplies for seven men to survive over five months. They would leave in the spring of 1672, heading for the Straits of Mackinac. Accompanying them would be Father Henri Nouvel, Marquette's replacement at the St. Ignace Mission. Once there, they would acquire two six-person Ottawa canoes capable of supporting a sail. With Father Marquette on board, they would make the exploratory journey and return to St. Ignace by early fall. If all went well, they would reach Montreal before the rivers and lakes froze over.

Since they would only be handing out gifts on this trip, Louis would bring two boxes of new model French muskets. He would add twenty axes, forty pounds of tobacco, twenty white clay pipes, and a good supply of salted pork and dry goods, including pemmican and jerky. They would trade with the Natives for fish or meat and be capable of hunting and gathering for themselves when needed.

On April 15, 1672, Governor-General Rémy requested Louis Jolliet to come to his office. Jolliet expected to hear that his commission was in place and that he could start ordering the needed supplies. However, as Louis entered the room, the severe look on the faces of the governor-general and his intendant surprised him.

"Mr. Jolliet," the governor-general began, "I told you I would fight for relief on the unfair taxation that has crushed the fur trade, and I've done just that. However, it has come at a price. It has been brought to my attention that vicious rumors about me have spread within the Royal Court in Paris. I just received a letter stating that as of April 8, 1672, I'm relieved of my position. My replacement will be Louis de Buade de Frontenac. However, I'll continue as the acting governor-general of New France until his arrival."

"I'm terribly sorry to hear that, sir," Louis said, shocked. "You've always been an honorable man. You have done what's best for the colony. All the coureurs des bois appreciate how you have stood up for them. Sir, will this decision affect the exploration of the Mississippi?"

"That's why I called you here. As acting governor-general, I can't approve new sources of funding. I can approve you to go, but I can't fund your commission."

"How can I proceed without funding?" Jolliet asked, his dreams falling to pieces in front of him. "The supply bill for a five-month adventure will be substantial, and the men, although my friends, expect to get paid."

"I'm sorry, Louis," the governor-general said, shaking his head. "It will just have to wait until Frontenac arrives. And that will not be until September of this year."

"Well then, I'll send my men out on a fur run instead," Jolliet said, looking rather disgusted. "They need work!"

"I'm afraid that's not possible. Frontenac is now both the governor-general of New France and the lieutenant general of the military. His first order was that no coureurs des bois be allowed to leave the Upper St. Lawrence, and he ordered the military to enforce it. He wants every man in the area to be available to help build a fort at the mouth of the Cataraqui River just before the St. Lawrence River enters Lake Ontario."

"He's insane!" yelled Louis. "How are the fur traders to make a living between now and when he shows up?"

"He suggested the men keep busy with odd jobs. They'll be rewarded sufficiently with good-paying military jobs upon Frontenac's arrival. Those are his exact words in the orders he sent."

Louis Jolliet left the office stunned. But he wasn't the only one upset. The men who were now out of work gathered at the governor-general's mansion, demanding justice. The military responded quickly, stomping out the uprising before it had even truly begun. Throughout the summer, the men found work where they could. Bishop Laval hired as many men as possible for restoration work on church properties; even so, many families suffered from a lack of income.

When Frontenac arrived in Quebec City on September 7, 1672, the male population was desperate for work. He posted announcements around town stating all men seeking well-paying jobs should assemble at the governor-general's mansion in four days. On the morning of September 10, an angry mob of coureurs des bois, engagés, and fur warehouse workers showed up.

Standing on the front balcony of his residence, Governor-General Frontenac addressed the crowd. "Gentlemen, I bring you great news. The taxation on the fur industry, the industry that created this fine city, has been lifted." A loud cheer arose from the crowd.

Then Frontenac held up a handful of papers. "In my hand, I hold numerous lucrative fur contracts ready to be signed by our brave coureurs des bois. The shutdown of fur collections has created incredible shortages in the furrier and haberdashery shops on the streets of Paris. Competition for prime fur has caused that industry to pay two to three times what they were paying just one year ago. What this means to you is that more money will go into everyone's pockets—including yours." Another rousing cheer erupted.

"However," Frontenac continued, "these promissory notes don't go into effect until May 1, 1673, when a French military regiment of our finest fighting men arrives."

The gathering of men went dead silent. Then, a voice in the crowd yelled, "But we need work now!"

"I know, I know," Frontenac said as he raised his hand to quiet the mob. "Those are the exact words I said to Jean-Baptiste Colbert." Just mentioning Colbert's name sent the crowd into a chant of, "Hang the cheating scoundrel."

"Just one minute!" shouted the governor-general. "That's why the Honorable Jean-Baptiste Colbert sent a sizable commission that will put every man here to work." Another hush went through the crowd.

"I'm prepared to pay a very generous one-month salary, in advance, to any man that signs up to build a great fort where the St. Lawrence River enters Lake Ontario. That land needs clearing and housing built for the arriving regiment. The new fort will ensure that all land west of that point in the St. Lawrence basin will remain secure in the name of France forever. I'm placing the great explorer La Salle in charge of building my military forts. It will be La Salle's first fort, but I assure you it won't be his last as we continue strengthening our French control throughout the Great Lakes area."

The same voices that had demanded for heads to roll a moment ago now screamed, "Where do I sign up?"

"Men," Frontenac said. "My ships in the harbor are fully equipped for the venture and are ready to sail. Registration will start tomorrow at the pier. I expect all that sign on to be on board and sober on the morning of September 15."

Frontenac gave the crowd a minute to absorb the information, then continued. "On May 1, 1673, the fur trading ban ends, and the coureurs des bois are free to begin their annual collections. Also, because of the demand for fresh fur, Jean-Baptiste Colbert decided that in addition to trading guns, the trade of brandy or rum to the Indigenous tribes will now be legal."

"Finally, there is one more thing you should be aware of," Frontenac said. "The second and third months of work on the new fort will be paid in full on May 1, 1673, at the end of each man's contract."

Louis Jolliet, aware of what Frontenac was doing and the bishop's feelings on providing the Indigenous population with alcohol, went straight to Bishop Laval. The bishop was outraged. "This is nothing more than legalized slavery. He creates a situation where desperate men have no choice but to accept his offer, then works them close to death for two more months without pay. Then, he has the nerve to name the fort after him. The man is immoral. And the trading of brandy and rum to the tribes is, in my mind, a mortal sin."

"Louis, do you still have the papers signed by Governor-General Rémy authorizing your expedition?"

"Yes," Jolliet replied. "But they're worthless without funding."

The bishop smiled. "The order from Frontenac says there'll be no fur trading until May 1, 1673. It didn't mention exploration. Tell your team not to sign on with Frontenac. I'll hire you and your men to work for me. The Church will provide the funds needed to gather your supplies under the guise they are for our missions. Your team can slip out of town under the cover of darkness as soon as you are ready."

"Is that legal?"

"Mr. Jolliet! The governor-general runs the affairs of the Monarchy in New France. I run the affairs of the Church. I'll claim you are on a mission to comfort and protect our western Missions."

• • •

October 3, 1672, in the middle of a late chilly night, a fully loaded voyageur canoe slipped out of Quebec City with Louis Jolliet, Pierre Moreau, Jacques Largillier, Pierre Porteret, Jean Plattier, Jean Tiberge, and a priest named Henri Nouvel. They arrived in St. Ignace on December 8th with a letter signed by Governor-General Daniel de Rémy and Jean Talon to conduct an expedition of discovery to the Mississippi, funded by the Catholic Church.

Father Marquette was overjoyed to see his friends. The thought of the team spending the winter at the St. Ignace Mission warmed his heart, and all thoughts of loneliness and depression melted away.

Seeing the positive effects the news had on Father Marquette, Louis Jolliet decided it best not to tell Marquette that it was Governor-General Rémy's signature on the paper, not Count Frontenac's. *Sometimes, it's best to let sleeping dogs lie*, thought Jolliet.

The coureurs des bois spent most of the winter adding a residence hall to the back of the St. Ignace Chapel. On May 17, 1673, two six-person canoes equipped with sails set out on their expedition, while Father Henri Nouvel stayed behind to manage the mission. Father Marquette, Jacques Largillier, Pierre Porteret, and Jean Plattier were in one canoe. Louis Jolliet, Pierre Moreau, and Jean Tiberge were in the other. They traveled to Green Bay and met the Menominee on June 1.

Chief Malomimis welcomed them, and Jolliet presented the chief with a new musket and a packet of black powder and lead shot. Before leaving Quebec City, Louis Jolliet had commissioned a blacksmith to insert a silver beaver into the stock of each gun. He anticipated they would be a big hit with the chiefs, and he was right.

Malomimis was thrilled with the gifts he received and took the exploration team to the top of the hill to see Pierre's grave. The chief smiled with delight as Marquette explained to his fellow explorers that the pile of stones, taller than the prairie grass, was the number of lives Pierre and Henri had saved. During a fine dinner prepared by the Menominee women, Chief Malomimis continued to praise the lifesaving work the two deacons had performed. He begged Father Marquette to stay for longer. Marquette regretfully informed him they would be gone in the morning. However, he promised to return at the end of their voyage.

The following day, the team entered the Lower Fox River and stopped at the St. François Xavier Mission at the De Pere Rapids. Father Allouez was excited to see them and happy to receive fresh supplies but felt compelled to ask whether something terrible had happened to Nicolas Perrot. He was concerned why Perrot had not shown up in the spring.

Father Allouez could not believe Governor-General Rémy was gone and replaced by Frontenac. He could not understand why the new governor-general had put a one-year moratorium on the fur traders. But even more disturbing was the news that the French Government had confiscated the few furs Perrot had brought back.

"Frontenac justified it by claiming Perrot had a fortune of fur hidden somewhere in a warehouse out west to avoid the tax," Louis stated.

"Perrot did have furs," countered Father Allouez, pointing at a pile of burnt logs already half-covered with tall prairie grass. "I helped him save what we could, but the fire spread too quickly. We only got out a fraction of what he had. What will become of Perrot now?"

"Well," Louis said. "The King's Court not only bad-mouthed the reputation of Governor-General Rémy, but they did the same to Perrot. I don't think any investors or military officials will be backing Perrot's adventures for a long time. He has married, and his wife is expecting their first child. Nicolas seems to have accepted the bad fortune that has befallen him. Like you, I know Nicolas Perrot. He may not be the most profitable trader, but no one should question his integrity."

"I agree," Father Allouez said. "I'll pray for him, his new family, and his future successes."

Father Marquette told Father Allouez that he'd promised the Menominee that he would return and spend time with them. Father Allouez suggested Marquette spend the next winter with him, and they could share a joint ministry with Sunday Mass conducted at both villages. The thought made Marquette happy.

In the morning, the explorers moved on, arriving at the Winnebago camp on Lake Winnebago on June 5. Again, they received a warm welcome from Chief Hoocak. Jolliet presented another musket and supply packet to the chief and answered concerns about Nicolas Perrot's whereabouts.

The explorers continued up the Upper Fox River and met the Fox chief, Meskwaki, and Sauk chief, Keokuk. Jolliet presented both men with new French muskets and made promises of continued fur trade in the absence of Nicolas Perrot. On June 10, they portaged the swamp and slipped into the Wisconsin River. On June 17, they reached the mouth of the Wisconsin River and saw, for the first time, the Great River—the mighty Mississippi. The entire team was in a state of awe.

Louis Jolliet would later describe the Mississippi in this way:

*It stood out as the River of Possibilities. The river that could take you to unknown places and possibly a shortcut to California, the China Sea, and beyond.*

Marquette pointed to the top of the bluff overlooking the Mississippi River. "Up there lies the grave of Henri Hébert. It's because of his sacrifices and premature death that all this is possible. I'll say a mass of thanksgiving there in his honor."

They all followed Father Marquette to the top of the ridge, where they located seven mounds. As they gathered next to the one closest to the river, Marquette said Holy Mass and passed out Communion. Louis Jolliet wept.

On June 18, they entered the Mississippi River. For eight days, Marquette recorded seeing gargantuan fish with long spoon-like noses, bison, wolves, bears, deer, turkey, and a menagerie of water birds and river animals, but no Indigenous people.

On June 25, they reached the Des Moines River, and Jolliet stopped to map the area. While exploring, he saw a single set of footprints heading off into the prairie. Jolliet gathered his crew and followed the footprints northwest until they came to a trail. Two miles later, they found an Indigenous village in a low-cut valley with over three hundred lodges. Four men carrying long white peace pipes approached them with friendly smiles. One was Peoria Chief Echohawk, who had moved his village south from Rock Island, and the other was the former Kickapoo Chief Kiakiak. With them were two village shamans.

"Welcome, Frenchmen and Black Robe friend, to my village," Chief Echohawk said. "We have prepared a fine feast for you. Have you come to bring us more guns? Our supplies are running low, and the Dakota Sioux still pose a threat."

"How did you know we were coming?" Jolliet asked.

"Kiakiak has been watching you for two days."

"We have not seen a person, much less a village along the river, in over a week," Marquette said. "No one has been in contact with us."

"We've moved most of our villages to the eastern shoreline and inland a few miles to avoid detection by the Dakota Sioux," Echohawk replied. "The war in the woodlands may have ended, but the Sioux haven't forgotten. I asked Kiakiak to bring you here. Who do you think left the footprints in the sand for you to follow?"

"You have met Black Robes before?" Marquette asked.

"Yes," Kiakiak replied. "We were with Black Robe Henri when he fought with us and died at the battle near the Wisconsin River.

I was the one who took Father Allouez to see Henri's grave. I told him Henri died saving Morningstar."

"Nokee and Morningstar were with Henri?" Marquette asked, excited by the news. "Do you know where the two of them went?"

"There's much you do not know," Echohawk said. "Eat and share smoke with us. There's much we can tell you."

They talked, smoked tobacco, exchanged gifts, and Marquette and Jolliet gave speeches. Then they feasted on cornbread, fish, and bison. Both Echohawk and Kiakiak were pleased with the new muskets they received. In exchange, they gave the explorers two buffalo blankets.

During the festivities, Kiakiak started up a conversation with Marquette. "Nokee and his people are living at the Grand Village on the Illinois River. Take this pipe. It was given to me by Nokee. It belonged to his father. Hold this white peace pipe, with white and red hanging feathers, high in the air when you approach a tribe, and your group will be recognized and welcomed. When you find Nokee—or he finds you—give it back. Tell him it has served me well."

• • •

The explorers spent a few days with the Peoria, then headed downriver. After they left, Kiakiak told Chief Echohawk that he would go to the Kaskaskian village and inform Nokee that they had seen his friends. Chief Echohawk asked Kiakiak to notify the Illinois tribes he encountered that a group of Frenchmen had entered their territory.

"Tell them to treat them well," Echohawk said. "In these changing times, we need all the allies we can get."

On July 7, the explorers reached the Missouri River. Jolliet went on and on about the width and depth of this massive tributary flowing in from the west. Marquette, confused by why Jolliet was so excited about one more river, asked, "What makes this river different from the others?"

Jolliet looked at him, stunned by the question. "Don't you see the incredible amount of water this system carries? It must drain an extensive section of the west and run for hundreds if not thousands of miles. This river may take you to California. It's possible we have found the elusive shortcut to the China Sea!"

On July 10, they reached another massive river. After pondering this discovery, Jolliet started to laugh. "What's so funny?" Marquette asked. "Don't tell me you discovered another route to China."

"Don't be silly. This river flows from the east. Judging from its size, this must be the Ohio River. La Salle claimed to have explored this river to the Mississippi. But he said nothing of the topography here or the size of the Mississippi. Let's take this river back to Montreal on our return trip and expose La Salle's lie."

"But I promised Father Allouez that I would spend the winter with him," Marquette said, looking disappointed.

"Alright," laughed Jolliet. "Let La Salle have his false glory. Our exploration of the Mississippi should be achievement enough for any man in his lifetime."

On July 16, Jolliet and Marquette's team reached the southernmost point of their journey: the mouth of the Arkansas River. They met the Quapaw tribe in a village called Kappa. As they approached, Jolliet spotted the Quapaw holding Spanish guns. The chief had a Spanish sword on his belt, and some of the women wore Spanish rosaries around their necks and had Spanish pottery. It was obvious to Jolliet that they had been trading with Europeans and were in frequent contact with them.

Jolliet immediately deduced that the Spanish weren't far away, and this river must end in the Gulf of Mexico. Jolliet spread the word to his crew to say nothing. Being fluent in Spanish, he would do the talking. He whispered to Marquette to hold up the white calumet peace pipe, and it worked. Jolliet had a friendly opening conversation with the Natives.

They spent three days with the Quapaw, confirming that Spanish explorers and colonists lived further downstream, and that this river led to the Gulf of Mexico and into Spanish territory. It strengthened Jolliet's belief that the Missouri tributary, flowing to the west, would prove a shortcut to California. However, fearing detection by the Spanish and possibly causing an international incident, they turned around and headed back north.

That night, Marquette wrote in his journal:

> We felt that we were exposing ourselves to losing the fruit of this voyage, of which we could publish no knowledge were we to fall

into the hands of the Spaniards. For they undoubtedly would have held us captive, at the least.

• • •

When they reached the Illinois River, a man in the distance waved for them to come ashore. The explorers paid him little mind, thinking it was one of the Michigamea fishermen. That was until Marquette stood in the canoe and almost overturned it.

"Stop," screamed Marquette. "It's Nokee!"

Nokee was at the Grand Village of the Kaskaskia on the Upper Illinois River when Kiakiak arrived. He immediately grabbed a canoe and headed downriver, intending to intercept the explorers on their return trip. As Marquette stepped out of his canoe, Nokee embraced him, saying, "Never is the sun so bright, O Frenchman, as when thou come to visit us."

They sat on the riverbank for hours, sharing stories and filling in gaps since they had separated back in the Soo. Marquette focused on mission successes won by Father Allouez and himself, and Jolliet informed Nokee of Nicolas Perrot's troubles. Nokee told them about Morningstar and Illiniwek and how little Illiniwek was already bossing the young children around.

Nokee suddenly grew quiet, then reached into his shoulder bag and pulled out two extremely weathered, leather-bound books. With a penetrating look, he said, "Morningstar insisted that I give these to you. She told me more Black Robes would come. She was right."

"In the name of God, can those possibly be what I think they are?" Marquette asked as his eyes fixated on the two books.

"Yes," Nokee replied. "These are the Black Robes journals."

Slowly, Nokee transferred them to Marquette's trembling hands.

"I wanted to bury them with Henri," Nokee said. "But Morningstar wouldn't let me. Maybe you can take these wavy lines that tell the story of my people and their ways. Maybe you can keep those stories alive."

"I most certainly can," Marquette said, choking back tears. "The material in these journals is priceless. I read some of their writing while we spent the winter together in the Soo. Henri's descriptions of the various tribes, their customs, manner of dress, and religious practices, both current and past, are profound—they are history in the making. The maps, created by Pierre, are more detailed than any I've seen. These journals will most certainly go to Paris. They'll be published and read by the entire world."

"That is good," Nokee said with a thoughtful smile. "No matter what happens, the souls of my ancestors will not turn to dust."

"Now I've something for you," Marquette said, and he reached into his pack and pulled out the three pieces of Nokee's calumet.

Nokee slowly assembled the pieces, almost religiously. He turned the pipe over, studied the markings, and straightened the feathers. In a soft voice, he asked, "Where did you get this? It belonged to my father."

"I got it from Kiakiak. He told me to tell you this: 'When you find Nokee, or he finds you, give it back to him. Tell him it has served me well.'

"And I'll add this as well," Marquette said. "It has done the same for us."

Nokee raised the pipe in the air. "Father, the struggles we've both endured have not been in vain. The stories of our ancestors will live forever. Their souls will walk in the shadows, and the Great Mounds will be respected and protected."

Nokee then turned to Marquette. "Travel with me up the Illinois River to the Grand Village of the Kaskaskia. You can visit with Morningstar and meet Illiniwek."

"Did you say the Kaskaskians?" Marquette asked excitedly. "I met the Kaskaskians at Chequamegon Bay. They were some of the kindest people I've met in the New World. I have dreamt of visiting them and starting a mission there. But first, I promised Father Allouez I would return to Green Bay and spend the winter with him."

"If it's Green Bay you want to reach," Nokee said, "why not go to Lake Michigan, then travel up the shoreline? The Illinois River is your best route. I'll take you there."

Marquette exchanged glances with Jolliet. Jolliet shrugged and said, "If it gets us to Lake Michigan quicker and shows us a route to the Mississippi without going through the Fox, I'm interested. The Fox can be rather testy at times."

"Then it's agreed," Marquette said. "We go to meet the Kaskaskians."

As the night started to settle in, they sensed an impending heavy rain. The explorers set up a temporary shelter using the bison blankets they had received from the Peoria village. Huddling next to a small cooking fire, they watched the rain clouds start to move in. They asked Nokee to join them, but he said he would rather curl up under a spruce tree and headed into the woods.

Marquette, anxious to see the condition of the journals, untied the tightly bound wraps holding the books together. He gently pulled out a map protruding from the edges of what appeared to be Pierre's journal, and something fell out. Marquette picked it up and handed it to Jolliet.

"What do you think this is?" Marquette asked.

"It's too big to be an arrowhead," replied Jolliet. "It looks more like a spear point."

"It must have some significance for Pierre to keep it," Marquette said as he opened the journal and slid the point back into the leather pocket. Marquette started to look for any notes Pierre had made on the object.

"If you want to preserve those books," Jolliet said, "you better put them away. A curtain of water is heading straight at us. All hell is about to break loose in less than a minute."

Marquette grabbed a section of deer hide, wrapped the journals tightly, and gently placed them deep inside his pack. They scrambled inside their makeshift shelter as the rain hit, knowing it would be a long, soggy night.

# Father Marquette

Nokee guided them up the Illinois River until they came to the massive village of Peoria. It was the capital city of the Illinois Nation, heavily fortified with log walls. Surrounding the area were extensive fields of ripening corn, beans, and squash. The explorers were amazed at the number of tribes assembled there. In addition to the Peoria, there were Tamaroa, Piankashaw, and Wea all mingled together.

As they entered the walled city, Chief Ma-ka-tai met them with a smile and invited them into his lodge to smoke, eat, and share stories. The Peoria people of the Illinois Nation used an Algonquian-based language, which made it possible for the explorers to communicate with them.

"Why are so many tribes located here?" Louis Jolliet asked over dinner.

"The Iroquois are attacking our outlying villages, and the Illinois tribes have come here seeking protection," Chief Ma-ka-tai said.

"When I return to Quebec," said Jolliet, "I'll tell them you need the support of the French military.. I'll let them know this would be a wonderful place to build a fort."

Ma-ka-tai looked at Louis. "I have heard of the guns the Kaskaskians received from the French, but no soldiers came. Tell them I need the soldiers and guns now." Louis promised to deliver the message.

Marquette was more interested in the history of the Illinois people. He learned that all Illinois tribes were direct descendants of the ancient Illini Mound Builders. They practiced a religion based on natural events, and the Sun God was their most powerful deity. They were fascinated by Marquette's description of his all-powerful God, who lived in a beautiful place called heaven.

Marquette promised to return and tell them more about this place where their departed souls could go and be forever happy. Marquette gave a sermon in Algonquian and intermittently sang prayers in Latin. When he did, Chief Ma-ka-tai and his council smiled and laughed, as Marquette seemed to be making bird sounds.

They spent two days with the Peoria people. Before leaving, Jolliet gave Chief Ma-ka-tai a musket and supply packet and promised to return with many more. Then they were off, heading upriver toward the Grand Village of the Kaskaskia at Starving Rock, where Nokee had moved his people.

As they approached the village, the scouts announced that Nokee had returned and brought with him six Frenchmen and a Black Robe. Morningstar grabbed little Illiniwek in her arms and ran to meet them. Setting Illiniwek down, she embraced Father Marquette and whispered, "Bonjour, Mon Ami. I've prayed you would come. Did Nokee give you the Black Robes' journals?"

Before Marquette could say yes, little Illiniwek stepped between them, pushing Marquette away. In a small but insistent voice, Illiniwek said, "No! My *ogiin*—my mother." Morningstar and Nokee laughed and told Illiniwek that these men were friends with Black Robes Henri and Pierre. Illiniwek looked up and was satisfied with the answer. He grabbed a stick and ran off to play with the other boys.

The group sat there laughing, crying, and enjoying each other's company for hours. Then Nokee told them it was time to meet Chief Ducoigia. As they entered the fortified village, Marquette estimated about fifteen hundred people lived there in seventy-plus dome-shaped lodges covered with reeds and bearskin floors.

Chief Ducoigia faced the same problem that plagued Chief Ma-ka-tai—constant attacks from the Iroquois. Jolliet gave Chief Ducoigia the last of the silver beaver muskets and made the same offer of French military support and open trade. Chief Ducoigia thanked them for the muskets they had received earlier from

Nicolas Perrot's trading team. But like Chief Ma-ka-tai, he needed many more guns and the immediate support of soldiers.

On the third day of being fed and treated well, Marquette started feeling sick. His dysentery was flaring up again.

"Is he alright?" Morningstar asked with a concerned look.

"Yeah," said Jolliet, shaking his head. "He has been eating various tribal dishes for five days now. Indigenous food doesn't sit well with him. We had better get him on the trail and serve him corn mush and pemmican. That seems to suit him better." They both enjoyed a good laugh.

Before they left, Marquette promised to return to the Kaskaskians, teach them his faith, and start a new mission. Nokee guided the explorers up the Illinois River to its headwaters, then turned up the Des Plaines River. They made a short portage to reach the Chicago River, which flowed south into Lake Michigan. At the mouth of the Chicago River, they met a group of Kaskaskian fishermen netting round whitefish. The Kaskaskians told the group that their village was on the Upper Des Plaines River, upstream of the portage they had just made. They had a friendly visit with the Kaskaskians and shared a fine fish dinner.

• • •

On September 1, the explorers said their goodbye. Marquette again promised Nokee he would return soon, and Jolliet promised he would try to get more guns and help from the military. The two canoes left the Chicago River and traveled 250 miles north along the Lake Michigan shoreline. Ten days later, they reached Father Allouez's mission, St.-François Xavier, on the Lower Fox River, just south of Green Bay.

Feeling as though he was on the edge of death, Father Marquette was glad he had told Father Allouez he would spend the winter in Green Bay—he couldn't go any further if he wanted to. The entire crew of explorers stayed for a month to rebuild the burned fur warehouse. Jacques Largillier and Pierre Porteret agreed to remain with Marquette and Father Allouez. Louis Jolliet, Pierre Moreau, Jean Plattier, and Jean Tiberge headed for St. Ignace. Marquette kept his diary but sent the original journals and maps of Henri and Pierre back with Louis Jolliet.

Louis Jolliet's team arrived at St. Ignace in time to catch the fall convoy heading to Montreal. Jolliet sent his three coureurs des bois back to Quebec with a letter to Governor-General Frontenac expressing the Illinois tribe's desperate need for guns and military assistance. Jolliet decided to spend the winter with Father Henri Nouvel to help him finish the work on the chapel. He would use the long winter to rewrite his notes and make copies of his maps.

The following spring, 1674, Adrien Jolliet arrived in St. Ignace accompanied by Thomas Pajot Jr., Jean Plattier, Jean Tiberge, and four engagés. They came in a fully supplied voyageur canoe, ready to trade. Adrien reported that La Salle was casting doubt on their discovery of the Mississippi.

"La Salle has claimed there will be no proof without Father Marquette and your journals," exclaimed Adrien. "He has told the townspeople that we are simply trying to steal his glory of being the first to discover the Mississippi."

Louis Jolliet was infuriated. He sent Adrien and his crew south around the Lower Great Lakes on their annual fur run but stayed behind to continue writing while waiting for Marquette's return. He promised them he and Marquette would join them in Montreal that fall with all the proof they needed.

On October 1, while Louis was waiting for the annual fur convoy, three trappers came down from the Soo looking to top off their summer collections. They informed Louis that the fall convoy was late because the month-long wind and rains had held up the arrival of the Lake Superior fur collections.

"Governor-General Frontenac was fit to be tied when he discovered you had gone off exploring without his permission," one of the trappers said. "Frontenac has officially announced that if he doesn't hear any proof from the expedition by the end of this year, he will appoint La Salle to explore the Mississippi." This news further enraged Louis Jolliet.

The following morning, Jolliet grabbed a two-person canoe and set off alone. He had finished redrawing his maps and left a copy of them at the chapel in St. Ignace, but took his original journal. Henri and Pierre's journals were so extensive that he didn't have time to make copies. Realizing the importance of including the two deacons' work in the 1675 edition of *The Jesuit Relations*, he transported their original works as well.

Louis Jolliet made substantial progress due to the rising rivers from the month-long rains. When he reached the Lachine Rapids, just upstream from Montreal, he pulled his canoe ashore to make the portage. At the bottom of the rapids, he could wait for a ship to take him to Quebec City. Jolliet was tired and dreaded the three trips necessary to transfer his canoe and gear to the bottom.

*I traveled over a thousand miles on this trip alone*, thought Louis. *I've been on dozens of rivers over the past six years and navigated countless rapids, including the Soo. Why should I be afraid of this one? After all, didn't Champlain run these rapids fifty years ago? He was more of a sea captain than a river rat!*

As Jolliet pushed his canoe into the current, it didn't take long for him to realize he had made a big mistake. The current was faster than he had anticipated, and most of the large boulders now lurked beneath the surface. He zigzagged between them, eyes scanning for their telltale spray. Then, an unseen rock caught the bottom of his canoe, throwing it sideways into a massive boulder. The canoe shattered in two. Louis and all his gear sank as his body crashed into another boulder. Battered and bruised, he was swept downstream, tossed like a ragdoll.

Dragged underwater again and again, gasping for breath, Louis was sure he wouldn't survive. Then, by some miracle, his arm caught on a boulder and swung him into a back eddy. Louis hung on for hours, his strength gradually draining. Then, through the grace of God, some Algonquin fishermen rescued him. They cared for him for ten days until the fall fur convoy found him and carried him to the ship.

Louis had luckily escaped with his life—but the two Jesuits' diaries, the history of Nokee's people, and all Jolliet's original writings and maps were lost to the river.

• • •

Jolliet returned to Quebec with injuries both physical and mental. The physical ailments healed in a few weeks, but his mind was in disarray for months. Bishop Laval tried to see him, but Louis refused to discuss the Mississippi exploration. Bishop Laval arranged to have Father Dablon visit Louis. He knew Dablon had spent the 1668 winter at the Soo with Louis, and that he could perhaps break the depression cycle Jolliet was in.

When Father Dablon showed up, he initially got the same response. Louis, lying in bed, moaned rather than spoke. "It is hopeless. All the proof we needed was in my canoe. Then, because of a moment of stupidity, it was gone. And now La Salle is going around Paris saying I'm a fraud, a delusional man trying to steal his glory of being the first to explore the Ohio and Mississippi."

Father Dablon saw these thoughts as an opportunity to get Louis Jolliet talking. "Louis, how do you know that La Salle wasn't the first to discover the Mississippi?"

"Because we saw the mouth of the Ohio River," Jolliet said. "We saw how the waters of two great rivers came together. La Salle never mentioned the topography, the vast prairie, or the Indigenous people that lived along the Great River. He has told everyone he found the route to China, but the Mississippi doesn't take you to China. It takes you to the Gulf of Mexico. We met the Quapaw Indians at the mouth of the Arkansas, and they had Spanish guns. The route to California is through the Missouri River. It'll take you far to the west." Father Dablon handed Louis a piece of paper and said: "Show me. Draw me a map." In minutes, Louis Jolliet drew a map with all the rivers they had seen from Green Bay to the Arkansas River.

"Now name them," Dablon demanded.

Jolliet did as he was asked, quickly and accurately.

"How did you do that?"

"Because it's all in here, in my head."

"Exactly," Dablon responded. "And that's how we'll recreate the work you lost."

"Did you say we?" asked Jolliet, quickly sitting up.

"Yes. I'll help you. Why do you think the bishop made me superior general of the Great Lakes Mission? It's because I spent thirty years in that country. I walked the land. All writings from the Great Lakes Jesuits now come to me for editing and submission to the Jesuits' journal in Paris. Didn't you tell the bishop you made copies of your maps and left them at the chapel in St. Ignace? We can retrieve them. When Father Marquette returns with his journal, he will verify every word. However, if you would rather sit around and let La Salle claim he was the first to explore the Mississippi, I can leave."

"Never!" Jolliet replied, with a new sense of dignity. "When do we start?"

"We start today," Father Dablon said with a grin. "We start with you telling me the whole story."

• • •

Back in Green Bay, Father Marquette had spent a horrible winter with frequently recurring bouts of his disease, keeping him bedridden much of the time. Some days, he was too sick to attend, much less say, daily mass. By mid-spring, with all the fresh wild foods becoming available, he began to recover, and by fall, he felt he had beaten the disease.

Father Marquette was determined to return to the Grand Village of the Kaskaskia and open his second mission. On October 24, 1674, Marquette, Jacques Largillier, and Pierre Porteret slid their canoe into Lake Michigan and paddled south along the western shoreline. An unexpected early winter storm hit, and they were lucky to make it to the mouth of the Chicago River. They erected a makeshift shelter and awoke to two feet of snow and bitter cold.

They decided to hunker down and wait for a break in the weather, but it never came. Ice began to cover the river, making travel by birchbark canoe too treacherous. They had brought only limited supplies, expecting a short trip—but now they were in serious trouble. Fortunately, Kaskaskian hunters found them and invited them to spend the winter with them on the Upper Des Plaines River.

Marquette suffered mightily from the extreme weather and his returning dysentery. His abdominal pain, cramps, fever, and bloody diarrhea became more frequent as winter dragged on. In the spring, Jacques Largillier and Pierre Porteret begged Marquette to let them take him back to St. Ignace or the mission in Green Bay, but he refused.

On April 1, 1675, with Father Marquette in a terrible state, they resumed their journey to the Grand Village of the Kaskaskia. They arrived on April 11, during Easter Holy Week. They found the village had swelled to five times the size they remembered due to the renewed spring offensive of the Iroquois. Morningstar and Nokee begged Marquette to seek help from the village shaman, but Marquette insisted that he had God's work to do.

Marquette declared his new Mission of the Immaculate Conception of the Blessed Virgin officially open, and on Easter Sunday, said Holy Mass to thousands of Indigenous people. Later that day, Marquette wrote in his journal:

> I spoke to a council of more than fifteen hundred chiefs, elders, and young men, who formed a great circle around me on a beautiful prairie adorned with reed mats and bearskins.

Marquette spent the next two weeks under the care of the village shaman and the watchful eye of Morningstar. But as his health failed to improve, he came to accept the inevitable—the end was near. He asked his two coureurs des bois to take him back to St. Ignace, where he could die. Nokee led a procession of a dozen Kaskaskian canoes around the southern shoreline of Lake Michigan, then turned north.

Marquette's condition worsened, and they had to stop at the Ottawa village on Pine River. Nokee, Jacques Largillier, and Pierre Porteret carried Father Marquette ashore. Chief Atowas and his people did what they could to keep the Black Robe comfortable, but Marquette was too weak. He died on May 18, 1675, on the sixth birthday of Illiniwek. They buried Father Marquette near the mouth of the river. Jacques and Pierre cut a birch tree into slabs and made a six-foot cross, which they supported with a pile of rocks marking the grave.

Then, Chief Atowas approached the two men, carrying an iron cross made from a bayonet. "Take this and tie it to the wooden cross," Atowas said. "It belonged to Black Robe Henri. He told me to keep it as a promise that the Black Robes would return and build us a mission. He said to hang this on the mission door to show that Black Robes keep their word. I've heard that Black Robes Henri and Pierre are dead. Their replacement lies dead at the edge of my village. Hang it on the cross, so if a Black Robe passes this marker, they will know I still long for that mission."

Jacques Largillier said a series of prayers at the grave site. Pierre Porteret fired his musket in the air to honor their fallen hero. Jacques ended the ceremony with a pronouncement: "So that no one will ever forget the great works this man has done, from this day forward, this river will be called the Pere Marquette."

• • •

Nokee and the Kaskaskians turned their canoes south, and the two coureurs des bois headed north. The only personal item of Father Marquette that Jacques and Pierre took with them was Marquette's heavily weathered leather-bound journal. Upon arriving at the St. Ignace Mission, Father Henri Nouvel couldn't believe the news.

He paced the floor of his quarters in a panic. "How could Marquette be dead? How is this possible? How can this be part of God's plan? My tenure here was to be temporary. Now, I'm the head of this mission. What am I supposed to do?"

"I don't know," Jacques Largillier said. "I suppose your superior, Father Dablon, would want you to stay until you are permanently assigned here, or until he finds a replacement. Pierre and I are heading back to Quebec City with the news. You're welcome to come with us if you wish."

"No, you are right. God has placed me in this predicament for a reason. I'll stay to maintain the mission and work to spread the word of our Lord."

"We'll tell Father Dablon and the bishop of your dedication," Jacques Largillier said.

"Thank you," Father Nouvel replied. "Now, there's one more thing I must tell you, and it is disturbing news. Louis rolled his canoe in the Lachine Rapids on his return to Montreal. He nearly lost his life."

"Is he alright?" demanded Jacques.

"Yes, he recovered rather quickly. However, he lost everything. Luckily, Father Dablon is working with Louis to recreate the whole adventure. Louis made copies of his maps, and I have them here. He instructed me to keep them hidden and safe."

"Here, keep this as well. It's the journal of Father Marquette. Hide it! This journal is the only surviving proof of the discoveries we made. Some were against us making this journey, and some desperately wanted to claim this victory for themselves."

Father Nouvel tucked Marquette's journal into a small dusty wooden box and placed it on a storage shelf. "No one will ever know it's here!"

• • •

By the fall of 1676, Louis Jolliet had finished his rewrites. But Marquette's missing journal still cast doubt on the expedition. Some believed Father Marquette was alive and hidden away as part of the ruse. Louis Jolliet wanted to clear his name by returning to the western Great Lakes. He needed to fulfill his promise of creating a trading network while supplying guns and military help to the Illinois tribes.

When he approached the governor-general with the idea, Frontenac flatly refused the request. "Louis, your problem has always been that you are a hopeless romantic," Frontenac said with a smirk. "Do you really think we have been giving guns to the Natives to defend themselves against other tribes? We're here to seek out allies that will join us in the fight if the English or Spanish try to seize our newly acquired western territory. The forts are there to protect our land and the resources they hold, not the people that live there. La Salle understands this, so I've already commissioned La Salle to explore that area and build forts."

"He will determine if the Illinois tribes are truly with us. How do we know they won't back the English with all those guns when the fighting starts? If there's any doubt, let the Iroquois eliminate that ungrateful group and save the French troops the trouble of doing it later. When La Salle finishes building my military fort at the mouth of the Niagara River, he will head to the western Great Lakes to build Fort Miami on the St. Joseph River. Then La Salle will build another fort on the Illinois River at the Peoria village you wrote about."

Louis Jolliet marched out of the governor-general's office in a rage. He went immediately to his brother's fur trading office and offered his services. Louis Jolliet would never return to the Upper Great Lakes. Instead, he would turn his attention to the far north. Louis Jolliet would spend the rest of his life trading with the Inuit and exploring the Hudson Bay and Labrador area.

• • •

In the spring of 1677, Father Dablon traveled to the St. Ignace mission. At the same time, Nokee led a convoy of thirty Kaskaskian canoes bound for the Ottawa village on Lake Michigan. There, the Kaskaskians dug up the body of Father Marquette, cleaned off any remaining flesh, and spread the bones out in the sun to dry. From the birch cross that had marked his grave, they fashioned a box, filled it with Marquette's remains, and bound it with pine pitch and spruce roots. Upon its lid, they lashed Henri's iron bayonet cross. In a solemn procession led by Nokee, they transported Marquette's bones north, heading for the mission at St. Ignace, the place he loved most.

On a dark rainy night in early June of 1677, Father Henri Nouvel, the replacement pastor at the St. Ignatius Jesuit Mission at St. Ignace, was jarred from his sleep by excessive pounding on the chapel door. He hurried to quell the disturbance before it woke Father Claude Dablon, the visiting Superior of the Western Great Lakes Missions. Slowly opening the door, Father Nouvel jumped back as a birch box came thrusting toward him. Carefully lashed to the lid was a musket bayonet. But instead of a blade, it supported an iron cross.

"These are the bones of Father Marquette," said a deep voice. "I must know if the Black Robes' journals made it to Paris."

Father Dablon suddenly appeared in the shadows and whispered, "Who is it?"

"It's a tall chief with a white peace pipe tattooed on each arm," replied Father Nouvel, swallowing hard.

"Is that Nokee? For God's sake, let him in! I'm afraid I have some troubling news to tell him."

Nokee entered, soaking wet, creating a pool on the floor. "I hate to tell you this," Father Dablon said, "but Henri and Pierre's journals were lost. Louis Jolliet stayed in St. Ignace for almost a year, making copies of his maps and rewriting his journal. And thank God he did, because he made the wrong decision to return to Quebec City alone. Near Montreal, he lost control and rolled his canoe in the Lachine Rapids, losing everything—including Henri and Pierre's journals."

"I'm here," continued Father Dablon, "to retrieve Jolliet's maps and Father Marquette's journal left here by Jacques Largillier and

Pierre Porteret. Father Nouvel has kept them well hidden. I've been working with Louis Jolliet in Quebec City as we recreated their exploration. With Jolliet's maps and Marquette's journal, proof of their discoveries will be complete. But I'll need your help to reconstruct the work of Henri and Pierre."

Nokee lowered his head as he stood up and backed away toward the door. "That will have to wait. The Dark Forces continue to torment me and stand in my way. The Iroquois raiders have intensified their attacks, and no guns or soldiers came. It's only a matter of time until this old warrior sees his last battle.

"A messenger from the Kaskaskian village caught up with us yesterday," continued Nokee. "He reported a massive Iroquois force had broken through the Eastern Alliance and was heading for the Grand Village. Morningstar and Illiniwek are there. The Black Robes' written word and French soldiers' support have failed me. Any chance of preserving our ancestral stories now falls on Illiniwek's shoulders. He's my last hope. I've already stayed too long—now I must go."

Father Dablon would spend the summer of 1677 trying to recreate an abbreviated version of Marquette's writings. However, the story of Nokee's people, documented so carefully by Henri and Pierre, would remain lost. Without the Black Robes' written words, Nokee's dream of preserving his history was dust in the wind.

When Father Dablon returned to Quebec City, Governor-General Frontenac asked to see Marquette's journal. Frontenac insisted his geographers and historians needed time to assess the manuscript and compare its entries to what Louis Jolliet had published. Father Dablon gave Frontenac the abbreviated version.

It would be months before Dablon would lay eyes on that copy again. In the meantime, Dablon hid Marquette's original journal within the archives of the Catholic Church in Montreal. That precious document would remain forgotten for nearly two centuries. As for the journals of Henri and Pierre—lost when Jolliet's canoe shattered in the rapids—it would take over three hundred years, and the tireless work of generations of archaeologists and anthropologists, to recover perhaps half of what was lost that infamous day.

# Epilogue

In the summer of 1678, Governor-General Frontenac presented La Salle with orders to build a series of military forts and retrace the path of Louis Jolliet. Accompanying La Salle was Franciscan Recollect Louis Hennepin, who had previously constructed the chapel and residences for missionaries at Fort Frontenac. His task would be to do the same at each fort La Salle established.

On September 1, 1678, La Salle set out with thirty fresh engagés from France. While the engagés completed the portage around the Lachine Rapids, La Salle and Hennepin followed behind at a leisurely pace. Taking a short break near a log jam in the river, Recollect Hennepin spotted the wooden frame of a sunken canoe. He waded out and dragged the shattered front half to shore. Both men looked at each other, the same realization dawning in their eyes.

"This canoe could have belonged to anyone," La Salle said.

"Yes, but it's where Jolliet said he rolled his canoe when it broke in half," Hennepin replied, eyeing the canoe with suspicion.

"Let's drag it into the woods where no one will see it," La Salle said quietly. "I don't want anyone going back claiming they've found proof that Jolliet's story is true. It was hard enough getting him out of the picture—and I have no desire to reopen that fight."

Both men grabbed a corner of the broken canoe frame and carried it well off the trail. As they dropped it onto the forest floor, a washed-out leatherbound book fell out of the bow. "Could this be one of the journals Jolliet said he was transporting?" Hennepin asked.

"I'll take that," La Salle said, grabbing it. Seeing the leather binding was void of any paper remnants, he raised his arm to throw the empty cover into the brush. As he swung back, something fell out.

Hennepin picked the object up and turned it around in his hands. "It's big for an arrowhead. It must be a spear point. Why would Jolliet save something like this? Let's throw it back in the river."

"No, wait!" La Salle yelled. "Give it to me. Every time we look at that point, it will remind us that we stuck it to Jolliet one more time."

When they reached the mouth of the Niagara River, construction of Fort Niagara began at once. By spring, the outer walls stood firm, and Recollect Hennepin's team had completed the chapel and residences for the missionaries. La Salle then dispatched Hennepin and half of the engagés upriver to the mouth of Lake Erie, where they were to build a sailing vessel on an island. On the way, Hennepin stopped and sketched a picture of Niagara Falls, claiming he was the first European to do so—a claim Adrien Jolliet would later dispute.

By the end of the summer, Hennepin's team had finished *Le Griffon*, a thirty-five-foot brigantine with two masts. Joined by La Salle and his men, the crew of thirty-two prepared to set sail for Green Bay. La Salle inspected the vessel and was pleased with its construction. But he informed Recollect Hennepin there was one more thing he wanted.

"Before we set sail," La Salle said, "take this spear point from Jolliet's wrecked canoe and embed it in the ship wheel. Each time I look at the helm, it will remind me that we beat Louis Jolliet at his own game!"

Upon the ship's arrival in Green Bay, the local tribes—who had seen few fur traders over the past three years—were ready to trade. La Salle and Hennepin unloaded all but five of the crew and filled *Le Griffon* with prime fur. Ignoring tribal warnings of an approaching storm, they sent the undermanned vessel back toward Niagara. *Le Griffon* was never seen again.

La Salle's team proceeded by canoe around Lake Michigan and built Fort Miami on the St. Joseph River. They then traveled to the Peoria village on the Illinois River. Hennepin and most of the crew stayed behind to build Fort Crèvecœur—Fort Heartbreak—while La Salle set out to reach the Gulf of Mexico. The two men would never see each other again.

While Hennepin was building Fort Heartbreak, Fort Niagara mysteriously burned to the ground. Meanwhile, La Salle—driving his men relentlessly—was ultimately assassinated by his own followers in the wilds of Texas. Louis Hennepin would go on to explore the Upper Mississippi, only to be captured by the Dakota Sioux. A French soldier and explorer eventually rescued him and brought him back to Quebec City. With La Salle dead, Hennepin falsely claimed that his team had reached the mouth of the Mississippi before La Salle. Harshly ridiculed, Hennepin moved to England and authored a book on his adventures. In doing so, Hennepin would divulge French military secrets to the English and face hanging if he ever again set foot in New France.

To this day, deep in the clear, cold waters of Upper Lake Michigan lies the wreck of *Le Griffon*. On top of that wreckage, embedded in the ship's wheel, is a thin, well-crafted, corner-notched projectile point with serrated edges. It's long as an index finger, shaped like an aspen leaf, broader at the base, and tapered to a sharp front point. It's too large to be an arrowhead, more closely resembling the spear points used by the ancient Mound Builders. It lies there, guarded by Nanabozho and his Dark Forces, waiting for anyone who might seek to disturb it.

# Acknowledgments

None of this endeavor would have been possible without the help of family and friends, who read early drafts, made suggestions, and provided encouragement. A special thanks to my wife, Ruth, who was there every step of the way. To the team at Mission Point Press, Jen, Tanya, Hart, Zinzi, Stephanie, Jeanne, Darlene, Heather, Julie, Terese, and Tamra the team coordinator, thank you for taking this manuscript from concept to completion in such a professional and caring manor. My hat is off to all of you!

# About the Author

**Stephen Rheaume** is a thirteenth-generation descendant of Louis Hébert, New France's first European apothecary and farmer, through Hébert's daughter Guillemette. Rheaume, a native of Michigan, earned his bachelor of science in fish and wildlife management from Lake Superior State University. For more than 30 years, he worked as a federal biologist and geo-hydrologist with the U.S. Fish and Wildlife Service and the U.S. Geological Survey.

His professional contributions include the authorship of fifteen government publications addressing hydrological and ecological dynamics within the Great Lakes basin. Rheaume's scientific background informs his narrative work, often weaving together themes of cultural preservation, natural history, and Indigenous knowledge systems. He resides in Williamston, Michigan, with his wife and family.

# Maps

Major Indian Trails - indian trails: Project.geo.msu.edu, Michigan State University, East Lansing, Michigan.

Mound Sites in the Eastern United States - https://www.loc.gov/resource/g3706c.ct012058r/?r=-1.342,-0.195,3.685,1.209,0: Smithsonian/C. Thomas.

Great Lakes Tribes circa 1600 map - https://www.mpm.edu/content/wirp/ICW-21, Milwaukee Public Museum.

# References

Berriman, S., *Upper Tittabawassee River Boom Towns*: The Sanford Historical Society, 1999.

Cassidy, J. J. Jr., Project Editor, *Through Indian Eyes—The Untold Story of Native American Peoples*: The Reader's Digest Association, Inc., Pleasantville, New York/Montreal, 1995.

Chaput, C., *Michigan Indians—A Way of Life Changes*: Hillsdale Educational Publishers, Inc., Hillsdale, Michigan, 1970.

Claassen, C., *Beliefs and Rituals in Archaic Eastern North America—An Interpretive Guide*: The University of Alabama Press, Tuscaloosa, Alabama, 2015.

Doane, N. L., *Indian Doctor Book—Nature's method of curing and preventing disease according to the Indians*: Aerial Photography Services, Inc., Charlotte, North Carolina, 1985.

Fitting, J. E., *The Archaeology of Michigan—A guide to the prehistory of the Great Lakes Region*: Natural History Press, Garden City, New York, 1970.

Flaherty, T. H., Editor-In-Chief, *The Spirit World*: Time-Life Books, Morristown, New Jersey, 1992.

Gardner, J. L., Project Editor, *Mysteries of the Ancient Americas—The New World Before Columbus*: The Reader's Digest Association, Inc., Pleasantville, New York/Montreal, 1986.

Halsey, J. R., *Retrieving Michigan's Buried Past—The Archaeology of the Great Lakes State*: Cranbrook Institute of Science, 1999.

Hinsdale, W. B., *The Archaeological Atlas of Michigan 1851-1944*: Ann Arbor University of Michigan Press, 1931.

Hofsinde, R. (Gray-Wolf), *Indian Fishing and Camping*: William Morrow & Co., New York, 1963.

Hothem, L., *North American Indian Artifacts—A Collector's Identification & Value Guide*-6th Edition: Krause Publications, Iola, Wisconsin, 1998.

Huggler, T., *Fish Michigan 50 Rivers*: Friede Publication, 1995.

Kavasch, E. B., *The Mound Builders of Ancient North America—4000 Years of American Indian Art, Science, Engineering, & Spirituality Reflected in Majestic Earthworks & Artifacts*: iUniverse, Inc., Lincoln, Nebraska, 2004.

Kern, J., *A Short History of Michigan*: Michigan History Division, Michigan Department of State, 1977.

Kern L. and Luter S., Editors, *Native Peoples: Indians of the Great Lakes: Curriculum Manual 6-Adults*, Michigan Humanities Council, 1998.

Kruger, A., *American Nature Guides—Herbs*: Dragon's World Ltd, Limpsfield, Great Britain, 1995.

Kubiak, W. J., *Great Lakes Indians—A pictorial guide*—2nd edition: Baker Books, Grand Rapids, Michigan, 1999.

Larned, W. T., *North American Indian Tales*: Dover Publications, Inc., Mineola, New York, 1997.

Leverett, F. and Taylor, F. B., *The Pleistocene of Indiana and Michigan and the history of the Great Lakes*: U.S. Geological Survey, Monograph 53, 1915.

Quimby, G. I., *Indian Life in the Upper Great Lakes: 11,000 B.C. to A.D. 1800*: University of Chicago Press, Chicago, 1960.

Rombauer, I. S., and Becker, M. R., *Joy of Cooking*: New American Library, Times Mirror, New York, 1964.

Silverberg, R., *The Mound Builders*: Ohio University Press, Athens, Ohio, 1986.

Spencer, R. F., and Jennings, J. D., et al., *The Native Americans—Ethnology and Backgrounds of the North American Indians*: Harper Collins Publishers, Inc., New York, 1977.

Tomelleri, J. R., and Eberle, M. E., *Fishes of Central United States*: University Press of Kansas, Lawrence, Kansas, 1990.

Waldman, C., *Encyclopedia of Native American tribes—Revised Edition*: Checkmark Books, New York, 1999.

Walker, H., *Indian Cookin'*: Baxter Lane Co., Amarillo, Texas, 1977.

**Online searches (All retrievable as of December 2024)**

**Native American Chiefs and Tribes:**

Chief Canaqueese - Canaqueese - Wikipedia: Wikipedia.

Tutelo tribe - https://en.wikipedia.org/wiki/Tutelo: Wikipedia.

Santee Sioux tribes - https://www.thenicc.edu/about/history/santee-sioux-nation.php#:~:text=The%20Santee%20were%20the,spot%20of%20the%20Mississippi%20Valley.%22: History of the Santee Sioux tribe of Nebraska, Nebraska Indian Community College.

Illinois Confederation - https://en.wikipedia.org/wiki/Illinois_Confederation: Wikipedia.

**French Nobility and Explorers:**

Simon François Daumont - DAUMONT DE St.-LUSSON, SIMON-FRANÇOIS – Dictionary of Canadian Biography: Volume 1 (1000-1700).

Samuel de Champlain - https://en.wikipedia.org/wiki/Samuel_de_Champlain: Wikipedia.

The Explorers - https://www.historymuseum.ca/virtual-museum-of-new-france/the-explorers/samuel-de-champlain-1604-1616/: Virtual Museum of New France, Canadian Museum of History.

Jean Talon - https://www.biographi.ca/en/bio/talon_jean_1E.html: Volume 1 (1000-1700)-Dictionary of Canadian Biography.

Louis Hébert - Search Results – Full-Text Search: 'Hébert, louis' – Dictionary of Canadian Biography: Volume 1 (1000-1700)-Dictionary of Canadian Biography.

Joseph Hébert - https://www.biographi.ca/en/bio/Hébert_joseph_1636_1661_1662_1E.html: Volume 1 (1000-1700)-Dictionary of Canadian Biography.

Jean-Baptiste Colbert - https://www.thecanadianencyclopedia.ca/en/article/jean-baptiste-colbert: by Samuel Veniere-The Canadian Encyclopedia.

Rene Robert La Salle - https://www.biographi.ca/en/bio/cavelier_de_la_salle_rene_robert_1E.html: The Canadian Encyclopedia.

Daniel de Rémy de Courcelle - https://en.wikipedia.org/wiki/Daniel_de_Rémy_de_Courcelle: Wikipedia.

Jean Nicolet - Jean Nicolet - Wikipedia: Jean Nicolet (Nicolet), Sieur de Belleborne, Wikipedia.

Marquis Alexandre Prouville de Tracy - Alexandre de Prouville de Tracy - Wikipedia: Wikipedia.

Louis Jolliet - https://en.wikipedia.org/wiki/Louis_Jolliet: Wikipedia.

Nicolas Perrot - Nicolas Perrot 1665-1689 | Virtual Museum of New France: Virtual Museum of New France.

King Louis XIV - https://history.info/on-this-day/1654-coronation-of-french-king-louis-xiv/#google_vignette: History.info., Coronation of the French Boy King.

**Roman Catholic Clergy:**

Gabriel Sagard - https://www.biographi.ca/en/bio/sagard_gabriel_1E.html: Volume 1 (1000-1700)-Dictionary of Canadian Biography.

Joseph Le Caron - https://www.biographi.ca/en/bio/le_caron_joseph_1E.html: Volume 1 (1000-1700)-Dictionary of Canadian Biography.

Claude Allouez - https://www.biographi.ca/en/bio/allouez_claude_1E.html: Volume 1 (1000-1700)-Dictionary of Canadian Biography.

Claude-Jean Allouez - https://en.wikipedia.org/wiki/Claude-Jean_Allouez: Wikipedia.

Gabriel Druillettes - https://www.biographi.ca/en/bio/druillettes_gabriel_1E.html: Volume 1 (1000-1700)-Dictionary of Canadian Biography.

Claude Dablon - https://www.biographi.ca/en/bio/dablon_claude_1E.html: Volume 1 (1000-1700)-Dictionary of Canadian Biography.

Jesuits - https://www.thecanadianencyclopedia.ca/en/article/jesuits: The Canadian Encyclopedia.

*The Jesuit Relations* - https://www.thecanadianencyclopedia.ca/en/article/jesuit-relations: The Canadian Encyclopedia.

Jacques Marquette - https://www.biographi.ca/en/bio/marquette_jacques_1E.html: The Canadian Encyclopedia.

Jacques Marquette - Jacques Marquette: Biography, French Missionary, Explorer: Missionary (1637-1675), Biography.com.

A guide to Jesuit Formation - https://www.americamagazine.org/faith/2013/08/11/novice-regent-scholastic-guide-jesuit-formation-and-lingo?gad_source=1&gclid=CjwKCAiAjeW6BhBAEiwAdKltMllyY6gQstqgVARdDhXMUVA4s5MJNfwG9E8kGyyx8KMK58e5N2KxmRoCkyEQAvD_BwE: James Martin, S.J., America-The Jesuit Review.

Recollects - https://en.wikipedia.org/wiki/Recollects: Wikipedia.

Jesuits - https://en.wikipedia.org/wiki/Jesuits: Wikipedia.

Bishop François de Laval - https://en.wikipedia.org/wiki/Fran%C3%A7ois_de_Laval: Wikipedia.

Cardinal de Retz - https://en.wikipedia.org/wiki/Jean_Fran%C3%A7ois_Paul_de_Gondi: Wikipedia.

Louis Hennepin - Louis Hennepin 1678-1680 | Virtual Museum of New France: Virtual Museum of New France.

Father Henri Nouvel - https://en.wikipedia.org/wiki/Henri_Nouvel: Wikipedia.

Father Pierre Bailloquet - https://en.wikipedia.org/wiki/Pierre_Bailloquet: Wikipedia.

**Food and Medicine:**

Tubocurarine Chloride - https://en.wikipedia.org/wiki/Tubocurarine_chloride: Wikipedia.

Coqueluche (Flu) - https://en.wikipedia.org/wiki/1510_influenza_pandemic: Wikipedia.

Traditional Animal Foods - https://reporter.mcgill.ca/encyclopedia-highlights-traditional-animal-foods-of-indigenous-peoples/: by Neale McDevitt, McGill Reporter.

Plant Gatherers & Conservationists - The Original Medicinal Plant Gatherers & Conservationists - United Plant Savers: Anderson M. K., United Plant Savers Medicinal Plant Conservation.

20 Wild Edible Plants - 20 Wild Edible Plants - Farmers' Almanac - Plan Your Day. Grow Your Life.: Farmer's Almanac.

Mushroom Hunting - Mushroom Hunting In Upper Michigan - Iron County Lodging Association: Iron County Michigan Logging Council.

Arctic Grayling - The Arctic Grayling: All You Need To Know - Trout Unlimited: The Arctic Grayling – all you need to know, Trout Unlimited.

Lake Sturgeon Spawning Season - Lake sturgeon spawning | | Wisconsin DNR: WDNR.

Coaster Brook Trout - https://www.fws.gov/media/coaster-brook-trout: U.S. Fish and Wildlife Service, Fisheries, Midwest Region.

How to make Pemmican - Pemmican | First Nations Development Institute: First Nations Development Institute, firstnations.org.

Making Bear Lard - Why Great Grandma Loved Bear Lard - Petersen's Hunting: Anthony Licata, Petersen's Hunting Magazine, March 2021.

Native Americans Making Maple Syrup - How did Native Americans make syrup? | WXPR: Gary Entz, WXPR Public Radio.

Native Wild Rice in Michigan - PowerPoint Presentation: Roger Labine, Lac Vieux Desert Band of the Lake Superior Chippewa.

Ambroise Pare, French Surgeon - Ambroise Paré - Wikipedia: Wikipedia.

1510 French influenza pandemic - 1510 influenza pandemic - Wikipedia: Wikipedia.

Birthing process - How Native American Women Gave Birth: Sherman Indian Museum, Riverside, California.

Pregnancy complications - What are some common complications of pregnancy? | NICHD - Eunice Kennedy Shriver National Institute of Child Health and Human Development: What are some common complications of pregnancy? – National Institute of Child Health and Human Development.

Morning sickness - Morning sickness - Symptoms and causes - Mayo Clinic: Mayo Clinic, Rochester, Minnesota.

Heart failure - Heart failure - Symptoms and causes - Mayo Clinic: Mayo Clinic, Rochester, Minnesota.

**History and Travel:**

Mound Sites in the Eastern United States - https://www.loc.gov/resource/g3706c.ct012058r/?r=-1.342,-0.195,3.685,1.209,0: Smithsonian/C. Thomas.

Jesuit Missions - Jesuit Missions amongst the Huron - Wikipedia: Wikipedia.

Fur Trade History (1670 to 1870) - https://eh.net/encyclopedia/the-economic-history-of-the-fur-trade-1670-to-1870/: by Carlos, A. M. and Lewis, F. D., eh.net/encyclopedia.

Chippewa Sauk War - https://prezi.com/p/tvi94msu1snp/chippewa-sauk-war/: By Timothy Dowell, Prezi.com.

Battle of the Flint River - https://www.mycitymag.com/battle-of-the-flint-river-fact-or-fiction/: My City Magazine.

Major Indian tribes and Trails-1760 - indian trails: Project.geo.msu.edu, Michigan State University, East Lansing, Michigan.

The Arrival of the Europeans - The Arrival of the Europeans: 17th Century Wars - Canada.ca: Government of Canada.

Fur Trade in Canada - https://www.thecanadianencyclopedia.ca/en/article/fur-trade: The Canadian Encyclopedia.

Quebec History (1663-1759) - https://en.wikipedia.org/wiki/Timeline_of_Quebec_history_(1663%E2%80%931759): Wikipedia.

Company of One Hundred Associates - https://www.thecanadianencyclopedia.ca/en/article/compagnie-des-cent-associes: The Canadian Encyclopedia.

The French and Iroquois Wars (1642 to 1698) - https://raogk.org/military-records/french-iroquois-wars/#google_vignette: The Beaver Wars, Random Acts of Genealogical Kindness.

Michigan Lakes and Rivers - https://geology.com/lakes-rivers-water/michigan.shtml: Geology.com, Geoscience News and Information.

Wisconsin Lakes and Rivers - https://geology.com/lakes-rivers-water/wisconsin.shtml#:~:text=Wisconsin%20Lakes%2C%20Rivers%20and%20Water%20Resources&text=Croix%20River%2C%20Wisconsin%20River%2C%20Wolf,Flambeau%20Flowage%20and%20Willow%20Reservoir.: Geology.com, Geoscience News and Information.

History of Niagara Falls - https://www.niagarafallsstatepark.com/park-information/history/: Niagara Falls State Park.

Kaskaskia Village - https://www.museum.state.il.us/muslink/nat_amer/post/htmls/hi_explore.html: Arrival of Marquette and Jolliet at the Grand Village of the Kaskaskia, Museumlink Illinois, The Illinois History Exploration.

European Contact - Native Americans:Historic:The Illinois:History:Contact: The Illinois History European Contact, Museumlink Illinois.

Jesuits in New France - http://nativeamericannetroots.net/diary/1291: 17th Century Jesuits in New France, Netroots.net.

Peoria tribe - History – Peoria tribe of Indians of Oklahoma: Peoria tribe of Indians of Oklahoma, Peoriatribe.com.

Jolliet and Marquette Expedition - The Jolliet and Marquette Expedition | Missouri State Parks: The Jolliet and Marquette Expedition at Illiniwek Village State Historic Site.

Exploration of the Interior - Expedition of Marquette and Joliet, 1673 | Wisconsin Historical Society: French Exploration of the North American Interior, Wisconsin Historical Society.

Jolliet's Journal - What Became of Jolliet's Journal? on JSTOR: Preview: The Americas, by Steck, F. B., Vol. 5 No. 2, (Oct. 1948).

Exploring the Mississippi - Marquette-Joliet Expedition - Encyclopedia of Arkansas: Marquette-Joliet Expedition.

Jolliet's Journey - Louis Jolliet - Students | Britannica Kids | Homework Help: Louis Jolliet, French-Canadian Explorer.

**Equipment and Trade Items:**

French Confit Pots - antique glazed french confit pot - Search Images: Microsoft Bing.

French Copper Hanging Cauldron - https://www.etsy.com/market/antique_french_copper_cauldron: etsy.com.

Tomahawks and Trade Pipes - https://peachstatearchaeologicalsociety.org/artifact-identification/pipes/tomahawk-trade-pipes/: Peach State Archeological Society.

Dutch Arquebus - https://en.wikipedia.org/wiki/Arquebus: Wikipedia.

Musket - https://en.wikipedia.org/wiki/Musket: Wikipedia.

Bayport Chert - https://arrowheads.com/michigan-paleo-and-bayport-chert/: by Todd Walterspaugh, Michigan Paleo and Bayport Chert.

Making Arrowheads - Making Arrowheads: The Ancient Art of Flint Knapping: The art of flint knapping, Alderleaf Wilderness College.

Birch Bark Canoes - https://historyonthefox.wordpress.com/2013/11/04/those-marvelous-ojibwa-birch-bark-canoes/: WordPress.com, historyonthefox.

The use of Birchbark by the Ojibwa Indians - https://folklife-media.si.edu/docs/festival/program-book-articles/FESTBK1981_03.pdf: Smithsonian Institution, folklife-media.

**Tribal Traditions and Legends:**

The Legend of the sleeping bear - Legend of the Sleeping Bear: Joel Lucas, Earth Magazine-The science behind the headlines.

Buffalo Dance - Buffalo dance - Wikipedia: Wikipedia.

Green Corn Ceremony - Green Corn Ceremony - Wikipedia: Wikipedia.

Feast of the Dead - The Huron Feast of the Dead - Wikipedia: Wikipedia.

Ghost Dance - Ghost Dance - Wikipedia: Wikipedia.

Medicine Bags - https://en.wikipedia.org/wiki/Medicine_bag: Wikipedia.

Wendigo - https://en.wikipedia.org/wiki/Wendigo: A mythological creature or evil spirit, Wikipedia.

Vision Quest - https://en.wikipedia.org/wiki/Vision_quest: Wikipedia.

Tattoos - https://en.wikipedia.org/wiki/History_of_tattooing#The_Americas: Wikipedia.

Wooden False Faces - https://en.wikipedia.org/wiki/False_Face_Society: Wikipedia.

Wampum Belts - https://en.wikipedia.org/wiki/Two_Row_Wampum_Treaty: Wikipedia.

8 Mystical Dream Herbs – https://lonerwolf.com/legal-psychedelics/: by Mateo Sol, Lonerwolf.

Effigy Mounds - https://en.wikipedia.org/wiki/Effigy_mound: Wikipedia.

Native American Moon Cycles - https://ojibwe.net/projects/months-moons/: Ojibwe.net.

Lacrosse (Tewaaraton) - https://www.oneidaindiannation.com/lacrosse-the-creators-game/: The Creator's Game, Oneida Indian Nation.

**Miscellaneous:**

Le Griffon - https://en.wikipedia.org/wiki/Le_Griffon: Wikipedia.

Paris Carnival - https://en.wikipedia.org/wiki/Paris_Carnival: Wikipedia.

Fireworks during the reign of Louis XIV - https://gizmodo.com/the-first-fireworks-displays-were-terrifyingly-huge-1600541130: Gizmodo.

Te Deum - Te Deum - Wikipedia: Wikipedia.

Vexilla Regis Prodeunt - Vexilla regis prodeunt - Wikipedia: Wikipedia.

The Pageant of 1671 - https://www.americanjourneys.org/aj-050/index.asp: American Journeys.

Marquette's Peace Pipe - 'Father Jacques Marquette Holding a Peace Pipe to Greet Native Americans, c.1673' Giclee Print | Art.com: Father Marquette holding a white Peace Pipe with White and Red feathers, Art.com.

Hunting and Trapping - https://www.mpm.edu/content/wirp/ICW-28: Milwaukee Public Museum.

Wingbone Turkey Calls - https://www.instructables.com/Wingbone-Turkey-Call/: by catman529, Autodesk Instructables.

English Doglock Pistol - http://myarmoury.com/review_mvt_doglock.html#-google_vignette: myArmoury.com.

Brain Tanning - https://theleatherguy.org/blogs/leather-101/brain-tanned-leather-what-is-it-and-how-do-you-use-it: by The Leather Guy, see the difference.

The Equinox - https://en.wikipedia.org/wiki/Equinox: Wikipedia.

www.ingramcontent.com/pod-product-compliance
Lightning Source LLC
LaVergne TN
LVHW040038080526
838202LV00045B/3385